ALSO BY BRAD LEITHAUSER

Hundreds of Fireflies (poetry)

Equal Distance (a novel)

A Seaside Mountain (poetry chapbook)

Cats of the Temple (poetry)

HENCE

A novel by

HENCE

Brad Leithauser

ALFRED A. KNOPF NEW YORK 1989

THIS IS A BORZOI BOOK
PUBLISHED BY ALFRED A. KNOPF, INC.

Published in the United States by Alfred A. Knopf, Inc., New York, and simultaneously in Canada by Random House of Canada Limited, Toronto. Distributed by Random House, Inc., New York.

Library of Congress Cataloging-in-Publication Data

Leithauser, Brad.
Hence.

I. Title.
PS3562.E4623H4 1989 813'.54 88-45259
ISBN 0-394-57311-0

Manufactured in the United States of America
FIRST EDITION

For Harold Leithauser
1922–1985

with thanks
and thanks again

For what could be a more bizarre and haunting tragedy than the death of a twin child?

EQUAL DISTANCE

Oh yes, quite so, I know it's queer,
My dear and gentle-hearted
Reader, for me to leave you here,
Before we'd even started.

ATTRIBUTED TO JORGE LUIS BORGES
THE GEOMETRY OF IMAGINARY VOLUMES

HENCE

ALSO BY GARNER BRIGGS

The Contract to Contract: Reflections on the Origins of Law

Legal Fictions and the Human Fiction: An Introduction

Life and Law: The Grand Synthesis (in progress)

HENCE

A Meditation in Voices by

GARNER BRIGGS

With a new introduction by

ROBIN ORRIN

THE REARGUARD PRESS

BOSTON

"In the End was the word . . ."

To my parents,
who influenced me somewhat

Manufactured in the United States of America

FIRST EDITION

For he that laughs is justly reputed more wise, than at whom it is laughed. And hence I think proceeds that which in these later formal times I have much noted; that now when our superstitious civilitie of manners is become a mutuall tickling flattery of one another, almost every man affecteth an humour of jesting, and is content to be deject, and to deform himself, yea become fool to no other end that I can spie, but to give his wise Companion occasion to laugh; and to shew themselves in promptness of laughing is so great in wise men, that I think all wise men, if any wise men do read this Paradox, will laugh both at it and me.

John Donne, *Paradoxes and Problems*

Many men think that I am like them.

Icelandic proverb

INTRODUCTION

Too much has been written about the death of the book for me to nurture any hope of profitably lamenting its passing here. Suffice it to say, then, that I was pleased—a pleasure in fact exceeding by far my own exiguous powers of evocation—when a few months ago I received a brief but graceful letter from The Rearguard Press, its purpose to inform me of their plan to reissue Garner Briggs's *Hence: A Meditation in Voices* in that supremely impractical, vigorously anachronistic, and reassuringly tactile form,— viz., a book. And would I be interested in assembling a few words by way of introduction?

Ineffability having been my plea in paragraph one, permit me in paragraph two volubly to observe, at the very least, that I felt jubilant, enlivened, elevated, and transported upon receipt of this request. Well, I hadn't a moment's doubt that I would be "interested"!,— oh, no, my immediate reservation lay rather in that request for a "few words." A few? For I felt stirring within me not a few, no, but a few *thousand* words (words by the chapter, words by the subsection), as I pointed myself toward the prospect of expatiating upon the quite peculiar author of this extremely peculiar book. And would I disqualify myself here at the outset, prove myself a soul unfit for my Rearguard task, were I to confess that for a moment I envisioned not a mere and so to speak introductory introduction, but rather a series of interlaced annotations, the whole to be housed, perhaps, in twin companion volumes? It was as though, in those short-lived but deliriously happy moments, I had landed within that era and world which it is my quiet job in some measure to recreate twice weekly for a fresh generation of drugged but ambitious young people,— that world in which phrases were meant to be ample, paragraphs leniently capacious, and books themselves fat with robust good health. Before long, needless to say, Reason, in the guise of that cordial but at bottom sensibly businesslike note from The Rearguard Press, reasserted itself, and I perforce abandoned all thoughts of my two-volume *Hence;* I am gratified to say, nonetheless, that even yet something of the moment's blissful delirium lingers. For the truth is that my fingers hum with their own sense of well-being as I pen (literally, with fountain pen and inkstand) these words of greeting. Welcome, reader, and God bless you.

You are reading these words while seated perhaps within a roaring aircraft some dozen miles above the surface of the globe; or within one of those atmosphere-controlled compartments that hurtle through horizontal subterranean corridors as the perpendicular twins to the automated compartments that race up and down the Miraplex supertowers of our pullulating megalopoli; or within a bathysphere; but in my mind you are sitting in a large, a rather lumpy, and a thoroughly stationary chair—a Morris chair, in fact—in the library of a ramshackle summer house beringed by such plentiful woods that the silence around you is apprehended as something dense and multitiered. A battered standing lamp, banished countryward many years ago by reason of its homely shabbiness, lobs a cone of golden light over your right shoulder, and, hungry for that selfsame light, hordes of furry moths flicker against the screen,— for it is nightfall. The book in your hands, this book, presents an agreeable heft, and you read slowly, with an impression of something almost illicit in the pleasure your eye takes in journeying over the page. You sense that the practice of solitude, and the habit of reading bred with it, have somehow become quietly sinful, and there is something rousingly romantic in the notion that soon you will carry this volume off to bed. Under such circumstances, surely I am entitled to call you dear reader, as you most surely are entitled to ask of me just what sort of companion it is, precisely, which you will find reposing beside you, when, deliciously late, you wake in the morning.

I would be frank, and I would have you see this book clearly . . . I would begin by admitting that I am filled with solicitous inner voices, each in its way intent on warning you yet again that you have in your hands a very strange book indeed,— warnings perhaps the better conveyed through an assurance that it never can seem so strange to you as originally it did to those of us who knew its author. Vividly, I am returned to that afternoon when *Hence* first fell into my hands. I am borne back to a blue windless fall afternoon,— one of those warm and cool, time-stalled, vertiginously blue afternoons that used to grace this New England town perhaps two or three days each autumn in the years before the Shift. In the absence of wind, the leaves were descending not in clusters but singly from the big silver birch my office window gave upon. (This, when birches were still common in my part of New England.) I had jabbered my way through a morning class and had an hour remaining before facing down a similar group, into whose pretty heads I must needs hammer my unwelcome notion that there was nothing self-consciously quaint about the Victorians, and under that splendid sky, I sauntered over to the town bookstore, where, beside a stack of books self-identified as "the official picture-bio" of a woman known as "The Lips," I found a handsome pile, five volumes high, of *Hence: A Meditation in Voices*. I bought two copies, not sure even today for whom I intended the second, and with all thought of lunch forgotten, returned to the friendly Morris chair in my office, where I began to read . . .

Came a knock eventually upon my office door, and the elevated, head-poking entrance of a blond young man, a basketball player, who with unwonted conscientiousness had come in quest of the missing professor. It seems I was already twenty-five minutes late for class. With a kind of desperation, I protested, as impatiently as incoherently, the onset of a sudden illness, sent him packing, and returned to my book . . . And it was evening, the deep blue sky had fallen noiselessly away to reveal a crisp scatter of stars, before I rose once more from my chair. My protestations of illness had come naturally enough, for in truth the book left me feeling heartsick. It also left me impressed, puzzled, splenetic, and amazed. To see myself, in the very first pages, referred to as "a rather insistent friend" . . . A *friend!* Oh, there was a measure of strict, inviolate truth to that, I suppose, and yet,— and yet was I, who had played if not quite a decisive, at least a central, role in so many of the book's events; I, who at a moment's notice had driven halfway across the country in the middle of the night on an insane errand; I, who had served throughout as hidden muse, at last nothing but a "friend"? Indeed . . .

It seems the book wounded me more deeply even than I acknowledged at the time, for when the request arrived from The Rearguard Press, so many years later, my own thoughts surprised me by the rapidity with which they detected an opportunity for,— for Revenge. I would set things right, I would even the score, I would restore myself to my rightful place! Now, at last, both of the brothers who serve as the principal parties of this book having prematurely passed from us, I could with quiet impunity correct, and expand, and clarify . . . Oh, I would of course be truthful! But I would pursue the truth evenhandedly, openly, slighting no one in my search . . . And in the end, I would offer up that accurate text which you, dear reader, so patently deserve.

But I chose in the end to play a greatly more modest role. Yes, true, in one or two places I have made trifling modifications, correcting here and there what was unmistakably a typographical error, or a simple oversight, and in the process necessarily adding or deleting a phrase, but I have left the quale of my friend Garner Briggs's *Hence* untouched. (Even to the point of reprinting, as a sort of *memento mori,* that prefatory page headed "Also by Garner Briggs," in which one finds a bold listing for "*Life and Law: The Grand Synthesis* (in progress),"— that long-planned *chef d'oeuvre* he never managed to complete.) But I am not at all sure this decision was a sagacious one. Of course I have on my side all sorts of pious conventionalities about the "sanctity" of the text, and the "perils" of editorial "tampering," but in my heart I think it moot whether an unaltered text can be said to represent fairly this particular book. The text cries out for revisions, and not merely such as may assuage the feelings of those souls who were slighted within it.

I considered for a time the possibility of providing the reader with a brief calendar of events. While my friend prided himself (rather too openly, I fear) on his longsightedness, it seems that the years have conspired to mock him, gradually making manifest how much his "timeless" book reflects the year—1993—it seeks to document. He assumes, again and again, a reader's familiarity with events long since receded from our ever-shortening collective memory. Was it unreasonable of me, then, to suppose that the reader might feel a bit at sea, and would welcome the solid spar provided by a simple chronological record of the events this "meditation in voices" meditates upon?

The deeper I pursued my task, however, the more complicated became this business of emendation. Yes, there were all sorts of simple errors that begged for correction (jumbled dates, distorted names, &c.), as well as larger distortions of personality,— but most of these inaccuracies revealed, on close inspection, their own logic or intention, often of a satiric or even faintly cruel nature. Consider for example an absolutely *min*uscule affair, that passage in Chapter XXVI wherein Garner reports, of his sister Nettie, that "Solicitude comes naturally to this woman who has seven children in her house." Well, in the eyes of Nettie (the mother, then as now, of six children), this was an infuriating error, whether viewed as a gibe at her fertility or merely another egregious instance of Garner's inattentions as an uncle. A mere typographical error, Garner claimed by way of exoneration,— and yet this was an error that survived the book's second and third printings. Naturally, I was eager, in my role as editor, to right this oversight at last,— until it occurred to me that what I actually faced was another of Garner's characteristically private ironies: a subtle and somewhat mean-spirited jab at someone (his brother-in-law, Gerry) whom he regarded as hopelessly immature.

Which squarely raises the, in many ways, thorny question of the, in many ways, thorny personality of Garner Tyler Briggs. If the request from the Rearguard Press helped me to perceive that resentments I thought long dead were merely slumberous, it also revealed a protectiveness I would not have thought still quick within me. How many times, while rereading this Meditation, did I long to soften a phrase, to excise a pomposity, to insert a slight, lenitive emendation that would cast our Garner in a better light! I worried that the reader would find him from the very first, from those impossible epigraphs he dug up God knows where, a cold and arrogant creature, whilst myself simultaneously aware that he often *was* a cold and arrogant creature,— but not of quite the sort this Meditation might suggest.

Oh, it was a choice irony, I would be the first to admit,— that I, with my decidedly obsolescent literary inclinations, would be calling for greater tightness and concision . . . But it was not so much Garner's prolixities I bridled at, as, rather, the quiet and gloating satisfaction detectable behind them. Wit was the intention, I suppose, and yet what inverted pride seemed to reek from phrases like "a journalistic prize of some reputation among obituarists" and "that institute of law and legal education across a dead river from the city of Boston . . ." How it would rankle him to hear me say this, but the truth was, in fact, that I longed to shelter him from,— from you, my dear but surprisingly formidable reader. I say "surprisingly" because I'd been struck anew by an impression (so contrary to all commonplace wisdoms) of the vulnerability of the dead. Or at least of the dead writer. In the end, each is turned into a mendicant. *A moment,* they implore, *a moment of your time . . .*

Admittedly, this is not a book that seems, on its face, the least bit supplicatory. In my recent rereadings, I have been unexpectedly met with the realization that to a fresh reader it might seem, on the contrary, rather close-mouthed and remote. But to those of us who knew the author, the book's appearance had a wholly other effect. We were alike astonished at how this quiet, sometimes chilly, and always eerily unbodied man had so exposed his family and himself. It seems he wanted to strip away their clothing,— literally, physically. And I can safely say that in the years when I saw a great deal of him, or as much of him as anyone did, Garner frequently astonished me,— but never so completely as when he made that curious literary leap at the end of Chapter V, transforming his book utterly by bidding good-bye not merely to the reader but in a sense to himself as well.

Having established, or so I should hope, unimpeachable scrupulosity as regards my editorial practices, I would now elaborate upon a secret that may hint of self-aggrandizement. I have always been convinced that, despite my conspicuous absence in this book (an absence which, in fact, only fuels this conviction of mine), the entire Meditation should properly be regarded as a response to me. In my own mind, nothing could be clearer than the fact that *Hence* represents Garner Briggs's not always conscious attempt to demonstrate that all of those antiquated novels I hold so dear— and which have provided me with a modest career and sinecure, and about which Garner uttered such bitter denunciations on the one occasion when I made the mistake of accusing him of "a failure to understand them"—were at bottom an offhand and tertiary achievement. Didn't *Hence* conclusively demonstrate to an obscure (if well respected, I'd care to think) New England Thackerayan that Garner Briggs, whilst composing a vast meditation on the future of life on this planet and the significance of legal truth (or whatever in God's name was Garner's goal in its writing), could also, collaterally, throw in much of the richness of an old-fashioned three-decker novel as well? I had no doubt then, on that day when the birch leaves were down-drifting through a fading fall afternoon, as I have no doubts now, so many down-driftings later, that the book was meant to one-up me,— or, as Garner himself would put it (seeking, evidently, by means of inverted commas, to suggest that his was an inner world so rarefied and exclusive that slang of even the most everyday sort seldom had access to it), to "one-up" me.

And the odd thing is that he succeeded far better than he, or anyone else who knew this brilliant but shall we say occasionally purblind man, had any reason to expect. Now it is true that Garner in person was actually an adroit, if rather shy, mimic,—a gift to which much of the Meditation's success might be ascribed. (And true, as well, that he had incomparable material to work with. The portrayal here, particularly, of his maundering, malaprop-ridden mother, which may seem viciously exaggerated, is if anything understated; Mrs. Briggs had the greatest gift for mangling the English mother tongue that I've ever encountered.) And true also, as I can attest personally, having known nearly all the people sketched in these pages, that he has, time after time, got their voices exactly, quirkily right. (Or all of the voices except, significantly, his own. The outside reader would never suppose that the urbane Garner Briggs who deftly quips his way through these pages suffered in real life from a stutter . . . If I could give this book my own subtitle, I would call it *The Stammerer's Revenge.*) But, *and this is the important thing,* he did far more than get the intonations down. He had clearly listened to those around him more closely—I'm tempted to say, more lovingly—than anyone would have supposed.

So,— I stand reproached. I stand accused. I stand—as others memorialized in these pages no longer do—under the sky, still on my feet, such as they are, tottering a bit but still gulping the earth's air, such as it is, still grateful and resentful in all the welter of my unresolved feelings and still earnestly imploring the reader to look kindly on my friend. Of older readers, I would beg that an effort be made to return passionately, but unsentimentally, to an era so unlike our own as to seem illusory. Younger readers are asked to hold skepticism in abeyance while attempting to apprehend that the (or so our own experts would have it) "millennial neuroses" recorded here were real and compelling enough to those who confronted them from the other side of the calendrical summit. And I am confident that anyone who makes these imaginatory efforts must come away impressed by my friend's prescience. For surely it *is* remarkable,— the degree to which what he adumbrated has in fact threaded itself into the complex, synthetic, "un-earthed" texture of life in our own millennium. One can profitably regard this Meditation as a dark prophetic satire, and if at times when painting the brave old world of "high tech and high glitz" Cambridge, Massachusetts, he was a bit heavy-handed in his satirical touches (mocha bagels indeed!), those who were there must come away impressed at how frequently what were once inaccuracies became verities in the fullness of time.

Surely, in any case, in these days since the Shift, no one on the planet can afford to laugh, as various friends of Garner's once laughed, at his dark broodings about the effects that "the globe's filthiest animal" would have on the world's climatic equilibrium.

Interestingly, one of the arguments about which he seems most tentative—the question of the interconnectedness of those "three media events" the Meditation touches upon—now seems so manifest that Garner's hesitancy looks rather puzzling. Perhaps he was daunted by the geographical distances involved . . . A chess match in Boston, a jackknife-wielding evangelist from Kansas, and the emergence of a nonpareil musical prodigy on a tiny island in the Japan Sea . . . But isn't it today abundantly clear that all three were, at least when viewed as "media events," reflections of a technological society's failure to come to terms with the offspring of its own technology? Don't they all reflect a common unease with that world which we had, and have, created for ourselves? And if that chess match has faded out of memory, and the jackknife's slashings, too, been washed away by other, more spectacular bloodlettings, isn't it delicious to reflect on how that little Oriental boy, whose round, bespectacled, queerly unchildlike face was then just breaking into our newspapers and magazines, has since become an enduring charmer whose music, looking selectively backward, will sail him futurewards forever? I have Tatsumi's music playing in the background even as I write these words, and if in that old country house wherein you have so shamelessly secreted yourself there is also a music system—preferably of that antiquated sort in which the tape hisses like soft rainfall through the speakers—might I suggest that you now turn it on? I would, myself, recommend the delightful, untroubled seventeenth piano concerto. It would make the perfect complementary voice as you enter the puzzling, dark, nettlesome, masterful literary singularity that is Garner Briggs's *Hence: A Meditation in Voices.*

ROBIN ORRIN
AMHERST, MASSACHUSETTS

HENCE: *A MEDITATION IN VOICES*

I

By nature, I am uneasy in a city . . . I write these words at the desk in the study in the apartment I've lived in for the past twelve years. My window looks out upon a busy avenue. One might say—even if I myself probably would not—that I live beside a sea of vehicles, whose tide goes in (work; downtown) in the morning and out (rest; suburbs) in the late afternoon. In any case, if one luminous morning I were to wake up blind as a bat, I would probably be able, in bat fashion, to fix the time and the state of the day merely by listening. At this point, the traffic's flow is in my blood. But blessed as I am with eyesight that seems almost implausibly keen, in light of my age (late-thirties) and "life-style" (a constant reader for three decades), my gaze is met each day as I seat myself at this desk by a highly particularized vision of an establishment called Burger Splurger, whose golden lights go off at about ten at night, and of Ben's Organic Pizza, whose green neon sign, topped with three red neon rosettes, goes off promptly at two, of Double Take, a photocopy establishment whose prosperity can be largely attributed—so reputation has it—to a willingness to circumvent those provisions of the U.S. Code (Title 17, § 107—"Fair Use") that restrict the reproduction of printed text in an educational setting, and whose cruelly bare strip lights go off at two thirty—or even later when the pace picks up toward semester's end—and of the Slak Shak, whose doors close at seven in the evening but whose orange neon letters blaze throughout the night. Very late, when all the other shop lights are extinguished, that orange glow burns with a serene commercial tranquillity upon the ceiling of this room. When I work at this desk until dawn—as frequently I do—the pink, enlivening glimmer of the new day mingles uneasily with that of the orange neon, dryly bathing the objects of my room in a cheerful, unearthly, ghastly glow of a sort which I associate with radioactive blasts. It is often the last light I see before retiring, and it lingers longer than one might suppose against the drawn screen of my eyelids.

I am made uneasy, as I say, and yet this is where I continue to live, continue to work.

There is a network of tunnels in that vast, pragmatic institute of law and legal education, situated across a dead river from the city of Boston, where I perform the task, penumbral and "classy" at once, of instructing future attorneys in some of the subtleties of jurisprudential philosophy. One can get almost anywhere on campus by means of them. There are vending machines within the tunnels, and lounges, and offices, and toilets, so that one can eat and work, take one's daily constitutional and do one's socializing, preen and "relieve oneself," all belowground. In the course of a day, one needn't inhale a single breath that hasn't first been seasoned by the place, hasn't already absorbed something of its floor polish and disinfectant, the enamel paint of its metal lockers, the peculiar weary jitteriness of its much-exchanged air. During the long winter, one has some plausible rationale for the presence of so many of us in those tunnels, but who can tell me why, on a magnificent spring morning in May, so many purposeful, pasty faces are seen underground? *Is there some interesting reason,* I inquire of myself as I, likewise subterranean, head from the lecture hall to the library, *why we have chosen a route that takes us out of the light of this incomparable spring morning?* Can it be merely force of habit? And how is mere habit ever to explain not only our own transitory presence here but the existence of the tunnels themselves? In the end, how are we to square what we know of geological time and evolution—of that eager-eyed, rapidly masticating tree shrew out of whose tiny, generous loins all of us are sprung—with the "naturally organic Power Snax" of those tunnel vending machines? Surely all such things must be synthesized, every stray scrap . . . Someone is peering at us—a literal lowbrow, who stands semiupright at the edge of a clearing, a jawbone in his hand—peering with an incomprehension so thick it makes him look wistful, and how are we even with all of our technology to fabricate the mirror wherein we will recognize ourselves, or our selves, at last?

I am made uneasy, and yet I find it difficult to leave this apartment, especially overnight. It is not merely the matter of deciding which books will accompany me, which remain behind, and the whole upsetting business of separating shelf-mate from -mate. It is also the attempting to sleep by the shore of another sea of sounds, and the drifting in the mornings through rooms not my own . . . and that sense of being surrounded on all sides by peripheral objects that, notwithstanding their own peripheralism, are demanding an immediate assimilation . . .

I mention some of my own personal and perhaps idiosyncratic tastes and habits because it happens that at the time when the events upon which this text would meditate actually commenced I was living, for the first time in years, outside my own apartment. Somehow having "given in" to the promptings of a rather insistent friend, I had agreed to share the rent of a vast summer house in western Massachusetts. The move was an unpleasant one and despair immediately overtook me on arrival. I was again struck forcibly, as only the confirmed, all-but-unbudgable urbanite can be, by how primitive country living inevitably turns out to be. One hears so much about the incivilities and aggressions of the city, but nothing there could actually prepare one for that sense each time one steps into the Great Outdoors of being surrounded by creatures who are literally bloodthirsty . . .

But then . . . But then, I must admit, an unforeseen and welcome change took place. I shifted my hours, and if they still failed to conform to that up-at-dawn and down-at-dusk regimen which the natural world seems so "keen on," they at least approximated what others would call a normal schedule. I went for walks. I even climbed a hill. I was reading Locke that summer, with a pleased, enlarged sense of admiration. It seemed that doors were opening at the ends of corridors I had thought doorless. It's the philosopher's dream, isn't it—to reach so deep an understanding of another thinker's thought that the latter's work can be dismissed altogether? And when one thinks about the fertile promise of a world in which Locke never existed, an unLocked world . . . I was to move backward, expunging them all, one by one—which is to say, I was making tremendous progress. Mine was that timeless, tantalizing prospect—what might it be possible to think once we'd cleared all past thinkers out of our way?

My progress was briefly interrupted by a phone call, or (more accurately) by the message of a phone call, for we had no telephone in that damp summer house and depended on a neighbor to relay our calls. I was to telephone my mother. This message was delivered by a tobacco-chewing, lantern-jawed, grizzled old Yankee who played the role of brusque New England farmer to such exquisite perfection that I found it difficult actually to hear what he was saying—so aware was I, during his aphorism-packed delivery, that it had required a lifetime of diligence to learn to talk and carry himself like this . . . He had taken what was surely an illusory stereotype and made it his life. I waited until evening, then placed my call from the telephone booth on the edge of a rural shopping center. "Doris," I said.

"Who is this?" Her question came with a familiar note of wary aggression, a familiar pride in her own toughness. Hers, too, was a long-cultivated role, this voice whose tone said *Mister, whatever pitch it is you're selling, I'm not buying.*

"It's your elder son. Garner. Calling from the wilds of Heath, Massachusetts."

Our connection was less than perfect, but still I could hear the intake of breath at the other end. She was, I knew, about to begin one of what my sister Nettie (who is normally not given to wordplay) once called a "warm-up dressing down"—a distinctive mix of advice, inquiry, reproach, and dire prophecy. But this time, the pause extended longer than I would have expected.

These little preambles of Doris's can usually be counted on to follow familiar grooves. I am to be scolded for my unwillingness ever to leave my apartment (and, specifically, to leave it for Key Largo, Florida, which I had not yet visited, although Doris had so mysteriously moved there many months before); Nettie for "letting her weight go"; and my brother Timothy for dropping out of college. It was as though my calling not from civilized Cambridge but from the wilds of Heath had disordered Doris and she didn't know quite where to begin with me. "Lord save us, *first* it's that you won't come see me but *now* you've managed to arrange it so there's no way of calling you, either."

"Doris," I said, "I think you're right. Leaving the Cambridge apartment was reckless. I *knew* it was reckless . . ."

"It's a question of what you leave *for,*" Doris pointed out. "If you're going to leave *for* somewhere, you could as well arrange to have it for some somewhere where there's a phone there."

"Doris, by the time I could have one installed, I'd be out of here."

"I lost your phone number," Doris accused me. "I needed to call you yesterday, or that neighbor of yours anyway, and I couldn't find the number. I looked everywhere."

"Put it in a safe place," I suggested.

"I'm not even going to mention the possibility of coming down here to see me."

"Florida in the *summer,* Doris? I wouldn't get a thing done. Besides, I don't fly—as you well know."

"Oh, it's not so hot here," she said. "Not that you would know, never having been. It's not so hot as Chicago. You know I never was so hot as Chicago that year we lived in Chicago. I've often thought they shouldn't call it the *Windy* City—"

"Could you speak up? I can't hear you over the roar of your air conditioner."

"I won't even mention coming down. Even though that would make it a little easier to get a hold of you, especially when there's maybe important news."

"What's your news, Doris?"

Another anticipatory intake of breath. "Well I expect you've actually honestly heard about Timmy."

"Actually honestly, I haven't talked to Timothy, or heard a word about him, in weeks."

"Isn't that exactly what I've always said? That he wouldn't be in the awful mess he's in now if you only'd kept in closer touch? *Some*one's got to be a father to that boy, Garner."

"I think you handle the role with great aplomb, Doris."

"Well I thank you, or I'd thank you if I thought you meant a single word of what you say. That's I guess what you call irony, isn't it, but if you ask me it's simply saying one thing and meaning another, and if you'd like to know what *I* call saying one thing and meaning another—"

"What's happened to Timothy?"

"Well, you know they've asked him to play some sort of *computer.* In chess. Against the Com*pu*ter."

"That doesn't sound like such an *aw*ful mess."

"In the spring. Or in the fall, and not this fall, but *next* fall. Which honestly don't you know means he's going to be spending every possible minute—"

"What sort of computer? Who was this who asked him, Doris?"

"We're talking another *year,* aren't we? And every single minute devoted—"

"What in the world are you talking about? Which computer are you talking about?"

"It's some sort of world championship," Doris said.

"Championship of what?"

"Or national championship. Of playing against the computer."

"There's no such thing. I mean as far as I know there's no such thing as any formal—"

"Well be that as may be, he has been chosen. I can tell you that on Bibled oath. Which you'd know yourself, wouldn't you, if only you once in a while called your brother?"

"How was he chosen?"

"He was *selected,*" Doris explained.

"On what grounds was he selected?"

"Well, he *is* the national champion." Standing in the phone booth outside the shopping center, I could see Doris vividly at that moment. She had lifted her chin slightly, in her maternal pride, and her upper lip, vertically fissured with the fine wrinkles of a prematurely old woman, had smugly protruded itself.

"That isn't quite right . . ."

"The junior national champion, if you're going to put me on the witness stand."

"But he isn't a junior any more."

"The point is," Doris said, "the *point* is that I'm afraid he's very keen on this, and I can just see him staying out of school another year just to play some big hulking machine that never had to worry a day in its whole life about where its next meal was coming from. I want you to call him, Garner."

"Why do you want me to call him, Doris?"

"Does there have to be a why?"

"Well, perhaps I think you have a 'why' in mind."

"Well the why is, I want you to find out about what all this is actually about. I want you to talk about his *plans.* He has plenty of time later to do chess, if he wants to, just the way his father did his coins."

"Doris, we've been through all that. *Non*sense—you've got to guard yourself against *non*sense."

She took this well. Or she didn't hear it—her imagination had moved elsewhere. "He seems to think there's real money in this crazy computer thing."

"There may be."

"You think so?" A quickening—an eager hopefulness for her strange third child, her surviving baby—had entered her voice.

"I'll find out what I can."

"And then call me? Call me as soon as you hear anything. Because I can't call you."

"Yes," I said. "I know."

II

THE TRUTH LIES all about us, and doesn't this help to explain why any accurate narration of these events proves so tricky an undertaking? For the moment, I seek merely to recreate two telephone conversations, the first of them between a then thirty-four-year-old professor of jurisprudence and his then sixty-two-year-old mother, the second between this same professor and his then twenty-year-old brother. And if even this modest ambition would appear unobtainable, how am I to hope to reproduce here a series of events that, however briefly, captured the world's attention?

The truth lies . . . and in this hoariest and most familiar of paradoxes I would look for fresh pleasure and renewed wisdom. If indeed the truth is deceitful, we must forbear from its direct pursuit. Rather, an oblique advance, going toward it with the queer, untoward gait of a crab . . .

The truth lies, and isn't it as though all sons and daughters of the English mother-tongue have been given with this phrase a warning from above? Advised, that is, not to trust too closely to appearances? Hints, warnings, auguries of revelation . . . And how tempting to postulate that if one could only catalog every tongue, and assemble all such clues, some full clarification would be at hand—that the truth awaits, eagerly, our recognition. In the meantime, we make our calls, send our voices across the wire-strung void, at times refusing to identify ourselves for the simple, playful pleasure of having others recognize us unaided: "You sound like a voice from beyond the grave," I began.

"Yeah? Garner?"

"You were sleeping?"

"Yeah. What time is it?"

"What time did you go to sleep?"

"Don't know. I guess sleeping," Timothy said.

There's always a certain awkwardness between my brother

and me, which we seek to overcome in all sorts of ways. This was one. On the phone, we always leap right in—as though to suggest that we'd spoken only hours before.

"Your schedule is stranger than mine," I said.

"Don't know, maybe. I was sleeping."

I suspect that I have some reputation for taciturnity among my colleagues and neighbors, but in this area I actually can't begin to match my brother, who when the mood strikes him can get by for whole days on a few grunted monosyllables. I mention this now, and will perhaps mention it later, because in what follows Timothy on occasion has a great deal to say—much of it of an intimate nature—and these "outbursts" can only be understood against the background of a reticence that often might seem surly.

Timothy is prone, as well, to abrupt fits of abstraction. He "drifts off" in the middle of conversations, no less when he himself is speaking than when he is listening to someone else. A friend of mine, who does not share my aversion to travel, once described Timothy as looking exactly like every second Nebraskan gas station attendant on the Interstate highway—a young man who had, apparently, learned to operate a gas pump only after prodigious mental effort, but on having mastered this single commercial skill had resolved to pump gas for the rest of his days. I've never been to Nebraska, but I suspect this observation isn't quite fair. And yet I would be the first to admit that Timothy can appear slow-witted—an impression he enhances by means of a lurching style of movement that makes him seem ill-assembled.

"So what's new over there?" I asked him.

"Nothing."

"Nothing?"

"They cut off my phone."

"It seems to be working satisfactorily."

"Oh it's working *now.* After I paid them nearly two hundred *dollars*. Just to throw a little switch."

"Two hundred dollars to throw a switch?"

"They said I owed them some calls. I swear I didn't get half the bills they said they sent. I swear they're stealing my mail. I wanted to cut the phone off for good but Mom said no. No, she'd pay the monthly service charge she said. So I said if it was so important to her, I'd let her pay it."

"So she's paying your phone these days as well as your rent . . ."

"Oh I told her I didn't need to move. I made that *clear.* I was happy where I was and if I moved it was for her benefit. These things can happen anywhere."

By "these things" Timothy presumably meant muggings . . . To see Timothy walking a city street, feet adrift and head stuck firmly in the clouds, one would probably not give him more than two or three unmolested days in the worst parts of Manhattan. But it took him nearly six months of living on the edges of Harlem before, one spring evening, someone pulled a knife on him a block away from his apartment. Doris of course ordered him to leave the city immediately, and Timothy said he wouldn't, and so a "compromise" was finally struck, and he was moved to an apartment on the "safe" Upper East Side. Timothy claims hardly to remember the incident, and that may be true, for he was unable, evidently, to tell the police with any certainty whether his assailant had been white, black, or some shade in between. Timothy's ability to expunge unpleasant thoughts does look—from the outside, anyway—quite remarkable. He claims, for example, to have scarcely a single memory of Tommy, his identical twin, although Timothy was nearly six when Tommy died. Tommy fell off a slide at the Robert Browning Elementary School playground in Victoria, Indiana. He suffered what appeared to be a minor bump and contusion, was ministered to by the school nurse, and came home from school at the usual time. Except for a white adhesive bandage, his little accident was apparently behind him.

He died that evening.

"I just talked to her. Doris."

"So how's Mom?"

Timothy resents, I gather, the way I address our mother by her first name, and he wages a little war with me over this. There is something quietly aggressive in the tone and frequency of his references to "Mom." Or perhaps I merely imagine this.

"She said you're going to play some sort of chess computer."

"Congam's."

"I beg your pardon."

"Congam. The computer company. Where do you live? They only make the fastest computer in the world. I'm going to be up against one of their best. And a new program they're designing at M.I.T. ANNDY. It's called ANNDY. Congam and M.I.T. How's that for formidable?" There was a coughing sound at the other end, or what a listener unacquainted with Timothy would have taken for a coughing sound; my brother has an unusual laugh.

"How were you chosen?"

"By phone call. Out of the blue. That was before the phone broke down."

"I mean, why you?"

"Why not?"

"Well, I don't know, if they're looking for somebody young, why not Kurza? Or Jeong?"

At that time, when all three young men were active players, both Kurza and Jeong were rated a little higher than Timothy was, although he had beaten them both at the National Junior Chess Championship in Minneapolis a couple of years before. That was during Timothy's first and only year at Columbia University. According to the seedings, he wasn't supposed to win that tournament, or even to come close; Kurza was favored to win. Since that great triumph, Timothy's play had been erratic (or so I was told—I could make no such judgments, since to this day I hardly know how the pieces move), and his future was unclear. There seemed some possibility, anyway, that the Junior Tournament was to stand as an apex, a glory he could never quite reach again.

The place of chess in Timothy's life was something that Doris had her own theories about. And—who knows?—she may have been right. In her universe, there was no question that the blame here (and there was no question, either, that this was a matter calling for a good deal of blame) could be laid at the doorstep of "that girl," his "high school sweetheart." That girl (whose name is Linda Faccione, and who I might helpfully reveal will reappear here later on) had "led him on for years" and in the end had "broken the poor boy's heart." By doing so, she had "unbalanced him"—pushed him so deeply into the world of chess that he "lost sight of the real world." Oh, this was all familiar territory, which I had been guided through time and again, and as I say, there may have been some truth in it. It would seem clear, anyway, that the girl had, indirectly, improved his game. By the time he reached Columbia, he had no interest whatsoever in his studies. No, he had enrolled there—it soon became clear—merely to submerge himself in the Manhattan chess world. And that first year, he won the National Junior Championship.

"Don't know," Timothy said, in response to my question about his being selected over Kurza or Jeong. "Maybe they wanted somebody American."

"I thought they were both Americans."

"American born. Could be big money in this, you know. Congam, they're big. They're colossal big."

"You'll still be going back to school in the fall?"

"Oh yeah. Well no, yeah I think no. Not yet maybe." He still sounded half asleep.

For all of Doris's urgent injunctions, I felt hesitant about pressing him. I'm not sure exactly why, but somehow I couldn't urge him back toward school. What was I supposed to do? Steer him eventually toward an MBA? Or hope to convince him to join the ranks of scrubbed, confident, unlikable faces to whom I deliver my ill-attended lectures? I must confess that I had some sympathy for him. A few years before, he'd been broadly acknowledged as the best in the country at what he did, for his age, and afterwards had entered adulthood (or at least the world of adult rankings) to discover that he stood . . . where? Tenth? Twelfth? Twentieth? His future looked uncertain. And yet he was working hard . . . In recent months, he had supposedly made great progress.

"I'll let you get back to sleep," I said. "But that is very good news. This computer business. Where will the match be held?"

"Cambridge." And again that queer cough of a laugh.

"Well. Well, I'll be there. I would probably have made it even if they had held it in horrifying New York, but it was kind of you to arrange all of this for my convenience."

"That's where M.I.T. is."

"Actually, I think I did know that. Yes, yes, I think so," I said, and we exchanged good-byes.

I stepped out of the phone booth. The air had turned sharply cool—one of those unsettlingly rapid drops in temperature so frequent out in the country. I was surrounded, I realized then, by thousands and thousands of crickets.

III

CRUELLY, MEMORY WOULD venture into that one zone of the past that never can be reconciled to the present—adolescence—in order to bring forth mother and teenage son as they stand arguing in quiet intimacy among the sparsely settled aisles of Brodie's Children's Wear, in the town of Victoria, Indiana. Outside, an autumn rain, cold with the promise of deepening coldness, is lightly falling in the premature dusk. Inside, the dispute centers upon the relative merits of two shirts—both plaid, one a quiet brown and green, the other a "louder" blue, red, and yellow—and doubtless by now the entire afternoon would have been long forgotten, had not the mother stated, "I'm fully partial to that one, it's got *life.*"

Like a bell, that's how the phrase rings inside the boy . . . He hears *fully partial* and knows the words are lovely in their way, rich with contradiction and reconciliation, and knows as well, even at that young age, that there is no point in trying to identify for her, who spoke them, their loveliness. The words come as a signal, a garbled message, to be decoded, years later, to be freed, only here . . .

Free as it is from the confines of physical rules of placement, and quick to grasp that the only logical way forward must often lead us backward for a time, the mind has always been the shortest distance between two points. In a moment, in a page or two, I will close up that summer house in Heath, Massachusetts, and will—per the landlord's instructions—set out poison for any way-worn mouse that might seek a home within its musty, warping borders; double-lock the door; and lodge the spare key on the shelf in the tool shed beside the rusty oil can. I will return to Cambridge and a warm, cool, timeless Indian summer will descend in a blazing of gold and blue. But the profundity of that blue would not have such depth except for, and its color can only be explained in light of, the blue of an antecedent sky, outspread years before over the horizons of a small midwestern town, our own Victoria. Nor would that gold possess so beguiling a luster were it not for an earlier, other, material gold. For reasons that I'm afraid would be all too transparent to a psychoanalyst, but which actually are far from simple, I dislike heights and have never flown in an airplane, but I am told that one need not get very high off the ground—half a mile up, perhaps—before the curvature of the earth heaves into view, and I would imagine there is a curious sort of floating attached to that vision, an alluring sense of skew lines, an inkling that the earth represents but one possible landing point. My story prepares to move backwardly forward . . .

Deep within the submerged, archaeological recesses of my late father's brain there glinted, rich but worn simple, like an old gold Roman coin, the hunger for a namesake. This was an appetite thwarted at my own birth by my mother's insistence that I be named for her father, who had died abruptly just two months before, the victim of a disfiguring accident in the lumber company where he had toiled throughout his entire adult life and from which he planned to retire in four months' time. My sister Nettie, who early on in life was singled out as a bringer of substantial disappointments to the family, thwarted him again by being born a girl. One might suppose, naturally, that his primitive dynastic impulse was assured of fulfillment when, a number of years later, the double opportunity of twin boys unexpectedly presented itself.

But to suppose this would be to reckon without energetic Doris, who with an equally primitive hunger, as well as a conviction that the naming of children was unshakably a maternal prerogative, hit upon the notion that identical twins required identical names—or names as close to identical as could be found. Negotiations went on for a couple of days. Doris had the advantage, sizable no doubt, of seeing her husband's position as wholly absurd. If one of the twins *was* to be named Boyce, she wanted to know, what was the other to be called? *What* name had any twinlike kinship to *Boyce?* My father, feebly, offered up Boris—but of course that wouldn't do at all. And *who* was to be the namesake and who the non-namesake? How was fairness to be achieved? she wanted to know. How could they, in *fairness,* give one of their children the handsome name of Boyce and the other the laughable name of Boris?

Fair in all things, Doris decided that the twins were to be called Tom and Tim. Or Tommy and Timmy, since she was flexible as well as fair. And how much closer to identical names could she, in all her egalitarian fervor, have come? This is a question which, in idle moments, I have often toyed with over the years. Craig and Greg? Gerome and Jeremy? Bart and Bert?

To an outsider, no doubt it would all seem a bit ludicrous, this attempt of Doris's to launch two infants out into the world as a matching set . . . But it would seem more pathetic than ludicrous to anyone who could page through the books and books of photographs she assembled over the years. Here are the two of them, two two-year-olds, in identical blue-and-white horizontally striped pajamas, and identical red-and-white horizontally striped socks; and here the two of them in matching bottle green sports coats and knickers; and here the two of them in sailor suits; and here the two of them in, yes, interchangeable Halloween costumes—a pair of diminutive hoboes, their faces streaked with burnt cork and (yes, truly, the photograph confirms my memory on this point) identical little yellow patches sewn onto the right knee of their identical little burlap trousers . . . One might reasonably suppose that Halloween in the Briggs household would have been regarded as a holiday from the continual task of human duplication, but no, Doris seems instead to have taken it as a call for a celebration and intensification of that great cause, identicality.

When Timothy was four or five, he developed an unacceptably self-assertive mole on his right cheekbone. This Doris had removed. Unfortunately, an infection crept in among the stitches, with the result that a small scar remained, and remains to this day. And although it is not known with any certainty, I strongly suspect that Doris considered making Tommy undergo the removal of a nonexistent mole, in the hope that a corresponding scar might follow . . .

Yes, you would regard Doris's exertions as laughable, and I would present them as laughable, but wasn't there conceivably something noble about her quest? Inexorably we diverge, all of us, as is our human destiny, even brothers nurtured from a single sperm and egg. For what I suppose might be regarded as unavoidable reasons, I have long been deeply interested in the phenomenon of twinship, and especially in monozygotic twins—a pursuit of knowledge that has led me doggedly through the clogged, mind-eroding prose of both the sociologist and the psychologist (worse even than the lawyer's constructions—of whose falsely exact, needlessly hairsplitting circumlocutions I might add only that I am tired of, and fed up with, them). And I have come away believing in internal forces that drive us—sister and sister, brother and brother—toward divergence. A force not solely in or of the mind, but of the physiognomy, the posture, the gait. As though the very bones of the identical twin's face, compelled so often to regard a mirror that is in fact no mirror, resolve to work themselves into features the earth has not yet beheld. What was

Doris's struggle but an attempt to counter the drift of a world whose every snowflake and rupturing wave is unique? To be a nonesuch is nothing. We are condemned to originality—although Doris, through her baby boys, meant to fight against that sentence with everything she had.

Those twins existed in a different, distant world, one out of touch with the present, with the Power Snax tunnels of my days and the Slak Shak glow of my nights, and yet I find it disconcerting, even now, to examine their photographs. Not surprisingly, the boys are easily confused, and I remark with some interest, as a quirk in my own psyche, that whenever a photograph contains but one child, I assume it to be Timothy. But when a photograph contains them both, when I am confronted by the children together and am compelled to distinguish one from the other, consternation sets in. I can't be sure of my own eyes. I don't know whether I know my own brother. I scrutinize, say, those two diminutive hoboes standing out in the backyard under a blue afterschool sky, each peering out at the camera with what looks like doleful resignation, and I am forced to say to myself, in effect, "Yes, let's see, yes, this is the Live One, on the left there, and the other, that's the Other."

It is a blue, an untroubled sky that hangs over that pair of vagrants, and in its matchlessly ravishing emptiness I locate my link, I leap forward to tell you that with the summer house behind me I returned to my classes, and delivered my lectures on legal philosophy to those dependably small if not intimate groups I attract each year. There is a bite to the evening winds, with a hint of menace to it, but striding out of the lecture hall in the mild early afternoon, having gracefully shaken off, like so many leaves from one's coat, a couple of grade-conscious students . . . emerging, I say, to a glimpse of that superior blueness, one knows instantly that the impression of passing time is an illusion. At the core of the universe, where all is balance and burnish, there can be no such thing as a forward-moving Time, or any other marring asymmetry. There are rings within rings, and the colors are blue and gold, at once deep and depthless.

One knows, on such a day, that nothing can ever happen, that every action is accomplished before it appears to occur—and yet, and yet there's something gratifying nonetheless, something jubilantly blue, in indulging that illusion by tending to life's little demands with all the punctiliousness they would request of us. I taught my classes that fall; rescued my apartment from its dusty somnolence; even reconciled Doris to Timothy's new plans . . . (I told her that this upcoming battle with the Congam machine—the makers, after all, of the world's fastest computer—would provide him with useful exposure to the business world. It would look good on a résumé. It would provide contacts and connections. Oh, I told her all sorts of things.)

One knows, on such a day, that nothing can ever occur, although all sorts of little "events" (illusory unravelings taking the form of fulfillments and surprises, quirks and coincidences) will obligingly come forward to "fill the time." A donkey will tumble off a ship and swim eight miles to the coast of Greece; a power failure will turn Buenos Aires fleetingly into a ghost town; a new pteropod will be disinterred by a septuagenarian Dane who, in taxonomic Latin, will christen the creature after his still-living mother. These were precisely the sorts of facts so dear to my father's heart. He gathered them up, all the tiny newspaper fillers, into a series of notebooks. He was a great collector, of coins and clippings, and together these two inexhaustible preserves extended their boundaries until they claimed nearly the whole of his life. Dear God, he would provide a sanctuary for them all! A carrot is exhumed in Oaxaca, Mexico, which with unmistakable puckishness resembles Emiliano Zapata. (*File that fact away . . .*) A goose in Winnipeg chokes to death on a golden egg—or at least a chocolate egg wrapped in golden foil. (*Save it . . .*) A man in Lisbon who has been deaf for fifteen years is awakened by the blaring rock-and-roll of his daughter's radio and his first words on that miraculous day are "Turn that damned thing off." And a young boy in Victoria, Indiana, plummets from a playground slide and comes home from school with a white adhesive bandage on his head. Clearly man was not born to fly.

This bandage makes him something of a family celebrity, especially in the eyes of his twin brother, who regards him, and the bandage, with awe and envy. There is worry that the wound will leave a scar, but after much discussion, and much repetition of the reassuring words of the school nurse, the dinner-table consensus is that probably it will not. The twins are sent to bed early, since one of them seems a little dazed or drowsy. And one of them wakes the next morning, and one does not.

One becomes a detached, hovering head, a thatch of sandy hair, a pair of blue eyes swimming in a domed blue sky that encloses a world where nothing ever happens.

IV

My meditation reveals thus far an irregular consistency, I'm afraid—or perhaps there is no harm in that. I would have the reader left worrying, just a little, as to whether we move any closer to that story about which, frankly, I suspect he has already read too much. I should perhaps have stated at the outset, but in any case will announce baldly now, that I have no interest in providing here the "bare facts," the "inside dope," the "intimate look."

To speak of an *irregular consistency* is to be reminded of the all but inedible oatmeal I was served at the Totaplex Hotel in Boston on the morning of the sixth game of the chess match. What they were charging then (I have not since returned) was four dollars per bowl. At that point, the glamour of his new life had perhaps faded somewhat for Timothy, but he still clung resolutely to his prerogatives as a guest of the hotel. He was not about to eat in another restaurant and at his own expense; nor about to breakfast in my apartment and at mine. A sweeping grandeur, or so much sweep and grandeur as was possible in someone who jerked and lurched around so much, had entered the flourish with which he would sign the bill at the close of a meal. He gloried in the hotel's absurd prices, as if these actually enhanced the quality of his free food and lodgings. The entire situation was all the more ridiculous given the indifference and even dislike he had always reserved for "gourmet dining." Oh, he was eating *money*—there could be no question that for him this was the ultimate commodity outspread on the breakfast table. He was managing, by judicious attention to the right-hand side of the menu, to consume day after day a twenty-dollar breakfast—and under such circumstances it mattered very little in what guise those dollars appeared.

Given how often and how publicly he complained about his lack of privacy, Timothy's decision to eat in the hotel restaurant rather than upstairs in his room may seem puzzling. In fact, he did run up astronomical bills for room service as well. But there can be no question about the enjoyment he took in looking affluent to the affluent. It delighted him to call loudly for the check—just as, I'm sure, it delighted the hotel management, as they steadily summed the bills against Congam's bottomless account, to have this week's minor celebrity seated where all the guests might see him. Didn't they not only indulge him, but encourage him, in all his mountainous whims? It must be recorded plainly that at this point Timothy was in a somewhat unsettled state. This is a complicated topic, about which I may eventually have a good deal to say, since there are so many misapprehensions to correct, but I would never deny that his behavior, even then, might have been termed "erratic." Something giddy and breathless had infiltrated his manner. To see him sitting there in the hotel restaurant was to see a kind of beleaguered monarch—one who wishes to believe that any problem can be disposed of with a wave of the royal hand, and yet who keeps receiving whispered, patchy reports that all is still not quite well in the kingdom.

I was deliberating over whether or not to send my bowl of cool and lumpy oatmeal back to the kitchen when our table was approached by a writer for a popular "newsweekly," who after the briefest of introductions struck right to the point: "But what does it mean to the *av*erage A*mer*ican, Timmy, who maybe doesn't even know a king from a bishop or a castle from a rook? This is the so-called royal game, and let's face it, we're hardly a nation of royalists, are we? I mean look at Tocqueville."

"Yes, look at him," I said.

"Now if you lose this match, and I'm sure you won't, but if you do, Timmy, what does that mean to the little man and the little woman on Main Street in Victoria, Indiana?"

"There is no Main Street in Victoria," I piped in. "And the people there are of no smaller stature than in Boston, or even New York." (It is perhaps not surprising that the occasional references to me in the press at this time were—as the saying goes—"unflattering.")

Such people are easy enough to dismiss (except perhaps in the physical sense), but what is one—what is Timothy—supposed to say when a Japanese journalist sidles forward, a pen tucked behind his ear, as if in imitation of those aggressive American newsmen he admires but cannot by nature make himself emulate . . . sidles forward, and says with a hesitancy that suggests insecurity with the English tongue, although in fact the words roll out faultlessly enough: "Pardon me, but one question, if you please. Do you think life is happy?" This particular encounter took place in a rest room on the M.I.T. campus, in those early days of the match before it, too, was moved over to the Totaplex Hotel (in order—so far as I can tell—to ensure that no journalist would have to face the inconvenience of a ten-minute walk). Pencil to notepad, our reporter from Tokyo is eagerly waiting, apparently in the cheerful expectation that at last he will be able to send home to his countrymen something that will clarify this whole puzzling story. A long pause ensues. And then, looking just a little crestfallen, and more than a little nervous suddenly, as if only now perceiving that his approach might somehow be flawed, the journalist continues, "But what do you feel is the purpose of man?"

It is a question I wonder whether my father ever asked himself. Presumably he had found some sort of satisfying answer, for in those monumental, back-breaking stacks of journals he left after his death there was not a single item or passage that might be called philosophical in even the most generous sense of that term. Not a single item that revealed any sort of probing, any type of quest. If one accepts without censure, as a "given," the structure and pastimes of his life, he would appear by all records to have been an almost preternaturally untroubled man.

He was, ironically, the son of an adventurous soul, of Ragnar Birgisson, born in Akureyri, Iceland, a sailor who for a time sought his future in the South Seas, where he caught malaria, and then moved to San Francisco, where he caught tuberculosis, and finally moved to a little town called Elizabeth—which, along with its neighbor Victoria, was one of the "regal sisters" of Founders Valley, Indiana. It was in Elizabeth that Ragnar's brother, Halldor Birgisson, had established himself. Halldor had clipped his name to Hal Briggs and—clipping in another fashion—had set up a profitable furniture-making business. Ragnar recovered his health sufficiently to marry, father a son, and take energetically to drink. He died five years later of what was evidently cirrhosis of the liver. Halldor, whose business had expanded to the storage and selling of grain, left no children and in time my father became his sole beneficiary. But what, in regard to his ancestors, my father actually inherited from whom—oh, there's the real question.

As far as my own memories are concerned, my father never went to work. Before I was born, he had apparently spent some dutiful years, or months, in the offices of the Briggs family business. But by the time I reached a memory-retaining stage of life, the enterprise had been sold and any conventional career was long behind him. As a child, I was of course only slowly able to perceive how singular his behavior was, and what an anomaly he created in that parceled-out, circumscribed world of Indiana's Founders Valley. He was for all the neighbors a unique and thoroughly enigmatic figure. Every other child of my acquaintance had a father who went off to work in the morning. That was what fathers did—but mine remained at home. *That* was what the Briggs family "did," so to speak—they remained at home. In fact, for a time in our household it was I, and I alone, who headed off, my lunchbox in hand, to work—which is to say, to school. Mother, father, baby sister would all bid me good-bye in the morning as I did that peculiar thing, departed from the house, and they would wait, like the court of Isabella and Ferdinand, for my return from *terra incognita.*

My father spent his days in his "office," a small, sunny, second-story room at the back of our big, wooden, gracefully mansarded house on Sweetwater Avenue—unquestionably the "best" street in all of Victoria. The office was strictly "off limits" to the rest of the family, including his wife. He divided his time between his coin collection and his journals. Both pastimes were pursued in an ornate, unhurried hand, as though he had all the time in the world at his disposal. He wrote drafts of letters to dealers and other private coin collectors, he drew up "tentative budgets" and "final budgets," he wrote off letters of inquiry and letters of thanks. And he often wore a large, potentially terrifying magnifying glass around his neck, in which a human eye could grow to monstrous, cyclopean proportions.

Doris inevitably describes her late husband with a contented series of negatives. He didn't drink. He didn't smoke. Didn't gamble and didn't chase women. Didn't curse and didn't raise his voice. He seems to have left her with little cause for complaint. One might see theirs as an unlikely alliance, this marriage between a poor, garrulous, uneducated Scottish-Irish girl of three-and-twenty and a quite well-to-do (as defined by standards obtaining in Victoria, Indiana), quiet, withdrawn, half-Dutch half-Icelandic bachelor of forty-four. But I can't picture *any* marriage that my father might have made as anything other than unlikely. I think I could trust myself to recount with greater verisimilitude the mating ritual and inner thoughts of, say, two pteropods than that courtship which brought my father and mother to matrimony. Some things are impenetrable. One must accept their union simply as a "given"—although for that matter,

I should perhaps somewhat contradictorily add that I cannot conceive of my father's having been married to anyone other than Doris, or she to anyone but my father.

The difference between my parents' ages may in actual practice have felt less imposing than the simple numbers might suggest. Photographs corroborate my recollections of my father as a man whose thick, brilliantined hair remained almost untouched by gray until the end of his life. His was an erect torso of medium size, slim and compact by nature, although in later years he gave way to a firm-looking stoutness. Photographs suggest a man who might have been athletic, although I haven't a single memory of his ever exerting himself physically for mere diversionary purposes—or for any other purpose, now that I look back upon it. His youthfulness made it all the more impossible to square his presence with a child's image of a "retiree." No, as I grew older, into my teens, and began to ponder life outwardly and actively, his dark, unbroken presence in that house became increasingly a Mystery—and one which, although perceived from the new, acute angles which age alone can bring, remains central to me yet.

. . . And a Mystery one might have expected to resolve itself when at last my father passed away, abruptly, leaving behind him his mountainous collection of journals. I was away, "back east," a college undergraduate at the time. The papers, as well as those coins that happened not to be stored in safety-deposit boxes at the Victoria Commonweal Bank, were left to sit untouched in his office. Years and years went by, and still they sat untouched. It was as though the injunctions that had prevented our entering his sanctum still held sway. His privacy must be preserved. I, for one, certainly felt no impulse to interlope into it.

The office remained intact, all but undusted, until some months after Doris came up with the astonishing news that she would soon be moving to Key Largo, Florida. None of her children believed her for a moment. We hardly believed her even when, in rapid order, she flew to Florida, purchased a condominium, and put the family house up for sale. But when a buyer was actually found, payments drawn up, and a "vacate date" arrived at, I drove out to Indiana to assist her. Now at last someone would have to come to grips with the dead man's papers, and who but I, the "scholar of the family," was up to the task? So numerous were the journals, and so bulky and heavy, that I could literally *feel* them there in the trunk of my rented car. They weighed down its back end; the car handled differently. Somewhere en route (actually, I can be rather precise on this point: I was in Pennsylvania, I had just crossed the Susquehanna River, it was late in the day and a light snow had started ticking across the windshield), my limbs suddenly warmed with a sense of grandiose intentions. Had I found my calling? Was this what it would feel like to find one's calling? Oh, how clear it all was suddenly! I would sort through every one of those papers with the greatest of care. I would plumb the mystery of that cyclops who guarded the numismatist's lair. I had, even then, inchoate forebodings that those papers would be dull, but in truth I gloried in the very promise of their dullness, which gave my resolution the more honor; I would stare right through the distorting lens of that dullness to look the cyclops eyes-to-eye.

But to speak of those papers as merely dull would be grossly misleading! It might be unfair to my father, who probably should be given credit for an unmatchable accomplishment—the compilation of the world's most boring monument—and would certainly be unfair to me, in light of what I eventually did with them. Their dullness was something I felt as a personal burden. As they sat stacked in my apartment, they weighed me down, as they had weighed down the car that brought them here.

His papers fell neatly into three categories. First, there were those concerned with coins. These included records of acquisitions, estimates, trades, etc., as well as elaborate reckonings of the value of various components of the collection. Second, there were daily, extremely detailed accounts of weather conditions in Victoria and Elizabeth, a log that missed scarcely a single day over a period of nearly thirty years. I offer one verbatim excerpt, which I copied as a record, a reminder, a reassurance for myself: "The steady rain which began shortly before noon gave way to drizzle at 2:15, which itself gave way to steady rain at 2:20." Third, there were newspaper stories. Sometimes, and particularly in the first few years of his journal keeping, these were taped or pasted directly into the pages, but the vast majority were *transcribed* in my father's handsome, painstakingly florid hand. Most of the stories that he had thought worthy of preservation were accounts of local Indiana news (the election of a new school board superintendent, perhaps, or the vandalization of a school trash receptacle), but here and there one found stories of curious or unusual occurrences taken from around the world (a donkey falls off a boat and swims eight miles to the shores of Greece; a carrot is discovered that bears a close resemblance to . . . etc.). He had transcribed thousands and thousands of news items into his quite plush and I suspect custom-made journals. The number of man-hours those journals represented was staggering to contemplate . . . And what, *what* was he thinking, that man, my father, as he would transcribe an article from the *Victorian Standard* on the renovation of Elizabeth's Capitol Hotel, scrupulously making note of all the typographical errors in the newspaper text? Did the annals he was keeping somehow seem of greater value than those parallel annals to be found in the files of the *Standard* itself? Did the events somehow become his own in the act of transcription? Did it seem to him that none of these events was real—that Toby Nagy's cow had not won a ribbon at the state fair, that snow had not fallen again for the third successive Christmas—until it was securely lodged within his journals?

There were few references to his children, and fewer to his wife. Neighbors appeared here and there, somewhat more often than did his family, which might lead an outsider to hypothesize that he had more dealings than in fact he did with the "outside world"—all of those people who were not of his immediate household. But most of these items (whose inclusion was perhaps to be justified under the heading of "local news") probably came from Doris.

He appears to have taken some special interest in the little girl who lived next door, whose name was Betsy Rolling. I remember her only slightly. She was blond, and I suppose was considered very pretty, and she was an extremely energetic child. From his office he could have watched her playing in her backyard. His interest in her was totally innocent, I am sure, or as innocent as any human being's interest in another can be. He recorded her fifth birthday, her receipt of a puppy one Christmas, her broken arm, the removal of her cast. Yet these references to "Betsy R." began to vanish as she approached her teens . . . She too was preempted, it would seem, by the weight of local news, of Indiana news . . . Probably no physical object in my life has oppressed me quite so unmercifully as those papers did. No, I'm sure of it: I have never known any physical object so oppressive to my soul. They were an insult to a mind that had been, at least potentially, a fine one. They were a final, damning indictment of a wasted life, and my relief was enormous when (one Christmas Eve, fittingly enough, as the ghosts of the past were flitting about me) I fed them book by book to the blaze of my apartment's little fireplace. It took hours, or so memory has it, and the books stank badly. Something in their glue, I suppose, resisted the blaze.

Consistency . . . The journals certainly did offer that. They were the most moving display I'd ever seen of the tyrannous, benighting, stultifying effects of a methodical mental consistency. No, my own meditation will not fall guilty of that fault, anyway. I will continue to proceed with an irregular consistency, which is to say, an inconsistent consistency, which is to say, with that unflinching comprehensiveness accessible only to paradox. I would have my words riddled with paradox. I would bring you (let the phrase be underlined, and later recalled) *something knotted up, and fantastical and stubbornly indirect.* And in this momentarily open spirit of resolution, of declaration, perhaps I should advise you that I am, very soon, going to plunge you more intimately into my view of things by making a farewell.

V

In the spring of 1901 (if I may induce you, just before you and I part ways, to take an auditor's seat inside my classroom), Bertrand Russell grew increasingly uneasy about certain logical uncertainties of a surprisingly troublesome nature. He was disturbed by the implications he discerned within the mathematical concept of class—and, in particular, of those peculiar classes of objects that are not members of themselves. "The class of teaspoons," he begins—quaintly, but there is a revolution stirring within his teacup—"is not another teaspoon, but the class of things that are not teaspoons is one of the things that are not teaspoons." At which, the student's inner eye is likely to squint for a moment—catching a misty glimpse of a mirrored mirror, perhaps, or a knot involuting into an infinite regress—and then to turn aside.

If, instead, one seeks resolutely to put oneself into a frame of mind wherein those mirrors are no mere mirrors, and that knot seems consequential, wherein it truly is the most consequential thing in all the world (as it was to Gottlob Frege, who saw more than a decade of slaving mathematical inquiry collapse with the realization that however hard he tugged upon this knot it would not unknot itself), we glimpse something else in the mist, and who among us could resist that light which promises us that once the paradox is recognized, and unraveled (when the knot is not a not any more), we would have our exit? . . . We would enter a system capacious enough to encompass the very paradox of self-reference.

Russell sits, like an overjoyed child, at the very summit of his Archimedean seesaw, perched on that lever by which the earth itself is to be moved . . . and yet why does it fail to budge? Why, instead, does the seesaw itself seem so rickety? He has erected (and is the last who will ever so erect) what appears to be a comprehensive mathematical system but—feel how it shakes!—there is somewhere a flaw in the playground he has built for himself. His is a system meant to last forever but—soon now—his forever is to meet another forever.

I was born into an age whose great privilege it has been to observe the first probing of the planet Mars—from early, speculative discussion, to unmanned flybys, to orbiters, to that culminating, initial successful soft landing in which, as perhaps never before, one planet reached out to grasp another. There it lies in our night sky, unchanged and unchangeable, the blooded planet (although of course less and less visible each year as the globe's most filthy creature works to shut out that troubling firmament). And there it lies, changed utterly. For a brief moment, fleeting as the blink of a sunspot, the minuscule spacecraft rips through the unresisting blackness. Those who should know consider it unlikely that this first true interplanetary probe will turn up any life forms on that frigid and windy skull, but of course the universe brims with wonders and who can say what we will find? The marvelous truth is that no one can say, no one on earth is positioned to know whether we will uncover a lifeless arctic desert or a place whose teeming life seethes and sways to the rhythms of micronic chemical chains more intricately jeweled than our own. It may be that those who should know, sifting and resifting calculations in their tiered fluorescent laboratories, refining and extrapolating, analyzing and extrapolating, have hit upon the truth—or it may turn out that superstition, myth, the untutored eye that has looked up, descried a red planet, and peopled it with the strangest creatures under heaven, is the far-seeing one. No one knows, although heading home from the town library in that summer of 1976, in those last few weeks before I left Indiana to head East (left for school, and for good), and looking up into the patchy morning sky, I know that soon we all will know. Soon the radioed analyses, and the cold photographs, will come falling back to earth, that great information-processing center, and we all shall know. Forever back into the past we have known virtually nothing about Mars; forever into the future, we shall know a great deal. And this is another of those junctions where forever meets and yields to forever—there on the streets of Victoria, Indiana, as a recent high school graduate (his youthfulness already revealing, to the sharp-eyed, a few threads of gray at the temples) saunters thoughtfully home, his head thrown back, a bundle of library books under his arm.

A boat—the fifty-five-ton *Discovery,* equipped with a crew of nineteen—sails from England on to Iceland and on to what will be known as the Hudson Strait, spills into what will be the Hudson Bay, ventures southward along its east coast, nudges into James Bay, fails to find what it seeks and drifts north, hurrying fast as it can now, for the cold is coming down like a wall. It is August, but up here, where the sun sheers so low in the sky, the cold, the killing cold, arrives early. Just a passage, a single saving strait . . . That is what the boat seeks, an unmapped waterway, linking one ocean to another, and through which riches, efficiency, glory will come streaming—the passage half of this crew will die in search of. Years later, the cartographic truth comes down: there is no passage. How could Hudson and his crew have been so foolish as to give their lives for a passage where there was no passage? The maps are drawn, refined, refined . . .

Weeks later, the news comes, literally, down. It arrives as a substanceless vibration across the black void and it announces the wisdom of the technicians: almost certainly, there is no life on Mars. Of course nothing has changed, the little planet glows bloodred as it always has, spilling its empty threat into the night sky, but of course everything has changed, since the threat is indeed empty. Its red has taken on another, less sanguinary, and I'm afraid less inspiring, shade . . . We have had to make an accommodation in this matter, as succeeding generations, for whom it will be a given, will never need to do. Our cranial cosmos—the great planetarium of the mind—has become a different place and why, one must ask, is the truth so often unwelcome? Why does the universe continually disappoint us? Something gradually acquired, is it, discontent as a tool of adaptation, an asset for the fittest? Or the eye that opens, by necessity of its own neurological construction, on a Euclidean world resenting being told that what it perceives is not quite there? Or might the source of most disappointment be external—are we merely seeing things straight on? Could it be that we are simply the first creatures on this fair earth sufficiently evolved to perceive that life itself is a raw deal?

In pursuit of such questions one might turn at times to a bookwormish Midwestern boy, only twelve and yet quite probing and contemplative, quite earnest and skeptical and methodical—in short, a young Garner Briggs—who, with a venturesome hunger that does not yet recognize itself as philosophical in origin, has taken up a quest that his family labels a hobby. He is the owner of a new microscope. It's a birthday gift, and he has been concocting a sort of home brew (a mix of mud, gravel, lint, nail parings, a few drops of milk, three balls of fuzz plucked in tiptoeing secret from his father's bathrobe, a polychromatic collection of human hair drawn from a family hairbrush, and, I'm afraid, some scrapings from his own ears and nose), which he has allowed to mature for over a week behind a curtain on his bedroom radiator. A gray-olive-brown that has no precise name, it has turned a deeply unpromising shade that is actually a sort of disguise. For the brew is full of riches. Garner has produced life.

Along with the microscope I—he—received a booklet in which is set out, in both name and diagram, a whole mad cageless zoo of cellular life, and now in a spiral notebook Garner begins to keep a scorecard of the life-forms that he has identified, that he has created. He, no less than his father, turns out to be a keeper of journals. He is the archivist for a world whose existence is unknown to our world and, for all the sense of duty he brings to his new employment, this is a task alit with passion. The truth is that he feels for them—those little scrambling lives. At bottom he already knows, perhaps, that their kick and throb express a wordless, inbred, outreaching dissatisfaction.

My task is to explain why a series of games played between an inarticulate, phlegmatic young man and a lifeless machine captured the imagination of millions of people who did not understand even the rules of that game. I remember sitting with

Timothy in his room at the Totaplex Hotel just at that time when it was becoming clear, if one may speak of clearness in regard to those days, that his match was expanding beyond what anyone had foreseen. Timothy (my "little brother"!) was becoming a celebrity.

"I want you to listen to this when you go home," Timothy urges and with slightly trembling hands places in my hands a cassette tape. "I got it Super Express, you know, twenty-four-hour service, from some guy in Ann Arbor." Trembling, too, ever so slightly, is Timothy's voice. The sudden new vastness of himself has created an echo inside him. "It's a song," Timothy confides. "About me you know. This guy, this history student guy in Ann Arbor, he wants me to help him market it, you know to offer my endorsement. You know, kind of an official song of the match," Timothy explains . . . and the simple act of recording his words here, just as he said them, disturbs me. Do I give a misleading impression about his state of mind? In truth, that reader is misled who would see here evidence of imbalance and nothing else, who would not see a healthy innocence, a boyish bedazzlement. How amazing—*how amazing it was for him!*—to discover that all those predictions he had been making for over a year, all those boasts about the "bigness" of the Congam match, had actually been great understatements.

"He wants to split the royalties fifty-fifty," Timothy tells me. "You know it's not a bad song. I mean I think you've got to admit it's kind of catchy. But if I'm going to endorse it, I mean make it the *official* song, I'm going to demand more than fifty percent." Timothy jerkily brushes a lock of sandy hair from his forehead. His blue eyes have narrowed in a pathetic and rather touching attempt to display a look of shrewdness, a hard entrepreneurial rapacity.

Well, I went home and actually listened, with mounting incredulity through the four interminable choruses, to that song. It was not at all what I had expected. This was no cynical attempt to exploit an emerging "news phenomenon"—although there were to be attempts enough of that sort before the whole affair was done. No, this was patently the work of someone who believed in what he was doing—some overage undergraduate, mind perhaps unhinged by hallucinogens, who had been moved by what he had seen in the newspapers and on the television, and who in his wakened passions felt the promise of some sort of personal release. Just as Timothy had emerged with such suddenness into the spotlights of renown, so, too, now would emerge this struggling songwriter from Ann Arbor, Michigan, whose song—so help me God—was entitled, "Timmy, We Believe in You."

And they did, by the millions, they believed in him . . . People all over the globe believed in him. They had invested their passions and their hopes in an abstraction that I, given my ties of blood, simply could not view as an abstraction. It confused me. In my own way, I was perhaps as confused as Timothy. What was it he stirred in them? The belief that his victory could somehow halt the invasion of all those machines that create in us each day both greater dependency and greater distrust? Did his "fans" watch the match with some of the assurance that early observers felt as the first biplanes were wheeled out, secure in the knowledge that if God had intended man to fly, He would have given him wings?

Maybe they did not know why they believed in him—but they wanted him, all the same, to *know* of their belief. If he could only *touch* an object of theirs, if the potent abstraction could somehow come down to lay a hand upon their world! He was sent requests for autographs and requests for his worn-out clothing, he was sent religious memorabilia, snapshots and confessions, poems and lucky pendants, a forty-pound clay bust of himself and a murky photograph that purported to show a boulder on the shore of Lake Superior into which wind and water had carved his initials, medical advice, a certificate entitling him to a free (and badly needed) teeth cleaning. He was sent a woman's undergarment, which I am told was in need of laundering.

They came from all walks and stations of life, his fans, but were united in their conviction that Timothy's victory would matter in some way that extended far beyond the Massachusetts

Institute of Technology, or even the "chain" of Totaplex Hotels. Theirs was a world in which purely symbolic action might have practical consequences—a world more hospitable and attentive than that other, which apparently surrounds us, in which symbol and seeker alike are borne helplessly forward on time's great crushing current. Somehow to believe, within that tumbling roar of interconnections, that the outcome of a mere game might rescue us from a hurtling descent into the gorge . . .

When my book *Legal Fictions and the Human Fiction* received a journalistic prize of some repute among obituarists, I delivered an acceptance speech which I am told dumfounded my modest audience by attempting in its three or four minutes to address a matter of genuine import. If I may indulge in the luxury of quoting myself (certainly a less venial sin than paraphrasing oneself, the technique by which most second and third books are written), I would repeat some of that address here: "Human law all but collapses once one removes from it the convention of the 'legal fiction,' that mythical being who pauses at the verge of each potentially destructive, illicit action to weigh its likely moral consequences. He reasons and he chooses.

"For hundreds of years, various philosophers, both 'pure' and jurisprudential, have told us that this model is unrealistic, and in the last few decades, particularly, the belief in rational choice, and what is typically called free will, has 'taken a beating.' An impressive weight of scientific, often neuro-biological, data has been assembled to further our suspicion that in actual practice, which is to say in 'real life,' the decision-making process diverges from our model. The experts may be right, and indeed the very resistance which their arguments engender may corroborate their rightness. But whether they are wrong or right, the mere plausibility of their objections leads us to a disjunction, a psychic schism, if you will, between what our experts tell us a human being is and what our everyday sense of ourselves remains. And it may well be that the preservation of law, which is to say of civilization as we know it, depends on the preservation of this inaccurate but convenient model. Which is to say, the continuation of society may well depend on the preservation of ignorance.

"We are told that the new models of humankind are preferable, because more accurate, and there is much to be said for this argument. We are told to welcome them because they are more interesting, which is to say more complex, and here what we have is . . . nonsense. No greater complexity exists than what we already have. Five people—yes, let us say five, five legal fictions—are afloat in a tiny life raft. A storm brews. Four are adults—a sickly old man, his healthy old wife, an accomplished navigator, a pregnant woman—and one is a child of fourteen. The little raft is overloaded and gradually it becomes clear that if someone is not tossed overboard the whole group will almost certainly perish. All five pause on the brink of a decision, and what is the fairest, the most equitable solution they can arrive at? The ancient paradigms are forever bringing us fresh problems of the best sort—which is to say, unanswerable ones."

Legal Fictions and the Human Fiction was subtitled *An Introduction*, words added not through that familiar academician's reflex which asserts that every scholarly book must carry a colon, nor as a display of false modesty. Much of what I said there requires amplification, and in a few cases I have modified my conclusions. But more directly and clearly than any other book ever to emerge in this country, *Legal Fictions and the Human Fiction* examines the question of what precise sort of entity it is that the law envisions itself being applied to. Humanity's perception of itself is altering, which is to say, humankind itself is being altered, and it is hardly clear how the law itself will have to alter. Eventually new legal fictions will be needed, since the need for Law runs deeper than the mere preservation of social order.

I suspect that nothing in the whole field of legal studies is so remarkable as that of our simple hunger for Law, this need for justice which we take with us even into the inanimate world. We move to the sixth game of the match, and Timothy has a decisive edge over the machine. Victory in this game is inevitable. Within the regulations governing the match, provision has been made that in such circumstances ANNDY's operators can resign on behalf of their machine. This is a provision inserted purely for Timothy's benefit; to spare him from needless exhaustion, he will not be required to pursue a foregone victory. Of course it is a provision of no possible use to ANNDY, or its makers, since the machine is indefatigable.

But Timothy—ashen-faced, and desperation blazing in his eyes, as though he stood on the threshold of another defeat rather than victory—refuses to let the machine resign. He would play on, and ANNDY must play with him. Now why would Timothy jeopardize the needed victory? It makes no sense . . . But after some shrugging of shoulders, some brief whispered consultations, it is agreed that the game will continue.

Timothy is driving his pawn to the queening square. His face has a peculiarly severe look: he is punishing the machine. He is pursuing Law. He is claiming Justice. And he is the Judge, he is the Lawman. The pawn would advance and there is no stopping it. In all the world, there can be no stopping it. Deeper, deeper must go that advance, until ANNDY is beaten, absolutely subjugated—the pawn queened, the king toppled. But when the game is concluded at last, and ANNDY's resignation accepted, Timothy rises with an uncertain look. Isn't it apparent that he wants to shake hands with the machine and not with its human operators? Triumph is on Timothy's pallid face, and a kind of stunned disbelief, but also isn't there a tinge of white-faced shame? One might suppose that having for a time ignored all the injunctions to halt, and having continued his forceful violation of this other mind, he has only now perceived, as he rises from his chair, that the victim of his advances is not living and has never been alive.

Has he escaped his own internal oppositions by projecting into the machine some aspect of himself? And having triumphed over it, must he now retrieve it, if he can, from the machine's cool, invisible core, in order to make himself whole again? If so, this has been an escape that is no true escape, and another method is needed . . .

I cling to all sorts of irreconcilable notions, one of which is that irreconcilability may itself be a principle of limited jurisdiction. . . . That there may indeed be some egress from the maze, that in the involutions of an infinite regress one may locate some aperture by which one can slide free of all previous reference. One must be wary, of course, and remain mindful of the mathematical chatter one overhears between the parabola and its asymptote ("Won't be long now—we're getting closer all the time . . ."). But I remain hopeful that if one begins with this recognition of confinement, and a yearning, which to be worth anything must be the most potent in one's life, for some release, we may go hence—may actually get somewhere.

I would go hence . . . and as I hope the rest of this account will make clear, my efforts on this behalf are stringent. Please accept these pages as the offspring of a yearning that says with clean simplicity *I want out.* I would have the reader accept this book, like its predecessor, as "an Introduction." I would present to the reader a deeper understanding of an event that dozens and dozens of journalists have already presented. I seek to be the best and deepest guide the reader has had, but if I am to attain my ambition it seems necessary for me now to bid you a partial but a permanent farewell.

VI

HIS EYES SEARCH in vain for his brother's face among the crowd of faces in Boston's South Station. The big clock tells him what he already knows. His train's twenty minutes early, which just goes to show how much they pad their scheduling in order to factor in for their own incompetence.

He feels nervous and alert stepping into this crowd of Boston people, still on the lookout for his brother; he feels himself entering enemy country. It's a pleasant sensation, all in all, for he comes readied for combat. He will leave this town in triumph. He can feel against his chest the business card of John Stanley Westman. It's tucked into the pocket of his flannel shirt. Would it be a good idea, he wonders again, to have cards made up for himself? On the one hand, cards suggest a certain professionalism; on the other, they're almost a confession that people don't know exactly who you are, or don't know how to get in touch with you.

He likes this sense of having come alone to hostile country, carrying nothing but a magazine and an overnight bag. Alone—without Imre, his trainer, who'd wanted to make the trip with him. But he'd told Imre to come up in a day or two. He'd wanted to arrive by himself. On his own—that's the point. Nonetheless, it's a relief when, some distance off, and his hair a whole lot grayer than expected, his brother materializes. "Would you believe it, the train was actually early," is how he begins to greet his brother, but he is interrupted—cut off at the start.

"Your arrival was indirectly heralded in one of our very local newspapers," Garner announces. It is typical of Garner to have something prepared-sounding to say, in place of any more conventional greeting. The two brothers shake hands. "I couldn't believe it, twenty minutes *early,*" Timothy repeats. He suddenly feels nervous—or a new sort of nervousness. He is never quite at ease with all of those intricacies that arise in meeting someone after a long separation. The handshaking, the exchanges of greetings—all of that sort of thing politicians and salesmen practice. He follows his brother to the mouth of the subway, and is explaining to Garner that John Stanley Westman of Congam Corporation has told him to keep taxi receipts, because Congam will reimburse him for all such expenses, when Garner interrupts again to say that the subway's probably faster, given the state of Boston traffic. And the subway, Garner adds, runs almost literally to the door of the Totaplex Hotel.

Timothy begins to feel better, exhilarated and sure of himself again, once they're seated on the subway. It reminds him of the city—New York City. He likes subways and that slightly subversive sense they give him of snaking from one place to another unseen by everybody up on the surface of the earth. He asks to see the newspaper article, and Garner draws from the inside pocket of his sports jacket a clipping from the Boston *Globe*. This article is short, and not bad as such things go. But it has his age wrong. He's listed as twenty-two rather than twenty-one.

Timothy vows to Garner that he will have them print a retraction. "It's not my age itself that's the issue. But it sets a bad precedent," Timothy says, and goes on (of course he hasn't a clue, poor boy, as to the inaccuracies and abuses he will soon be subjected to—but these must come in time, and in their place, which is not here) . . . and goes on, "We have to make sure they get things right right from the start."

The lobby of the Totaplex Hotel is awesome. "Some arrangement, huh?" Timothy marvels. There's a big waterfall that clatters into a pool in which a bust of the Venus de Milo rises on a pedestal. A sort of Moorish portico, inlaid with mosaics, stretches over the pool, which is also surrounded on all sides by low, flat couches in solid fluorescent colors. Timothy suddenly feels uneasily conspicuous—failing to perceive, somehow, that nothing and no one could be out of place in such a place.

Timid, nonetheless, Timothy finds himself uncharacteristically conscious of what he is wearing, and he darts a quick glance at his brother. Undiscerning as it is, this glance confirms Timothy's nervousness—for Garner seems to be as dapper as ever. (Garner in fact is wearing a pale gray shirt of broadloom cotton with a Viceroy collar and French cuffs; a darker, almost charcoal, pair of gray wool trousers; wing tip shoes; a blue and gray wool sports jacket, made in Belgium, with single vent back and two-button front; and a gray-, blue-, and red-striped Italian silk-twill tie held in place by an unobtrusive white-gold tie tack . . . *Held in place* and *unobtrusive,* yes; and just so, as promised, henceforth his own voice and presence must be.) When the two brothers make their way up to the reception desk, the woman behind the counter turns, predictably enough, not toward Timothy, in his flannel shirt, dungarees, and yellow and black footwear designed for some indeterminate athletic activity, but toward Garner. Perhaps a bit surprisingly, but only a bit, Timothy, too, turns to Garner for clarification.

Timothy's is a short-lived nervousness, however; once the actual business of checking in is behind them, and he has successfully operated the credit-card-sized plastic rectangle that serves as a room key, he's a confident and expansive soul once more. He sets his dusty overnight bag on top of one of the room's two double beds, and tosses his magazine on the other. It lands cover upwards and a grave Oriental face, that of a Japanese boy, stares up at the ceiling. Timothy turns on the television, remarks appreciatively, "Good picture, huh?", adds, "Food for peanut brains, it's incredible," and snaps it off. He lurches into one of the room's two armchairs, leans back, lunges forward, and draws from his shirt pocket a business card, which he hands to his brother. Timothy gives his brother time to digest the card's information before remarking, "John Stanley Westman, this is the guy, all right. He's very upper level at Congam. And he said I'm supposed to call him if everything isn't to my personal satisfaction."

"Personal as opposed to what?"

"It's an expression," Timothy explains.

"Yes . . ."

"I'm supposed to see him tomorrow." There is something winsome in Timothy's manner, which mixes so incongruously pride and deference. He has had heretofore little, indeed almost no, experience with the adult world of commerce—this is evident even in the scrupulous way that Timothy recites the man's three names, and in the gingerly way he handles the business card.

"And what are you going to wear?" Garner asks him.

"Wear?" The word might as well be "where" for the fuddled tone in which Timothy asks it. "Well, I brought a tie," he answers, with a shrug at the crumpled overnight bag on the bed.

Garner cocks his head slightly and lifts one eyebrow. It is an expression he often calls upon in his dealings with his younger brother—one which, for all its years of service, still rarely fails to have its intended effect: it disconcerts Timothy, just a little. "It's one you gave me," Timothy adds. "Coupla Christmases ago. And I brought other shoes, too."

"If you show up looking the way you do now," Garner says, "this Mr. John Stanley Westman is naturally going to suppose that his company is putting you up in the wrong place. He's going to think you belong somewhere a good deal less expensive."

This observation represents a logical If-then proposition to Timothy, who gives it the moment's serious reflection that any substantive deduction requires before—jerkily—nodding his assent. "Muh," he says—a sound that is, apparently, a hybrid variant of a close-lipped "Mmm" and an open-mouthed "Uh-huh."

"We could go now if you would like."

"Muh."

"I could go with you. You don't know the clothing stores around here."

This last is a small joke, since Timothy obviously does not know the clothing stores anywhere. But Timothy seems to accept this remark, too, as a logical proposition.

"How much you think'll cost?" he asks at last. "I'm asking only because of course I'm going to have my prize money soon, but I didn't bring all that much with me. On account of Congam's paying for everything," he explains.

"We can put the bills on my credit card. You can pay me back later," Garner suggests.

So—through the carpeted hallways, down the elevator, into the lobby with its indoor cataract, go these unlikely brothers, and from there out into the street. This early-October day has turned cool. What appear to be rain clouds amass overhead. Timothy pauses on the sidewalk, lifting his long chin as if the better to sniff the air, and says, "I should call the Boston *Globe.*"

"Maybe you'd better wait until we finish our shopping."

"I have to call Mom. I told her I'd call her when I got in." This remark is, vaguely, aggressive.

"You can do all of your calling from the hotel."

"I have so many things I have to *do,*" Timothy sighs, although the impression he gives, standing there nervously on the sidewalk, is a completely contrary one: he's waiting, heedless as a child, to have his empty day planned and filled up for him.

Garner naturally shies from escorting anyone dressed the way his brother is into his own clothiers. Instead, he leads Timothy into an anonymously large but perfectly reputable shop on Oldfellow Street. He asks Timothy, again with a mild, playful hint of sarcasm, whether he happens to know his own shirt size.

"Fifteen, thirty-four." Timothy seizes eagerly upon this chance to hold his own, to be on solid ground at last: "That's fifteen neck, thirty-four sleeve."

"Yes . . ."

French cuffs, of course, are impossible for Timothy, who would never be able to manage cuff links. Garner steers his brother instead toward two simple but evidently well-made (gauntlet button, vertical seam at the shoulder yoke, etc.) shirts, one white and one a very pale lilac. Although Garner prefers pure cotton, preferably Egyptian cotton, for himself, generally, he chooses for Timothy a blend of cotton and synthetic fibers—a material of greater practicality for someone unlikely to change his shirt each day, or even every other day. Timothy, his flannel shirt wadded into a plastic bag, wears the new lilac Oxford cloth out of the store.

The two brothers move along to a shoe store just off Oldfellow Street, where with great if imperceptible finesse Garner steers his younger brother away from the monstrous mongrelized "shoe boots" that immediately catch his eye and on to a fine pair of English brogues of a brown that is only a shade or two lighter than black. The bill, once two pairs of brown socks of a wool-and-cotton blend have been added to it, comes to $130. Timothy leaves the store with his new shoes on his feet.

"You can pay me back when you win the match," Garner says. "With your prize money."

"If I don't win, I only get half the money."

"In that case, you only have to pay me half of what you owe me. You see I'd like to have a stake, a fundamental stake, in this match, too," Garner says. In truth, the money suddenly seems all but irrelevant to him. This is fun. Garner has his own mobile mannequin on hand, and (for one day, anyway) his brother will be turned out in the most tasteful and dapper of fashions.

Dark rainclouds have continued to thicken overhead and the crowds are scurrying along. With Timothy having now safely crossed the threshold of presentability, Garner conducts him to a little shop on Edgemore Street. Here, Garner's friend Achille Ariana, who has worked in this store for more years than Garner has been alive, greets the two of them with festive warmth. This is an establishment that generally does not stock "ready to wear" slacks, but a pair of cotton-and-polyester chinos are found in Timothy's size. Timothy proves a little difficult to fit in a pair of trousers. For all the narrowness of his chest and waist, his hips are surprisingly ample. A second pair of trousers, a dark gray wool not dissimilar to those that Garner is wearing, seem quite promising, although they would require a few alterations. But for one of his favorite customers, Mr. Ariana is willing to move mountains—or at least the mountainous tailor, Mr. Miccinelli—and the pants are promised by tomorrow. Timothy selects a regrettable red and cobalt-blue necktie for himself, which Garner is careful not to censure, and Garner selects for his brother a second necktie—this one in alternate rows of fine ivory-colored diamonds and lavender rosettes on a sandy background. It "goes" perfectly with Timothy's new lilac-colored shirt. In fact, the tie so appeals to Garner that he searches until he finds another just like it, for himself. "We'll be twins," he proposes, and this offhand and perhaps somewhat careless remark leaves a queer stillness in the air. Garner certainly feels its queerness, anyway, although he isn't absolutely certain that Timothy, who has been looking a little dazed ever since this unprecedented buying spree began, actually notices.

The remark calls up a ghost, that of Tommy, Timothy's identical twin, who died at the age of not-quite-six, and probably no one outside the Briggs family could ever quite understand the curious, unresolved place that little Tommy, or at least his ghost, continues to hold among the surviving members of the family.

One might suppose that a decade and a half would have proved a sufficient interval for a full reconciliation to have been achieved. But the death has not yet been accepted; it has left an unaccountable unspoken guilt, or a kind of shame—a mutually constructed web of secrecy similar, perhaps, to that which might have been woven around an instance of family madness a hundred years ago.

"You need a haircut," Garner tells his brother as they step out into the street once more. Garner is hungry, and just a bit tired of playing the role of guide and counselor, but it is getting on toward late afternoon and the barbershops will not remain open much longer.

Timothy assents readily enough. "Okay," he says. "All right." It is as though he has gone completely soft beneath his crisp new clothes; he seems to have lost all of his normally formidable reserves of rebelliousness.

If required to characterize it, Garner with his taste for paradox would probably describe his relationship with Timothy as "distant but close." Theirs is a physical distance rarely bridged by telephone calls or letters, and yet, Garner would suppose, they are united by profound feelings of attachment and mutual concern. Still, Garner is hardly prepared for the tender feelings evoked on seeing his younger brother in the barber's chair. The way that unkempt head pokes out from the barber's voluminous snowy sheet—yes, Timothy seems a mere boy again, and an upwelling of affection burns Garner's esophagus. The moment is reverberative, an echo of what must have been many occasions, although he has forgotten them all, when as a young man he led his baby brother to a barbershop (Red's Barber Shop, although Red had long ago become a snowy-haired man), on Soldiers Way in the little, pretty town of Victoria, Indiana, where the two brothers, though separated by half a generation, grew up.

In the lobby of the Totaplex Hotel, Timothy shakes a few raindrops from his freshly cut hair, for the two of them have not completely escaped the coming downpour. "Welcome Plastic Surgeons" reads a bulletin board beside the Moorish fountain. Among these people who make their ample livelihoods by transforming human appearances, Timothy moves as a transformed person. He even seems to be walking with less of a slouch than usual—as though the new clothes constrain him and he cannot immediately succumb to all of his old habits. It is while the two brothers are riding the elevator up to the fourteenth floor, probably, that the storm finally breaks. In any case, when Timothy unlocks the door to his room, a harsh clatter can be heard against the big window. Timothy goes over and throws open the curtain. The Boston skyline has been obliterated. A vertical river streams down the glass. Timothy glances around the room. Pride in his new lodgings is unmistakable—and, again, affecting. "Some spread, huh?" he asks, and adds, "I guess you could call this adequate shelter from the storm." A cowlick has sprung up on the back of Timothy's pruned head, just where, Garner notices with a sense of bracing satisfaction, it always did when Timothy was completely a boy.

VII

THE FIRST THING he does, after the storm has died down and Garner finally says good-bye, is to remove the new clothes, carefully. He isn't himself inside them. He hangs them up in the empty hotel closet. There are two kinds of hangers. There are normal, cheap plastic hangers, the kind you get from the dry cleaners, and there are hangers made of wood. The wooden ones, though, cannot be removed from the central clothes bar. It isn't a hook that attaches them to the bar but a closed metal loop. It surprises, it disgusts him—the realization that people who could afford to stay at this hotel would steal clothes hangers. But after a moment it makes him laugh as well. They're all petty crooks, he thinks, the rich, they're no better than anybody else. Oh, he has known for a long time about their being crooks, people who think their money puts them above the Law . . . But to see them as *petty* crooks, that does have to make you laugh . . .

Timothy Briggs stands in his undershorts in a room on the fourteenth floor of Boston's Totaplex Hotel, feeling unsure of himself but confident that some sort of clarity is imminent. In just a moment, some inner directive will make itself heard; it is, he knows, only a matter of waiting to be told what to do. He hesitates at the sight of his dungarees, which he has retrieved from their plastic shopping bag, and then, just as he'd expected, he realizes what ought to come next: he needs a shower. It is as though his new clothes, in all their clean stiffness, still linger on his skin, and even though he showered this morning, and usually does not bathe more than twice a week, their unfamiliarity must be rinsed away. He pads into the bathroom, locks the door, and peers into the mirror over the sink.

The face in the mirror startles Timothy. He had forgotten all about his haircut. He closes one eye and narrows the other to a slit, which brings the image in the glass, somehow, closer to the one he knows. He reaches up and runs his fingers lightly back and forth over the sharp part in his hair, to soften it, and the effect of this, too, is reassuring.

Timothy spends little time outdoors and yet his face takes and holds whatever sun it gets, remaining always a shade or two darker than his forever pallid neck and chest. His face never tans, exactly; the sun seems instead to draw it toward a yellow, sandy color. His hair is a similar sandy shade, as are the almost invisible freckles that saddle his fine, slightly prominent nose. His is a remarkably monochromatic face (his teeth are a deep, disturbing yellow, and even his corneas are more yellow than white), and one in which the features seem to disappear into each other—sandy eyebrows into sandy brow, sparse sandy whiskers into sandy jawline . . . All except for the pale blue eyes, whose pupils seem dwindled, as though the light they encounter is perpetually too bright.

Timothy discovers on the sink two little bars of soap wrapped in pale green paper. TOTAPLEX is printed on each in dot-matrix blue letters. While the unwrapping of an ordinary bar of soap means nothing to him, these promise to be different: he yearns to open one of these smart little packages. It is as though, merely by being small, these green bars are transformed into gifts, designed expressly for him.

It occurs to Timothy that he might use one of the bars now and take the other back with him to New York, but this possibility recalls to him the wooden coat hangers in the closet, and all the thieving that goes on in a hotel like this, and he resolves not to remove from this room a single item that isn't his own. He considers, instead, asking the woman at the reception desk whether he can take one of them home. But she may think this a little peculiar. It could even put her into an ethical bind—in which her duty to please the customer would push her to condone a theft.

As Timothy steps into the shower he discovers two additional similar-sized bars of soap in a covered dish beside the tub. Clearly the hotel has estimated a level of soap consumption far in excess of his actual needs. He calculates that if he uses soap sparingly, and is careful not to leave it in the drain, one of these little bars should last him a week or so. And couldn't he then pack one of the other bars for home, having merely redistributed what is, through the hotel's own computations, his own soap? Possibly.

Beside the light switch there are two additional switches. Both are labeled. One says FAN and the other says HEATER. Standing on the bath mat, dripping freely, he tries the HEATER switch but nothing seems to happen. Then he realizes that a coil on the ceiling has begun to tick and glow. He lets them all run, LIGHT, FAN, HEATER, while he stands drying himself with a monogrammed towel. TP the towel says, in little dots meant to represent again a dot-matrix computer printer. They call this place a "high tech" hotel and you've got to admire the way they keep letting you know it, right down to their towels. TP stands of course for Totaplex, but Timothy smiles to think that somebody unintelligent might think of Toilet Paper. He dries his body carefully. When he steps back into the bedroom, dressed in the same pair of undershorts, he experiences a hunger so familiar that it need not rise to full consciousness in order to be identified. Much as a heavy smoker might wake up and feel a need that will be met by actions that are not fully conscious (fishing a cigarette from an open pack, lodging it on lower lip, flicking a lighter, setting flame to end and drawing deeply), Timothy drifts toward the overnight bag on the bed. His chess set is inside it. He pauses beside the bag, however, as one semiconscious hunger is tugged at by another. He waits. He knows that in all likelihood he need only wait for the thing to declare itself; he will be told just what to do. And sure enough, it comes to him—the magazine. He had been reading an article, on the train, which still calls him, hours later.

He goes over to the other double bed and picks up the crumpled *Time* and stares once again into the small, indrawn eyes of the Oriental boy on the cover. The face holds Timothy. Behind its smooth, impassive features, Timothy detects the powers of an enormous intelligence. As a chess player, he prides himself on his ability to read in another's face the mental reserves within. In this case, the words below the face would suggest something boyishly cute: MA-CHAN: THAT MUSICAL MIRACLE! the caption reads, but the overall impression of this face is not cuteness but, for all its youth, formidable strength.

The flat, planar lines of the boy's Eastern face stir inside Timothy a remote resentment. If some "musical miracle" *must* come along (and it may be that the appearance of any prodigy, even one well outside the chess world, undermines him a little), he would much prefer that it not arrive from Japan. And yet—and yet, Timothy finds so much that is appealing in this Ma-chan's story that, reading along, he actually winds up rooting for the kid. The article describes a kind of battle—and what an amazing mix of forces these are! This little kid, only twelve years old, matched up against musical experts and theorists working in the biggest universities and orchestras in the world. As big as M.I.T., as big as Congam . . .

So far as he knows, Timothy has never heard a single note composed by Ma-chan, whose real name is Masahiro Tatsumi, and even if he were to sit down and listen to an entire symphony, he would still feel unqualified to make any serious evaluation. Classical music (in fact, music of any sort) isn't something that interests him all that much. But the controversy itself couldn't be clearer: there are those who want to believe in Ma-chan and there are those who do not. And the believers would tell you he is already writing music that Haydn or Mozart would have been proud of, while the nonbelievers would say he's nothing but a skillful mimic. That's the trouble with music, Timothy knows, which is supposed to be so much like chess, but isn't at all, really: in the world of music, one never had to admit to being checkmated. This Ma-chan could write what Mozart, Beethoven, Tchaikovsky, Sousa, all of them in heaven, would freely admit was the greatest symphony ever written, and still the critics on earth could go on denying it. With chess, at least, no one could take away your accomplishment. Maybe they don't put your face on the cover of *Time*—that's the trouble with America, none of the mental discipline you need to love chess the way the Russians do—but if you're a winner you can always tell the experts to go shove it.

His stomach aches a little, and it seems it has been aching for some time, in fact, and Timothy realizes that he has become extremely hungry. Being in Boston has shifted everything around. In one of his letters, John Stanley Westman promised that Congam would be paying for all "ordinary expenses, including meals," but Timothy doesn't know quite how to proceed on this. What is "ordinary," after all? He could order up something by room service, which would probably mean the meal bill would be added to his overall bill, but something might go wrong, and anyway Timothy doesn't like the idea of having to pay somebody a dollar or two just to carry a sandwich upstairs. He wishes, as he has a number of times in the last few hours, that Imre was here to advise him—not that Imre was ever much good when it came to any sort of super-fancy place like the Totaplex Hotel.

Timothy waits and then an idea occurs to him. There's a sort of brochure on the desk—a big fancy deal in laminated plastic that looks like a menu but has a cover that reads "ABOUT US . . ." He goes over to study it.

"We are your TOTAlly modern, your business and pleasure, your working and resting, living- and leisure-comPLEX . . ." The phrasing, the use of capitals, seems peculiar—until Timothy perceives what he suspects is too subtle for most people to notice right away: the capital letters spell TOTAPLEX. He likes this touch. Riddles, codes, games . . . he doesn't care for them indiscriminately. In fact, sometimes they make him quite angry—when they seem childish, silly, or a simple waste of time. But this sort of cleverness, in which one tier of meaning is conveyed without bothering anyone, so that those who don't recognize it don't even see that they don't see, sets up a sort of pleasant tickle in the recesses of his brain. With an expanding sense of pleasure and well-being, he reads about Boston's Totaplex Hotel, which is equipped for teleconferences and FAX transmissions and video presentations; which offers computer terminals on a rent-by-the-hour basis and a "communications expert" on call during working days and twenty-four-hour phone transcription services; and which includes a swimming pool, a Jacuzzi, a weight room, a multireligious center, and a "gamut-running strictly rotated" art gallery; and whose elevators lead down into an underground shopping mall. "It's incredible," he says to Imre, as if Imre were here. It's an exclamation squeezed pleasurably out of Timothy's chest, and he can feel Imre's heavy, happy nod of disbelief.

He turns to the page marked ROOM SERVICE and looks first to the right-hand side (the prices are ridiculous) and then to the left (the food sounds complicated). When eating out, Timothy generally avoids any menu item that carries a long description.

Better, he concludes, to go down and check out the restaurants in the lobby. And he can take Mr. Westman's letter with him, on its Congam stationery, just in case there's any problem. Just a little guiltily, envisioning Garner's lifted eyebrow of disapproval, he slips back into the pants and shirt he had on before the shopping spree began. As a sort of compromise, he decides to wear the new shoes. These are stiffer than they look. He likes the way they shine, though, in the light of the corridor, and in the light of the elevator on the way down—but as he enters the lobby, he senses that people may be staring at his feet, and to make himself less conspicuous he takes somewhat smaller steps than usual. He is carrying in his right hand the issue of *Time,* rolled tightly into a tube, and he slaps it a couple of times in the palm of his left hand in a casual sort of way. Hesitating just a moment, he enters Colette's Cafe, which even though it has a French name seems to be, Timothy is relieved to see, an informal coffee shop. When he begins explaining to the hostess who seats him that he's a guest of the hotel, a guest of Congam Corporation, she cuts him off by announcing that he can charge the meal simply by presenting ID and his keycard. Timothy nods at her as she marches off, leaving only her perfume in his nose. He'd hoped to be asked to produce the letter from Westman.

He'd hoped, too, to order a couple of hot dogs, but there are none on the menu. And the only hamburger, called a Totaburger, doesn't sound like what he wants. It weighs in at a third of a pound, which almost certainly means it's too big to get your mouth around. Timothy doesn't like hamburgers he can't get his mouth around. He asks the waitress, who appears to be Spanish, or maybe Oriental, to divide his Totaburger into two smaller burgers, but she doesn't understand—or, more likely, pretends not to. Eventually she calls over a waiter, but Timothy knows instantly that this is somebody who will be no help at all, since he's wearing eye makeup. Not lavishly, but it's there. And he has that manner, that very theatrical usually New York manner, of suggesting that he isn't really a waiter—but only somebody who is *playing* a waiter, and so of course must act as though never in his whole life has he met such a peculiar request. After listening to Timothy repeat what he wants a couple of times, he says, in a tone of huge relief, as though he has just now cut his way through Timothy's maze of confusion, "What you're asking for is an extra *bun . . .*"

What so annoys Timothy about all of this is how anybody could pretend to misunderstand what can be so precisely expressed. "What I am asking for is for two hamburgers, each weighing approximately a sixth of a pound and each on a bun—you can charge me for the extra bun—and the *one* order of french fries that usually comes with a Totaburger, and two Cokes."

This ordering of two Cokes is of course another invitation to feigned confusion. But it's Timothy's usual practice, and he sticks to it now. It always seems better, on the whole, to put up with having to repeat the order than to put up with thirst in the event that service turns out to be poor. The waiter says, "Oh, are you expecting someone?"—which is a response Timothy has heard dozens of times before. "Should I set another place?" he also asks, but this calls for no answer, since he isn't really asking. He is merely working out an exit line that will carry him toward the kitchen.

Timothy opens the issue of *Time,* turning again to the article about the "musical miracle." His eye falls randomly upon a paragraph beginning, "If the Eighties were Japan's 'Decade of Boom and Bloom,' then the—" and then the map alongside pulls his eyes away. The idea of growing up on an island, like Ma-chan, is deeply attractive. Timothy studies again the location of this group of four islands, the Okis, out in the Japan Sea. He'd never heard of them until recently—but apparently no one else had, either. One of the troubles with chess is that you can't really study it in complete isolation, you need competition sooner or later, although on Iceland they do all right. To some extent, it all depends on the island. They have the highest per capita rate of grandmasters in the world, the Icelanders, and this statistic encourages Timothy, since his grandfather was Icelandic. Timothy has never been there, but the phrase *Icelandic blood* vibrates for him. It's one he has heard hundreds, thousands of times on his mother's lips. (For her, it explains a great deal about the men in her family.) The ideal island (Timothy supposes, entertaining anew an old vision of a better world) would lie a little ways off the east coast of

America. It would be devoted solely to chess, with a chess library and all the best players given free accommodation, year in, year out, and Timothy feels an old, bitter disappointment that such an island doesn't exist. It would take money, and the Western governments would never come up with that.

Almost more interesting to Timothy than Ma-chan is Ma-chan's grandfather. Timothy examines the old man's face once more. His name is Zentaro Katsuoka. He is white-haired and kind looking, his ancient face creased with a big grin, but below the picture the caption reads, THE WORLD'S MOST GENIAL STEELINESS. Timothy likes this phrase, which sets him thinking about Imre, his own trainer. Imre has been great, yes, indispensable in all sorts of ways—but, Timothy has to ask himself, doesn't he maybe lack that final measure of fanaticism? Would anyone ever use the word "steeliness" to describe him? Imre has been teaching him patience, which is a great virtue and something he somehow never learned before, and also to love purity, an absolute cleanliness on the board, elegance that may not be so rich as what the most complicated mid-game offers but which has satisfactions all its own. Which is to say, Imre has been teaching him balance. Imre has been great—there's no denying that. And yet, Timothy feels qualms in his stomach as he scrutinizes that white-haired face whose grin has all but swallowed up its pair of tiny eyes. Timothy reads, entering in mid-sentence: ". . . he is quite firm on this point. No, the boy has never heard a single note of post-Mozartean music. Surely a jingle on the radio? he is asked. A stray melody at a friend's house? No, no, not a single note—at least since the boy came to the island ten years ago. Movie music? Television scores? The incredulous reporters wait for him to back down, to qualify, to admit an exception. And again that wide grin breaks, that genial steeliness shines forth. *Zenzen*, Katsuoka confidently pronounces. Which means Never."

There is comfort to be had, though, in all the similarities between this Katsuoka and Imre. It was at Imre's prompting, after all, that Timothy has stayed away from tournaments this past year, in order to go back to square one. Like Ma-chan, Timothy has been spending his time "underground," and he feels ready now, like the "musical miracle," to burst into glory.

The arrival of the food catches Timothy off guard, deep in thought, and he is embarrassed by the little lurch of surprise with which he responds to the waiter's "Here we are." With bustling motions that feel a little defensive, Timothy clears a place on his plate and pours a broad pool of ketchup, which he salts heavily. He enjoys ketchup with most of what he eats, but he doesn't like having it sprawl directly on top of his food. Instead, he likes to dip his food into it—hot dogs, hamburgers, onion rings, omelettes, french fries, dinner rolls, sandwiches. It's another habit that Garner disapproves of. Garner's always joking about "ketchup fondue," but in fact it's neater this way, and you have better control over how much ketchup each bite is receiving. And less spilling, too.

Timothy's eyes jump here and there over the article as he eats. He reads that Katsuoka-san once played with a Tokyo symphony, that he was one of the finest violinists in Japan at that time, but actually never quite a world-class musician—and in this way, too, Timothy is reminded of Imre, who was once the champion of Hungary but never quite, quite of world class. Timothy returns to the opening of the article, which he liked the first time around: "He tips the scale at thirty kilos—which, as he will translate readily for any American not yet at home in the metric system, is sixty-six pounds. Even in Japan he is considered small for his age, but from the Land of Miniaturization now emerges what may be the most stunning—and exportable—package yet to . . ." Timothy wonders how tall he himself was at the age of twelve. He can't remember, but there would be records, school records, back in the Robert Browning Elementary School. Back in Victoria, Indiana, which is thousands of miles from the Oki Islands in the Japan Sea.

But what most interests Timothy is something that the article only touches upon. The key here, obviously, is Ma-chan's education. To Timothy, the notion of never going to school, of soaking up one's entire education at home, is powerfully appealing. It fills him with hope, with anger. Always he feels himself pressed on all sides to finish his schooling, by people who don't have the vision to comprehend that he may already have spent far too long in schools as it is. Timothy wonders—wonders constantly—whether his game might now be a good deal further along had he never gone to school. If he'd only met Imre sooner! If he'd only spent every day, full-time every single day, studying chess, what might he not have achieved by now? The question torments him. The possibility must be faced that a big mistake was made, and so long ago that it can never be remedied now—that he has already lost the heights he would otherwise have attained. That they are out there, those heights, that they are real, and he may never climb them. He jabs a handful of cool french fries into his ketchup pool and crunches down upon them.

Of less interest to Timothy, though evidently of major interest to the writer for *Time,* is the affection that Katsuoka feels for the very music he has forbidden his grandson. Timothy does not know what to think when he reads that in Katsuoka's eyes all of Western music took a wrong turn with Beethoven. Timothy reads the last few lines of the article: "His hand leaps again to bow across that invisible instrument. 'But this does not mean that Beethoven's music is not beautiful. I myself used to play his violin concerto—although it was much too difficult for me,' he modestly adds. His floating hand freezes as he lowers his voice to make a confession. 'Sometimes, when the boy is out with his mother, I will listen to that concerto. Or at night, when the boy is sleeping, I listen with my headphones.' And that transforming grin, joyful and sly, breaks across his face once more."

Timothy studies his bill. He wonders whether tipping would be classified as an ordinary expense in Congam's eyes. And partly because he isn't sure, and partly because he isn't happy with the service, he leaves a tip of only eleven and a half percent. He exits quickly in his shiny new shoes and heads into the hotel newsstand, where he buys a copy of *Newsweek.* As he ascends in the elevator, alone except for the Muzak that is piped inside it, he wonders when was the last time—if ever—that he bought two news magazines in a week.

He takes off his shoes the moment he enters his room and pads over to the window. It's a huge window, really, stretching almost from the floor to the ceiling. That alien skyline—Boston's—has emerged out of the rain but is now fading into the night. The buildings are beginning to light up and on that thin block of distant deep river water visible between two buildings a little boat goes by, rowed by a single person. Timothy has traveled here and there to various chess tournaments but he has never been put up in such luxury. To stand at this window, looking out, produces a hollow feeling low in his chest or high in his stomach. It is a little like hunger, this feeling, but it is assuaged a bit when he spreads his arms and places his hands, palms flattened, on the glass. Looking out upon the foreign, miniaturized Manhattan of Boston, he is aware of the possibility, although it does not quite coalesce into words, that he has indeed climbed to some sort of pinnacle in his life. He is a silhouette, Timothy Briggs, and is aware of himself as a silhouette: a sandy-haired young man staring out with a slightly opened jaw upon a rain-washed city, his mind working, sifting and seeking to reconcile both the vast, sweet promise of this skyline and a queer sense of oppression that hems him in on his other three sides. Only what lies before him, only the city is open. It's lit with opportunity. And the opportunity on the one side, and the oppression on the others, seem to have come to a kind of balance inside him, a stalemate of pleasure and anxiety, and then it is as though a minuscule subversion occurs—some minuscule, momentous shifting of the pieces by which everything is altered. They would hurl him, if they could—those forces that hem him in, they would hurl him right through the glass, to fall where there is only pavement to break your fall.

He lurches back from the window. Through vectorial distributions of power he is moving, as always he moves, even if sometimes he might ignore them: but they are there, the alignments, the air's assembled, compacted energies always are there. He removes his set from his overnight bag and snaps it open. The air clots around this new entrance; it is struggling toward a future of sharper axial alignments. Between his sandy eyebrows, a single vertical furrow bifurcates his brow. Although he has a complicated mid-game position in his mind, he begins at the beginning, which is the way he likes to begin: he clears the air a bit by setting the thirty-two pieces, one by one, on the squares they were born for. He lingers in motionlessness a moment, as if sizing up an unseen opponent, an opponent that is a machine, just as the city out there on the other side of the rain-dotted glass is a machine, horizontal and vertical acres of machinery, yearning to grow as everything yearns to grow, then boldly, yes, equal to it all, Timothy Briggs, with a windy rush-release of energies, advances a pawn.

VIII

THAT POUNDING, which is so insistent, and so stupidly repetitive, turns out to be a knock at the door. From great depths of sleep, where the source of a colossal humming resides, and from a dream retrievable only in jagged-edged fragments, in which his assailants have been holding his legs, to stop him from kicking out against them, Timothy is summoned—up to a view, as his eyes snap open at last, of his room at the Totaplex Hotel. His legs have been held by the tight sheets of the bed. There is another knock at the door. Because he has been sleeping in his flannel shirt and his socks, he has only to slide into his dungarees to be fully dressed.

Timothy opens the door and finds Imre standing in the corridor. Joy, surprise, relief spring upwards inside him to thicken all words of greeting in his throat. "Uh," he says as the two shake hands. "Yuhh."

Imre bustles into the room in his clipped, rapid way—those

movements that are so much Imre's and no one else's—swings his big suitcase in a happy arc and lets it drop to the floor. It makes quite a thump, despite the room's carpeting.

"Books!" Timothy says.

"The best portable chess library in America. Puh," Imre adds—a familiar little snort that serves him as the equivalent of a wink or grin. He looks pleased with himself. He, too, is cheered by this reunion.

"So how dya like the room?" Timothy asks him—but Imre doesn't answer. His attention has already gone elsewhere. He hunches over the chessboard on the desk, utterly silent for almost a minute, then wheels around to make a stabbing accusation: "Sacrifices! Always those sacrifices."

Timothy has little to say to this. He can only drop his eyes, shrug, and feebly mumble, "Just investigating . . ."

"What is it with you, you always need to be giving something away, give it away just to see if you can get it back? You don't believe me, believe I'm right when I tell you how much better it is not to give anything away in the first place? Fireworks." Slowly, despairingly, Imre shakes his huge, bespectacled head. "Always the fireworks . . ."

So disproportionately large is Imre's head, and his hands as well, that in photographs he often looks achondroplastic—dwarfish. The impression is quite misleading. In fact, he is a man of about average height; he is as tall, for instance, as Timothy's brother Garner. Yet even in person, a sense of something compressed, or stunted, remains. When he goes out on the street, in his ragged clothes and his thick, powerful eyeglasses, which bulge his eyes to enormous proportions, he is apt to draw stares—especially from children, who perceive him as something of a freak. His speech, too, fosters misconceptions. The thickness of his accent, and the lumbering idiosyncracies of his delivery, suggest an incomplete hold on the English tongue. And yet his grammar is often a good deal sounder than Timothy's own. "Fireworks," Imre says. "You saw what happened to Jeong in Amsterdam? Against Broner?"

"Oh well hey Jeong's crazy," Timothy says.

"Who do I hear saying that? When he plays so much like you? He'd sacrifice his king if only they'd permit such a thing."

Imre's huge hands scramble over the chessboard. He rearranges the pieces with brisk violence, setting them down with little knocking noises. Timothy goes over to investigate. "Thirty-two minutes Jeong looks at this position," Imre says, "and then what does he do? Doesn't he bring the bishop all the way out here?" Knock. "But let's just say he pulls the bishop back." And this time, instead of rapping the piece upon its proposed spot, Imre slides it soundlessly backwards, one diagonal space. "Wait," he barks, an order seemingly addressed not so much at Timothy as at Timothy's hand, which has sprung eagerly toward the board. Imre glares at it until it makes a full retreat into Timothy's lap. "Broner's going to bring the pawn up then? So, you think so? But maybe, then, just maybe the knight comes over . . ." Knock, knock. Pieces dance. Timothy's hand reaches out again and this time is permitted to shift a piece.

It is like a conversation between the deaf, this flood of hand signals, with its overlapping stops and starts, this onrush of motions that simply cannot keep pace with the thoughts that fly before it. Imre proposes a plausible line of discourse, Timothy counters with an objection, and Imre—proudly, having foreseen this very objection—immediately thrusts forward a pawn. Timothy's hand goes to his chin, to stroke the sandy stubble thoughtfully. "Muh," he agrees at last. "Neat. Yeah. Yeah."

Imre modestly shakes off the compliment. "Puh," he says.

"Oh yeah, neat. That's neat."

Chairs are pulled up. An hour passes, or maybe two. Timothy does not seem to notice when Imre rises at last and goes into the bathroom. And when Imre returns and says, "Some sandwiches?" Timothy does not respond. Accustomed to having his questions ignored at such times, Imre repeats, a little louder but without a hint of impatience, "Some sandwiches?"

Timothy looks up from the board. "We can order up room service. It's free. I checked it out and it's free."

But Imre does not respond as Timothy had hoped; he simply shakes off the suggestion and goes to his suitcase and takes out a large brown paper bag, from which he removes two sandwiches wrapped in cellophane. Again there's no acknowledgment from Imre of the fact that Timothy has brought the two of them to these almost unbelievable lodgings; they are climbing, together, visibly climbing the long chess ladder to the top, and they have never been this high before. Timothy accepts the offered sandwich and begins to unwrap it. "How many did she pack? That thing looks e*nor*mous," Timothy says, of the brown paper bag. Betty, Imre's wife, would have made these sandwiches this morning. Timothy has eaten hundreds of Betty's sandwiches over the last year. Imre rarely goes anywhere without a little sackful of them. They come in two varieties, either bologna and cheese or ham and cheese. They are made with white bread, sliced diagonally after the crusts have been removed. The result is a sandwich that has no top or bottom—a symmetry that Timothy finds quite pleasing. He likes these thin sandwiches of Betty's, which are always so easy to eat when one is huddled over a chessboard, and which keep well, too. You never quite know how many hours or days they've been sitting in the bag, but they generally taste the same—just fine. In fact, they often seem fresher for the time they've spent in the cellophane, which allows the bread to absorb something of the meat and cheese.

To have Imre across the board is comforting for Timothy. This is true even if no words are exchanged, even if each of them is off alone in his own field of concentration. Just by being nearby, Imre rechannels the energies, disperses the problems, widens the possibilities. It's liberating. Imre brings discipline, and the nudging reach of a potent imagination. Timothy knows this particular imagination intimately—there is no other mind in the universe he knows half so well—and therefore he can accept as incidental, as almost unreal, whole areas of Imre's life that others might think significant. Timothy has very little sense of Imre's politics, of his thoughts about either the Hungary he left behind or the America that he has made his home. Timothy has never asked, or thought to wonder, as to why Imre and Betty have no children. Betty is simply there—a colossal kindly drowsy woman who spends her days happily enough watching soap operas.

They make a peculiar, a "colorful" pair, Timothy and Imre—or so, within a few weeks' time, the news media would have it. Little of the peculiarity is perceived from within, however. What Timothy senses in Imre is a benevolence he does not need to question, a set of complementary ambitions and hungers, a like-minded exploratory drive. And Imre, what does he find in Timothy? According to the news media, Timothy represents the son he never had—and, oddly enough, there may be some truth in that. Oh, it's hard to say, given the dense privacy of what goes on inside that impossibly oversized head of his, but he is clearly devoted to "the kid," as Imre usually refers to his pupil. He admires the kid's capacity for work, and the belligerence the kid brings to the game, and the ultimate finitude of that belligerence—for Timothy can be tractable as well, if need be. The kid wants to learn. And Imre finds also in Timothy something which he once found in himself perhaps, and which may be the greatest treasure in the world—a sense of untapped potentialities, the possibility of achievement so great it exceeds all reasonable ambition. Imre broods upon a secret, one which he has only hintingly intimated to Timothy, and separately, confidentially, to Garner as well: in these last few months, astonishing progress has been made. Timothy himself cannot yet see how far he has come. Imre has watched the kid's mind expand, and go on expanding, week by week. Imre has felt himself placed beside a force that is larger, more powerful than he is—while managing, nonetheless, to guide it precisely, the way a man might guide a horse. And for Imre, too, this is an intimacy that knows little compulsion to probe into those areas that might be thought congenial to intimacy. He has never inquired, directly or indirectly, into why the kid shows so little interest in girls. There had been a girl once, Imre knows, a couple of years ago, but she has disappeared, and Imre is content to leave her there; there's no need to bring her up now. Imre has satisfied himself that the boy's interest does not lie in the other direction, which would be, or so Imre supposes, even worse for the boy's game than a wild taste in women. And that satisfaction is all that Imre needs.

Plunged deep in thought, both men jerk upward, in marionette fashion, when the phone on the desk top sounds. "Hello," Timothy warily offers.

"You promised to call me the moment you arrived."

It is Doris, Timothy's mother.

"Mom. Hi, just woke up. Imre's here."

"Your plane could have crashed without a single survivor and you wouldn't have called me."

"I took the train up."

"Oh not you *too.* The last thing this family needs is another person scared to fly. And I don't suppose you've seen your brother."

"Seen him I guess it was yesterday. And I wasn't scared, only it was just cheaper. We went shopping. I bought new clothes, shoes pants shirts, the works."

"New *clothes,*" Doris says, and Timothy knows he has hit upon just the right note; she sounds very pleased, suddenly.

"Garner picked them out. He helped me pick them out."

"Well, he's the one to do it. I swear he always makes me feel *shabby,* with even his fingers, studying the material of what I'm wearing. I've always believed in looking nice, if I may say so, and I'm not one of those more-than-sixty-year-old women you see down here in dungarees, to say nothing of the bathing suits, now don't you get me started . . ."

"Okay," Timothy says.

"But the amazing thing is, how he's always been like that, even just a little boy no higher than a doorknob, he was a real clothes horse to put the rest of us to shame. You know he gets that from his great- . . . No, that wouldn't be . . . Charley was *my* uncle . . . Let me see . . ."

"What's the temperature down there?"

Ever since her move to Florida, Doris relishes being asked the temperature, and Timothy (unlike his two siblings, who have never fully acknowledged their mother's leaving Indiana) is quite accommodating on this point. "Se-ven-ty-se-ven," Doris says.

"Seventy-seven," Timothy marvels.

"Se-ven-ty-se-ven."

"There's a clipping about me, about the match, in the Boston *Globe.* I'll send it down."

"A clipping?"

"In the Boston *Globe.* I'll send it down."

"I'll be watching for it." For years now, Doris has served as the chief librarian of the Timothy Briggs Archive. Timothy knows that he needn't keep any sort of record of his own doings; he merely has to send along to her the tournament results, the trophies, the occasional newspaper clipping, and she will do the rest. They are in close touch, mother and son. Doris finds it a difficult proposition to talk to her eldest child, Garner, whose endless sarcasm can be extremely off-putting. And, as she herself freely admits, she isn't "as close as a mother should be" to her second child, Nettie, who lives in Todsville, Pennsylvania. Perhaps—Doris has often speculated—the two of them were simply *meant* to fight. Otherwise, why would they do it so often? It had been something of a relief for Doris when Nettie moved out of the house.

In any case, Doris feels little need to talk regularly with her two older children. They are the sorts of people who can take care of themselves—Nettie, particularly, who at sixteen had been ready to move out, to up and marry. But her Timmy was another story. He was one who needed constant watching and had always needed watching. Even as a child, an infant, he had been accident-prone—always far more so than his twin brother, Tommy. When Doris ponders what she calls the Accident (there is only one in her life), she still cannot quite accept that it would have been Tommy, the older of the twins, who slipped from the playground slide, rather than Timmy, the baby. To her, it still felt as though a mistake had been made. As though God Himself had momentarily confused the two little identically dressed boys.

"Is the Boston *Globe* a magazine?" Doris asks. She is looking out her kitchen window onto a parking lot. A newcomer to the condominium complex, Wilbur Harrington, has just pulled in and is getting out of his car. Doris watches Wilbur with special attention because she feels quite certain that of all the peculiar people in the complex he is the one who is not merely peculiar but truly disturbed. She begins to tell Timmy about some of the crazy things the Harringtons, both of them, said at the last condominium meeting. But as she is ascending toward the very *worst* detail, the one outrageous bit she has been saving for the close (the way crazy Wilbur Harrington has been spotted walking around the complex with some sort of enormous bowie knife dangling from his belt), Timothy says, "Chacall me back later, Ma? Imre and I're in the middle of something."

Doris has never liked to be rushed off a phone and she clears her throat huffily. If Timmy is by far the best among her children at carrying on a decent phone conversation, he can be quite abrupt at times. He lacks some social graces—she would have to concede that. As she is pondering her next remark, Wilbur Harrington comes into view once more, opens up the trunk of his car, and removes from it a cardboard box—quite a long box, the kind of thing you might store a rifle inside. "How can I call you back later when I never know when I'll be waking you up?" Doris says.

"Sokay. Call any time."

"You know when you're staying in a hotel, you have to follow normal hotel hours to some extent. That's only common courtesy to the maids."

There is no response. It is as though Timothy has already hung up the phone. "How *is* the hotel?" Doris asks him.

The pause extends, and yet when Timothy's voice does return, it is warm with reawakened life. "It's the lap of luxury here, Ma. Milk and honey, fourteenth floor, the works. I can see *boats* from the window."

"It's really *ritzy?* It's really specially *nice?*" The vision goes right to her heart. Lord, how this image—her Timmy settled in some extravagant Boston hotel—pleases her.

"It's the lap of luxury, all right."

"Timmy," she says, in a sharp tone, for she has remembered something important. "Now what have I told you about ordering liver and onions at hotels?"

"I never eat liver. Other than liver sausage. Sometimes."

"You remember what happened to me at that hotel in Gary when Uncle Kendrick was having his pancreas out. God save us all, no one ever *was* so sick. In fact, I was sick the other night—Tuesday night. This time, I think it was the Jell-O, I do think they overdo the limes down here. The whole *meal* was green, salad, spinach casserole, Jell-O. I don't think a person's stomach was ever meant to eat so much of just one color, do you?"

"Muh."

"That's just common sense," Doris agrees with herself. "Timmy, are you listening to me?"

"Yeah, sure, Mom, I will," Timothy replies, with some sense of gratitude, even though in fact he is scarcely listening to her. His mind has learned to filter out the particularities of his mother's injunctions and to extract from them a simple, supportive concern; he is comforted by her advice. It is all part of an ancient and reassuringly unvarying ritual between them. "Call me later," Timothy advises her again.

Even as his hand is stretching out to cradle the phone, his eyes have returned to the board before him. A greased inner sliding and locking takes place, as he feels himself being frictionlessly routed from one network of tensions and comforts to another. The chessboard has been pulling on him throughout, composing a series of mounting demands that he can only now accommodate; and, as requested, he again yields to them utterly.

The position before him is one that was first arrived at by two chess programs, DUCKIT 2 and FLYER. Imre has been restudying the games of DUCKIT 1 and DUCKIT 2 and DUCKIT 3. They, too, were born at M.I.T., like ANNDY, Timothy's opponent in the upcoming match; you might call them ANNDY's parents. DUCKIT 1 was a good program for its day, but that day is now nearly ten years gone, and Timothy doesn't see much point in looking over its games. DUCKIT 2 was a good deal better, a real advance, and DUCKIT 3—well, that was a much bigger advance. Some of its moves were quite amazing. It was scary—it was almost scary how good it could sometimes be. But according to Imre, even DUCKIT 3 had all sorts of hidden weaknesses and wasn't nearly so strong as it looked. For one thing, it was too materialistic—which was the usual case with computers; they wanted to "grab, grab, grab," in Imre's words, "like people with credit cards," without peering down the road to see what it would eventually cost them. And DUCKIT 3 played a relatively weak endgame—though Timothy's own endgame, as Imre was forever pointing out, had its shortcomings. "Impatience—always impatience," Imre would moan, and strike his head, and crack those oversized knuckles of his. Still, even Imre had to admit that DUCKIT 3 was some kind of tactical genius. Whatever it lacked in long-term strategy, it often made up in its ability to strike out suddenly, like a cobra, if you let your guard down. Staggering—how quickly it could turn a game around.

But what Imre didn't know—what perhaps no one actually knew yet—was just how big an improvement ANNDY would be over DUCKIT 3. Imre was counting on the fact that weaknesses found in the DUCKIT prototypes might still be there and exploitable in ANNDY. But in one of his chess magazines Timothy had read an interview with a graduate student who'd helped design ANNDY, and *he'd* said that the new program represented a "whole new generation" in chess machines. It was hard to know how to take this. It might only be boasting. ANNDY had looked *good*, there was no question of that, in its few published games. And in its one big tournament, the national computer championship in Atlanta four months before, ANNDY's record had been awesome. Five victories, no losses, and no ties. And four of the victories were quite impressive. It took hours of analysis—more time by far than you would ever have under game conditions—to dig out some of the flaws in its play. The fifth game, though, had been badly botched on both sides, and so, inevitably, Imre had insisted on going over and over it, searching for the hidden causes of ineptitude. The chink in the armor was what Imre called it.

But there was always the possibility that that game represented nothing more than some simple bug in the program, since corrected. Timothy questioned the value of spending so much time with ANNDY's games, so much time trying to discover ANNDY's true nature. No one really knew—that was Timothy's point.

The phone trills, and again the two of them leap at the sound. "Hello," Timothy says.

"Tim? Tim Briggs?"

"Yeah." Timothy amends this: "Yes?"

"Jack Westman here."

Timothy naturally pauses, since he knows no Jack Westman. "Tim Briggs here," he parrots, which produces a chuckle at the other end of the line.

"Listen, I'm afraid I'm going to have to shoot our dinner plans. Things coming up from all over, God I'm sorry. But how about a drink instead? Could we say ten o'clock at the Viaduct? That's the corner of Chapman and Stanton streets, right around the corner from you. It's owned by a friend of mine who's losing fistfuls of money, so we shouldn't have any trouble finding each other." And again there is a chuckle.

It has taken Timothy a moment to realize that this "Jack" is John Stanley Westman, and that "shoot" apparently means cancel. But having caught on, Timothy says, "Muh, sure, okay. Ten o'clock? Chapman and Stanton streets?"

"You'll recognize me because I'll be reading an enormous financial report and wearing a very bored expression."

There is another pause—as though Westman at the other end is expecting a comment, or some laughter. "Okay," Timothy says.

"Great. See you then, Tim." And in a different sort of cheerful voice, one that is perhaps a bit more businesslike, Westman adds, "Looking forward to meeting you, Tim."

Timothy does not know quite how to reply to this, either. "Sure. Me, too, John—Jack," he says, as he hears the phone click at the other end.

Gently, as if there were still an open ear at the other end,

Timothy cradles his own phone. "That's Westman," he explains to Imre, whose eyes are invisible behind the thick, light-drowned lenses of his glasses. "He goes by Jack. As a name. I'm going to meet him at ten." Timothy feels himself outmaneuvered, and slightly ashamed, for he had planned to present a tougher front to Westman. But he hadn't expected such a young-sounding voice, and such a young manner. Timothy thinks about Bobby Fischer, who demanded so much and got so much in Reykjavík, and suspects that in his very first challenge he has fallen short. There are going to be problems, he knows there will be problems as this match goes on, and in order to bargain properly he must remain always in a position that commands total respect. And yet, that call had caught him off guard . . .

"You hungry?" Timothy says. "Go get something to eat?"

"I got more sandwiches." Imre goes over to the brown paper bag on the bed and fishes out four sandwiches and an unopened bag of Chuck's Chockablock Chocolate Chip Cookies.

"I'll get us some Cokes," Timothy says.

"Maybe just one for me." Violently, with no thought to future storage, Imre rips open the bag of cookies, places two of them into his mouth, and resumes his hunkering position at the chessboard. When Timothy returns to the room, two cans in one hand and one in the other, and says, "Do you believe it? A buck each! They really rip you off here," Imre does not answer. "A buck each, they really rip you off here," Timothy tries again. He, too, is used to having to repeat himself. The tone of Timothy's complaint is proud rather than indignant; the exorbitant prices of the vending machines are but another indication of the luxury of the Totaplex. Timothy examines the two sandwiches Imre has left for him on the desk top. "What kind do *you* got?" he asks.

Imre lifts the top first from the sandwich he is eating and then from the one that waits for him, unwrapped, beside the board. "Ham," he says. "Both ham."

"So are mine. I was hoping bologna."

"Bologna, there's bologna in there." Imre, grunting, rises, forages a moment in the brown paper bag, and returns with another cellophane-wrapped sandwich. "There's lots of bologna."

But Timothy doesn't unwrap the new sandwich. Instead, he steps over to the window and throws open the curtain. There, once more, the city lies outspread before him, Boston, gold and silver in the fading light. "Pretty impressive, huh?"

"Mmm," Imre agrees.

"You ever been to Boston, Imre?"

"Mmm."

"How many times?"

Imre swallows the last of his sandwich and takes a deep sip from his can of Coca-Cola. "I don't know. You, have you been to Boston?"

"Sure. My brother lives there."

"How many times?

"I don't know."

Timothy paces back to the desk and reaches into the bag of Chuck's Chockablock Chocolate Chip Cookies. They are small, but generous enough with the chocolate chips. He puts two of them simultaneously into his mouth and snaps them under his teeth, realizing in that moment of satisfyingly crunchy submission that he actually has become quite hungry. He washes down the cookies with a long swig of Coca-Cola, washes down another pair with a couple more swigs, and unwraps the bologna sandwich.

"How is it?" Imre asks him.

"Mm. Good," Timothy answers, which is true. It's delicious, in fact. "My compliments to the chef." Timothy grins at him, his yellow teeth flecked around the gums with little spongy knots of white bread.

"Puh," Imre, grinning himself, replies.

The two of them eat in silence for a while. "What time you need to leave here?"

"About ten," Timothy says. "It's just round the corner. And I want to be a couple minutes late."

"Don't go irritating anybody you haven't even just met," Imre advises. "It's like sacrifices. Always trying to make up the lost ground."

"Oh, just a couple minutes, Imre. He'll probably be a couple minutes late himself. And I don't want to be sitting there alone in some stupid Boston bar."

"They drink a lot in Boston," Imre says.

"They do?"

"Sure they do."

"More than in New York?"

"Half again as much," Imre says. "Probably."

"And people always think New York's the leader in everything," Timothy says. "It's so damn ridiculous."

The profanity, which has slipped out unwillingly, doesn't seem to bother Imre. As a rule, Imre doesn't approve of swearing, and Timothy has come around to seeing things from his trainer's point of view: swearing is nothing but a way of trying to put strength in what you said when you suspect it isn't really there. It's really weakness, Timothy has come to understand—just a crutch for stupid minds. Still, from pure force of habit, now and then a banished word slips out.

"I'll set it for nine forty, then." Imre tap-taps at the buttons on his Korean digital watch, a "jogging watch" that can do all sorts of things even though it cost only fifteen dollars. Although it's impossible for Timothy to imagine Imre running around a track, the alarm and stopwatch have actually proved extremely useful. Imre on the whole is no better than Timothy at keeping track of the time, but the watch's tiny, almost private beepings have provided him with a means of regulating his life. And the watch means that Timothy needn't worry about the time; Imre will make sure that he gets where he needs to go.

Imre returns to the chessboard but Timothy, nudged again by restlessness, crams another pair of cookies into his mouth and slides over to the window. There he closes the curtain—the lights of the city make him uneasy—and goes over to throw his lanky body upon one of the double beds. He spreads his new magazine,

Newsweek, over his face, to shield his eyes, and finishes chewing his cookies in a private semidarkness. From Imre's vantage point, at the desk, the resulting picture of Timothy is (or would be, were Imre to glance up from the chessboard) rich in ironies: here is the aspiring star, sprawled in his filthy clothes on a luxurious double bed, his head replaced by a magazine, and his face by the face of an Oriental boy . . . Below the solemn Japanese face, one word is blazoned in cherry-red letters: PRODIGIOUS! "You know," Imre says, "I don't think it does such harm. To fianchetto queen side."

"Mm?" Timothy deliberately restrains any show of interest. He resents the claim, the pull of Imre's voice. For he'd had a sense just now, as he's had before while lying with eyes closed on this bed, of a faint but colossal hum that encloses this room. It draws him—down—with its own claims, its own pulls. And also he disapproves of what Imre is doing—even if he must acknowledge the wisdom in it—and he wants Imre to know of his disapproval. Timothy does not dare disagree when Imre reminds him that he is no match for ANNDY's knowledge of the openings. There isn't a human being in the world who could compete with ANNDY there. They've every one been programmed in, a complete encyclopedia of opening lines—millions of moves in all. In opening after opening after opening, ANNDY can go ten, fifteen, twenty, twenty-five moves simply "from book"—without ever analyzing a single position. And *if* ANNDY doesn't need to pause for analysis in the opening, *then* ANNDY's going to have a lot more thinking time in the middle and endgame. There's no arguing with that . . . But the implication, as Imre sees it, is something Timothy cannot quite accept. Imre, who is always advising Timothy to "play the man and not the board," has recently modified his old rule. "You must play the machine and not the board," he insists. And what this entails is trying to force ANNDY out of book by coming up with some unexpected move early on—something that won't be found within its memory bank of opening moves. Not the *best* move, no—but the best *unusual* move. There is wisdom in this argument, but its underlying principle—the cultivation of the unfamiliar for unfamiliarity's sake—offends

Timothy. It seems a kind of corruption, this decision to play if not badly then less than one's very best. And yet, Imre's observation about the bishop raises all sorts of tantalizing possibilities. Timothy lifts himself from the bed, driven both by simple curiosity and by a desire to prove Imre's line of play—indeed, Imre's whole approach to the machine—unsound.

When, some hours later perhaps, the little alarm on Imre's watch begins its mild beeping, Timothy says, without glancing up from the board, "I've still got a little time."

"You're going to change your clothes?"

"Yeah. I guess so." Then, "I got some new clothes," Timothy remembers. He goes to the closet and draws out the pair of chinos on their hanger. "See?" he says.

Imre nods at him without looking up. "Nice," he says.

"Garner helped pick them out."

"Very nice. Isn't that what I always tell you—if you want something, go to an expert? Specialization—it's the wave of the future."

Timothy puts on the new slacks and after a moment's flustered uncertainty, glancing from the white shirt to the lavender one he wore yesterday, and which still looks pretty good, he settles on the former. His stomach's all aflutter as he crosses the room in his sharply creased pants and stiff new shirt, to get his new shoes, which are over by the television stand. "You think I'm getting overdressed?" he asks Imre.

"I don't think so. It looks nice," Imre tells him.

"You want to walk over there with me? Get some air?"

"Okay." Imre's hand dips into the bag and comes up with a handful of cookies. "Sure."

The two of them get into an elevator with a middle-aged couple who seem quite formally dressed. In fact, Timothy notices, the man is wearing a tuxedo. No one speaks, but Timothy can hear Imre chewing one of the chocolate chip cookies. He gives Imre a prompting tap on the wrist and after a pause Imre hands over a couple. Timothy has just slipped both cookies into his mouth when the man in the tuxedo turns to him and says,

"Pardon me, but have you the time? I'm afraid my watch is jet-lagged." He smiles at Timothy.

Timothy smiles back, with closed lips, and nudges Imre, who says, "Nine fifty-seven."

"Thank you," the woman says to Imre, then says to her husband, "Three thousand miles to look at some spray-painted balloons and chicken wire, I simply fail to see the point, I'm afraid."

Timothy and Imre, hanging back, give the couple a good deal of space when the elevator doors open. "What was all that about the chicken wire?" Timothy whispers.

"I'm not sure, but I think some show. Modern art," Imre says.

"Modern art," Timothy repeats, happily. Modern art is one of the things, he knows, that no one need feel the slightest bit embarrassed about not understanding—quite the reverse, in fact. The hotel lobby, in its magnificent gold lights, its fountain and potted trees, is for both of them a somewhat intimidating place, and it is with a sense of shared relief that they step out into the street. "It smells good," Timothy says. "Maybe the air here smells better than New York."

"I wouldn't know. You know I lost my sense of smell in 1971."

Timothy often overlooks this fact—if it is a fact. He would dismiss it outright, as another of Imre's weird medical complaints, were it not that the specificity of the date somehow gives it a certain credibility. "Maybe you're better off. The way the air is in New York," Timothy says, and laughs.

"I don't miss it. Ten thousand years, humans won't have a sense of smell at all. It's unnecessary. It's just an evolutionary throwback."

"You think so?" Timothy says.

"Absolutely. People getting more specialized all the time—that's the wave of the future."

"Imre Szendrei, the wave of the future," Timothy interrupts.

"Let the bloodhounds do all of our smelling for us. Puh." Imre laughs.

They have reached the door of the Viaduct. The place really

is just around the corner. Timothy hesitates. The look of it, swank and sophisticated, makes him a little nervous—and all the more so when two pretty, done-up women clatter up the sidewalk and push open the front door without a second thought. Timothy doesn't know what the drinking age is in Massachusetts, and normally wouldn't care, because he doesn't drink and usually doesn't go into bars at all. But he has brought no identification with him and sometimes people don't think he's twenty-one. He hopes he won't be tossed out at the door, which would hardly be the way to begin negotiations with Westman. "You want to come in?" he asks Imre.

Imre peers at the bar's tinted, nearly opaque front windows. He lifts a hand, as if to touch the glass, then lets it drop. "I don't know . . ."

Imre could be talked into coming in, Timothy senses, but senses as well that it might be wiser to enter alone. He knows that people often perceive Imre as a little peculiar, and it is important with Westman to make a solid no-nonsense first impression. "Well I won't be long in any case . . ."

"Sure," Imre says and then, perceiving that he is being granted his liberty, adds cheerfully, "Yeah, okay, okay, good, I'll be back at the room."

"You may need something." Timothy holds up the plastic key card.

"Yeah, good. Good, that's good," Imre chants. "You're thinking now. Good, you're *thinking*."

Imre watches Timothy push open the door to the bar and then he strides off toward the hotel. His sense of relief and pleasure, already running high, is driven to a sweet apex of joy when, in placing the key card in his pants pocket, his knuckles bump up against a circular shape. Two such shapes, in fact. He has no recollection of storing any cookies in this other pocket. He must have done it absentmindedly, while studying the chessboard. He sets one cookie, whole, on his tongue, while saving the other, with a light-headed feeling of anticipation, snug in the palm of his colossal right hand.

IX

I'M SUPPOSED TO MEET SOMEONE is what Timothy prepares to say, if intercepted by a host or hostess at the door, but no one challenges him. The Viaduct is a quiet, medium-sized, badly lit place, and it's hard to see who's here. There are maybe twenty people scattered at the booths and tables, but only one solitary man, who looks much too young to be John Stanley Westman. On the other hand, he *does* appear to be reading some sort of financial report. Timothy shuffles up toward his booth, planning to ask *Are you Mr. Westman?* But while still some ten feet away he pauses and, instead, he clears his throat.

The man at the table looks up. "Tim?" he says.

"Mr. Westman, hello," Timothy says.

"*Mis-ter West-man,* oh Jesus how about Jack? Jack's fine." This man, Jack, laughs warmly, pumps Timothy's hand, motions him to take a seat on the other side of the booth. Big, sweeping gestures. "So you're going to tackle the monster machine," he says.

"Muh. Soon," Timothy says. He sits down.

"I envy you that opportunity," Jack says. He is blond, broad-shouldered, and good-looking. He is wearing a tan suit and a bright blue tie whose loosened knot hangs quite a ways down his chest. "You'll be going up against the Congam C-4. Jesus, that's one hell of a machine. So frigging fast it boggles the mind. Abso-positively boggles the mind . . ."

This is a side to the upcoming contest to which Timothy has given little thought. His interest is in the program, ANNDY, and not in the machine on which ANNDY will be run. He senses that Westman is trying to psych him out, and replies, "Well the machine's only as good as the program."

"I really do, I envy you that chance. To go up head-on-head against Congam and M.I.T. That's a mighty tall order, cowboy. Aren't you intimidated?"

Timothy looks this Jack squarely in the eye and declares, "I'm not the least bit worried. Not the least bit."

Unexpectedly, Westman guffaws at this—guffaws right in Timothy's face, and with such force that Timothy can feel it puff against his cheeks. "Oh I do like that. That's the spirit, all right. Ohhh, the pluckiness of youth!"

The sudden wistful way in which Jack delivers this last remark is what you might expect from somebody twice or three times his age; in fact, Jack doesn't look that many years older than Timothy himself. He is somebody who has only just reached that age where Timothy wouldn't know whether to call him a kid or a man. "I wish you luck," Jack continues. "I hope you kick our corporate ass. Do us a world of good."

Timothy, who doesn't know what to say, nods rapidly. Perhaps because it is difficult to visualize a machine opponent, over the past few months he has thought of John Stanley Westman as the embodiment of his enemy; but Jack seems completely sincere in all this well-wishing. And doesn't seem the least bit put out at the thought of Timothy's obliterating ANNDY.

Timothy's nodding is interrupted by the appearance of a waitress, who announces wearily, in a sort of slow rush, "Sorry fellas about the delay the regular bartender fell off his motorcycle again and what can I get you now?"

"Again? You say he fell off it *again?*" The grin that Jack shows the waitress is different from the one with which he'd greeted Timothy, who realizes that Jack is flirting with the woman, even though she's almost middle-aged and pretty stringy-looking.

"It happened last week, too."

"He's supposed to be pouring for the *cus*tomers, not for himself." Jack laughs at his own joke and the waitress laughs with him, although Timothy can't decide whether she's just humoring a customer or actually thinks this is funny. Or whether she's flirting back.

"What can I get you?" Jack asks Timothy.

"What are you having?" Timothy counters.

"I thought maybe some Remy Martin," Jack says—a name Timothy doesn't recognize, although he thinks he hears the word *rum*. "Make it a double," Jack tells the waitress.

"I'll have a rum and Coke," Timothy says.

"And maybe some zucchini sticks," Jack says to the waitress. "That sound good, Tim?"

"Zucchini?"

Timothy *would* like something to eat, something hot—although he generally doesn't like vegetables, except corn. And except potatoes, which hardly count. "All right. Sure," Timothy says, decisively even though his approval is extraneous; the waitress has already recorded their order and departed.

"You in school, Tim?"

"Columbia. Not right now, though. How old are you?"

The question apparently seems a bit abrupt, or peculiar, to Jack, who flashes a grin—Jesus, this guy does a lot of grinning—before saying, "Twenty-seven." Timothy does have to concede that the guy has an impressive smile. Those big teeth shine in the darkness of the Viaduct.

"How long you worked at Congam?"

"Three years."

"Where did you work before that?" Timothy has a sense of having this guy maybe a little bit on the run, although Jack's slippery, amused, confident manner is tricky.

"I was in business school."

"Where?"

"Stanford," Jack says, which leaves Timothy—who has never even been to California—with little hope of a continuation.

The waitress returns with their drinks. At the top of Timothy's, the liquid's all but transparent: nothing but rum. The bartender forgot to stir it, evidently. Lifting the glass without tilting it, Timothy takes a deep slurping sip, in the hope of finishing the rum at one go and thereby leaving himself with a glass of almost unadulterated Coke.

"To your coming triumph," Jack says, and sips deeply from

his own drink, which has arrived in a glass that is different, smaller than Timothy's. "How long you been playing chess, Tim?"

"Oh, I've played for years, Jack," Timothy says, pleased to counterstroke with the other's name. "But I only started seriously, I mean really seriously, a couple years ago."

"How much time you devote to it?"

"I don't know. A lot."

"Are you a monomaniac? I'm no expert, Lord knows, but my understanding is that most chess champions are monomaniacs." There is a pause, during which Timothy sifts his responses and Jack, as if to clarify the meaning of *monomaniac,* adds, "I mean have you got other interests as well?"

"Sure of course lots of other interests," Timothy replies, just a little indignantly. Jack is obviously waiting for him to elaborate, but it is as though the liquor has already gone to his brain: Timothy experiences an utter loss of words. Nothing remotely suitable comes to mind. He would like to reply that he is interested in philosophy, and is devoted to trying to figure out the deeper meanings to things, but he always feels self-conscious about mentioning his philosophical leanings; they seem so scattered and unbookish when compared to his brother Garner's. Timothy feels Garner's presence at times as a weight, an impediment, but it is hard to talk about this; indeed, it is hard, sometimes, to think about this. "I mean I have all sorts of interests."

Jack laughs and then, balling into a fist the hand that isn't holding his liquor glass, reaches across the table to tap Timothy lightly on the bicep. "Just kidding," Jack says. "Joke, joke, joke. I should tell you, incidentally, that we may be joined any minute now by a third party, a certain Victoria—" But even as he is introducing the possibility, his face alters and a pleased, avid gleam fires his eyes. He lifts his free hand, waves. "Vicky," he calls.

"I'm sorry I'm late, but actually I should be praised like hell for pulling off a miraculous escape," this unforeseen third party, this young woman, Vicky, says to Jack, and the rapid, scooting way in which she slides in beside him leaves her black hair bouncing. "You must be the chess player," she says to Timothy, who as he takes her outstretched hand feels a mouselike skitter of nervousness run across his chest. He has an immediate and potent sense, on meeting her eyes, of her unmanning prettiness.

"Vicky Schmidt, Tim Briggs," Jack says.

"Someone's going to push old Raber down an elevator shaft," Vicky says to Jack. "And it's not such a bad idea. But you know, I'm sure he'd sur*vive* it. He'd land on some furniture pads or something at the bottom, brush himself off, and climb out like nothing happened. He wouldn't notice that anything *had* happened. That's the last bit of shoptalk you're going to hear from me tonight," Vicky says to Timothy. "I just had to get that out," she says to Jack.

Vicky turns back toward Timothy with her eyebrows coaxingly uplifted, as though awaiting some sort of expected response. And not knowing what else to say, he asks her, "Who's Raber?"

"Oh God you don't want to *know.* You definitely don't." Vicky giggles. Jack laughs with her. The waitress comes and Vicky orders a Campari and soda, Jack another Remy Martin. Timothy tells the waitress that he is *All right for now.*

"Where are you from, Tim?" Vicky asks him.

"I live in New York. But I grew up in Indiana."

"Another midwesterner," Vicky says.

"You're from the Midwest?" He asks this eagerly, cheered at the prospect of sharing such an important bond with her.

"Oh not me," Vicky says. "Jack. He's from Minnesota."

"Edina, Minnesota. Fair and innocent Edina . . ." Jack says, or sings. "Oh why did I ever leave you for the harlotry of the big city?"

"Where are you from?" Timothy asks Vicky.

"I'm a local. I'm from Constance," Vicky says.

"Is that in Massachusetts?"

"You never heard of it? Nobody ever heard of it. I'm so crushed," Vicky says and pouts at Timothy. "It's about a hundred miles from here, but you know"—and she leans forward in a confiding sort of way—"you're probably better off not *know*ing. It's like Raber." Jack guffaws at this, as Timothy realizes that Vicky perceives herself (it is a key to her self-image, surely) as a girl who is sharp-tongued in a sophisticated, sardonic way. And the fact that, for all of Jack's laughter, she doesn't appear to be all that funny—well, this creates an enticing vulnerability.

"Vicky works in public relations. She'll be your publicist, Tim," Jack says.

"And Jack works in entertainment. He'll be your gag writer," Vicky says. "And pimp."

Jack tap-taps at Vicky's wrist—as if weakly imploring her to stop. "No, actually, Tim, I was teasing," he says. "Vicky is one more happy Congam employee. I'm told she basically holds the Boston office together."

"Me and a thousand others, all of who ought to be out looking for new jobs."

"Don't believe a word of it, Tim. Vicky *loves* Congam. She sleeps with her W-2 forms under her pillow."

"You know what I'd like to know? . . ."

Vicky turns to address this inquiry to an invisible fourth party, seated at the end of the booth. ". . . I'd like to know who *is* this guy? I mean," she continues, and to Timothy this miming is quite charming, quite exciting, somehow, "who is this guy who knows so much about my *personal* life?"

Although she has promised no more "shoptalk," Vicky soon returns, after a few more questions for Timothy, to the subject of Congam. For some ten or fifteen minutes she and Jack discuss projects and people that Timothy knows nothing about. It's actually a welcome shift in the conversation. Timothy has been having trouble assimilating these two, Jack and Vicky, and is glad for the chance to observe them in peace. It is, in addition, a pleasure merely to look at Vicky, to study her in conversation with someone else.

Timothy's face is rubber-jawed as he watches the young woman; his lips have drifted open. When someone stirs him in this way—which doesn't happen all that often, it isn't "just a matter of looks" for our Timothy—he can stare at her endlessly.

He supposes, vaguely, that women don't notice when they're being looked at . . . And if, in fact, this is one of the things they're quickest to notice, Timothy is less resented than one might think. For his modest intentions are patent—his is a mellow-eyed, slack-jawed admiration that contemplates no advances.

Turning to Timothy at last, Jack says, "So how you like the Totaplex? Accommodations okay?"

It is clear from Jack's manner that he expects gratitude. Instead, Timothy says, in a voice that unfortunately turns rather shrill, "Jack that's something I need to talk to you about. I mean I mentioned in my letters, there's just got to be a separate room for Imre. Imre Szendrei, my trainer."

"You have a *trainer?*" Vicky seems quite impressed by this. "Just like Rambo or something?"

"Rocky. Rocky's the boxer," Jack says. "By the way, *Rocky XXVII* just opened in heaven. The saga continues."

"Oh *Jack,* don't even bring it up," Vicky says. "I swear, the whole thing's so morbid . . ."

"I meant it respectfully," Jack says. "Stallone was one great American kick-ass."

"What an absolutely gruesome—"

"It wasn't all that gruesome, as such things go—"

"*As such things go?* Huh? *What* things? I mean of all the unprecedented—"

"Well it was only fitting and proper. Look at what he'd been doing to those gooks over the years. The only thing that made the shall-we-say mishap so gruesome is that five hundred cameras happened to be running. But that's the whole point, and besides, that was Sylvester's dream—that's the American dream: to spill one's guts out while the cameras—"

"My trainer's name is Imre Szendrei," Timothy says. "He's a Hungarian, he was once the best chess player in Hungary." Vicky does seem impressed, and Timothy feels himself getting sidetracked. "I'm going to need to concentrate," he tells Jack. "And that means my own room."

"Well I don't think that's going to be any problem."

"Now I *am* willing to accept a *slight*ly smaller room than I've got now," Timothy continues. He had been expecting stiff opposition from Jack and feels bewildered at meeting agreement instead. He doesn't know whether to offer his follow-up line: *As a show of good faith . . .*

"Sure, we'll get it all worked out, why don't you call me tomorrow in New York? I'm taking a morning shuttle."

"Okay," Timothy says and then, suspecting himself guilty of too much flexibility, adds, "It's absolutely necessary."

The waitress returns, at last, with their zucchini sticks. "Oh God I'm starving. I didn't know you'd ordered anything, Jack, you're a genius," Vicky says—which Timothy hears with some envy and a great deal of misgiving: even as a joke, nobody ought to call Jack a genius, because it demeans the word. "Another round," Jack tells the waitress, without consulting anyone. Timothy had again been planning to refuse a new drink, this time with the phrase *Maybe later thanks.* "And some of the mushroom caps," Jack calls. That flirtatiousness which he'd earlier shown the waitress has utterly disappeared—or has been rechanneled. Timothy wonders (and the possibility hits him with a painful shoving suddenness) whether Jack and Vicky might be lovers.

Now if, moments before, Vicky was trying to dispel any such impression by asking the ghost at the table *Who is this man who knows so much about my personal life?*, her intention had been lost on Timothy. He has not been listening as attentively as he might, although he has been taking in a great deal nonetheless. He has noticed, already, the slight crookedness of Vicky's lower two front teeth, the prominent mole on her jaw, the lighter, smaller mole on her neck where an Adam's apple would be, if women had Adam's apples, the faint, almost imperceptible lipstick, her fine white queenly hands and forearms. He understands anew that Jack does indeed represent the opposition, and feels himself being summoned to battle, but without anything solid beneath him, as though his floating, flailing legs meet only air where charted, plotted ground should be. He has no clue, he knows he has no clue, as to how Jack really thinks and operates. But the ultimate design of Jack's manipulations—oh, Vicky!—has become unmistakably clear.

X

AND WHO COULD HAVE *foreseen the string of circumstances that would lead me here?* Garner asks himself. He is sitting, oddly enough, in a large room on the fourteenth floor of Boston's Totaplex Hotel. He is waiting for his brother to emerge from the bathroom. Meanwhile, he is wondering whether the English calf-leather brogues toward which he steered his brother so dexterously two days before might in fact have been a mistake. At least as much as pets do, shoes come in time to resemble their owners—obligingly bending shape and manner to the figure above them. But there are limits to what even selflessness can do. Meanwhile, in the high-ceilinged courtroom of the mind, Garner follows one question with another: *And is this a beginning of something for Timothy, or a sort of culmination?* And would a somewhat more casual shoe have been more appropriate?

Garner today is to accompany his brother on an introductory foray into the M.I.T. campus, where they are scheduled to meet one of the people responsible for ANNDY, the world's highest-ranked computer chess program. Garner is, on the whole, glad to be giving these hours to Timothy. His pleasure's no doubt partly that of a conscience cleansed, since he often feels naggingly guilty about how little time he allots his brother. Yet what he mostly feels today is a guiltless joy that delights in itself, in its own warmhearted beneficence. It is inspiriting merely to observe Timothy's excitement and pride in having landed in what he continually calls "the lap of luxury." There isn't yet anything the slightest bit alarming in any of Timothy's exuberance . . . No, to watch Timothy playing urbane host—"Garner, can I order you up some room service?"—is unexpectedly and profoundly satisfying.

And Garner is pleased, too, for the opportunity of a close look at ANNDY. This match has been talked about for over a year, but only in the last few days has Garner begun to appreciate some of its more incisive ironies and implications. It offers a potent symbol, the sort of stark confrontation that historians are apt to seize upon—partly for convenience' sake, but only partly—when speaking of intellectual watersheds. Man versus machine. Chess as a simulation of war. The human military commander versus the mechanical commander. A program designed to commit—or so the Freudians would have it—a form of patricide. Oh, this is fine! Garner would owe it to himself to be here, to be following this match, even if his brother were not its central protagonist. A machine will be performing a "creative" task—and what does this tell us about that artist whose medium is the chessboard? And where will this lead us? What sorts of "creative" pastimes will machines have mastered in ten years' time, in fifty? He has spent a good many hours in the last few days poring over books that in some way might begin to shape and clarify the issues for him. Lightning-like, thoughts are darting and arching in Garner's head this afternoon, as he sits in a desk chair in his brother's hotel room, watching Timothy prepare for an encounter with "the enemy."

It is not only good to be sitting here, Garner senses, but *useful.* And it will be useful to talk to ANNDY's programmer. He feels inspired, and excited to be feeling inspired. The intimate truth is that Garner, despite having so boldly declared in his *Legal Fictions and the Human Fiction* that "the mind that has glimpsed the enduring beauty of true theoretical inquiry can never succumb to despair," seems to be undergoing in these past few weeks—or would it be fair to say months?—what in the language of biographers is almost inevitably called a "crisis of confidence." He has begun, again, to question his methods; to wonder whether his own field of inquiry is, in some fundamental way, too straitened. And to spend any time in Timothy's company, which provides such a raw and undiluted example of intellectual occlusion, is for Garner necessarily to confront the question of whether his own inner gazing might be focused upon too small a board. The upcoming, unprecedented match—Briggs vs. ANNDY—rings with the promise of freshly excavated lines of thought, and isn't it possible that in this last decade of the second millennium we are approaching wonderful new models (and hence a cleaner philosophy) of the nature of human decision making? Which is to say, of course, new impingings upon the legal fiction itself—that ratiocinative Benthamite man who poises collectedly between pleasure and pain, rectitude and lawlessness.

"It's time to go," says Garner.

"Mmm." Really it is somewhat astonishing for Garner—how anyone so little interested in his own appearance could spend as much time as Timothy does in "getting ready" to go somewhere.

The phone rings. "That's Mom I think," Timothy says. "You want to get that?"

Garner reaches for the phone with an unusual eagerness. He looks forward to his mother's surprise, and her pleasure at visualizing her two sons together. "Good afternoon," Garner says.

"Tim?" The voice is female, but not Doris's.

"No, this is Timothy's brother, Garner. Garner Briggs."

"Oh, hi, yeah's Tim there?"

"Just one moment please."

Timothy takes the offered phone warily. "'Lo?" he says. "Oh. Hi. Everything's fine. I mean okay. Things are okay. Tonight? Well I don't know. I mean—I don't know. Really? Really? Yeah, really? Seven o'clock? I guess I could. Okay. I guess so. Muh, yeah, okay, see you then." Timothy returns the phone to its cradle and answers Garner's mildly inquisitive glance with a sheepish expression. He draws a business card from his shirt pocket. "That's her," he says.

Garner would not have needed to overhear the telephone conversation, or even to see the anxious look on his brother's face, in order to guess at some childish infatuation. Merely to observe the proud but deferential and thoroughly protective way in which Timothy hands over the business card would have been sufficient. There are areas of experience the two brothers never discuss, but much can be conveyed regarding them nonetheless; it is as though reticence makes Garner all the more observant. He examines the card—that of a Victoria T. Schmidt, an employee at the Boston branch of Congam Corporation—and passes it back to Timothy, who has been awaiting its return with hand outstretched, as though to foil any attempt on Garner's part to pocket it. Timothy turns the card over to show Garner a scrawl of numbers. "That's her home phone. She said I had to meet her tonight to straighten out our media agenda. Imre's going to be angry," Timothy says, with what appears to be relish at the prospect. Imre at the moment is asleep. In his first battle with the giant Congam Corporation, Timothy has managed to induce them to pay for a separate room for his trainer. "He doesn't approve of doing anything social the night before a game. Though this is actually business . . ." There's a flash of a yellow grin at the tail of this remark, a little exultation in his own shrewdness. "So: you ready to go?" Timothy asks, with the blithe impatience of someone utterly unaware that he himself has been the source of all delay.

Oliver Conant, the chief programmer of ANNDY, turns out to conform with almost laughable exactitude to Garner's clichéd image of the typical M.I.T. graduate student. Actually, this is one of the great, quiet joys of Garner's life—the discovery, time and again, of people willing to the point of eagerness to embrace the stereotype that would encompass them. Conant is small and bony and homely, pasty-faced and pimply, with thick black plastic-framed glasses and a high voice that cracks and squeaks in moments of excitement, which are frequent with him—at least when he is discussing the future of computing machines. "ANNDY's looking at some three hundred and sixty-five thousand positions per second. Per *second.* In less than ten years, say by the year 2000, ANNDY'll be looking at a *mill*ion. And at that point ANNDY'll defeat the world champion. If, if the world champion isn't *scared* to go up against ANNDY."

"And my brother, he serves as a sort of warm-up?" Garner says. "A rung on the ladder?" And why is it, Garner wonders to himself, that science buildings invariably smell so bad? The three of them are sitting in a tiny, unsightly, fungible office in a huge, unsightly, fungible building on the M.I.T. campus. One can understand why biology buildings, with their vatted, fraying pigs and frogs, their high-strung rats gazing pink-eyed at the strip lights overhead, must reek a bit, but why does this deadly acrid odor make its way into the nooks and crannies even of buildings devoted to the inorganic sciences?

Conant doesn't seem to know quite how to meet Garner's bantering note. When he finds his voice, it emerges in a splutter of qualifications. "Oh I don't make any guaran*tees* about this match. We've still got lotsa *work* to do. We're only just getting *star*ted. Who *knows* where all this will end?"

And why—Garner continues to muse—does this project, the creation of what is at bottom a strategical war machine, inevitably fall into the unclean hands (literally so: Garner has already registered the black crescent moons of urban sediment beneath the young man's fingernails) of someone like this Oliver Conant? And yet—yet even as this line of inquiry beckons, Garner realizes that its ungenerosity, its plain anger, derives partly from recent personal frustrations. There is no denying his own resentment of science—there is only hoping that this resentment is adequately complicated and deferential. He must constantly make himself face the possibility that he has flawed his investigations, fatally flawed them, by failing to pursue scientific inquiry, especially in regard to neurology and the functioning of the brain. Only a person of supreme intellectual recklessness could, in Garner's position, ignore the possibility that answers to all of his bedeviling jurisprudential questions will eventually be found, and can only be found, in the computerized siftings of EKG studies on rhesus monkeys, or from tables born in rat mazes, or from statisticians and teams of workers who have constructed programs too complex to be grasped in entirety by any single mind—the possibility, that is, that in our time legal philosophy as a solitary, a nobly eremitic, activity is inherently constrained. And doesn't his own distaste for science derive from some remote yearning for an "aristocratic" outlook? Some vaguely British conviction that a "gentleman" steers away from the soiling frictions of the material world? How much, he has to ask himself, has he been motivated all along by a desire to "keep his hands clean"?

Dirty-fingered Oliver buoyantly explains that ANNDY is actually the brainchild of two people besides himself: Albrecht Zehnder and Ivan Sestanovich. Timothy, who has said very little since the initial shaking of hands, grunts in recognition at the name of Sestanovich, who is apparently some sort of chess expert. He has evidently never heard of Zehnder, though, whose name is quite familiar to Garner; indeed, only the day before yesterday Garner dipped into one of Zehnder's books, entitled *Playful Machinery* or something of the sort. Garner had previously known Zehnder only as the author of some curious essays, utopian and misanthropic by turns, in *The New York Review of Books*. But *Playful Machinery* had added up to more than Garner had expected, and it seems that even those who don't like Zehnder's views must acknowledge him as one of the world's leading experts in the field of thinking machines. He's a man whose message would appear to be that human salvation lies in the imminent arrival of mechanical intelligences that will supersede us, and he has coined a slogan ("Let's save the world for our machine-children") that has, as intended, irked some people.

If Oliver Conant shares his mentor's faith in the salvational future of technology, he displays none of that underlying gloating bitterness which Garner associates with Zehnder. Conant seems purely cheerful as he says, or squeals, "For me, this is just the be*gin*ning. When I'm finished with ANNDY, I'm going to teach the machine to do jazz improv . . . You know, jazz improvisation. It's going to be so good you won't know which one's Louie—Louis Armstrong—and which one's my computer. Wynton Marsalis," Conant goes on. "Keith Jarrett."

Garner kindly fights down his urge to laugh at this. Even though he has himself no large regard for jazz, Conant's prophecy seems deliciously ludicrous. How rich it all is from the sociological point of view—this clumsy pimply white boy who thinks he has found the magic machine by which to enter the brooding bruised world of the black jazz musician. Dr. Conant, I presume? What more laughable ambition could this young man, who clearly has never possessed even a momentary sense of "cool," have possibly latched on to? And yet, a familiar voice in Garner's head (a philosophical, or perhaps even lawyerly voice, whose business it is to invert any quickly accepted proposition) observes that the "absurdity" or "impurity" of an inventor's motives may prove irrelevant. Who knows what "really" led Alexander Graham Bell to discover the telephone—urges to converse with his buried ancestors? necromancy? hubristic impulses to address the Lord? And what does it matter, so long as, merely by hitting a few buttons, the thing actually works?

Conant leads the two brothers to the Lester C. Topples Auditorium, where the match will occur. The auditorium is locked. Inset in the metal door there's a dirty window, its glass veined with thin, reinforcing strands of wire, and the three of them in sequence peer down into the dark auditorium. One can make out, but only just, the stage on which the match will be enacted. The name of the auditorium has been painted on the door, and someone (Garner notices) has crossed out the first of the two P's in TOPPLES and added a final S, thereby creating TOPLESS. Someone, presumably a student at this elite institution, thought this a clever stroke . . . With some bright exceptions, graffiti as a rule depresses Garner; it's one of the reasons why he generally doesn't like to use public rest rooms. The private mind, on public display, is such a disheartening thing.

As the culminating stop to the tour, Conant conducts the two brothers to another fluorescent-flooded room to show them ANNDY—or what aspects of ANNDY are apprehensible to the naked eye. There is a teletype hookup and one of the largest television screens that Garner has ever seen. Its vast, vacant field of muddy green comes vibrantly alive as Oliver tap-taps at his keyboard. A big, keen-edged, black-and-white chessboard blooms upon the screen. The pieces are set up. "Let me just ask it a question," Oliver says. He taps again and the board vanishes. An inquiry appears in its place: HOW 'BOUT A GAME, ANNDY? Oliver pecks at the keyboard once more and a new message appears: YOUR PLACE OR MINE, OLIVER? Another tapping, and another question: WHY DON'T WE DO IT RIGHT HERE, ANNDY? And another answer: OOH, I LIKE YOUR MIND . . .

Garner does not know what exactly he was expecting from ANNDY, but surely nothing like this. The machine's blend of technology and ribaldry, sophistication and puerility, seems in its way astonishing: almost despite himself, Garner feels dazzled and overwhelmed. And feels, in the midst of his head-shaking wonder, a flickering stab of pity, and a touch of something like fear. How, how in the world is his brother ever to compete against this screen, and against the computer that fires it, and against the whole stacked complex of laboratories and libraries, the blueprints and feasibility studies, the federal grants and the teams of technicians—the whole massive monster that ANNDY embodies?

"ANNDY has all *sorts* of messages," Oliver says from his seat at the teletype. There is something poignant as well in the manifest hunger for approval that emanates from America's next Louis Armstrong. "ANNDY'll tell you how things are going, what its evaluations are, when you made a mistake. ANNDY's the politest, friendliest opponent a chess player ever had."

Timothy has nothing, not a word, to say in response to the machine. Oliver's demonstration, which extends for some ten or fifteen minutes, is increasingly directed not at Timothy but at Garner, who in politeness feels he must at least offer occasional words of interest and praise, although the various configurations and evaluations that blaze and vanish upon the screen are all but incomprehensible to him. And even when the display is over, when Oliver nervously repeats his good-byes (sensing, perhaps, that he has fallen short in some way), Timothy says almost nothing. The two brothers wend their way wordlessly out of the vast building's oversized rat's maze. Garner respects what seems to be an implicit request for silence. Not until the two brothers are walking along within sight of the Charles River, which has taken on a primitive golden glow in the dusklight, seemingly fiercer than the setting sun which engenders it, does he say, "And what were your impressions of Oliver Conant?"

Timothy curses, which is uncharacteristic of him, and continues, "Talk about your classic nerd . . ."

"Your classic what?"

"Nerd. Jesus."

"Nerd?" Garner feigns unfamiliarity with the term. And Timothy, with an amusingly mild show of surprise (is there *any* limit to Timothy's belief in his brother's insularity?), turns to a definition of sorts. His words emerge with unexpected rancor: "I mean did you see those glasses? And all the pimples? And his fly, you saw about his fly, how it was halfway down the whole time?"

"He did seem to fit a certain type, or mold . . ."

"I mean here's somebody nobody ever liked, nobody likes now, nobody's ever *going* to like, they go into computers, or building ham radios, it's a nerd's way of making friends they can never have."

Garner is secretly pleased to hear his own views of Conant echoed, but in a spirit of mischief he says, "And a chessboard is somehow different?" There's even a slight touch of cruelty, perhaps, to the question—but also a deep intellectual curiosity: Garner very much wants to hear his brother's ideas about this.

"Oh I don't mean chess players aren't nerds. A lot of them are. Steinbrenner is. He's your classic nerd. But so are a lot of law professors."

"No veiled accusations there, I hope?"

"It depends on the *person.*"

"I see," Garner says, only now perceiving, as his brother amplifies the definition, how important this term "nerd" is to Timothy. It would seem he has almost defined his own identity in opposition to it. And the failure of an undiscerning world to distinguish him instantly from the ranks of nerds, the carelessness of others in their designations—oh, this infuriates him! The world is dismissive; the world is indiscriminate; it is too stupid even to see that chess is matchlessly beautiful and that he, the artist, Timothy Briggs, is nothing, *nothing* like a nerd . . .

The world's shortcomings in this regard are also Garner's own, actually, since he is one of those people who cannot quite understand what the game offers. To Garner, the pieces and the positions must remain mere symbols for larger figures and processes. He can't help condescendingly seeking to "look beyond" the surface of the chessboard. And who could? Garner knows that any psychologist would likely interpret Timothy's obsession as some sort of involuted response to the death, so "repressed" in Timothy's psyche, of his twin brother—but of course there is nothing that Timothy could ever do with his life that would not be amenable to the same interpretation. Timothy could sell cocaine or be elected to Congress, train as an Assyriologist or take up astrology, turn to fashion design or become a Faroese citizen, and still his path in life would be regarded as a struggle to surmount the Oedipal guilt of his brother's descent and disappearance. The very adaptability of this interpretive system, its ability to bend a ductile truth around any collocation of facts, however wayward, makes it suspect to Garner's way of thinking. The actual truth, he senses, always proves more rigid and stiff than that; it is elastic but tough, and in the end asserts its own shape. And it is something, Garner is intuitively convinced, that the unwary could bark his shin against quite crisply in the dark.

XI

When the phone rings this time, Garner is alone in the hotel room. And thinking it must be Doris *this* time, Garner picks it up and announces in a voice meant to sound almost comically urbane, "Top of the evening."

There's a squawk at the other end. "*Wot?*" Oh yes, this is Doris all right.

"A good evening to you."

Doris responds with an accusation: "Somebody must've connected me to the wrong *room.*"

"Well, I suppose that's possible, Doris. Fallibility is ever the rule, even in Boston's finest 'high tech' hotel. To whom did you wish to speak?"

A deep, assimilative silence pours through the receiver in Garner's hand. "Gar-ner," Doris sighs. "*What* are you doing there?"

"I'm visiting my brother. I am providing him with paternal guidance."

"What are you *doing?*"

"I'm waiting for Timothy, actually. He's waking up Imre, who has obtained a room down the hall. I honestly believe those two keep stranger hours than I do."

"And it isn't healthy, the sun comes up and goes down when it does for a *reason.* That's as clear as day. You remember your father's friend Terry Gunnarsson—"

"Another one who suffered so badly from cold Scandinavian blood if I'm—"

"I think he proved once and for all that the human animal . . ." A short intake of breath is audible, and another pause opens, in which—such is the quickness of understanding between these two, mother and son, even though they talk so rarely—Garner can read across the wires of the phone a regathering of Doris's features. A canny gleam has entered her eye. A clear resolve. A fixed inquisitiveness. "Garner," she begins. "I want you to tell me how Timmy's doing."

"Doing? Well, he seems fine to me."

"Well, he seems *odd* to me. He seems very *odd.*"

"Odd? Well yes, I suppose one might even say eccentric, if that term didn't suggest such British overtones—carrying breadcrumbs for the pigeons in the cuffs of your pants and all of that. But no odder than usual surely."

In the weeks to come, Doris's observation, and his own flippant reply, will hauntingly return to Garner. While at times he can be—it must be said—dismissive of Doris's rapid, nuance-free character analyses, she does on occasion exhibit impressive intuitive powers. Garner will be forced to question, soon, how much he should have been able to foresee . . . And later still, when for different purposes and with different designs he finds himself seeking to recreate the chess match in some coherent if deliberately fragmentary collection of words, Doris's warning will return once more—this time as a cautionary signal. She will remind him of his observational shortcomings, his sometimes shocking and dispiriting inability to perceive human realities outside himself.

"I just wanted to tell him that that man Rabbitt's on TV tonight."

"That man Rabbitt?"

"The preacher. The one who's always bleeding," Doris says, and although Garner remains invitingly silent, she does not choose to elaborate. Unlike Timothy, who is willing to believe that Garner's ignorance about anything pertaining to "pop culture" is near-absolute, Doris at bottom seems convinced that her elder son whiles away his days reading newsweeklies and his nights watching situation comedies. She treats his occasional expressions of bewilderment as an affectation. In this particular case, admittedly, Garner does know to whom she refers (there can't be anyone left in America who by now hasn't heard of this enigmatic man with the laughable name), but perhaps it peeves him ever so slightly that she would simply *assume* that he knew.

"Timothy is quite interested in him," Doris says.

"He is?" Garner asks, intending her to catch his note of skepticism. But later, Doris's shrewdness on this point, too, will look impressive.

"Oh it's fascinating, he's fascinating," Doris bubbles on. "There's no one like him. He's so *primitive.*"

"I wouldn't suppose that would make him all that singular, Doris. You say he's a hemophiliac?"

"What?"

"This bleeder?"

"He's a great one for blood brothership, that's what he is. And I'll tell you something, Garner, he'da gone to the lions without a shiver, and that's not something you can say about your average preacher. You must've seen pictures."

Garner has not only seen a number of the mesmerizing, ghastly photos of the notorious "Reverend Rabbitt" (including one unforgettable tableau, in which that lankily photogenic figure, his upraised hands streaming with blood, is delivering a sermon to a congregation whose upraised, answering arms drip blood as well . . .); he has also discussed the Reverend Rabbitt at some length with a colleague at the law school, David Fein. Fein—something of a lunatic himself, but without question one of the country's leading constitutional scholars—had actually been briefly retained on Rabbitt's behalf. It seems (or so Fein would have it) that the city of Boston, among others, had been guilty of curtailing the Reverend's right of assembly and freedom of religion through the machinations of its Board of Health. One might just suppose that there *were* sound reasons of community health behind the curbing of any mass, unsterilized bloodletting—but Fein didn't quite see it that way. On the other hand, Fein was on rock-solid ground in arguing that just because this particular Reverend made many people uneasy was no reason for allowing the latter to muzzle the former. And Fein was right, too, in pointing out that a country in which various state courts had condoned peyotism in the Native American Church could not in the long run prohibit what were in fact mild acts of self-punishment and self-mutilation, especially when these were carried out with unimpeachable sincerity in the name of godly fellowship.

"And my brother has taken an interest in him?"

"*Ev*erybody has. You seem to live in your own world, Garner."

"Each of us does."

Doris's reply is neatly eloquent: "But yours is farther away. Only visible through a telescope or something."

Like Timothy, Doris was forever inflicting punishment on the English language—achieving through loquacity what Timothy managed to accomplish with brusqueness. And like Timothy, if somewhat less frequently, Doris had an occasional way of throwing out an adroitly penetrating conclusion, thereby periodically compelling Garner to inquire whether she had more wits about her than he generally credited her with.

"He's on at seven thirty, you can tell Timmy."

"Who's 'on,' and 'on' what?"

"Rabbitt. The preacher. On TV—which incidentally is short for television."

She is doing quite well, actually. "I'll convey the message," Garner says.

"And take care of him," is Doris's final plea, delivered in an abruptly plaintive whine.

"Hold on a second . . ." Garner calls, for he thinks that he might hear familiar footsteps approaching the door, but she, with her stylistic flair for the melodramatic, refuses to dilute her entreaty with the humdrum formalities of a good-bye; Garner is holding a disconnected phone by the time Timothy steps into the room.

"You missed Doris," Garner says.

"She'll call back. There's no waking Imre. None. He sleeps in a different world."

"Mm?"

"It's a little joke I came up with. You know how sometimes people say that somebody lives in a different world?"

"They say it often. In fact, by a rather neat coincidence, Doris just a moment ago—"

"Well, Imre sleeps in a different world. He becomes a bear or a hippo or something." There's affection in Timothy's laughter, but also an odd sort of pride; somehow it vindicates him that Imre, so obviously, "isn't like other people."

"You know you're late. Or we're late."

"Not really."

Garner reconsults his watch. "Well, of course I was speaking only temporally . . ." He has agreed to accompany his brother to one of the hotel bars, the Rendezvous, in order to meet the woman whose business card Timothy still carries in his shirt pocket. Garner demurred when first asked to come along. Timothy's invitation had seemed but one more attempt to flaunt a newfound eminence. But Garner changed his mind when he perceived, as Timothy repeated his request a second time, and then a third, the insecurity behind it.

Although Garner has only the haziest notions of what sort of woman might constitute Timothy's "type," this Victoria T. Schmidt, who introduces herself as "Vicky," proves nothing like what Garner would have predicted. She is a little older and a lot more sophisticated; she is also better dressed (if a little sloppy in coordinating the shades of blue in her shoes, skirt, and scarf—and perhaps unwise, too, in her choice of exaggeratedly long pendant earrings) and more "made up" than Garner would have foreseen. Still, she is undoubtedly a pretty young woman, and in her eager self-congratulation—in the way she immediately announces that she has succeeded in convincing a local television station to send a crew to the game tomorrow—there is something quite winsome.

"I think the *Globe*'s going to interview you," she tells Timothy. "And the *Christian Science Monitor* is a definite. And the *Herald*'s a pretty solid probably. And there may even be a stringer from the *Times*. That would be a big help in getting the other papers to cover. I mean, I expect this to build. I really expect this to build," Vicky says. "But I think we're off to a flying start."

Timothy, just a bit tardily—for he did not at first recognize this as a plea for agreement—jerks his head up and down. A little to Garner's surprise, he has ordered an alcoholic drink, a Campari and soda—exactly what Vicky is drinking. Vicky does most of the talking. She seems, at first glance, rather too formidably sharp-tongued and cynical for Timothy, but she is very quick to laugh—

a low, throaty sound which breaks at times into a young girl's irrepressible giggle. Garner begins to perceive, across a distance, some of the reasons why his brother has become so smitten. Although Timothy, his eyes soft-focused upon her, manages to answer her occasional questions only in bare monosyllables and Garner offers little by way of conversational assistance, Vicky's talk rattles along agreeably and appealingly enough. She asks the two brothers about their upbringing, and their interests, talks about her hometown of Constance, Massachusetts, and about Congam Corporation and the upcoming match.

When Timothy excuses himself and, lurching just a little more than usual perhaps, wanders off in search of the men's rest room, Garner says to her, "You seem to be feeling more excited about this match than my rather subdued brother is this evening."

"I *am* excited. This should be fun. Of course I don't have to go up against that damned machine." She giggles, eyes him across the table, and sips from her pretty drink. He feels, in both her profanity and her giggle, that she is testing or appraising him. "And it's fun for now, anyway, to be calling up the papers and the TV stations. I mean this is *new.* This isn't what I usually do at Congam."

"And what is it you usually do?"

In a good imitation of a schoolgirl's wide-eyed surprise, Vicky exclaims, "Why, whatever they *tell* me, Garner! Nothing has changed since I was a little kid in a Saint Mary's of Constance blazer doing what the nuns told me to do. I mean I am a very obedient and docile *person.*" She giggles at this. Could it be, Garner wonders, that she is flirting with him? In any case, and by anyone's standards, those eyes of hers are striking, captivating. "No, actually," she continues, in a matter-of-fact manner that might be described as businesslike, "what I am, Garner, is a simple cog. I am a tiny part, perhaps a not quite reliable part, in the great machine of Congam International. *We're going to sponsor a chess match,* they tell me. *Wo-kay, we're going to sponsor a chess match,* I reply. *And we want you to call the newspapers and television studios,* they say. *Wo-kay,* I answer, *why don't I call the newspapers and television studios?* My job isn't to question why they do what they do, Garner."

Garner is struck (as often happens, too, in the company of his students) by a realization that he is in the presence of a much younger person who commands, on one level, a good deal more social fluency than he himself. This is not a lack he regrets, on the whole, but it would be foolish not to note its existence. "Why did they decide to sponsor the match?"

"I don't know, it seems a pretty good way to demonstrate what this new machine, the C-4, can do."

"Sort of a publicity stunt?"

"Exactly." The readiness of her reply is followed, after a censorious pause on Garner's part, by a hasty afterthought: "I mean in a *way*. I mean, it's the nature of the company, isn't it? Always looking for ways to demonstrate some product to your average Joe Ignoramus? Hell, what's ten thousand dollars to them?"

"Ten thousand dollars?"

"I thought that's what Tim's getting for the match."

"Twenty," Garner corrects, with a subdued feistiness. "Twenty if he wins."

"Well, I hope he does. Garner, you got to realize that nobody at Congam, least of all any of the younger people, are actually going to root for the *com*pany. You give them your *life* when you take the job—fifty, sixty, seventy hours a week. You're not going to give them your loyalty, too."

When Timothy returns from the bathroom, Vicky says to him, "Oh, you missed my sermonette. I've been preaching the gospel according to Congam."

"Sorry," Timothy answers, with uncalled-for gravity. He looks oddly pale.

"And speaking of preachers," Garner says to his brother, "I forgot to tell you earlier, per Doris's instructions, that on television tonight some minister is appearing who apparently entertains his entire congregation by bleeding all—"

"Oh *God*," Vicky interrupts. "Reverend Rabbitt! I *love* him. I mean have you *seen* him? He's better than old reruns of MTV, with those cheekbones and those crazed sexy eyes, doing his *Not since Jesus Christ himself*—"

"I'm afraid I've never seen him."

"Oh, he's amazing all right," Timothy says.

"No, honest to God, I mean it used to be he'd nick the end of his pinky finger or something, you know a covenant sealed in *blood* and all that, but now it's his whole *palm*. I mean what this is, this really is a slasher film for the fundamentalist set. Don't you see? You've got to love him, standing up there with his arms out"—Vicky throws her arms cruciform—"blood *gush*ing down, telling us all in this wonderful big gruff voice that the Second Coming is nigh. Nigh!" Vicky explodes in giggles. "Oh, you've got to see him, Garner. When's he on, when's he on tonight?"

Garner consults his watch. "Well, actually I think the program has just begun . . ."

Vicky's head swivels to and fro. "Do you believe it, they don't seem to have a TV in here? They ought to have a TV in here."

"I've got one. Upstairs. We can watch upstairs. Come on, let's all go up and watch upstairs. Come on, Garner," Timothy says, with a curious strained urgency in his voice. "Come on, you've got to see him." This is the longest string of words that Timothy has managed to put together all night.

"Oh that's okay," Vicky says. "I mean I'm sure he'll be on again. We can always see him some other time."

"Maybe some other time *would* be better," Garner says—aware (as his brother evidently is not) that the last way for Timothy to impress this woman would be to reveal at the outset his habitual squalor.

"No, come on. Please," Timothy says with that same straining urgency. "Please. This'll be good. We'll all watch him. Just a few minutes," Timothy says.

Timothy's urgings are oddly persuasive. No one wants to cross him, anyway. And so it is that the unlikeliest of quartets, and the unlikeliest of scenarios, materializes: here they are together, Timothy, Garner, Vicky, and a just-awakened Imre, assembled before a television in a room on the fourteenth floor of

Boston's Totaplex Hotel. "I don't think he's bleeding yet," Timothy says, squinting hard at the screen. "No, he *is,*" Vicky cries. "No, look, Timmy, look he already *is!*"

"I am not asking you, the Lord is not asking you, for an hour of your time on Sunday mornings. The Christian religion is not a hobby. It is not a weekend activity like painting or gardening. Or softball," the Reverend says, and Garner, who owns no television set and sees no more than two or three films a year, watches in a sort of numb, unbelieving fascination. Although both weary and skeptical of words like "star quality" and "personal magnetism," he perceives immediately that there is something remarkable about this gangling man with the lank greasy hair and the sharp-eyed, vulpine face. And the voice, deep and clear, is marvelous. Oh, he is a spellbinding orator—that's clear within moments. This is a level of demagoguery that most politicians and preachers, in their ardent little hearts, would sacrifice half of their remaining principles for. "The Lord is asking you for a to-tal commitment. He is asking for your eyes and your ears, your mind and your heart, the blood of your veins—"

"Blood!" Vicky calls. "He's getting it on now . . ."

"—and the bones of your bodies. He is asking you for your past and for your future, your days *and* your nights. He is asking you to cleanse yourself, to free yourself from the impurities that all of you—"

Garner cannot quite make himself believe that what he is viewing on the screen is a transmission of an actual event. In the early years of motion pictures, audiences would sometimes hurl objects at the screen, and on one occasion some terror-overcome soul even (Garner once read somewhere) emptied a revolver at it, in what seemed self-defense. Garner this evening is experiencing the opposite illusion: he can't quite accept that these people in the pews who sit before the Reverend Rabbitt are genuine people, who have come to partake in the word of God. Nor can he make himself believe that the Reverend's sermon is marching upon that goal toward which it is so manifestly and ineluctably marching. No, the numbness and the incredulity can only deepen: he watches in a sort of bedazzlement as, at last, with the Reverend's prompting, members of the congregation step forward to face the little individual blades (sterilized and hygienically packaged, in accordance with the recent directives of various boards of health). "The Lord does not want you—" the Reverend Rabbitt intones, with an almost ferocious bitterness. He is standing cruciform at last, and the blood streams fluently from his palms. "—unless you are willing to make a total commitment. The Lord does not want you," the Reverend repeats, and there is a kind of clever genius, surely, in this cold, inhospitable phrasing. "—unless . . . unless you are ready to give yourself *wholly.* I ask you *not* to come forward," the Reverend continues, as the herding drive toward the sacrificial altar thickens. "—unless you are sincere. Please, please now—" he beseeches, and it is as though he is momentarily helpless, and in a near-panic, before that advancing wave which he himself has summoned. "—please, please stay seated, hang back, hang *back,* stay in your seats all of you, do not make your blood covenant with the Lord, unless"—and here the Reverend regains his poise—"unless the blood in your *heart* flows with Him as well. Do not come forward, no no dear God," the Reverend cries and his deep voice breaks under the brunt of his anguish, "do not do even this little tiny small thing for Him, who bled for you, who died in hammering pain right up there upon the cross for you . . . No, I call on you to *stop,* to *stop,* to *stop,*" the Reverend roars, but one might as well ask the tide, the wind, the avalanche to halt. "Unless you are willing to offer Him all of yourself, body and soul."

It is with a sense almost of peril, and an effortfulness which in itself is a little frightening, that Garner tears his gaze from the television screen to survey the other three people in the room. For all of their differences, they are identical in their dazed, submissive looks of absorption. Imre's huge, pumpkin-sized head cranes anxiously forward; Vicky is chewing fiercely, or sucking fiercely, on the end of her thumb; and Timothy sits rubber-jawed, mouth agape. All are unreally pale, as though the blood has been drained from their faces.

"Wasn't he *great,* didn't I tell you he's better than MTV?" Vicky cries when the bleeding Reverend at last has faded from the screen. She giggles, as though to make a joke of what she has witnessed, but still her face wears the papery, fragile pallor of one recently released from a trance. "I mean isn't he fabu-lous?" she goes on, unconvincingly. "Isn't he great?" she asks them all again.

Timothy says nothing. He merely watches Vicky, with the same glazed, overmastered look he'd given the screen a few minutes before.

They were mesmerized . . . The three of them were absolutely mesmerized, a voice in Garner's head announces when at last, an hour or so later, he unlocks the door to his own dear apartment. He is telling himself that what was truly extraordinary this evening was not the Reverend's performance per se, but the hypnagogic state which he managed to create within that room in the Totaplex Hotel—as well as within the herded masses at his feet. But when, later still, having plunged with little success into a dense stretch of jurisprudential reading, Garner at his desk momentarily closes his eyes, what he sees is not the others in the hotel room, and not the milling, blood-letting congregation, but the berserk Reverend himself, who had revealed no flicker of discomfort as the blood coursed down his upraised arms.

Garner attempts to resume his reading. There's a subtle shift in the room's lighting, signifying the extinguishing of the lights at Ben's Organic Pizza across the street. Which means it's a little after two o'clock. Garner turns off the desk light, letting emerge into prominence at last the unhealthy orange glow of the Slak Shak sign. The long day is over. And the chess match and all the spectacle, the interviews and the blood-pounding clamor—everything, everything, everything—is about to begin.

XII

SORRY 'BOUT THAT . . . HOW 'BOUT ANOTHER? . . . SORRY 'BOUT THAT . . . HOW 'BOUT ANOTHER? is the message that starts to flash across ANNDY's screen when Timothy, playing Black, resigns on the thirty-eighth move of the first game. Laughter and a ripple of applause arise from the medium-sized audience within the medium-sized Topples Auditorium. The closing moments, effectively captured (it turns out) by the crew of a local television station, make a vividly dramatic scene: a white-faced, shocked, and furious Timothy, rising from his seat; refusing the outstretched hand of a jubilant Oliver Conant; declaring with uncharacteristically clear enunciation, "You can take your machine out of this zoo and just *stuff* it"; and stalking clumsily off stage, past that screen which continues to extend its lighthearted apology: SORRY 'BOUT THAT . . . HOW 'BOUT ANOTHER?

So unexpected and precipitous is this departure that a moment passes before Garner realizes what has happened and takes up the pursuit. And by the time Garner, trailed by a couple of journalists, reaches the long corridor outside the auditorium, Timothy is nowhere to be seen. As the presence of the two journalists somehow seems to render mandatory, Garner hastens over to the door below the sign saying EXIT and sweepingly throws it open. He cocks his head toward the stairwell but hears no footfalls. "He seems to be gone," Garner announces.

"Sore loser," one of the journalists says.

"He did lose the game?" says the other.

Garner returns to the auditorium to confer with Imre, who is shifting pieces around on his portable chess set. "He's gone," Garner says.

"He won't go far . . ." Imre does not glance up from the board. "Now that move, that number twenty-seven," Imre says. "Stupid. Stupid, stupid, stupid."

"Well, yes, I'm sure . . . But I do think it was very hard to concentrate." In fact, Timothy had been not at all unreasonable in calling the match a "zoo." He might also have called it a farce . . . How *was* he supposed to concentrate, with ANNDY's inexhaustible run of lame jokes busily flashing upon that television screen? And the screen itself had been (Garner was fairly certain) visible from where Timothy sat, burning its silly messages upon the peripheries of his vision . . . But what did it matter whether Timothy could see it or not? He must still have been aware of it, since ANNDY's little quips had stirred titters and sometimes open laughter from the crowd. DID YOU REALLY MEAN THAT? and CAN'T WE BE FRIENDS? and HAVE I MADE A BOO-BOO? WELL I'M ONLY HUMAN . . . Of course Timothy should have raised a protest at the very outset . . . But that wasn't like our Timothy. No, with his usual unvoiced obstinacy he had attempted instead to triumph in silence over the world's most outrageous chess opponent.

If the complex flow of the game had been a good deal too deep for Garner, he'd been able nonetheless to follow with perfect clarity the stages of his brother's rigidifying anger. And as Timothy had fallen behind, which according to Imre had occurred very early in the contest, a dogged, dumb determination had clearly solidified. Timothy's mortifying outburst at the conclusion of the game was, at least in retrospect, inevitable.

Garner leaves Imre huddled over his chessboard and wanders over to watch squeaking Oliver Conant being interviewed by the television crew. "Well you *see,* you *see,* we never could decide whether it was a boy or a girl. Sometimes we called it *he* and sometimes we called it *she.* So that's how we settled on ANNDY, which is kind of a boy's name and kind of a girl's, so that whatever which way you call it, you can't go wrong. ANNDY is actually short for Anndy the Androgynous Androidal Answer and also for A Nice New Dandy Yardstick for the Mind." This raises a nod from the interviewer, whose ultimate ambition—or so his blond, bland, horsey good looks would suggest—is to present his television station's nightly sports roundup. In any case, he clearly is delighted to have such a picturesque little jerk on his hands, and Oliver, encouraged by the nodding, continues in a now familiar fashion: "You see, ANNDY is just the beginning. I'm working on a jazz trumpet program now." Although Oliver is not wearing the pants he wore yesterday, he has again neglected to secure the zipper—an omission that, Garner speculates, may serve him as a sort of unconscious trademark, a way of identifying himself immediately as (in Timothy's words) a classic nerd. "And when I'm done," Oliver vows, "you won't be able to tell whether it's my program or Louie Armstrong, whether it's my program or Miles Davis!"

Is it unfair, Garner asks himself, to suppose that the glee the computer scientist commonly feels when speculating about the duplicability of human behavior springs from an underlying sense of himself as less than human? Isn't he in effect saying to the rest of us, *See? Even you, who have so often called me clumsy and empty and soulless, are nothing better than a machine?* It is only a fool, surely, who would underestimate the degree to which feelings of inadequacy and spite motivate the scientist . . . Or the philosopher, for that matter.

Garner returns to where Imre sits, still pondering so intently his chess positions. "Do you think he went over to the hotel?"

"Maybe. I think so," Imre says.

"Perhaps I should go over and see if he's there."

"Mmm, I'll go with you." With one sweep of an enormous hand, Imre removes the pieces. Flipping the board over with the other hand, he scatters them into their little green felt storage bin. "Okay," Imre says. "Okay now."

The two men walk in silence through the ugly handbill- and poster-plastered campus. Garner never knows quite how to "approach" Imre. He would like, if only it were possible, to express gratitude for the way in which Imre has provided Timothy with a guidance and discipline which Garner himself, as the older brother, might normally have been expected to supply. "So he played badly?" Garner asks.

"Like a child. Just like a child," Imre says.

"Well, the surroundings were hardly intended for good concentration."

"The surroundings can be changed . . ." Gloomily, Imre shakes his head.

"Harder to change human attitudes, is that it?" And Garner laughs lightly at this.

"Puh," Imre says. "He's too big a problem for old Imre. That brother of yours."

"Oh, he's *always* been a problem" is Garner's cheerful reply. He feels oddly exhilarated on this day of disappointments. Perhaps it is merely the open breadth of the river (for the two men are now crossing the bridge from Cambridge into Boston), with its sailboats and sculls creating complex, ranging networks of crosscurrents invisible to those who actually navigate the waters. Or perhaps it is this panorama of Boston in the dusklight, the taller apartment buildings catching a high-flung gilt magnificence. It's lovely, the way the mere curvature of the earth contrives to erect this simple, daily model of the human condition, whereby illumination is extended in the end only to those who have mounted to the uppermost reaches. And the rest labor in semidarkness.

When the two men stand before the door of Timothy's room at the Totaplex Hotel, it is, by implicit agreement, Imre who takes charge. He knocks and when there is no answer he announces, "Hey, hey there, hey now."

The door slowly swings open as a plaintive voice within replies, "Hi." Garner is somewhat surprised, and maybe even a little hurt, to receive from Timothy (who had evidently supposed Imre alone) a fleeting grimace. "Quite an afternoon," Garner says.

"Hmp," Timothy snorts. He shuffles over to the desk chair but does not sit down; Garner, too, lingering beside the door, remains on his feet.

"I just came by to see if you're all right," Garner says. "I've got to get home now, I'm afraid, but I wanted to see whether you're all right."

"I'm okay."

"I just wanted to make sure that everything is all right. Everything's all right?" Garner asks his brother.

"Okay. Everything's okay."

"Well." Garner exhales loudly. He is not wanted here (which is fine—it means, after all, an invitation to freedom), but there's no attempt made to disguise the fact that he isn't wanted here (which isn't fine—it creates an awkward situation). By way of easing into a farewell, Garner extends his hand to his brother, simultaneously recalling how Timothy had refused Oliver Conant's handshake; but this time, Timothy takes the hand that is offered him.

"A lot of games still to play," Garner says.

"Sure." Timothy keeps his gaze downcast.

"Well, I'm rooting for you," Garner calls as he retreats down the corridor. "You know, I'm right behind you."

"Thanks," Timothy says—and only now does he lift his gaze. He runs a hand through his sandy hair and calls again, as the elevator doors slide shut upon his brother, "Thanks." Then Timothy retreats into his room and clicks shut the door, ignoring an impulse to double-lock it behind him. "Christ," he says. He goes over and sits on one of the two big beds. The room, illuminated only by the light from the window, is nearly dark. The days are growing short. Timothy takes a deep breath and makes an announcement: "The match is over."

Imre, too, takes his time before speaking. "Don't be stupid . . ."

"No, I mean really *over*. I called Westman in New York and told him I was quitting."

This time, the silence runs even longer. For a great stretch of seconds, the rich gray room is absolutely still. "Okay, what did he say?" Imre asks.

"He wasn't there. He was in a stupid meeting. I left a message."

"Don't be stupid," Imre says. "Call him back. Leave a new message."

Timothy repeats "It's over," his voice breaking this time. His eyes have turned glassy with tears; even in the dim light, Imre can see them shining, waiting to break. Timothy takes a deep breath, regaining some control over himself, and says, "I'm a chess player, Imre, you know that . . . And I don't play chess in that kind of a zoo."

"We'll get 'em to change things."

"Maybe you think we ought to move the match right over to the zoo. Maybe that's what you think, Imre. Hold it in the monkey house is maybe what you're suggesting now."

"Okay, what were you doing on that twenty-seventh move?" Imre asks.

"I was being *stu*pid," Timothy cries. "That's right, I was being *stu*pid."

"It was stupid."

Another pause. "Gofrawock?" Timothy says.

"Huh?"

"You wanta go for a walk or not?"

"Okay, okay now you're thinking," Imre says. "Now you're starting to think."

Because Timothy refuses to wait for the elevator, they take the stairs down to the lobby—thirteen flights, or actually twelve, since the hotel has no thirteenth floor. On the street, Timothy sets off at a furious clip, with Imre huffing a step or two behind. Suddenly Imre is very busy—for he not only must huff and puff on his stubby legs to keep up with lanky Timothy, and insert here and there into Timothy's flood of talk a necessary word of qualification or caution, but must also keep track of where they are going. According to the terms of an unspoken but longstanding agreement, whenever Timothy takes off like this on a wild, headlong tear, it is Imre's job to steer them home.

"Don't be stupid," Imre says, and "That's just plain stupid," and "You don't want to be stupid now." It is a little amazing, really, how effectively he can guide his pupil with so limited a range of advice and reproach. In that ongoing, strategic game which comprises their personal relations, Imre exhibits a mastery of pacing. He understands when he must let Timothy freely rant and rave, and when to intercede with only the mildest calming string of reservations, and when to throw himself against Timothy with an answering, unyielding vehemence.

"I'm a chess player, not a circus performer," Timothy says.

"We'll get things changed," Imre soothes. "The next game will be all different."

"There isn't going to be any next game."

"Don't be stupid," Imre says, but soothingly. "Don't be stupid."

"I'm not going to play a dumb machine," Timothy cries.

"It's just a dumb machine"—soothingly still.

"Look, you'll get your money," Timothy says—shouts, really—at Imre. "I'll make sure you get your cut, if that's what you're so concerned about."

"My, my, you're getting stupider"—dolefully now. Imre follows this up with a heavy shake of the head and declares, "You really are getting absolutely too completely stupid for me."

"How am I getting so *stu*pid?" Timothy shrieks. They are crossing a bridge, Imre isn't sure of its name, across the wide Charles River. The roar of traffic alongside cuts the noise of Timothy's voice somewhat, but not enough that other pedestrians on the walkway aren't noticing. The sky has grown dark and the windows of the buildings of this strange little city are burning with yellow flames. "I just want to know *how.* I just want to hear you tell me right here this minute exactly how it is I'm becoming so stupid if you please."

"I suppose I'm after the money, right? Now is that it? Is that it, I ask you?" And Imre has raised his voice at last. "Now if money was what I was after, well couldn't I just have gone into the construction business, like my brother Janos, who is so stupid no one could ever believe how stupid he was and who went on to become a millionaire?"

Imre almost never speaks of his past, or of his family, but he does mention occasionally his brother Janos, who lives in Brooklyn Heights and drives a Cadillac. Timothy has never met Janos, but the man is no less real for that. He serves as a touchstone for Timothy no less than for Imre. It is an axiom not open to question between the two chess players that in his pursuit of the game Imre has sacrificed the life-style of a millionaire—which has fallen, by default, upon his younger brother Janos, who even in earliest childhood revealed what might be called precocious depths of stupidity.

"Am I after the money? Is that what you think, that I'm after the money?" The question would appear to be rhetorical, and yet Imre, with that instinct for knowing just when Timothy is to be pressured, now supplies an additional prod: "Well okay, okay am I?"

The reply, quiet and sulky, is a child's—and yet, as an expression of renewed loyalty, Imre finds it fully satisfying. "No. No you're not," Timothy admits.

The two men have crossed the bridge. They walk in silence for a while. "You want a sandwich?" Imre says.

"No. Well I don't think so," Timothy says.

"You haven't eaten a thing in hours."

Imre draws from a voluminous pocket of his voluminous overcoat two somewhat flattened cellophane-wrapped squares. With his wife so far away, Imre has taken up the task of making the sandwiches. These aren't the same, somehow, even though Imre would appear to have followed Betty's formula exactly: ham-and-cheese or bologna-and-cheese on white bread; sliced diagonally; crusts removed . . . They taste different—not as good, actually. But Timothy doesn't have the heart to tell Imre this. He unwraps the offered sandwich. And even if Betty's are better, these are still pretty good. And he hasn't eaten a thing in hours.

"I don't know, Imre." This emerges more mumblingly than usual, since Timothy's mouth is full. "I just don't see this match as a plausible scenario."

"You know what I see? I see two scenarios." There is something a little outrageous, and deliciously absurd (even Timothy can hear it) in Imre's use of "scenario." It calls up Hollywood, films and television shows, a world of deals put together by people chatting on the phone with their sunglasses on—a world in which, as in America itself, Imre must remain an outsider. "Now in the number one scenario," Imre says, "you quit the match, you go away looking like a loser, you give up the extra ten thousand dollars you get if you win the match, you probably give up the first ten thousand because of breach of contract, maybe I'm not a lawyer but that's certainly the way it looks to me, and probably they make you pay the hotel bill as well, including the phone bill.

"In the number two scenario," Imre continues, and his voice has taken on a sort of glow; the pleasure he derives from the irrefutable tightness of his argument is unmistakable, "you go back, you beat the machine, you come away a winner in every way, and you get the full twenty thousand.

"Personally, I have not one doubt at all that you can beat the machine. I don't often go telling you things like that—what's the point building your overconfidence? But I have no doubts myself, personally. Okay, sure, these days everybody does nothing but only talk about what these machines can do. They're telling you this one's playing at the twenty-four hundred level, that one's playing the twenty-five hundred. Two hundred thousand nodes a second, three hundred thousand. But you and I, we know a little secret, don't we? They're not as good as all the numbers say, are they? Numbers are just numbers and they're overrated, okay, and it's as simple as that. People aren't used to them is what it is, and people get antsy against them and they do something stupid, the way you do something antsy and stupid today, and the machine comes out looking like some big genius brain, doesn't it, when actually it's just stupid in its own particular stupid way. ANNDY's stupid, too, if you'll just learn to let it be stupid. I tell you, *You got to let its own stupidness come out.* That's your job. Just letting its own natural stupidness come out. That's it, that's all, everybody's got to have a job, there's no free lunch, and that one's yours—letting out the stupidness. Okay, sure, this ANNDY's smart in the *short* term, the six moves, the eight moves, maybe the ten moves in, you and I can't compete with it. But fifteen moves, twenty, it's blind, it's like Imre without his glasses . . ." Imre halts on the sidewalk and actually plucks his glasses from his face. Timothy has almost never glimpsed his trainer's face bare, and to gaze upon it now—that clotted, overstuffed physiognomy blinking sightlessly away in the streetlights of Boston—is unsettling. "How many moves, how many moves were you seeing ahead," Imre blindly goes on, "in that game against Jeong in Minneapolis? Twenty?"

"Closer to thirty really," Timothy answers his trainer. He wishes Imre would return the glasses to his face. Feeling himself helpless in Imre's swaying hands, Timothy goes on, "I mean not every implication, obviously, but I saw the shape of the endgame. Right down to that weak knight's pawn."

"Twenty, thirty moves . . . How is ANNDY going to compete against you? Don't I always tell you it's not going on in a vacuum, you got to play the man? Well now, now you got to play the machine. I have no doubt. No doubt personally," Imre says, restoring his glasses to the waiting dents above the bridge of his nose. "You're going to leave this match a winner." At some point in the last few minutes a change has occurred and Imre has taken charge of their walking pace. He halts again, and Timothy halts with him. And it turns out that the two of them are standing before a sandwich shop in whose window a public telephone is visible. "Call him," Imre says.

"I'll call him when I get back to the hotel."

"You've got to cancel that message," Imre says. "It's better it doesn't reach him at all. That's the smart thing to do."

Timothy sighs in a loud, thoughtful way, as though still attempting to make up his mind, and glances searchingly up and down the street—but at this sound and gesture Imre realizes, with an inner jubilation he is careful not to reveal, that he has won. Timothy shrugs, pushes open the door of the sandwich shop, and says "Wait here" in a brusque tone meant to reassert his autonomy. And when someone answers at the other end of the line, Timothy turns his head, as if to forestall the possibility of Imre's reading his lips. Imre, for his part, turns his head, as though to signal his own intention of giving Timothy all the privacy he needs.

Timothy's conversation lasts less than a minute. "Okay, what did he say?" Imre asks when Timothy, taking his own sweet time, shuffles out of the shop.

"Westman? He's still in a meeting."

"Did you leave a new message?"

"Sort of," Timothy says.

"Did you leave a new message?"

"Sort of."

Imre ponders for a moment. "Call the girl," he says.

XIII

"WHAT GIRL?" Timothy says.

"The woman. Miss Schmidt."

"She's left work by now. I don't have her home number."

"Maybe it's in your shirt pocket . . ."

Yes, it is indeed, and to draw forth the trim little business card, while being watched so closely by the vast eyes that float in the deep lenses of Imre's spectacles, is sufficiently mortifying that Timothy possesses no opportunity of further protestation. Docile now, in a dutiful daze, he returns to the phone and deposits his coins. He is internally debating the question of how to identify himself (*Hello, this is Timothy; hi, this is Tim*), and whether to include his last name, when a woman's voice answers.

"Hi—Vicky? Is that Vicky? Yeah? This—"

"It's the television star! Have you seen yourself on the news?"

"No, oh God no, you mean I'm on the—"

"It was *fab*ulous. It really was, it made me so *sorry* that I'd missed the game itself."

"What did they show? I mean how long was the actual—"

"But I suppose I really ought to be offering condolences, not congratulations. Are you still upset about the game? That was what was so dramatic about it all . . . You seemed so up*set* . . ."

Abruptly, and for the first time in hours, ever since he committed that blunder on the twenty-seventh move, the game subsides and brightens a little in Timothy's mind, so that it no longer looms as the largest and darkest thing there. The frustration and confinement and the despair the game brought on give way to something else—an opening forth, an airy feeling of incomprehension. Without his even thinking about it, his televised image has been going out to thousands and thousands of strangers, going out without his approval or inspection, and without any hope of retrieval.

"You seemed *so* upset . . ."

"Yeah, yes, well I kind of was. Am. Sure. Listen," Timothy says. "I called Westman and told him the tournament's off. I'm a chess player, I'm not a circus performer." This last announcement is more satisfying this time around than on any of its previous iterations—so much so that Timothy serves it up again: "What people don't understand about me is that I'm a chess player, not a circus performer."

"Off? How can the tournament be *off*? I mean this is only the first game, I'm just getting started. Everything is just beginning to—"

"I'm afraid it's a completely unworkable situation."

"You're up*set*. You're really up*set*," Vicky cries in an altered, sympathetic tone that undermines Timothy; her voice, with its capacious feminine sympathy, its plea for confessions and confidences, erodes any sense he has of his own dignified reserve.

"Listen, have you had dinner yet?" Vicky asks him.

"Yeah. Sort of. Not really," Timothy says.

"Can I take you out to dinner? Please? I mean I want to talk about *all* of this with you."

Internally scrambling for some sort of maneuvering room, Timothy experiences a shadowy, bewildering sense of this woman's breadth and variability, the rapidly modifying roles she assumes in her personal dealings. Her attractions are powerful, and intertwined, and they leave him feeling, much as the news of his television appearance did, at once helplessly dispersed and faintly ill.

"You got to understand, things aren't workable. This whole setup utterly lacks workability."

"Where *are* you? I seem to hear trucks and things."

"Well I don't really know, I went for a walk and I don't really know where I am." Timothy laughs. He enjoys making this confession. Someone could interpret it as an admission of weakness, as though he is saying that he is basically lost, really—but no, Timothy savors the adventurousness of it all. The whole thing speaks of his fine indifference to any mere location, his confidence that he can return—make a comeback—from anywhere. "I mean I always get where I'm going somehow," he explains to her.

"Well if a certain woman you've befriended recently was to be standing in the lobby of the Totaplex in, say, half an hour, with her handy Congam credit card in her hand, do you think she'd be stood up?"

"Mm? You want to meet me in half an hour?" This would seem to be what she is saying. But her ways of expressing things can be a little confusing, and it's better to be absolutely certain, Timothy figures.

"Yes," she says. "I want to take you out to dinner. I want to talk to you, Tim."

"Okay." Timothy sighs into the phone, right into her white ear. "Okay."

"See you then," Vicky says, and is unfortunately off the

phone before he can say again, as he suddenly yearns to, *I'm afraid this is a totally unworkable situation.*

"I'm going to meet her," Timothy announces to Imre. The phone call leaves inside him a considerable residue of confusion, and embarrassment, and so there's great comfort to be had in Imre's response—a pleased nod and a contented clearing of the throat. "In a half hour," Timothy goes on. "She's going to take me out to dinner. How far we now from the hotel you figure?"

"Forty, forty-five minutes maybe."

"You think I'm going to be late, then?"

"Maybe," Imre says.

"We could take a cab," Timothy suggests doubtfully. Cabs often make him a bit nervous. The busy meter is a little too much like a running chess clock for him to sit in comfort. "If I keep the receipt Congam would reimburse me."

"We could walk fast," Imre says.

"We'll walk *fast,*" Timothy says. "Really *fast.* We'll get there in half an hour."

As it turns out, it takes the two of them just under forty minutes to reach the Totaplex. Timothy's eyes dart here and there throughout the lobby but Vicky is not to be found. "Imre, you don't think she left?"

"Just late. Everybody a little late," Imre says.

"You think I should go up and change? You could wait here for her."

Imre bites down thoughtfully on his plump lower lip. The prospect of meeting this young woman alone, on his own, and in this grand hotel lobby, clearly discomposes him. "You look fine," he says.

"Maybe I should at least go up and brush my hair?"

Imre reaches again into the pockets of his overcoat and withdraws a black plastic comb that at first appears to be monogrammed. But the initials, Timothy notices, are TP—another gift of the hotel. "Here," Imre says. "You look fine."

Timothy is running the comb quickly through his hair when,

behind him, a woman's voice says, "Haven't I seen you on television?" His hand jumps and as he swings around he tries, guiltily, to shove Imre's comb into a back pocket of his dungarees. He misses, though, and the comb falls to the floor. "You're late . . ." he counters. In the edge of his vision, he sees Imre stoop for the comb.

"Oh I know, God I'm sorry, I hope I haven't stranded you, will you be joining us for dinner, Imre?"

"No, no. No," Imre says, huffing a little from the exertion, and then adds, drawing upon a little-used wellspring of formality reserved almost exclusively for dealings with either pretty women or police officers, "I am afraid I must decline."

"You've already eaten?" Vicky asks him. In her heels, Timothy notices, Vicky is taller than Imre, and makes him look even denser, more compact. This really is Beauty and the Beast . . . That head of his looks big enough to be made into two normal-sized heads.

"Puh," Imre affirms, and then says, "Yeah. Yes, thank you."

"Well maybe another time, hm?" Vicky says. "Will you consider the offer open?"

Timothy watches their little exchange in nervous fascination: evidently Vicky hasn't yet realized that one doesn't attempt this sort of talk, full of jokes and sophistication, with Imre.

But Imre again attempts, and surprisingly seems to pull off, a kind of gallantry: "I look forward to that opportunity," he says and, appearing pleased with himself, mumbles a good-bye and shuffles off.

"So where am I taking you?" Vicky asks Timothy. "I mean it's a we-can-go-anywhere situation, this'll be courtesy of Congam, what would you like? You want to eat ethnic?"

"Eat what?"

"Ethnic *food.* Chinese or Japanese. Or Spanish. And there's quite a good Thai place, actually, not far from here."

"I don't generally like foreign food," Timothy says. "Except Italian. Does that count?"

"Sure, sure that *counts.*" Vicky's deep laughter is warm and complimentary, as though generously suggesting that he has pulled off a little witticism. And as he examines his remark in retrospect, it appears that he actually did intend it partly as a joke on himself. It is as if Vicky understands that in all sorts of ways he is shrewder and funnier—better company—than he might immediately let on.

"I know quite a good little Italian place. Hm? Come on," Vicky urges, and touches—glancingly, with a tap that reverberates through him—his arm above the elbow.

"Do you like your job?" Timothy asks as they step out of the lobby. The night is cooling toward a promise of rain.

"Can I tell you a secret?" Vicky says.

"A secret?" Timothy says.

Vicky leans toward Timothy, cups one hand beside her mouth as though about to impart something in a whisper, and then says at normal volume, "It sucks." Her low, throaty laugh breaks into a giggle. "No actually it's okay, except they work us too much. There's always something. Now we have to fight off the Japanese challenge. I don't think there *is* a Japanese challenge. I think Congam owns Japan lock, stock, and barrel. And they've cooked up this 'challenge' to make us work harder."

Ahead, traffic thickens, halts—to let a screaming police car through. The racing, blue-blazing car is followed by another, and then another. Still, for all the noise and rush and flashing lights, it's hard for Timothy to take crime in Boston seriously. It isn't real, somehow, the way it is in New York. He recalls the night—a very cold, drizzly spring night and he'd been wearing only a thin windbreaker—when he was mugged . . . Or, if not quite recalling it, he feels a porous, hunching tightness in his chest which has come to represent that night for him. "Have you been reading about Tatsumi?"

"About the what?"

"Ma-chan. That Japanese kid. The composer. They're saying he may be the greatest genius, musical genius, of the whole century."

"Oh, yes, him, well I'm sure it's all a Congam plot. I don't know how or why, but I'm sure the whole thing was cooked up by Congam."

"I wish he was an American," Timothy says. "People are getting the wrong idea about us."

"And what idea's that?"

"Well, you know that we're not fanatical enough. That we've grown fat."

"I hope you're not making any accusation . . ."

"Well, that's what they're saying . . ."

"No, I meant—" Vicky giggles. "And are you fanatical, Tim?" she asks. "Or fanatical enough?"

Timothy hesitates over his reply. There appears to be something faintly mischievous in Vicky's voice, as though she means to pull his leg. He decides, however, to answer her seriously. Carefully, but seriously. "I believe in working hard," he declares. "I believe that people can get good at all sorts of things, if only they work hard."

"And you're good at what you do?"

"Well I want to get better." This sounds a little indecisive, and Timothy adds, "Well, I am getting a whole lot better, actually."

"Well God, I mean really you're the national *champion* or whatever it is."

"No, no I was the junior champion, eighteen and under. I guess you could say I'm one of the best players in the country. I haven't played so much in recent months. And well the ratings, they're not always the most—"

"And you only—how old are you?"

"Twenty-one. That's not that young. Kasparov was world champion at twenty-two . . ." These words are vast, they are dispersed like water vapor across the city's night, and yet for all their dispersion Timothy can actually feel them, pushing up against the very bones of his face.

"Was he American?"

"Oh no, geez, I mean he was Russian. They've all been Russian, well of course except for Fischer, ever since—"

"They're going to get the wrong idea about us. You've got to do America proud, Tim," Vicky says, and touches him, again fleetingly, on the upper arm. It's the left arm, this time, balancing that other touching, whose reverberations still linger. They are walking beside a travel agency in whose windows stands a cardboard poster showing a man and a woman strolling down a beach. GREECE, it says, and below that, ONLY WHERE THE WORLD BEGAN. The man and the woman are both wearing powder-blue bathing suits, and the beach is an endless stretch of pink-white sand, and Timothy's mind goes out, Vicky beside him, to that distant burning pastel littoral. ANNDY, Oliver Conant, the loss today, the blunder at move twenty-seven—all of these might as well not exist. Far more real, Timothy knows, is that grain by grain infinite unrolling, the trees on one side and the sea on the other, and overhead that fierce Mediterranean sun which dries your hair in moments.

The restaurant Vicky leads him to is small, with red tablecloths and candles. To arrive at a place of this sort, with a woman of this sort beside him—the prettiest woman, in fact, with whom he has ever had a meal alone—is a matter of hand-trembling excitement for Timothy; he has to remind himself that his job tonight is to be tough with her. He must make his grievances known . . .

Although the menu goes on and on, it does not appear to include either of Timothy's two favorite Italian foods, spaghetti with meatballs or lasagna. "You want to start with an appetizer?" Vicky asks him.

"Maybe some garlic bread. You think they got garlic bread?"

"I bet they do. I thought maybe I'd have the prosciutto and melon."

"Okay," Timothy says.

"And some wine. You want to share a bottle of wine with me?"

"Okay," Timothy says.

"Tim, you do know, don't you, that I'm so sorry you lost the match today." As she volunteers this, Vicky leans forward and cups her chin in her palms. A golden candle burns fuellessly in each of her dark eyes. "You know I'm rooting for you all the way."

Timothy doesn't know what to say to this. "Thanks. Thanks a lot," he replies, although in fact what he wishes to tell her is *I love you.* The words are prepared, packaged, ready to go, inside his head. He wants to explain to her that if she would only accompany him to that shore glimpsed in the travel agency poster, if she would walk beside him with the sun stirring up all sorts of black rainbows in her hair, he would gladly give up his chess forever. And all those years of pushing one wooden piece after another, of slowly working your forces across that invisible, charged, tripwire fence which separates your own half of the board from your enemy's—oh, he would just give it all up! And even while he senses that he can never quite walk down that abundant shore with this girl who now sits across from him, he does not quite understand why that scenario should seem so utterly impossible. Where is the barrier? And *who* has erected it? After all, people do do such things. You see it on TV all the time, and in the movies, the magazines. That beach is no fantasy. It's *there,* the sun was blazing on it this very day! Probably. And he could pay for the trip (during their whole time together she would never once have to unzip her purse) by means of his tournament money. Or, at least (at *least,* at the very least), he would be satisfied if the two of them could just sit down together and rationally analyze why it is that this scenario, which is so clearly the finest one his life has to offer, is unworkable . . . "But I can't play the way things were set up today. It's an absolutely unworkable situation," Timothy says.

"Well I'm sure we can change things. I mean if I only knew what exactly—"

"That damn screen, going on and off, now you tell me how I am supposed to concentrate, huh? Does anyone ever stop and ask, How is he supposed to concentrate?"

"Well we'll move the screen. I mean my goodness, you shouldn't have to be looking at that. And what else, what else do you want, Tim?"

"And that goddamned Oliver Conant?"

"That goddamned who?"

"Oh, ANNDY, he's one of its designers. He's always fidgeting, and whispering in his horrible ratty voice, and playing with his damn pimples."

"Well we'll simply tell him to leave his damn pimples alone. We'll send a solemn directive to that effect on Congam stationery. No damn pimple play during the chess match. Go on, go on, what else do you want?"

What else does he want? He has a sense, looking into her eyes, of need—of having a great many things he wants to ask of her. But he had been anticipating opposition from her . . . And as with Westman, what he meets instead is agreement, bottomless agreement. Her willingness to indulge him, the obvious concern she feels for his own well-being, makes it a little difficult to think. He has a sense that his list of grievances is long, but somehow he cannot bring anything specific to mind.

He is saved by the appearance of the waiter—or is at least diverted from a knotty problem to a simpler one. What does he want to eat? "You go first," he says. "I need a minute."

Vicky orders a bottle of wine, prosciutto and melon, and saltimbocca. Timothy had planned perhaps to order whatever Vicky ordered, but he has never heard of saltimbocca and is reluctant to take so large a gamble. On any restaurant menu, even an Italian one, he always finds a surprisingly high proportion of things that he doesn't see why or how people actually eat. Disregarding his suspicion that he should order something that costs roughly what her entree costs, Timothy decisively announces, "I'll have the steak, the bigger one, without the sauce, and well done. And some garlic bread. And house dressing on my salad."

Timothy looks at Vicky to see whether his somewhat un-Italian order will be met by anything like disapproval. She smiles back at him. When the wine arrives, she fills his glass before turning to her own. Timothy wonders whether, as a reciprocal gesture, he ought to fill hers, or whether, as the man at the table, he ought perhaps to fill both glasses. Or does the fact that she is paying for the meal reverse all such expectations? There are no doubt rules that govern such matters, but one of the things he likes best about Vicky is the leniency she exudes—as though nothing he could do would offend or disappoint her. He has a sense of her as a woman who makes allowances, who accepts him as he is. She drinks deeply from her wine, and Timothy in response drinks deeply also.

"The messages on ANNDY's screen, they have to go," Timothy says. "All of them. Nothing on the screen but a chessboard."

"All of them? But I mean I think they a*muse* people. You know not everybody can follow the game itself. I mean *I'm* certainly not smart enough to follow what you're up to. I mean I think they make the match more interesting to people. I think they make people more interested in *you,*" Vicky says. His glance lifts from her handsome neck, with that little mole where the Adam's apple would be, to her candlelit eyes. It is no longer the cores of the burning black irises that pull one in, but rather those golden flames that flicker against the snow of her corneas. Or, rather, there are now two competing centers, like the foci of an ellipse, and a gap between them into which a man might tumble headlong.

"All of them," he declares, from the brink he stands upon. "They got to go."

"But couldn't we just keep the messages so long as *you* couldn't see the screen? I mean then they couldn't bother you. You wouldn't even know what they said."

"I'm a chess player, not a circus performer," Timothy says. "I mean if this were Russia, where they actually appreciate chess, I'd have financial support and whole training programs—"

"Oh but you don't *want* to live in Russia, Tim, where all the women are plumbers and telephone repairmen. They wear big muddy boots and enormous key rings at their waist that jangle, clunk, clunk, clunk, when they walk." Her lovely left hand, which has a delicate gold chain strung around its fair wrist, darts out as if in joking remonstrance toward Timothy's on the tabletop, as if to touch him a third time. Instead, the hand halts and lingers, less than an inch away.

"People don't seem to see that *I'm* the human being in this match. I mean we seem to be arranging everything for the machine's convenience . . . when *I'm* the human being in this match."

"You seem very human to me," Vicky says, and follows this again with that sweet, rumpling, disarming low laugh of hers. "Have a little more wine."

XIV

"He has a winner, just maybe. Just maybe . . ." The words pass hesitantly from Imre to Garner, delivered in a trembling whisper. "Just maybe . . ." Imre repeats, more to himself than to Garner. The crowd assembled today, for the second game of the match, is double what the first game attracted; the Topples Auditorium is nearly full. "Just maybe . . ."

But only a few minutes later, after an exchange of pieces, Imre is shaking his head in dismay: "No, drawish, it looks drawish."

"Beg your pardon?"

"Looks like a draw."

"Well that's still better than a loss," Garner whispers in reply, hoping to hearten Imre—although in fact this dimming of hopes, the projected receding of victory's darting, elusive light, strikes Garner as deeply sad. Money, renown, pride, self-satisfaction, it's all drifting away, and he feels acutely Timothy's anger and helplessness up there on the stage—his sense of being invaded and spied upon. Timothy is furious with an opponent he cannot see, one whose little jokes and wisecracks keep eliciting titters of laughter from an audience that includes photographers and television crews. The moment is being recorded—immortalized—and the audience itself waits eagerly for another outburst. For it turns out, unforeseeably enough, that Timothy is "telegenic"—or so Garner has heard from one of the camera crew—and that his little tantrum after the first game "made good television." In any case, that first game's tableau of shame (ANNDY's blinking screen, Timothy's shocked face and refusal to shake hands, the embittered words and headlong departure) had been quickly snapped up by television stations around the country.

And so Garner is grateful to see that—today, anyway—the television crews are destined for disappointment. The game dwindles, as Imre predicted, into an untelegenic draw and, though obviously furious, Timothy checks his anger at least enough to accept Oliver Conant's handshake. WHEW . . . is the message on ANNDY's screen. I THOUGHT YOU HAD ME THERE . . . WHEW . . . I THOUGHT YOU HAD ME THERE . . .

It may be simple peevishness that inspires Timothy after the match to remark to a Washington *Post* "Style Section" reporter that he will "beat ANNDY or die trying." One has to wonder, anyway, whether it would have occurred to the reporter to describe Timothy as a "modern-day John Henry" had this offhand remark not been made. And if Timothy had not been characterized as our modern John Henry, is it possible that the tone of the entire match might have been altogether different? That it might never have caught the public imagination in quite the way it did? When, some time later, Garner sorts through all the yellowed newspaper and magazine clippings, seeking to understand something he had never before (and has never since) observed at close range—that queer, fleeting, obfuscatory modern phenomenon known as a "media event"—he notes how rapidly the journalists (after a quick scurry, one would suppose, back to the lyrics of the folk song) seized upon this "John Henry" theme. In the modern media age, a news story must have (or so Garner has repeatedly read) a simple "handle" or "slant." And what a handle Timothy was providing! It almost writes itself, doesn't it? HE'LL STOP THE MACHINE one of the headlines promised, with a subheadline adding, "Or Says He'll Die Trying." And one can't help pondering as well what the effects on Timothy were of seeing his absurdly romantic "do or die" remarks seized upon so eagerly. What fears and expectations did this create? When everything was turning out so badly at the outset, did Timothy feel that his personal end must be near? And toward the close of the match, did his continued survival seem a betrayal of a vow?

Shuddering inwardly, Garner watches his brother being interviewed after the second game. "No more wisecracks on ANNDY's screen. That is nonnegotiable demand number one." Timothy's eyes are burning with fury and frustration. "If that's what people are coming here for, and if they're too stupid to understand the game itself, then they can just stay home and watch reruns of MTV." *Click-click* go the cameras, freezing that scowl which blackens his face; *click-click* and *whir-whir* and they have captured that threadbare rent in the elbow of his rumpled flannel shirt. "It's time people started thinking about human *be*ings and not ma*chines*," Timothy cries. And *click-click, whir-whir,* they are taking it all in. Timothy is being tricked, hoodwinked, made a fool of . . .

And yet the joke is on Garner, it would seem, who discovers the next day, and the next, that whatever rash or surly remark his brother lets fly, it somehow emerges, after being clipped and cooled into film snippet or newsprint, as appealingly brash—becomes spirited, pithy, sharp. This Timothy Briggs is a "real character" and oh, how the cameras love him! In their glass eyes Timothy becomes an oddly waiflike and all but irresistible creature. The cameras choose to ignore the yellow of his teeth and to reproduce faithfully instead the admittedly fine bone structure of his face; to transmute a distressing grubbiness into an ingratiating dishevelment; and to shrink him as well, until no longer is he a lanky and awkward six-footer but a winsome adolescent, a boy touchingly in need of adult attention—as that rip in the elbow of his shirt attests. The whine of his voice becomes a beguiling boyish tenor and his flashing shows of unreasoned defiance are signals of a healthy—an All-American—drive for victory. It is as though the journalists' need to distort the essence of this match is being abetted through the connivance of the inorganic tools of their trade—as though the light meters, and the rolls of film unspooling themselves in the darkness of the cameras' bellies, the audio microcassettes and the firing matrices of the television screens, all are collaborating to convert Timothy into some sort of youthful emblem of hope. He is to become a spunky David, who would slay with the primitive slingshot of his wits the Goliath of the Modern Corporation. He is the John Henry of the Computer Age, who will go up against the Machine not physically but mentally, and will beat it down.

Given so many newspaper and magazine clippings, set out before him ("From Clash to Cliché"—*The New Republic;* "Zoo Story"—*Vanity Fair;* "Dark Dogmas"—*The New Criterion;* ". . . And Everyone's a Loser"—*The Nation*), Garner thinks, as he sometimes does, of his father—that eccentric and eremitic figure who, in effect, dedicated the last years of his life to the newspaper clipping. What *would* it have been like for that man to see block after block of newsprint emerging in response to one of his own flesh and blood? What would it have been like for him—as an ancient but still proudly erect patriarch from Victoria, Indiana—to stroll among the cosmopolitan news gatherers, to watch the television crews in action, to chatter with the journalists? The thrill of a lifetime? One that would stir at last a warm rapturous pulsing in his frosty Icelandic veins? Or would it have been (as seems the more likely) an irrecoverable blow? To realize that these hustling people, aggressively deaf to nuance and qualification, were the very ones to whom he had pledged his life . . .

When the last brief petulant interview has been concluded, Vicky Schmidt approaches Timothy, and Garner watches her closely. He sees her head come dipping forward—an unexpected move, evidently, from Timothy's point of view—to leave upon that pallidly freckled cheek a rosy splotch of lipstick. "You were *fab*ulous. You're on the way to victory now. I just *know* you are."

The lipstick all but vanishes as Timothy's cheek pinkens. "Thanks," Timothy says. "But I shoulda won the game." Then, visibly collecting himself, he adds, "There's not going to be any more of ANNDY's wisecracks." It was at Vicky's prompting that he'd permitted the messages to flash today on ANNDY's screen. "That is a nonnegotiable demand."

"Did the man from the *Phoenix* interview you? He seemed really sorry he got lost the other day and missed the whole thing."

"I don't know. I don't know who interviewed me," Timothy says. "And another thing. Why doesn't Westman return my phone calls? I called him four times yesterday, and he only returned one call."

"He was probably in a meeting."

"That's what they *said.*" Timothy's tone is triumphant. "You know, that's just what *they* said—that he was in a meeting."

"Probably because he was in a meeting. Listen, I'm sure he'll return your calls. I mean he's the sort of person who returns your calls. He's very conscientious, though maybe he wouldn't want to hear me say it. And I'd like to stay, but listen I've got to run. Lord help us, the Japanese have no doubt cut all their prices by twenty percent while I've been here. But Tim, you know I can tell you one thing—that everybody at Congam is just delighted with you and everything and how the match is going. Delighted, delighted, delighted," she chants, and, with a sharpshooter's eye, leaving but a single mark on the target, manages to kiss Timothy precisely where she did a moment ago.

Timothy's head may be full of his nonnegotiable demands; or he may merely be reliving the grazing touch of those glossy lips on his cheek; but in any case, he's in something of an abstracted state as he saunters back toward the Totaplex Hotel, his brother on one side of him and his trainer on the other. He hums loudly for a time, in his tuneless way. And then he announces, "Mom's coming up here the day after tomorrow."

"Oh good Lord, good Lord . . . For whatever reason?" Garner intends this as a sort of joke, but it rankles Timothy, who replies, with a laboring dignity, "Well, to see *me* for one thing. And to see the match. You know I was on TV down there. In Florida. She was very excited."

"I can imagine."

"And Nettie may come too."

"Well I should have figured," Garner says, who hears in his brother's words the chilling threat of houseguests. "And maybe we can get Father along, too. Summon him up by Ouija board. They can all stay at my place. And Tom as well. After all, I don't see the point in excluding anyone." *Tom.* How peculiar the name sounds, spoken aloud like this. *Tom,* the missing twin, *Tom,* the life snuffed out because a child's tiny hand failed to find the railing on a playground ladder, *Tom,* who is so seldom mentioned in the Briggs family. Garner is not quite sure how, or why, or when, this policy of silence was established. Mr. and Mrs. Briggs had presumably decided that the remaining twin might find it too upsetting, during the years of his growing up, to hear mention of his missing counterpart. Perhaps it was believed that in time Timothy would forget about his twin—as, evidently, he *has* forgotten. He claims to have no recollections of that funeral for which, one more time (a detail that grows, with each passing year, more incredible and positively macabre in Garner's mind), Doris dressed her twins identically. Two trig little boys, one paler than the other, each in a gray flannel suit and a gray-and-blue bow tie. *Tom, Tom, Tom . . .* It is the beat of a primitive drum, the call to the most base and superstitious sector of the mind, where the heedless utterance of a tabooed word invites destruction.

"Don't let's talk about the game, Imre," Timothy orders, as he throws open the door to his hotel room. He goes over and plops himself in the big armchair by the television set. "I don't want to hear a word about anything yet."

Imre merely shrugs in reply and takes a seat in the desk chair.

"I'm hungry," Timothy announces. His tone is adversarial. With every remark, he seems to be anticipating opposition. "Let's order up some food."

"Order it up?" Garner says.

"Room service. Everything comes courtesy of Congam."

"Well I don't think their hospitality is meant to extend to my meals."

The reply is quick, barbed, almost vicious: "Why don't you

let *me* worry about them, huh?" This is an almost unprecedentedly open hostility—which, after a flurry of blinks, shifts into a look of gloating slyness and a quieter confidential tone. "You let me handle the Congam boys, Garner, *okay?* Okay now fellas, I'm going to order me up that cheeseburg dinner. Okay now, what are you fellas craving? Imre, you wanna steak?"

"Cheeseburger."

"Garner?"

"Cheeseburger," Garner says, taking all of his cues from Imre.

"A Coke?" Timothy says.

"A Coke," Imre says.

"A Coke," Garner says.

"How many Cokes you guys want?" Timothy asks.

"One."

"I think one will do."

Timothy dials room service and to Garner's astonishment says, in an absurd forcible tone which implies that he will brook absolutely no back talk: "Okay, this is what I'd like. I want three cheeseburger dinners, an order of onion rings, three of those double fudge brownies, and four Cokes. And for God's sake, don't put any ice in the Cokes. By the time they get up here, they're nothing but water. For God's sake, put the ice in an ice bucket, huh?"

There's a spooky, abrupt look of satisfied tranquillity upon Timothy's face as he snuggles the phone into its cradle. His cheeks are flaming red, as though he has just triumphantly withstood a sharp blow. The lanky, sandy-haired young man who rises decisively from his chair, hurls open the curtain to reveal the Boston skyline, and glances appraisingly around the hotel room is someone Garner has never seen.

XV

INTO A SENSE of unwanted but irresistible motion, which is like being swept up in a crowd, one packed so thick you can no longer move as you'd wish, and even the inching motions of the crowd itself no longer seem expressions of any human will, but only a complex working out of contrary vectorial propulsions—Imre wakes. Even before he opens his eyes he realizes that the object toward which he is being drawn is a chessboard, on which has been enacted an unalterable defeat. His eyes open upon what might as well be his own room, given the interchangeable wallpaper and the crackless, snowy ceiling, but isn't. Timothy is asleep in the room's other bed. Yes, right, it all comes back: Imre hadn't wanted to leave the kid alone.

Defeat, another defeat, the second in three games, and for the first time since arriving in Boston Imre had undergone real despair. He has grown heavy with despair. His knee releases a substantial, resentful crack as he rises from the bed, and in his T-shirt and voluminous boxer undershorts Imre pads with weighted slowness into the bathroom. He prepares the shower carefully, with many minuscule adjustments to the hot and cold taps.

As he steps out of his undershorts, Imre thinks of his wife Betty, alone in the Bronx, and how last night, at the kid's insistence, he actually went ahead and telephoned her. Everything, and now the cost of the call, too, was supposed to be paid by Congam. But Betty hadn't liked receiving a long-distance call and even after being reassured that nothing was wrong and the call would not be charged to either of them, she'd still sounded antsy. It had been inconsiderate to call her, and yet Imre had been reluctant to tangle again with Timothy, who was so dead-set on the call's being made.

Despair streams over his shoulders as the strong water cascades from the showerhead, waking the sleep out of his bones to make clearer and clearer the hopelessness of his situation: the problem isn't so much the bad chess the kid has been playing as the kid himself. Generally, Imre knows that he knows how to handle Timothy. And there's a pleasure in that, a very sizable pleasure, for in many ways this has become the new central game in his life, and like any good game it's a complicated one. He has felt his mind shaping itself around the task, for this game, like any good game, shapes the mind that would play it. The goal is clear and yet extremely tricky: to make the kid a champion. There are forces shaping themselves out there, and an opponent that will not show himself, and here, too, is a key element in this good game: nothing is given to you. You even have to discover the rules of the game yourself, and this, too, is all part of the game, which might be called Psychology. And Imre feels the boy slipping away somehow, like so much water down the drain. He feels himself losing at this game, and there is nothing to do but to play along in search of a break: to hold on, to wait and see. Imre soaps the pallid, stacked folds of his middle and wonders how much it's all the fault of the girl, Miss Schmidt, the one the kid seems so taken with. These long, buried creases on his belly, where one ripple of flesh rolls over another, must always be washed with care. If they're not, the skin there, which doesn't get enough air, maybe, will turn red and start to itch. There are many things that need thinking about but Imre can scarcely bear to recall the way the kid stood up after the game yesterday and began spouting nonsense at all of the reporters. Imre winces at the thought of that—Timothy up there spouting his nonsense: "I am *not* John Henry. I repeat: my name is *not* John Henry. My name is Timothy Briggs. I repeat: my name is Timothy Briggs." No sense, no sense at all . . . Even after Garner explained the whole thing, especially who this John Henry was, still it made no sense: the boy knew better than that. Because there's no point, there's just no point, in even answering people as stupid as that. Those reporters knew just exactly what his name was, and if they wanted to call him something else, what was the point in telling them different?

Sometimes when he showers, perhaps because the steam is so much like a cloud, he thinks of the time, the one time, he flew in an airplane. Less than two hours in all. Detroit Metropolitan Airport to La Guardia Airport, coming back alone from Uncle Gyorgy's funeral. It had been gray and snowy when he left Detroit, and gray and rainy when he reached New York, but in the meantime the girl who sat beside him on the crowded plane was richly suntanned. A blond girl, and so tan that her skin was darker than her hair, and in her lap a green notebook, a student's notebook, which she never opened. The name Alexandra Seaward was written on its cover in a childish hand. She never opened the notebook, instead she fell right to sleep, her head thrown back, and when the aircraft broke through the clouds the sun, falling eagerly through the window, lighted up each of her closed blond eyelashes and the little bit of peeling skin on the tip of her upturned nose. Sometimes, particularly in the shower, Imre thinks of that.

Later, needing to set his mind at rest, he'd looked up Seaward in various borough phone books and had been a little relieved to find no listing. He'd counted on that and was glad to find in this case, too, he'd been figuring correctly: somehow he'd just *known* that she wasn't from New York.

Steam has clouded the mirror over the sink and Imre with one of his huge hands swipes it clear to peer blindly at that squat troll's face he knows gapes blindly back at him. He doesn't like to wear his glasses when he shaves. His little bag of toiletries is down the hall, in the bathroom of his own room, and so he shaves with Timothy's razor. He also borrows, after a pause, a sweet little mound of shaving cream. It's a luxury he doesn't permit himself usually, and like most luxuries it's a weapon against you in the end, but the feel of the stuff on his face, light as a heavenly cloud, inspires Imre with the first touch of real hope he has known since yesterday afternoon. What was so dispiriting was that this time around, unlike the first two games, there wasn't any sort of reasonable excuse. The machine had simply taken the kid's game apart: jumped on a slightly stupid bishop advance and gone on and gone on to grind out a victory. This time, there'd been no distracting messages on the screen, which had been moved way up front anyway, where the kid couldn't see it. This time, the screen kept itself under control: no jokes, no complaints, no questions . . . Just the game position, and sometimes ANNDY's evaluation of where it stood: up four hundred and eleven one-thousandths of a pawn after ten moves, and 1.232 pawns after twenty, and 2.501 pawns after thirty . . . Not until Timothy resigned, and there was no more worrying about laughter from the audience, did a message flash on ANNDY's screen: COME BACK SOON, YOU HEAR? . . . COME BACK SOON, YOU HEAR?

In T-shirt and undershorts and glasses, Imre returns to the bedroom, unsnaps the catch on his little chessboard, and sits down at the desk and begins to play through yesterday's game. He halts on Timothy's fourteenth move, when the bishop had advanced so far on the wing.

"What game you playing?"

"You're awake," Imre says.

"That's yesterday's game, isn't it. Isn't it? *Well isn't it?* Goddamn it, Imre, do I have to wake up to that? I mean don't I get to take a Goddamn pee before I have to look at that?"

There it is, the profanity again, and this time, rather than retreating from Timothy's anger, Imre faces it squarely: "What were you doing with that bishop? What kind of stupid thing is that? What were you doing, huh?"

Timothy has sat up. "I was being *stu*pid," he cries, and waves his arms around. "I mean I *know* it was stupid. What do you think, he doesn't *know* it was stupid? What do you think he is, *stupid* or something?"

Timothy rises from his bed with a huff, and in his undershorts and loose socks, which have tumbled down over his ankles, he marches with all possible dignity into the bathroom. "I mean am I allowed to take a simple preliminary pee first? That is all I am inquiring into here. Does he get to take his own simple preliminary pee around here first? That's the full extent of what he wants to know."

"We're roughly a quarter of the way through the match, you know."

"You know I'm really glad you pointed that out," Timothy calls from the bathroom. "Because *I* don't know how to compute simple fractions myself. He's too stupid to compute simple stupid fractions himself, so he needs you around just to tell him how many games are left."

"Now you're getting crazy," Imre says. "Now you're really getting crazy."

Timothy stamps back into the room and picks up the phone with a brisk, snapping motion and punches at the little game board of its buttons. "I want a cheese omelette," he says, "with french fries instead of home fries, a minute steak, well done, an orange juice, and a Coke without ice, with an ice bucket on the side." Timothy lowers the phone. "Okay, so what do you want, Imre?"

"Nothing . . ."

"Double that order," Timothy barks into the phone. "Yes. Yes, yes, the whole entire damn thing." He hangs up.

"You're getting crazy," Imre says. "You're being crazy now."

"*I'm* being crazy? No I'm not being crazy. I'm being *stu*pid. You can't even keep straight what you're saying to me." Timothy has raised his voice still higher, so that it's nearly a shout. "And what does it say about *you*, Imre, that you're spending all your time with this stupid and crazy person, huh? Maybe *you're* the stupid and crazy one, Imre."

Imre knows he cannot sit idle in the face of these words, which lash him like a blow, but even as he's sorting out an answer the kid comes forward and—a rare physical contact between the two of them—punches him on the shoulder, as if to say the whole thing was nothing but a joke, and goes over and collapses with a groan into a chair. The kid looks over and his face breaks, suddenly, into a queer grin, or a grimace, and he emits a strange high little explosion of laughter: "*Bah-bah-huh-ha-ha*. Okay, okay," he cries. "So when I win the next game, Imre, well then I'm only down by one, right?" And now, all innocence, he grins like somebody's stray puppy dog . . .

"You're going to win the next game?" Imre asks him.

"Yeah, sure, I'm going to win the next game."

"You can win the next game if you want to," Imre says.

"And I'm going to win the next game, okay? Okay, I'm going to win the game, okay?"

"Okay," Imre says. "Okay. So you're really ready to play now."

"I'm ready." Timothy has come over and sat down and already settled his gaze upon the board. "You know I'm ready."

"You going to play smart?"

"Smart. You know I'm going to play smart. Nothing but closed positions, just like you told me. The computer doesn't play well against closed positions. Lots of pawns. ANNDY doesn't know how to handle pawns. The Caro-Kann, the Queen's Gambit. Everything just like you say, Imre. Smart, smart, smart," Timothy chants and with a sly, self-delighted expression on his face withdraws the bishop from that square to which he advanced it yesterday and substitutes instead a surprising rook's pawn advance.

"Mm?" Imre questions.

"Muh," Timothy asserts, with some confidence. The move is an interesting one and Imre, too, inclining his huge head, bends to the board.

"That's the one all right," the kid announces happily. "Just let ANNDY chew on that . . ."

"Mmmm," Imre replies.

And the two of them jump when, some minutes later, there's a knock on the door. "Oh," Timothy says in a small voice, and a dawning pink of guilty comprehension laps across his cheeks. "Heya. Soon huh? Well. That's our breakfast."

XVI

THE FOURTH GAME, which ends in a draw, is "very, very dull," according to Imre, who offers the judgment in a voice that to Garner's ears sounds jovially contented. Imre, too, apparently yearns only for the predictable, the uneventful. Anything—anything except another outburst, another crushing defeat. While it may be true that Timothy needs a victory (needs at least two before the match can end in a draw, and three if he's to win it outright), Imre seems quite unconcerned about the prize money. For Imre, too, there's satisfaction enough in seeing the offer of a draw accepted, in watching Timothy meet Oliver Conant's outstretched handshake, in hearing Timothy speaking rationally to the few assembled reporters.

Meanwhile, what Garner sees as the key question here—just how worried is Imre about Timothy?—goes unasked. It isn't one that Garner is about to pose directly. No, he prefers studying Imre for some sidelong hint that his own unease might be shared . . . or, better yet, might be unfounded. But surely Imre, too, must find it unsettling—this weird, humming, remote tranquillity which in the last few days has settled over Timothy. "Very, very dull," Imre concludes, and deep satisfaction echoes in the judgment.

These are not easy days for making judgments of any sort—or are not for most people. Doris, though, seems to be facing no such difficulties. She has been in town some three days now, long enough to form and express very forceful conclusions about Oliver Conant and M.I.T., and about the Totaplex Hotel and Congam Corporation, about the current life-styles of her three children, and about, especially, the "cold atmosphere" of her eldest boy's apartment—for she has come as a houseguest.

Hers has always been the vigor of unreflective certitude. This is a trait of great utility in the waging of any sort of argument—of which, so far, there has been one spectacular instance. This (a private affair between mother and youngest child) occurred on her very first night in town. The exact details have not yet been revealed to Garner. But there is no question as to its gravity, since mother and son are still barely on speaking terms. Timothy himself has said nothing about it to Garner, which given the healthy reserve between the two brothers is not unexpected; but it is odd, even a little dismaying, that Doris of all people would turn tight-lipped.

Mysterious as the whole thing is, it would seem clear, anyway, that Timothy's response has been to retreat into a peculiar, humming tranquillity. Humming literally, for in the back of his throat he seems to be turning over again and again the notes of an unidentifiable song, as though he has utterly given himself over to the task of its recovery. He has never before in his life shown the faintest real interest in music, and one can only suppose that the notes work as a kind of "white noise," insulating him from his surroundings. It is as though Timothy hums to keep Doris, in all her volubility, at a distance—to keep the world at a distance, including his indefatigable machine opponent. For Garner is fairly certain, though he cannot quite hear it from his seat in the Topples Auditorium, that in the roots of Timothy's throat a low humming continues, rolling over and over upon itself, even as this "very very dull" game unfolds.

In any case, Timothy hums throughout dinner. It is left chiefly to Imre to field Doris's questions, to respond to her observations and complaints. The meal takes place at a well-known seafood restaurant which has almost certainly not been visited by a Boston native in the last twenty years. Surely these are all out-of-state visitors—Texans, Iowans, Hawaiians, Michiganders—who have come, like Doris, in pursuit of what is widely and redundantly advertised as "truly authentic New England clam chowder." It has "everything of the sea in it but the sand."

From the first moment when, a Visitor's Guide to Boston brandished in her hand, Doris expressed what she actually called a "hankering" for this chowder, Garner knew they were headed toward an expensive mistake. But he has been in no mood to argue with her. In fact, he hardly wants to exchange the simplest of words with Doris, of whom in these last few days he has seen much too much. Her mysterious argument with her younger son has driven her fast into the unwilling arms of her elder. Garner has taken her to tour the Bunker Hill Monument and the USS *Constitution* and Paul Revere's depressingly cramped house.

Doris feels just a trifle unwanted, perhaps, and ought by rights to serve as a fully sympathetic figure, but in her spirited way she appears to be doing her level best to seem nothing of the sort. In this unconscionable restaurant, she has evidently decided to teach her sons a lesson . . . She will subject them to the deprivation of all maternal attention by lavishing her attentions utterly upon Imre. So, while Timothy takes refuge behind the all but impregnable wall of his humming, and Garner takes refuge (as he does perhaps once a year) in alcohol, following up a first martini with a second, Imre listens with a heavy, masticating steadiness to Doris's musings upon the true meaning of chess. "I don't see how anyone can devote so much of their time to a game, even pinochle, and I *do* know how to play pinochle. I couldn't do it," Doris says, "devote my days to that tight little board. Me, I'm too interested in *life.* Of course you have the advantage of being Hungarian. They're not so life-centered, are they? They make natural chess players, don't they?"

"I think so, oh, yes," says Imre. "In fact, among women—"

"Of course Timmy's an Icelander. That's where he gets that. That's where his father got that passion for coins. Garner. Garner—" she calls her son, through the icily transparent wall he has erected in front of himself, "you know I met some Icelanders recently. They were vacationing in Florida. Only they weren't real Icelanders."

"Where were they from?"

"Oh, they were *from* Iceland. I mean that's where they live. But they weren't true Icelanders at all, if you follow me."

"Whatever do you mean, Doris?"

"Oh now don't you start that, because I won't be lawyered to. I expect I know an Icelander when I see one. After all, I was *mar-*

ried to one for nearly thirty years." And having delivered this unshakable refutation, Doris turns back to Imre and, with a sweep of her hands to signal that she is unqualifiedly his once more, says, "Now you've never been to Florida and it's a place that takes some explaining. I could explain all night and there'd still be explaining left over." And as though intent on actually verifying her claim, Doris goes on unbrokenly for ten, fifteen, twenty minutes. The "mini-mart" near her home. The true Cubans and the other Cubans. The drugs along the beaches. The alligators—moving in, zeroing in upon her residence, week by week. Garner watches this woman, Doris, his mother, with an incredulity that familiarity somehow fails to blunt. She cannot possibly be as old as she would seek to suggest. Why, then, has she chosen for herself this circuitousness, this doddering inattention, this wholehearted embracing of the elderly person's prerogative to abdicate all responsibility when it comes to making an anecdote interesting or focused? He looks at her, this woman with needlessly ill-fitting dentures and hair dyed a gray that shades into blue, and he momentarily experiences, in this crowded and atrocious restaurant, one of the strangest sensations a human being can know: he feels motherless. Surely, he is closer kin to ANNDY, that amazing nice new dandy yardstick for the mind, than to this woman.

Letting her celebrated bowl of chowder go cold, Doris prattles on about Florida, and a life ever so much more pleasant than what Indiana offers a woman of her advancing years, and all of her talk has a familiar and a needlessly forceful ring. She returns too often, if only for the purpose of disparagement, to that little, snowbound, cloud-bound midwestern town, and this, too, is depressing: she has never extricated herself from the place. To belittle Victoria too strenuously is only to belittle oneself, since the town does not amount to enough even to serve as a means of adequate negative self-definition. It is too small in every sense to offer anything but an ignoble confinement. A few ghosts, a few deficient stores, some mediocre schools and streets long past their heyday, and there you have it, for good and all: Victoria, Indiana. "The thing about that town, Imre," Doris is saying, "is that they don't *appreciate* a person there. That's why I had to leave it. I could have tolerated what-all and whatever, if only in their hearts they *appreciated* you there."

"And just how," Garner says, "were they supposed to register their appreciation?"

It's a thickheaded question, Doris's weary shake of the head makes clear. "Why, through their be*ha*vior," she explains. "It's not a place, Imre, for anyone who believes that people ought to believe in people." One must admire the way she perseveres in this actually somewhat delicious charade that in Imre she has located, at last, the sort of discerning and sensitive soul in whom an aging but lively woman might confide the flowing intimacies of her heart. "The town has a great many *charms,* I'll grant you that, but if I were you I wouldn't go there looking to be appreciated for who you *are.* It's an ungrateful town. You'd think after you'd spent a life in a place, they just might eventually realize they owe you a little something."

"Oh, Doris, what in the world does Victoria owe you?" Garner asks this in a slightly higher, thinner voice than normal, one whose tone might reveal, even to a stranger, his kinship to Timothy. Yet if his head is fuzzy with drink, he is not so disoriented that he fails to recognize the peculiarly disabling, self-dwindling feeling that any adult must feel on growing angry with a parent; for this is anger that makes a child, a boy, of you once more.

"Owes *me?* Who said anything about *me?* Don't you see it's *all* of us? You know, you are a Briggs after all, and the Briggs family practically built the town of Victoria, and half the town of Elizabeth besides."

Of all the absurdities that have dropped from Doris's lips this evening, this call to time-forged, dynastic loyalties strikes Garner as by far the most absurd. To begin with, she is asking her children to place themselves within a family tree that branches down from old Boyce Briggs; and if Garner has momentarily perceived himself as motherless this evening, he has never, never been able to link his father to any sort of forebears whatsoever. What could be clearer than the fact that that remote, erect old man in his unbreachable study, his eyes fixed upon his tarnished coins and yellowing newspaper clippings, never had a mother or a father, a sister or a brother, a cousin or a grandparent?

"If it was just *me,*" Doris continues, "if only *I* was the only one who was treated that way, I wouldn't mind. I'm not one to go grudge-harboring. But you know, Imre, my friend Harriet Dwiggins, my closest friend for thirty years, she gave her *life* to that town, she literally died in its confines, God rest her soul, and was she ever appreciated for making that supreme final sacrifice?"

Garner does not reply, *Of course she wasn't because the bloody bitch was an absolutely irredeemable old windbag who did nothing but feel sorry for herself endlessly and who would also appear, Mother, to have helped nurture in you your own unaccountable feelings of entitlement and self-pity, evidence for which I find in the way you make your friend sound as though she fell in pitched battle on the plains outside Victoria, Mother, instead of in a lounge chair suffering from emphysema acquired by smoking three packs of cigarettes a day until the day she died;* instead, he signals to the waiter and murmurs, "The check, please." Although she had probably been Doris's senior by less than ten years, Harriet had always been, even in Garner's earliest memory, an old woman—an old woman who, as he'd perceived at a precociously early age, sipped each hour of her existence on bile. The staple satisfaction of her days had been the recounting of the calamities which life had dealt her—and life, it must be said, sharply attuned to her individual appetites, had dealt these with a liberal hand.

"Harriet Dwiggins. She was a rare woman, Imre. An extraordinary woman."

Imre nods gratefully in receipt of this information. He seems prepared, if need be, to listen to Doris for hours on end—and without any means of insulating himself. Or perhaps one should view the impressive amount that Imre eats as his own form of compensation or self-protection; he actually has consumed six dinner rolls before the entrees have arrived.

In any case, when the meal finally concludes, its final stages rushed a bit in deference to tonight's television schedule, Garner rises from the table, head bobbing a bit above its wash of two martinis, and discovers, as he steps with his brother out into the street, that—yes—Timothy is still humming.

XVII

THE FOUR OF them make their way to Timothy's room at the Totaplex Hotel and range themselves before the dying campfire glow of the television screen. A hush, at last, temporarily falls.

The program, a "talk show," is one that Garner has never seen. There is of course nothing—not a thing—to be said about television. Before it, words are impotent and one's choice is unmistakable. One can simply pretend it isn't there, or one can hang openmouthed in front of its cheery succession of lights, stunned and horrified by the realization that millions of people day and night find it irresistible. Tonight's guests are a pair of young, blond women—one of whom is wearing a military camouflage outfit (although it has an untraditional, deep V-neck) and a pair of red high heels—and the topic under investigation this evening is the disadvantages of being physically beautiful. Our host is a trim, bespectacled man with beard but no mustache who carries an unlit pipe in one hand. "I would imagine that it's a problem all the more problematic because most people refuse to take it seriously," he offers as a preliminary conclusion. Cut to a "station identification," which consists of a middle-aged woman dropping to her knees as though in prayer before a larger-than-a-man-sized bottle of "drain declogger"; a car emerging with a papery crash through a portrait of George Washington; a woman weightlifter cracking a walnut in the crook of her elbow; the members of a stock exchange rising from their anachronistically ticker tape–overladen desks to sing a paean to a deodorant soap;

the intimate tangoing of two biped coffee beans. And back to our host who, stroking the belly of his pipe with his thumbnail, asks the woman in camouflage whether, knowing what she now knows, she would still choose to enter show business. The camera closes upon her face for this moment of soul-scrutiny. "Well I suppose I would, Frank," she concludes, "but this time, I would go in with definitely lowered expectations." And more talk, more crossing of legs, more stroking of the pipe . . . ("You know, I read he doesn't really need those glasses," Doris says, "and that they're just for wearing to look more intelligent." "He doesn't look all that intellectual," Timothy says, "if you ask me he—" "Shh," Doris says.) And over to the trunk of a sports car, out of which, one by one, a team of crew-cut boys emerges dribbling beach balls. Of course all of this is aggression of the cruelest sort, and one might conclude from an hour in front of this screen that those frequent lamentations one hears about an America grown affluently soft are unfounded: we are fighters still, who willingly undergo grueling psychological warfare nightly. Or one might make no such remark, since there is nothing to be said.

The problems of being physically beautiful clarified, if not solved altogether, the two actresses are kissed into that void where the camera does not venture. Off like rabbits they scamper. And the next guests are a trio of evangelists, one of whom is a Rabbitt. Garner is surprised at the relief he feels on seeing the controversial "Reverend" materialize. Somehow that fine-featured, cadaverous face, with the long lank dirty hair, is almost reassuring—even welcome. A palpable expectancy fills the hotel room. "They *hate* him," Timothy says with a kind of gleeful admiration. This is the first real outward show of emotion he has displayed all day. His eyes are pasted to the screen. "Those other two, they just *hate* him."

In acknowledgment of the serious turn tonight's program has now taken, Frank, our television host, actually lights his pipe, although he does not yet smoke it. He speaks straight into the camera. "In this country, the Christian Fundamentalist Movement and its ministers are too often lumped together. In fact, the

Fundamentalist Movement encompasses a wide range of differences and life-styles. These might begin with dress—" and here Frank pauses to let the camera swing from himself to the three seated ministers. One is wearing a blue suit and a red tie, and the next is wearing a blue suit and a red tie, and the last one, the Reverend Rabbitt, is wearing what looks like a windbreaker over a greasy denim work shirt. "But they go far deeper than that," Frank continues.

Judging them purely on their look of well-fed vapidity, Garner initially supposes that the two blue-suited ministers have been selected expressly to make the orthodox wing of the Fundamentalist Movement look ridiculous—that Frank, or whoever it is who selects Frank's guests, is working on behalf of the Reverend Rabbitt. It soon grows clear, however, that Frank's loyalties, or at least his conceptions about what will make "good television," place him on the other side. He is out to hunt Rabbitt, although he goes at it indirectly. He first asks the plumper of the two blue-suited ministers, a Reverend Whiteburn, to say a few words about the ground breaking of his new Whiteburn Bible College in Arkansas. This may be necessary ground breaking of another sort, the presentation of a "balanced" view of the Fundamentalist Movement, as well as a demonstration that Frank is interested in more than the controversial, undeniably gory dissension that the Reverend Rabbitt represents, and yet it seems that Frank himself—and who can blame him?—is irrepressibly bored by all of this. It isn't long before he has turned the conversation to a more lively note. "Why all this emphasis on *blood?*" he is asking the Reverend Rabbitt. "In a world of so much bloodshed already, including the death just this past month of all those thirty-three schoolboys at Harrow School, the alma mater of Winston Churchill, whom we must never forget was one of the most unquestionably important statesmen of the entire century, and that left the whole world weeping, why more *blood?* It seems so, I don't know, so"—and Frank gives quite a passable impersonation of someone undergoing an involuntary shudder—"so *primitive.* It gives me the *willies,*" he confesses in a microphoned aside to the studio audience, which replies with a sympathetic roll of laughter; they, too, share his squeamishness. And they are clearly fond of their Frank.

"Religion *is* primitive," the Reverend replies in that odd, arresting voice of his. Months and months later, when Garner has occasion to comb through the clippings and microfilms to see how others at that time characterized the Reverend's voice, he finds that one magazine calls it "gravel-bottomed," and in another the voice is "as dry and flat and as timelessly fertile as a Kansas plain." Uh-huh . . . But there is undeniably something powerful and compelling, *morally* compelling, about that voice. "It certainly has nothing to do with the modern world," he goes on, "if what you mean by the modern world is a pack of skyscrapers constructed by the greedy vermin for the greedy vermin, or if you mean a drugged nation, or if you mean the daily vermin-feeding garbage of television . . ."

The nervous, tittery laughter in the studio audience, exhilarated and nettled, is silenced by a magnanimous flourish of Frank's pipe. "Well now, Reverend," he says, "those are harsh words about television, which in fact brings pleasure to millions of Americans every day, including shut-ins and the seven point seven million of us whom we mustn't forget are hospitalized or bedridden on any given day of the year, and who may have no other means of entertainment at their immediate disposal, and yet you yourself consent to appearing on my show." And the aggrieved, just faintly hurt-sounding manner with which this "my" is delivered represents a little masterstroke; one might almost believe that this is not a multilayered, multimillion-dollar electronic complex to which the Reverend has been invited, but an intimate parlor, wherein the Reverend has committed a gross breach of guestly good manners. "Can I ask you, can I ask you, Reverend, why it is that you're here exactly?" Frank concludes, to loud, hooted applause from the audience. They have seen themselves fully vindicated.

"Welll," the Reverend begins, with a sad swaying of his head. He drawls this word, so that, although his accent is definitely more midwestern than southern, it emerges almost as *wail.* "I can assure you, sir, it is highly distasteful. It is highly distasteful, for me personally, to be here. But I do have my message to deliver. And to deliver it I must go wherever I must go. Our Lord Jesus went among thieves and prostitutes. I too go among thieves"—and here the Reverend, with an indeterminate shuffle of his hands, may mean to designate his two brethren in God—"and prostitutes." And this time there is no mistaking it: his sweep of the hand includes Frank himself.

Whooped laughter, and a kind of confederate gasp, and an anticipatory *ooh* of excitement from the heated-up studio audience. Oh, Frank may be their darling, but their hunger for some sort of scandal or violence—for good television—runs deeper still.

"Who you calling a thief?" the Reverend Whiteburn thunders, or tries to thunder, for he doesn't quite have the voice for thundering, and the Reverend Rabbitt in a strikingly smaller voice, tinged almost with a crackerbarrel folksiness, replies, "Wail, isn't it odd that *you* would jump to that conclusion . . ."

Laughter, unified grateful laughter, surges, and a crisp demanding swell of applause: the audience wants more.

The Reverend Whiteburn begins to hold forth, but he is cut off abruptly in the most effective way possible: the camera leaves him, in the blink of an eye, to focus upon Frank, who may well have snatched it away with a flick of his pipe. Frank's expression, by contrast, is self-congratulatorily calm and disinterested.

"And tell me," he says to the Reverend Rabbitt, "just what is your message? That we ought to bulldoze New York and go back to living in mud huts?" Scattered, piecemeal laughter, but not of the collective magnitude our Frank was evidently seeking. "Or that we ought to scar and disfigure ourselves with knives and razor blades, in a country in which a violent crime is on average committed every—"

"You are not listening," the Reverend replies in what is now a big voice of complementary but somehow far more impressive calm. "My message is much more revolutionary than that. My message is that we have to return God to our hearts. Even you, sir." With a modest fluttering of his hands, the Reverend motions to quell the eruptions of laughter this creates, as though genuinely eager not to discomfit or discredit his host. There is a superb plangency to the woeful, wistful way he adds, "He has been gone from there for a long time . . ."

And there is undisguised aggression on Frank's face, and an unmaskable impression that he knows himself getting the worst of it, as he says, "Then how is your message any different from anybody else's, hm? So what makes you think you're so special, hm?"

"Perhaps I say it more passionately." With a magisterial sweep of his hand the Reverend brushes a lank greasy lock from his forehead. The eyes are burning in that fine white skull face of his. "I say that religion in our country has sold itself. It has sold itself to the tobacco industry and the real estate firms, to the car companies and the liquor companies, to the football teams and the newspapers and the politicians. It has sold its soul to television and radio. We need to reclaim ourselves, to purify. It is time to return, to return, to return."

"And these two other gentlemen who were kind enough to appear tonight"—no doubt about it, Frank is floundering—"I presume that you're actually alleging that these men of God aren't alleging that we need more love in this country where a new homicide occurs on the average every eight minutes? That we need more purity? You know, Reverend, you have a reputation for being unwilling, or unable, to work with the other branches of the Christian church, with other evangelists."

"Oh they *hate* him," Timothy cries gleefully.

The Reverend Rabbitt deliberates. "Well, you see things have changed quite a bit for me these last few months. I have the people behind me now, and suddenly the so-called ministers who always scorned me and spat upon me with their eyes are letting me know, in so many words, that I might now be welcome to a portion of their pie, and that there's plenty of that pie to go around for all of us in the what you call the Fundamentalist Movement. But don't you *see?*" the Reverend beseeches and seems suddenly sincerely aggrieved by the simple dead-end obtuseness of this man, his television host. "I don't bargain—no, sir. I don't compromise—no, sir. I don't traffic in corruption, and that's what that offer is—it's corruption. No. No, *I want the whole pie,* because God himself wants the whole pie. These men are compromisers, but Jesus had no use for compromisers. 'I will follow you as soon as I have seen to my father's funeral,' the would-be disciple said to him, and Our Lord replies, 'Let the dead bury the dead.'"

"He doesn't *work* with any of us, simply because no sane person would work with *him.*" The camera jumps eagerly upon this. The Reverend Whiteburn is a big, broad, jowly man and the flesh of his face is visibly aquiver with rage. "Because he is a crazy man. A fully demented lunatic is what he is!"

"*Look* at you. Just *look* at you." The Reverend Rabbitt manages to infuse these words with an incomparable degree of scorn and disgust—as though he had never beheld under Heaven any creature, crawling or squirming, hooved or scaled, that quite so revolted him. "Getting yourself up there every Sunday morning, saying"—and the Reverend Rabbitt's voice leaps up into an oddly unsettling falsetto—"'*Touch your hand against mine on your home television screen,*' saying '*Send me money, send me money, send me money.*' Just *look* at you. Sitting there in your toupee and your *make*up. Sitting there for all the world with your face all made up like some slick little miniskirted bar hostess, saying '*Send me money, send me money, send me money.*'"

Garner has often heard and read the expression "to splutter with rage," but probably not until now has he actually seen a demonstration of what this entails. The sounds that issue from the Reverend Whiteburn's throat as he rises from his chair are prelinguistic, or prehuman; they are the sounds of a laboring animal. And when the words in fact do emerge, as he approaches the Reverend Rabbitt with a rhetorical shaking of his fists, it is as though *he,* tossing out his accusations of insanity, is mad beyond all hope of retrieval. "You're a *satanist,* that's what you are. The American people need to get a good close-up look at you, and what they'll behold is a cloven hoof and a great big—"

What the American people, including those four who sit breathless in a room in Boston's Totaplex Hotel, actually behold is something that most of them have seen on film countless times before. In Westerns, in spy thrillers, in costume romances, they have watched their reliable hero step forward, as the Reverend Jack Rabbitt now does, to drive a fist crashingly into the face of his opponent.

The blow, just as happens in the most satisfying cinematic simulations, knocks the Reverend Whiteburn backward to drop him heavily upon his ample bottom. And somehow, deep in the pandemonium that follows—the shouting in the studio, the clamor in the hotel room—one sharp image surfaces. In the Reverend Whiteburn's bloody open hole of a mouth there's a new gaping vacancy: his front teeth have been knocked out.

Blood is flowing freely and Timothy has leapt to his feet. "Did you *see* that? Did you *see* that?" he cries, over and over. Frank's little homey studio vanishes in a twinkling, and deeply shaken households all across America are steadied by the image of a Siamese cat in academic haberdashery delivering a lecture on the subject of a dog's nutritional needs. Timothy swings his fist back and forth in powerful imitation of the Reverend's blow. Then a spookier sound, a kind of shouted snort, breaks from his throat. It is the culminating strangeness to all the strange sounds that have emerged recently from Timothy's larynx, a kind of diabolical snort: "*Beh*-huh-hah!" he bellows. "Beh-huh-*hah!* Now he'll need false teeth too, huh? Makeup, a toupee, and now *false teeth too!*"

XVIII

HE SENSES OUT there, beyond the edges of his vision, as he takes the pawn—not with the bishop, which everyone, including

ANNDY, would have expected, but with the knight—Imre. He is offering ANNDY a free pawn, and he knows ANNDY's going to take it. He senses Imre's forward-lunging shock, elbows on knees and head pitched into those huge-knuckled hands, all of that massing nervous censure and all the frantic scrambling attempts to trace the strategic lines. And the possibility of Imre's anger, that stern lecture even now preparing itself for delivery, this raises the stakes and increases the sweet, dangerous racket in his veins. He is off alone, in a high deserted angular terrain and braver than anyone knows, for they can't understand it or envision the least bit of it, bravery like this. ANNDY takes the pawn.

And when, soon, he offers ANNDY another pawn, this one on the king's side, he feels this time Imre's mind dogging along close behind his. Imre sees, it doesn't take him long at all to see how this pawn will be retrieved. Yes, Imre is right there with him. Inside the head there's a loud but muffled whirring, like the sound of a gas stove in the next room when the flame's turned up all the way, only louder, but still he can feel Imre so close beside him. ANNDY thinks for eighteen minutes when forced to trade its bishop for a knight. Trouble, it smells trouble, and knows enough to push its analysis another half-move deeper than usual. But the answer's not to be found there, not a half-move deeper, or two, or three, or even five: it's all too deep, too high, for ANNDY.

A profound reevaluation is going on. ANNDY, too, has begun to grasp the shifting current of the game, deep, right down deep in the cold pooling microlabyrinths of its circuitry, but all the machinery in the world at this point can do precisely nothing. *Yes.* ANNDY has taken a blow and all the computations in the world cannot undo the damage.

There's a kind of leakage, like a crowbar to the abdomen of a robot, the oiled wafers mangled and an ooze like blood around the edges of a wound, a sweet needed easing and a deeper wounding driving, and none of it can be halted. "ANNDY doesn't like this," Oliver Conant says, though he himself can't see why it is that

ANNDY, still technically up a pawn, is hurting. But ANNDY is hurting . . .

And ANNDY's going to be liking the game less and less, five moves down the line, ten moves down; ANNDY has begun to grasp it all now, has felt the first precision-tooled advances of a raiding party that cannot be stopped. They have connected at last, come together, he and ANNDY have, and ANNDY sees just exactly what he sees: a white rook perched firmly on the seventh rank.

ANNDY is going so deep, and so far, three hundred and sixty-five thousand nodes a second, twenty million positions a minute, roads and roads and roads almost without number and all of them leading to that towering rook on the seventh rank. Like the spokes of a wheel, the infinity of lines slicing through any particular point, but this particular point is the human rook erected at the hub of the world. Millions and millions of positions glimpsed and evaluated, and all so fast they go beyond a blur, they race on into invisibility . . . And not one of them skipped or slighted, not one dismissed at the outset, but everything tagged and stored, tagged and stored . . . Yes, yes, ANNDY is vast, ANNDY is the biggest mind in the world really, there's no use denying that, and all so clean, so beautifully pristine, with none of the world's stink and sewage getting in: just that endless hunger, that ravenous insweeping call for more positions, more positions, more positions, and yet ANNDY is missing some something . . . Something's been left out, or a pettiness has crept in, and ANNDY's greedy, for pawns, for the small stuff, too greedy and small ever to dare to lift its gaze down and out to the real beyond, where, already, the farthest future shapes are assembling themselves.

It is odd to feel this so acutely now, as the machine slowly is being cornered, all of its calculations coming together to produce nothing but a defeat, but he has never so clearly discerned those billions of numbers ANNDY's forever sifting, that generous-lapped mountain, the Everest of calculations upon which it perches. ANNDY is vast, but he knows, as the flame whirs with a loud steady slap-slapping inside his head, that Timothy Briggs is vaster. He is being drawn upward, and upward with a refining flame, when he sets the rook down, thump in all its ponderous masonry, on the seventh rank, thump, himself inside it, high in the tower, as he knew he would be, his face inside it, thump, and all of the walls of ANNDY's defenses fixed to crumble. "ANNDY doesn't like this *at all*," Oliver says.

At this utterly safe height, high in the laddered tower, he can feel his own knowledge branching magnanimously outwards, descending in sweetened sunny rays to touch the separate intellects in the audience. What Imre has seen for some time, and ANNDY for not quite so long, grows more and more apparent, until Garner can see it, and the little kids from the Boston Chess Club, and squirming bony-hipped Oliver Conant, who can't manage to keep his fly up, so that a bit of pink shirt tail pokes through today, and the television crew, and the journalists, and even Vicky, too, who hardly knows how to move the pieces—Vicky, who sits as such a potent dark configuration of entanglements there just beyond the board of his vision. He perches at such an elevation that Oliver's voice reaches him thinned by distance: "ANNDY's willing to concede this one."

Soon, or a little later, "ANNDY's had enough . . . Good game," Oliver says, and this time extends his hand. The shaking of hands awakens a bank of applause in the audience and Oliver turns toward it and gives a kind of wave and backs away into a defeated dark. And with Oliver gone, everyone is looking only at what is visible of Timothy Briggs now, and his eyes are burning in the bright flaming light as he, too, waves and nods at them. Forces are regrouping themselves. There has been a release and another sort of leakage, a puncture through which are somersaulting voices, lights, eyes, and the bigger, hungry eyes of the television cameras. Meshed microphones are held before him, with those cameras hungrily running, and he feels the whole of this as a sort of spilling in reverse, a huge and unregulated outward upflow, holes through which everything in the auditorium is cascading. He is being asked questions, one stacked upon another, but the words are not there by which they might be answered. The words will not group, they scatter in a wandering spotlit babble beneath that massed permanent tower on the seventh rank, whose stringent lessons about life's perfectability are every moment being retreated from. And then comes a question, *What does your victory today show?* to which it turns out he has the one significant, the perfect reply. "I think this should give everybody hope . . ." He addresses these words to all of them, the microphones and the papers, the blank newspapers with boxes reserved for his photograph, the faces waiting on the other side of the camera's eye. Everything is spilling outward into place. "That's what I'm trying to do here. I'm trying to give people hope." They ask him to step over to the edge of the stage, closer to ANNDY's screen, and that's all right. They want to take photographs that will have ANNDY's screen in the background. They can't see much of anything, of course, nothing of what really happened today, nothing of what ANNDY's really like, the mountains of numbers below which they live their whole lives, but that's all right. They're blind as bats but it's all right so long as you explain things very clearly to them, because they would like to understand, truly, but they just don't have the minds for it. They want to be told what all of this means. "ANNDY's a fabulous piece of machinery," he explains. "There's no doubt about that. But it can't compare with the human mind. People need to understand how special they are."

And ANNDY, it turns out, has been elaborately prepared for a loss like this. They knew it all along, Conant and the rest of them, that the loss was inevitable, otherwise why should they have gone to the trouble of preparing all of these messages? OUCH! YOU'VE GOT THE SMARTS THAT SMART and YOU REALLY KNOW HOW TO HURT A GUY and OOH, I THINK I MUST HAVE DRUNK TOO MUCH LAST NIGHT.

The messages are flashing, nearby, behind him, as he explains it carefully to all of them out there. "This isn't John Henry all over again. This isn't a battle of muscle but of mind and that's a whole new something else. People need to see that they can do anything, once they put their minds to it." He feels his words going out, across his waiting country, and feels the need people have, from one wired, plugged-in coast to the other, for these very words. A regrouping, a disciplined reorganization from above is required in this country, and soon, by which what is at present random and all but powerless will be made efficient and powerful. The pieces, the material, are out there—have been there all along. "What I'm going to show people, in this match, is that the machine can never replace the human being. That we're special. We need to go right back to that idea. This match stands for something. It stands for something big."

They are laughing, and that's all right, for it scares them a little, and therefore they're looking for laughter, and that's what ANNDY serves up to them: JUST LET ME SULK FOR A WHILE and YOU'RE A BIG BAD BRUTE YOU ARE. They are laughing, but that's just nervousness: they *want* these words that make them jittery, they know they need to feel his voice expanding still further before them: "You know people have been calling me John Henry, but I'm not John Henry. I'm Timothy Briggs. This is a different kind of a story. He didn't use his *mind.* We're at the dawn of a new millennium and these are new issues and people need to see with their minds what this means. They don't think hard enough." He doesn't want to hurt them, but this is something they will have to face dead on. There are things they will have to face, and with this cool, crystallizing realization he feels also a kind of anger, or impatience—something smoldering hot—shrugging upward through his human insides, up to his throat. "Sometimes ladies and gentlemen, you honestly don't think hard enough."

Laughter, like monkeys at the zoo they are always wanting to retreat behind laughter. ANYONE FOR TENNIS? asks ANNDY, and adds, after a moment's thought, IT ONLY HURTS WHEN I LAUGH.

XIX

IT'S AS IF the lights suddenly stop swimming and a thudding stops; a rapid kind of coming down, or catching of the breath, takes place, and Timothy feels more clearly than before the well-intentioned flowings in the air around him. He shakes Imre's hand, and then Garner's, who says, "I didn't expect both a victory *and* a peroration—congratulations," which Timothy supposes is meant as wit or irony but in any case it seems harmless and can be allowed to pass. He stoops to accept a hug and a kiss from his mother, who says, "That's my *boy,* the television star. I wonder if they'll show this in Key Largo."

"I expect so," he tells her.

When Vicky comes forward to congratulate him, she clutches his right hand in both of hers as she leans forward to kiss him on the cheek, not far from the mouth, really. "Didn't I tell you?" she says, and these are words that thrill him. Just like a stick across the pickets of a fence, that's how they rap and clatter along the insides of his ribs. "Well, didn't I tell you victory was on the way?"

"Yes," Timothy admits. "You did."

"Hello, Imre," Vicky says. "And is it appropriate to congratulate you?" She extends her hand. "I suppose so. You're the trainer, after all."

"Oh yeah, you can congratulate him all right," Timothy says.

"Puh," says Imre, and adds, with an abrupt courtliness, "it is a very happy day for all."

Courtly as Imre might seek to be, he neglects to perform the introduction that so obviously waits to be made. And Timothy, too, fails to step forward, despite the suggestive, prodding tilt to Vicky's head. So, unasked, Vicky again extends her hand, and says, "You must be Tim's mother. My name is Vicky Schmidt."

"Oh it's Doris, dear, you'll be calling me Doris won't you,

huh?" Doris accepts the hand eagerly. She peers hard at this young woman who has just kissed her son.

"I work for Congam Corporation," Vicky says. "You know, the tournament sponsors."

"Do you make up the sayings, dear?"

"The what?"

"The maybe you call them sayings? On the TV screen? They're really *very* clever."

I'D SELL MY SOUL FOR A BREW is ANNDY's newest message.

"Oh no, that's ANNDY. We don't have anything to do with that. ANNDY's a chess program made here. At M.I.T. At Congam, we make the computer that ANNDY runs on. The famous Congam C-4 Gigacomputer. Actually, I don't make the computer, either," Vicky says, and giggles. "Golly, I don't know *what* I do, Doris."

"Well I'm sure you do it well. It seems so *com*plic*a*ted. These computers playing chess just like the boys always do."

"I guess it *is* complicated," Vicky says.

"I'm sure *I* don't understand it all," Doris says in that emphatic and faintly pugnacious way she has, as if anticipating resistance. Vicky, or Garner, or even trainer Imre, might well be about to insist, *Oh, no, you do understand it all! You do!*

"Well this is just such a *dream,* isn't it? I mean wow, how the match is going. We hardly *dreamed* it would build this fast. The *New York Times, Time* magazine, *tel*evision."

"Timmy was on TV in Key Largo. That's where I live, Key Largo. I'm not *from* there, but that's where I live."

"Oh he was on all over the country! He's going to have to hire a theatrical agent pretty soon."

"I'm *from* Indiana. Do you think so?"

"Mm?"

"An agent?"

"It honestly would not surprise me."

"There may be real money in it. Now I wouldn't know, dear," Doris concedes, "but I've heard it said, that there may be real money in it."

"Listen, if you'd all like to, I'd like to take you all out for a quick bite of something. I mean courtesy of Congam."

"We'd all like that, wouldn't we?" Timothy says, and when Garner politely demurs, and by way of persuasion Doris points out that *it won't take but less than an hour,* Timothy adds, "Mom, Garner's got lots to *do.*" The truth is that Timothy feels his brother's gray dapper presence as a weight upon his own lifting exaltation; feels that Garner would be out of place at a celebration of this sort.

So the little victory party assembles itself. Garner departs, with another of his probably ironic observations ("We *all* have a lot to do"), and Doris elaborately concludes the business of donning her coat and gloves. Actually, it's a temperate October evening, with a breeze carrying the smells of autumn but the warmth of summer, and Vicky wears only a lightweight white wool cardigan in place of a jacket. "Maybe we better let Tim choose our destination," she says to Doris. Imre and Timothy—or "the boys" as Doris calls them—are walking a few steps behind the two women. "He seems to be a pretty fussy eater."

"It's not how he used to be. He was little, he was the best eater I had. And I've done everything a body can. But it's just a stage, I think, just a very, very long stage. He just always needs somebody around to encourage him to eat more different things."

"Well, if you want to encourage him, there's a really good Szechuan place nearby."

"Szechuan?"

"Chinese," Vicky says.

"Oh I don't much like foreign food. On account of the flavors, dear," Doris explains.

"And there's a decent steak place. I mean the food's surprisingly decent, and if you're willing to accept the ambience purely as—"

"Steak," Timothy calls from behind them. "That's it. We'll all celebrate with *steak.* That's just perfect."

And—yes—he finds it perfect. To sit in the candle-starred constellated interior of the Steering Wheel, feeling the warmth of his victory inside him, and the warmth of a rum and Coke drifting searchingly in the upper reaches of his chest, with his mother on one side and beautiful Vicky on the other, and with Imre across the table, so proud, prouder than anyone else could be because Imre alone understands just how brilliant the playing was today—this is for Timothy the setting for an exhilaration that will not keep still. His fingers drum on the tabletop, his rhythmically clapping knees come together with fierce, sweet concussions. He would like to calm down, since just the pure watching of Vicky and his mother in conversation is a fascinating and an exciting thing, but he feels also an urgent need to speak his mind, and about anything under the sun—about chess and New York City and Garner and about the confusions the American people are feeling these days toward computers and about the John Henry folk song. He downs his drink just moments after Vicky finishes hers and he orders another.

"Do you always carry a briefcase?" Doris asks Vicky. "I've never even owned a briefcase."

"Well you haven't missed a thing, Doris." Advancing on a little wave of giggled laughter, Vicky's hand slides forward on the table, as if reassuringly to pat Doris's hand, although in fact the younger hand halts and no contact takes place. Apparently, it's a mannerism of hers, this near-touching. "I mean you make it sound really *glam*orous. Mine's full of all sorts of nasty *business* papers."

"Oh but it is. Really glamorous. You see, I see the ads, and they're always carrying briefcases now. The women. Even down in Key Largo, I don't miss any of the ads," Doris boasts.

Garlic bread, salads, potatoes, and steaks arrive simultaneously. Each of the steaks sports a little steering wheel in whose center is an initial or pair of initials—MR, MW . . . Medium, Rare, Medium Well.

"Do you live here in Boston, Vicky?"

"Well I do now. But I grew up in Constance, Massachusetts, not so far from here. Actually," Vicky says, "I was born in Chicago. But I hardly remember it, we moved when I was four."

The look that Doris gives the young woman is sympathetic—fondly pitying, even. "They moved because of the heat, dear?"

"The what?"

"Your family? You see we spent nearly a summer in Chicago and so I know all about all that. In all my life I never was so hot. It's a different *kind* of heat there. Course you know what I'm talking about."

"Maybe because of the lake?" Vicky says. "I honestly don't remember much."

"Maybe it's the slaughterhouses," Doris says. "All those animals. Breathing."

"I wonder if this cow's from Chicago," Timothy says. "I mean our steaks."

Imre clears his throat. "They're probably not all from the same cow." It's the first remark he has volunteered since coming to the restaurant. He doesn't often speak up like this in any sort of mixed group, although he will on occasion, as now, conscientiously tighten any looseness in his pupil's logic.

"Okay, okay make that cows with an *s*. Plural," Timothy says with a show of impatience, although it's clear that he enjoys this process of correction. He glances around the restaurant and everything he sees—the candles, the Tiffany lamps, the crushed red velvet on the near walls, the understated mural of an automobile racetrack on the far wall—pleases him.

"It's a hard life," Doris says. "Farming is."

"I'm sure," Vicky says.

"And what does your father do, dear?"

"Well, he's dead actually. He died when I was a kid. He used to work for the phone company."

"Ohhhh," Doris sighs. "You know Timmy's father died when he was a boy too. I will never understand it, these people always dying. Whenever will it stop?"

"Let's hope within our lifetimes," Vicky says and, as she so often will at her own remarks, giggles. Surprisingly, Imre responds with a rumble of laughter. Timothy, too, after a moment in which to ponder the remark, joins the laughter, as does, after another moment, Doris. Vicky looks pleased with herself, a little flushed, when she excuses herself to go to the ladies' room.

Vicky is still within sight, though retreating rapidly, when Doris, too, excuses herself. She follows Vicky through the doors of the ladies' room and finds her alone before the row of gleaming washbasins, brushing in rapid strokes her lovely, thick black hair. "Doris," Vicky says, "you don't have an aspirin, do you? Or something stronger?"

"Headache, dear?"

"Cramps. Every damn month, I get such horrible cramps."

"Yesss." Although a little put off by the directness of this response, and the profanity, Doris places a quelling, sympathetic hand on the girl's arm. "Dear, they'll get much better after you have some children. You'll get so you hardly notice."

"People don't just say that, Doris? I mean it's not just a trick to keep the human race alive?"

Doris feels a pleasurable sense of purpose mount within her, which compels her to squeeze the strong young arm. "Things get better," she declares, staring up into the girl's face, into the girl's dark innocent eyes. "You'll see that in so many ways things get *better.*" Doris pauses, ransacking her mind for some method of dealing with this familiar and yet always vexatious sensation of understanding so much more than she can say. She has a poignant feeling that this girl is vulnerable, despite the briefcase and all the rest—a vulnerability matched by Timmy's own. And the mutual lacks of these two young people, the need they have for each other, prompts Doris toward some healing message—whose words unfortunately do not arrive. In their place, Doris says, "You mustn't overdo. I have a sense of people, call it second sight if you wish, but I can tell things very quickly. And I can tell you overdo."

"I probably do," Vicky says, and hears herself giggle loudly in a stupid-sounding sort of way. It makes her uneasy—to have this gray-haired woman standing so close, gripping her arm, speaking so earnestly. There's something desperate—that queer unfocused desperation common to old people—in Doris's face, which is revealed so harshly in the light of this bathroom. "You don't have that aspirin, do you?"

"Aspirin?"

"My cramps," Vicky says.

"Yes. Oh yes, I think I do." Doris fumbles in her purse. "One or two, dear? Maybe you better start with the one. They can be hard on the stomach."

"Well, two, please, actually, I mean if you can spare them. I've got a very strong stomach. You've got to, if you work for Congam." Vicky gives the woman a wink, to signal an end to this conversation, and Doris, after a moment's further scrutiny, winks in reply—although this may be only a stray fluttering of her eyelids. It's unclear, too, what exactly brought Doris into the ladies'. Was it merely to talk, Vicky wonders, or has she forgotten her business here? In any case, Doris exits beside her.

"Would you look at that?" Vicky says. "They've already pulled out the chessboard."

"You boys will have to put away your game," Doris grandly announces as she marches up to the table. "Honestly, don't the two of you know when it's time for proper dinner conversation?" And by way of demonstration, once she has reseated herself, she begins, "Now I have a question, Vicky. Is your name really Victoria?"

"Victoria Teresa Schmidt. It's the best my parents could do, I guess," Vicky says.

"You know Timmy lived, we all did, in Victoria for a time. That's Victoria, Indiana."

"Yes, Tim mentioned that."

"Though some of the time, long ago, the Briggses lived in Elizabeth. They're the twin cities, Victoria and Elizabeth, the twin cities of Founders Valley. Maybe you've heard of them?"

"I have. Tim mentioned them."

"They're a wonderful place to grow up in," Doris says. "There aren't many good places left to grow up in."

"I suppose that's right."

"Young people today don't know what they're missing, but if they had it, they'd know what they were missing you can bet. Oh, Victoria's a fine place for growing up in, but it's a hard place for growing *old* in. They don't always appreciate a person there. My friend Harriet, that's Harriet Dwiggins, my best friend for more than thirty years, she actually died there. She gave the whole of her life to the place, and what did they care a single iota? Oh, it's a hard place for dying in."

"No one's going to die," Timothy says. "They're going to cure death in our lifetime."

"If they don't, we're dead," Doris says. Once uttered, the remark strikes her as witty, in a slightly naughty way, and although she herself is the only one to find it amusing, she gives it a generous laugh. "If they don't cure it," she repeats, "we're all the rest of us *dead*."

Dishes are taken away. Timothy and Imre order hot fudge sundaes. Vicky requests a cup of coffee. Doris tells the waitress, "Nothing for me," and adds, "but there's no hurry on that." It is to her that the bill is finally delivered. With a grand, splay-fingered descent she settles her right hand upon it. But, "No, no this is Congam's," Vicky declares, and neatly extracts the bill from the outstretched hand. "This is Congam's way of saying thanks. Everybody, the whole company, is just *so* pleased with your son."

In the face of such disarming words, Doris must drop all struggle for the bill. She says instead, "I wonder if today was on TV in Key Largo."

"I wouldn't be surprised . . . I wouldn't be surprised at all."

"It's a beautiful city. Boston," Doris remarks, when the four of them again stand outside the restaurant, although the view actually before her is nothing more than an old brick building with plywood slabs over the windows. "Do you live far from here, Vicky?"

"Oh it's just a shortish cab. You three, you might want to walk back, actually. I mean the Totaplex isn't far from here at all. Which means you'd be going that way"—she points to her left—

"and I'm going this way." She points to her right. "Well. Well hasn't it been great fun."

"Oh no, no, you mustn't walk unaccompanied and alone by yourself at night, my dear."

"Oh it's really just round the corner . . ."

"Timmy, now you're to walk the young lady. And you make sure she gets into a proper cab all right. You must excuse me, Vicky dear, but I'm suddenly so very tired suddenly I couldn't walk an extra step and I think I'll just head over to the hotel, if Imre wouldn't mind guiding me."

"Well, if you're really tired, we can *all* go catch a cab. There's a stand right around the corner."

"Oh no, no a little walk," Doris insists. "That's just what I need for my fatigue." She steps forward and takes the girl's hand and once more peers intently into her young, lovely eyes. "Now you remember what I said. About overdoing? And I hope to see you again soon."

"I hope so too. It's been fun."

"Good night, Ma," Timothy calls. "Good night, good night, good night." "That was a real game today, you're thinking now," Imre says, by way of farewell. "Oh, I'm *thinking* all right. Good night. Good night. Good night," Timothy calls. He can hardly believe the opportunity that by chance has come his way: he hadn't expected to have a moment alone with Vicky. He waves farewell to his mother and to his trainer and, with Vicky at his side, eagerly sets off.

"It's nice of you to walk me to the cab," Vicky says.

"You shouldn't walk at night." Timothy hesitates but then makes a confession: "I should know. I was mugged a while ago."

"You were? Where?"

He loves that easy, quick-flowing sympathy in her voice. "In New York. It was late. I'd been playing chess. It's not like they got away with much money, I didn't have much money. Not on me."

"How many of them were there?"

"The funny thing is," Timothy says, and his stomach tugs itself into a knot at the words, "I hardly remember it." But having made one quite intimate confession, he's ready to tender another: "Sometimes I hardly remember things. It's so funny."

"I don't blame you," Vicky says. "I mean, some things it's better to forget."

"It's so funny," Timothy goes on, and a sense of his own mixed daring and bewilderment revolves inside his head. "Because I remember other things. I remember other things so much better than *any*body else. I remember other things so many other people have forgotten forever."

"Yes." A moment of silence falls. The two of them round a corner, which opens a view of the Boston skyline, and Vicky says, "It's a real nice night, isn't it?" and it's as though, with the abrupt vertical view, and these words coming horizontally from her lips to his ear, a multidimensional realignment takes place, in an instant, and he beholds as though for the first time, as though just this moment it had loomed out of a gray cloud, the true essence of this city, Boston, which is gentler and fairer and so much more generous than New York. This beguilingly intricate, this gold-lit city, which he had perceived as enemy territory, actually belongs to him. Boston—it is the spoils of his victory, and in the pearllike strings of its streetlights, and in its walkways and trees and wandering boated river, in the greens and yellows and reds of its changing leaves, and in the other, brighter greens, yellows, reds of its traffic signals, it has all been waiting for him.

"From my hotel room, boy, you can really see this city." Only after the remark is out does he understand—and this ought to be embarrassing—that it might be interpreted as an invitation. But Vicky's reply, rooted in the bottomless hospitality of that invisible corporate conglomerate which has recently begun to feed him and to house him, to change his towels and sheets, to pay his phone and utility bills, is reassuring: "Well, I'm glad you like it. We aim to please."

Timothy does not know how to begin to say everything he needs to say and inside him an awareness of his own clumsiness stampedes into a sort of panic as they swing around another corner to face, right across the street, a hard-shining line of cabs.

"You've taken me out to eat twice now," he says. "I feel like I need to repay you."

"Well you don't. I mean need to feel that way. I mean I'm not entitled to your gratitude. Since it's Congam's paying for everything."

They cross the street together. There is no way to arrive where he must arrive, apparently, except by venturing right to the always risky center of things. That's where the forces are meant to converge, where the hidden victory must lie. "Oh but you are," he tells her. "Entitled to my gratitude. Because you helped me win today." The look she gives him seems encouraging, though somewhat puzzled, and a voice within his head warns that he'd better pull back his forces. But another voice within his head, one heard intermittently this whole day long, informs him that if he will only proceed directly, with power and intelligence enough, there is nothing in the world that can be denied him—not even this girl. He continues: "I mean I'm aware of your presence while I'm thinking. It's very hard to explain. It's not like I'm looking at you or anything, but I'm aware of your being there physically. I mean the way we're all here physically. That helps me win, that helped me win today."

"Oh that's so *sweet,*" she cries and there can be no question about it: she is genuinely touched.

"You help me, Vicky." Timothy wants to ask her whether there might be anything of hers he could hold on to, just for luck—as knights before tournaments used to be given a lady's scarf. Or perhaps a lock of her hair. But merely to have said *you help me, Vicky,* had nearly cracked his voice and he doesn't quite dare, or simply doesn't know how, to ask her this intimate favor. And he feels the metal cabs out there waiting to carry her away.

He wants to kiss her. He steps forward, alit with the fiery conviction that she can truly be his, and yet—yet something within him falters. *This is the wrong place,* an urgent internal voice advises him, and in a jolted panic he fumbles instead for her hand, even though his head has already canted awkwardly forward, and—

And Vicky comes to the rescue. It's *she* who rescues *him;* she seems to glimpse into the heart of all his crossed intentions, the odd jumble of voices he's hearing today, and she draws her face confidently forward to kiss him on the cheek. So simple. Once you see it, it's always so simple. And while this isn't quite the kiss he'd wanted, yet it is enough, and more: he's grateful, ever so grateful to her for this, as he is for her closing remark: "Good night, Champ."

His head may be a wild muddle and yet he knows that he needs this very sense of feeling grateful, and all the reassurance it can bring, if ever he's to quell the jangling tumult within. There are no words for any of this but there is danger everywhere, he is frightened, and it might almost seem that all of the chessboard's most brilliant, far-flung combinations are but a narrow, tremulous rope bridge spun across a darkness that, with the shredding of a few fibers, would swallow everything. Her furry white sweater gleams in the night. She gets into her cab.

He waves to her and she—oh, he adores her for all of this!—she turns around to wave at him.

XX

SHE TURNS AROUND, smiles and waves, turns back and, slouching toward comfort, lets her head drop against the back of the seat. She is nearly asleep when the taxi halts before her building. In all of her heavy-headed tiredness, she goes off without a receipt—which always makes reimbursement just a little sticky at the office. "Damn," she mumbles, unlocks her apartment, and finding the place much too warm (the thermostat must be on the blink again), unbuttons her sweater. She goes into her bedroom to see whether anybody has called and finds that her answering machine's little green message light is flashing.

She plays back the tape. It's a familiar voice, a man's, and quite up-front in its delivery, with none of that hemming and hawing you so often get when people are asked to speak into a machine. "You are a genius. No doubt lots of guys leave messages on your answering machine telling you you're a genius"—pause—"so you don't know who this could be but this could be Jack Westman. Could be and is. And if I ever run for political office, I want you for my campaign manager. Perhaps we could discuss political strategies over a sushi dinner. Which is to say, I'm coming up to Boston to see you this weekend. Call me for details."

Vicky removes her royal-blue mid-heel pumps and puts on a pair of powder-blue beaded suede moccasins. She pads into the kitchen and pours herself a very weak Campari and soda. It isn't so much a drink she actually wants as a cigarette, though she gave them up almost two years ago. It's always this way. She won't think about smoking all day long, and then at night, coming back to a solitary apartment, that high squeezing hunger in the chest will get at her, almost as strong as ever. She sips her drink on the way to the bedroom, begins with her free hand to unbutton her blouse, sets her drink on a coaster on her bedside table, consults the Rolodex, and punches the numbers on her push-button phone.

"Jack Westman here."

"Victoria Schmidt here. Good Lord you're actually at work. Or at the office, anyway. I would've called you at home first, only I didn't have the number."

"It's the same number. Congam *is* my home. I sleep here and I wouldn't feel *right* sleeping anywhere else."

"Oh please . . ."

"I have no other life. Unlike certain television stars I know. And now that you're a multimedia star, I've decided to come up and visit."

"What the hell are you talking about?"

"My sources in Boston tell me you were on TV. Standing beside young Briggsy."

"What sources? What are you talking about?"

"You were on Boston TV. Standing beside the boy who made Congam cry uncle. And probably New York TV, too, I wouldn't be at all surprised."

"But I wasn't standing beside him."

"Well, *near* him then. Vincent says he saw you. Definitely you."

"But the camera wasn't even *on* me."

"Or so you thought. Honey, those guys are clever. You know—always trying to throw a pretty face on the screen."

She would ignore this, normally, but now she confides, with an enthusiasm she can't quite quell or conceal, "You know, I've never been on TV before . . ." She turns to glance at her face in the bedside mirror but sees only her neck, her open blouse, the top of her powder-blue brassiere. She hunches and finds that her eyes look tired, her hair's a mess. It's her very first time on TV and she wonders where she might get a copy of the broadcast.

"He's going to make you famous. You're going to make him famous. Briggsy and Schmidt, I can see it up there now. Seriously, you've got to bag this business and jump into the ad game. You'll be a kajillionaire. I'll be your manager."

"I told you before, I think they call it a pimp," Vicky says, and she's pleased by the gruff snort of laughter at the other end. Somewhat surprisingly, she likes this Jack Westman. As a general rule, she has no use for his type. The world is too full of them—these can-do, aggressively flirtatious men. But he's better at it than most—much funnier—and he's very good-looking besides. And he knows how to listen, with very little watch-me-listen in his style; you don't get a sense with Jack that he's quite so completely in love with himself as most good-looking men are.

"Listen, seriously, I'm coming up there this weekend, and I thought I might take you to dinner. Saturday night?"

"Jack, I've got a friend coming in to stay with me this weekend."

"Is that a male sort of friend or a female sort of friend?"

"Doing a little digging, are we?"

"It's for the tabloids. One of those The-girl-you-see-on-the-boob-tube-isn't-what-she's-like-in-real-life stories."

"Her name's Marian Sowder and I've known her since junior high school and I've got to be specially good to her because she's just broken up with her perfect shit of a boyfriend."

"A little R. and R. in the Boston singles bar scene, huh?" The laughter at the other end, as though sensing itself to be unshared, abruptly halts. "No, no just kidding, jokey joke joke," Jack says. "I'm sure she's very sweet. Is she very sweet?" Vicky can feel at the other end of the line the way that Jack is absorbing new data, weighing plans and probabilities. What he wants to know, of course, is whether Marian is pretty. "Oh I think any really decent guy would think so," she says, switching the phone from hand to hand in order to unbutton her cuffs. "Can we put dinner on hold? Kind of see how things stand when Marian gets here?"

"Call it a definite maybe?" Jack says.

"Speaking of dinner, I just got back from dinner with Tim, and his mother, she's up from Florida, and his trainer, Imre. Have you met Imre?"

"Good Lord, and now I am really *truly* impressed. Lady, the things you won't *do* for Congam . . ."

"No, it was fine really, even the mother, Doris, although she did seem a little eager to marry me off to her son."

"Now *there's* a real catch, huh? Wow, I mean you've got yourself a real live wire there. To say nothing of a real hunk."

"Oh come on. Come on, he's tremendously sweet." All the buttons on her blouse undone, Vicky opens her mouth and twists her jaw to study the mole on her lower left cheek, which lately seems to have grown more prominent. She can't decide whether or not to have it removed. It's distinctive in its way, and some men have told her it's very sexy, but she doesn't like the way it breaks her jawline. "And you know actually he's quite good-looking."

"Is it okay in this liberated day and age to confess that I will never understand women? What do women want? as Karl Marx once asked. Was it Karl Marx?" Jack laughs loudly. "What is it that makes them select the absolutely *most* pathetic loser in any room and call him a lady-killer?"

"Why don't they all pay homage instead to the brash young rising stars of Congam Corporation—is that it? You know, you're not as good-looking as you think, Jack." She shrugs her shoulders out of her blouse.

"And another thing, another thing I don't understand, I don't understand why in today's liberated world men are still expected to go around telling women how good-looking they are and women are always free to tell a guy he looks like something for the pooper-scooper."

Vicky giggles at this. "Am I being a bitch again, huh? It's just this thing that comes over me, Doctor . . ."

"I think you like the kid because he gets you on TV."

"No. No in fact I'm *not* being a bitch," Vicky answers herself. "Every time I think I'm acting like a bitch to somebody, it turns out he completely deserves it."

"*Men* . . . Is there any question that they're absolutely the very worst sex in the world? Honestly, Vicky, have you ever met a worse sex than men?"

Letting him hear the sound, Vicky drains her drink with a clatter of ice cubes.

"They call me a brute, an insensitive clod," Jack goes on.

"If the shoe fits . . ."

"But the shoe *doesn't* fit. Don't you see, don't you see it never fits for anybody around here. *This isn't me,* I scream quietly. I'm not a Congam rep, I'm really a scuba instructor. And you go down the halls, you hear these wee little whispery voices—*This isn't me,* they're all saying, *I'm really a paleontologist,* or *I'm really an astronaut,* or *I'm really a sheep farmer . . .*"

"We're the generation that's going to change all that. I want you to realize your inner dreams, Jack."

"Do you? Do you really, Vicky? Well, that's good news—hey listen, why don't I call you tomorrow, and in the meantime you can call this, this—"

"This thing Marian?"

"Maybe we could all go out. I got a friend lives in Somerville, maybe we could all go out. He's a super guy."

"She's a *very* sweet girl," Vicky says, "and I feel it's my bounden duty not to let her anywhere *near* you, and the kinds of super friends I know you've got. I mean honestly, Jack, how would I ever forgive myself?"

XXI

"MMP," SAYS IMRE, "mmp, mmp," and, easing a bit, "Puhhh." ANNDY's position in game six steadily, decrementally is coming undone. . . . It is as though roles have been reversed, and Timothy become the slow, grinding, extractive machine. Up there on the stage, he even sits immobile like a machine. He plays today with none of his usual fidgeting, as if in a sort of trance, from which he emerges only to lock another piece into place. He is crushing the machine beneath him. "He's listening to me. He's finally listening to me," Imre whispers to Garner.

Things seem sufficiently under control for Garner to wander out to the corridor for a drink of water. There he meets a friend, a philosopher from M.I.T., who introduces him to another member of the M.I.T. faculty, a big outlandishly dressed man who has a familiar face. He is someone a person notices. This is Albrecht Zehnder, the father—or the godfather—of ANNDY. Oliver Conant is one of Zehnder's graduate students.

A curious, ritualized bit of academic volleying follows, as both Garner and Zehnder acknowledge a familiarity with the other's work, but only of the dimmest sort. In fact, Garner has long wanted to meet the celebrated Zehnder, whose gift for provocative statement, packaged as toothy little aphorisms, is forever getting him into the newspapers. "We don't have the right to impede our machines," Zehnder has postulated, and "Human beings may be smart enough, but only just barely, to make themselves obsolete."

"ANNDY seems to be having a bit of trouble in there," Garner observes.

"It's the monkeying. We monkeyed with the program last night, after losing that last game, and somehow we glitched it up. Laid a real egg in there. You look at those crazy things it's doing with its pawns." Zehnder is a big, stooped, paunchy, disheveled, cheerful figure. His is a form of sartorial outlandishness which, at least in academia, is generally reserved to faculty in the natural sciences—a voluminous Hawaiian shirt, tight black denim trousers, and high-top lime-green gym shoes. Of course law professors, too, have their own eccentricities of dress, but for better or worse these rarely take a form that might plausibly lead a small child to mistake the wearer for a circus clown.

"Maybe you should have left well enough alone," Garner says.

"Oh no, no, we likes to monkey. You might say we're monkeying animals, us computer scientists. Course we wouldn't go monkeying if winning was our primary goal. But hell, we're trying to learn something in here."

As seems to happen so often lately, Garner feels within himself a solicitous bristling, a sense of rankled loyalty on behalf of his brother. Zehnder's suggestion is disturbing, even infuriating—the notion that, although Timothy has plunged his whole soul into this contest (to the point where his brain seems, in best modern-day John Henry fashion, to be buckling a little underneath the pressure), ANNDY's makers regard the entire match dispassionately, as an experiment. Standing there in all his cheerful, clownish bulkiness, Zehnder would seem almost a cruel figure. . . . Yet when he says, "I think I need some coffee, you guys wanna go out for a coffee?" Garner accepts unhesitatingly, even though his friend—the performer of introductions, the link between Zehnder and himself—declines the invitation.

A surprisingly bitter wind rips across the M.I.T. campus. The sky on this late October day has become an unyielding, wintry gray. But Zehnder wears no jacket over his Hawaiian shirt. He crosses his arms as he walks and says, "Weather. Some weather."

"I've gotten a bit interested in this business," Garner says, "thinking machines and all the rest."

"I can't stand it," Zehnder says. "The notion that fall is really here."

"Winter is likely to follow . . ." Garner points out.

Zehnder leads Garner to a student "dive," a cafeteria, just off Massachusetts Avenue. Garner knits his hands, still numb with cold, around a cup of tea. Zehnder tears hungrily into a sizable wedge of something which a chalkboard menu identifies as Marco's Cherry Cheesecake and which has a chocolate chocolate-chip cookie crust. "I think I read an article of yours," Garner goes on. "Something about 'machine rights.'"

"Lots," Zehnder says with his mouth full. "I've written lots about machine rights. Myself, I see myself as a freedom fighter. More and more, this is where your *real* freedom fighters, the ones who don't mind bloodying their knuckles a bit, are going to be found. . . in the ivory tower of the academy."

"And you don't doubt that they'll be entitled to rights?"

"Oh, I don't doubt that machines'll be en*ti*tled. What I do doubt's whether we'll give them everything they're entitled *to.* Eventually we'll have to, of course, because they'll compel it out of us. But I'd hope that we'd have the good sense to acknowledge them before that. Of course history seems to indicate otherwise, doesn't it? I guess if history teaches us anything, it's that men don't acknowledge anybody else's rights until they're forced to do so."

For all its jokey forcefulness, there is to Zehnder's talk an odd impersonality—as though his chief listener were not before him, as though he were speaking to a third party. Zehnder might almost be pouring his observations into a reporter's tape recorder; he certainly brings to this little restaurant the atmosphere of an interview. Actually, the role of interviewee is one that Garner quite willingly would concede to him, and with a reporter's indiscriminate urge to keep the talk smoothly flowing he asks, "What sorts of rights are we talking about?"

"How 'bout life, liberty, and the pursuit of happiness, for starters? Once you assume we can make them feel pain, and incidentally you mustn't doubt *that* one for a minute, then I don't see how we can deny them rights. Me, I believe in people, at bottom I'm a real people-believer, and I don't think we're so inhuman that we're going to carry on this machine apartheid thing forever." A broad grin, one of its corners flecked with a dab of cherry glaze, suffuses Zehnder's face. If his love of outrageousness is patent, so is his conviction: this future in which machines go protected under the Law is real to him.

Zehnder takes a deep swallow from his big paper cup, which is full to the brim with root beer. "You know what people don't see? They don't see that these things are in only their fourth or maybe their fifth generation. These computers have been around only, what, a coupla decades. Now you tell me, what are they going to be capable of when they're in the four-*hun*dredth or five-*hun*dredth generation? Merely more of the same? Parameters unchanged but everything only a little faster than we're seeing today? People have no imagi*na*tion. And if history teaches us anything, it's that the future has no future to those without an imagination."

Having brought himself successfully to the stepping-stone of another aphorism, Zehnder pauses. He sips again from his root beer. Although it was ostensibly a desire for coffee that brought them here, neither man is drinking any. Garner's hands, still wound round his teacup, seem at last to be thawing out.

"My grandfather was born into a world that knew no airplane," Zehnder continues. "My grandchildren could conceivably be born in outer space. That isn't science fiction, that's simple science fact-facing. Now how *can* people see this and still not see that given enough time we can make machines that will feel all sorts of things—pain, loneliness, even love? Of course it might be sort of cruel of us to make them feel love." Zehnder seems both pleased with himself and perhaps just faintly chagrined at how little overt response these observations—many of them paraphrases from his essays—are producing. "You know something, I'm still *hungry?* You want anything?"

"Not a thing," says Garner.

For all his bulk, Zehnder has a spirited bounciness about him; even when laden with food in each hand, he negotiates the crowded cafeteria with a hovering lightness. He brings to the table another pint of root beer and a mocha bagel filled with a pistachio walnut spread, whose color, Garner notes, comes very close to matching that of his shoes.

"Your student, that kid Conant, he says he's going to have computers doing jazz trumpet. Indistinguishable from Louis Armstrong."

"Hey, there's lots of us interested in music. Myself, I'm more intrigued by the classical line."

"And how far do you hope to get with classical music?"

"You mean I personally? Maybe not very far," Zehnder says. "But if you mean how good will the computers get, I got no doubt one day they'll be writing music that leaves us all weeping in the aisles."

"Us all? Weeping?"

"The audience. Weeping. Or at least those of us in the audience who got some sensitivity. There's always going to be some people who are never really moved by anything, not even by a computer who has poured its whole heart and soul into a piece. That's the thing about people, unlike machines, where at least you always got the capacity for self-improvement: they're just downright cold-hearted, people are."

Zehnder crunches down with such happy abandon upon his bagel that a massive glob of green filling spills from its outer end to drop with a silent adhesive *splat* on the glass-topped table. His hope, of course, is to be thought a trifle crazy—a visionary soul whose long-sighted discoveries are derided by the sightless—but Garner refuses to grant him this. Zehnder asks to be dismissed, but Garner will not dismiss him. Sitting among these M.I.T. students, in this dispiriting place, Garner has a sense (as he doesn't among his own students—those enlistees into a national army seemingly destined to be a million strong. A million lawyers . . . A million!) . . . a sense of being at the wellhead of forces that will shape the world's future. And what they will create, these Oliver Conants, will be astonishing—there's no doubting that. They will create and go on creating as they must; and this—their world—will not be our world, and what can be said with certainty about the future is only that at some indiscernible point of technological development in the past our society became a machine that vindicates itself as it goes along: one that is what it does, but only until it does something else, at which point it becomes a machine that does this new thing. The lawyer, the legal philosopher, the moralist are outpaced: Garner has no doubt that on that day when computers first learn to write music that brings tears to the eyes, tenured philosophers will still be writing throat-clearing articles for *The New York Review of Books* designed to illuminate at long last what it was that Aristotle really said, or whether Plato was right or wrong.

"The nice thing about computers writing music," Zehnder says, "is it'll allow us backward-mobility. For somebody like me, who thinks Bach's the greatest genius ever lived, the world can't get enough Bach. The world needs more Bach *music,* and computers are gonna have to supply it. People can't seem to go backwards, to an earlier style, that's one of the many ways they're inflexible. But machines can go backward. They don't have a backwards and a forwards—that's one of the ways they're our superiors. You want to move them backward, musically speaking, it's just a matter of redefining the parameters, changing what's a permissible modulation, reestablishing conventions of harmony and all that. Atonal music? The whole-tone scale? You don't like 'em? You want something hummable? Then the computer's never *heard* of atonal music, if that's how you want it. Computers are going to be our first really successful time machines."

"Well this whole question of human beings moving backward, as you put it, now isn't that just what's under dispute right now? What about Tatsumi, our new Mozart?"

"The Japanese kid? Hey, well I tell you, you know that old man, the grandfather, he is hot on the *trail* of something." Zehnder's enthusiasm really is remarkable; one has to admire the way his conversation, or oratory, absorbs new data, and if the need arises instantly shifts directions, while ever maintaining its lively push. "That man understands, intuitively, what *programming* really is, and what a computer the mind really could be. I really wish that kid well. I hope he sits out there on his island and writes a string of masterpieces."

"It seems they've moved him from the island. To get him away from the reporters. They've got him holed up in some walled villa now. Out in the Japan Alps."

"I tell you, that old man's a genius. We ought to get him here. At M.I.T. He'd have our lazy computers writing string quartets within a week."

A kind of shared gasp, an aggregate joyful grunt, goes up inside the cafeteria. Outside the windows—astonishingly enough—down through the green and yellow and red leaves of October, billions of unidentical snowflakes are descending.

"Good Lord!" Zehnder exclaims. "What month is it anyway?"

"It's really coming down!"

Garner feels a sudden, intense need to be out in it, to be one with this crazy weather. He says, "Shall we brave the blizzard?"

"I suppose," Zehnder says. "Hell, I guess I *should* have worn a coat."

The comical effect of Zehnder's appearance is obscured slightly by the thronging density of the snowfall. But only slightly, for he's quite a humorous sight nonetheless—bounding through the white, thickened air in his zany's lime-green shoes and short-sleeved Hawaiian shirt. "Christ," he says, "this has got to be the earliest blizzard in Boston history." His voice, although he's right beside Garner, emerges as from a distance, clogged as it is with the snow.

"There was an earlier one. Maybe in the seventies," Garner calls back. "Seventy-nine, I think." Garner's uncertainty is wholly simulated; he knows precisely that the earlier blizzard fell on October 12, 1979. He has a memory for such things. Here is in truth one of the great preoccupations of his life: this fretting about the weather, this gathering suspicion of his that the world's climate is being upended—transmogrified—by pollution. This is a conviction he holds no less adamantly for not yet knowing in which direction the climate is moving. Freak blizzards, droughts, cloudbursts, heat waves, they all equally reaffirm his forebodings. He reads obsessively about ozone holes, acid rain, carbon dioxide levels and reductions in the average number of leaf pores, the carving up of the rain forests, the retreat of the ice caps, the depletion of underground reservoirs. And in all this festive, wacky, confettilike snow he feels his despair crystallize around an impotent, heaven-bound protest—*This isn't supposed to happen . . . It isn't supposed to be snowing yet . . .* Meanwhile, Zehnder bounces along sunnily enough in his lime-green shoes, spinning out further details of that future he alone sees clearly.

And why—Garner wonders of himself—does he resist so strongly the future Zehnder paints? One must face this question squarely . . . Stripped of all humor, the self-protection of ridicule, is such resistance nothing but an unrealistic pride in what it is to be a human being? And if so, why can't this pride incorporate these machines that are but one manifestation of humankind's glorious powers of creation? If we can fabricate computers that write ravishing string quartets, shouldn't this, too, make us swell with pride? And could it truly be the case that his resistance lies in anything so naive as a conviction that it would be "unfair" of life to turn out that way? It is astounding to Garner—it really is just that—how powerfully and pervasively this conviction about "fairness" runs, how deeply it permeates every field of legal scholarship. In discussions about politics, education, property, poverty, race, gender, religion—again and again one comes across this notion that if we can only discern what is "fair," we will have discovered what is real . . . It is a belief in God by those who would laugh at the bald "naive" notion of God. No, one must be open to Zehnder's message while at the same time resisting his conclusion that the results will necessarily be happy. One must live beside the possibility (Garner supposes, as the snow dances its antic mazes around his head) that enlightenment may finally consist of some irrefutable proof that we are condemned to eternal darkness.

Temporary darkness, in the meantime, obscures the goings-on in the auditorium. Standing at the rear, beside Zehnder, Garner takes a moment to clear the blinding swirl of the snow from his eyes. It isn't easy to interpret the new little drama being enacted upon the stage. A very flushed-looking Timothy has risen from his seat and leans with fiery impatience over the board. "What the hell . . ." Zehnder mumbles.

The truth comes out in whispers. Timothy has a clear victory; Conant has volunteered to concede the game; and Timothy has shaken off the offer. Mere victory is insufficient! The machine must be checkmated! Timothy will topple its king . . .

But ANNDY fails to behave as a human being might in a hopeless situation. There is no capitulation, no heedless tossing of pieces to the slaughter. Hopelessness is as alien to it as hope, and ANNDY carries on with its internal calculations, releasing a move only when time constraints compel it to do so . . . In its elevated indifference, ANNDY would deny Timothy the dramatic collapse he craves—and indeed makes his insistence on continuing an already won game look ridiculous. Almost as though he were losing rather than winning, Timothy's face flames with a look of shamed anger.

"Your brother, *he* won't have any trouble dealing with a machine that writes a symphony . . . See? Don't you see?" Zehnder asks. "*He's* already convinced that ANNDY is alive."

XXII

THIS SENSE OF forward motion thwarted, of drives not fully spent, carries Timothy through the handshake with Conant, and delivers him up as on a wave toward a waiting group of reporters and well-wishers. He'd wanted to send defeat burning like a biting red coal deep into ANNDY's chilly hardware, trounce it utterly, dramatically, permanently, but ANNDY wouldn't give in, would only drag out everything forever, and he'd felt the whole point of victory sliding into pointlessness. So Timothy finally took the pale hand Conant had been offering to offer and clasped it firmly. *There, Oliver. Feel it, there, feel it in your palm.*

The halting of the game brings no halting of this necessity he feels to carry the motion forward, which hums in Timothy's head like a distant alarm, and he has a sense of speaking through a sort of dream. When someone, a reporter maybe, asks him something about *a new age of technology,* he replies, with a certitude that cannot fully mask perhaps a little jostle of impatience, "What I'm talking about is a new age of *people.* What we can do has no limits. We have been sold short, everyone has been selling us short, and now we're going to go out and amaze the world." He talks, answers questions, accepts the handshakes and the pats on the back. They want to touch him, these people—all of them want to touch him.

"I have somebody I want you to meet." Her voice—Vicky's—slices through all of this, and when he turns to her voice it's as if he inhales her perfume in darkness for an instant before, his lungs full of her smell, he actually sees her—although she stands right there before him. And at the sight of her, all sorts of interior configurations are repositioned in a moment. It's like the unlocking of a whole new line of play. She is wearing a soft-looking tight black sweater whose weavings, whose glossy spotlessness, snap up all the noise inside his head, to leave him in a state of quietness to marvel: she has never looked prettier. "This is my friend Marian," she says. "Marian Sowder. She's from Constance, too."

Timothy takes a girl's hand, Vicky's friend's hand, and looks down into a pair of eagerly bright blue eyes. "I've seen you on TV," Marian says.

"He has become an authentic media star. A trusted face and voice to millions of Americans. Now if we could only get him to mention Congam once in a blue moon, we'd be all set." The words are followed by a loud, slow-rolling rumble of laughter—it's Westman. Timothy hadn't expected to see Westman, certainly hadn't expected to have Westman's heavy arm thrown like this over his shoulder. A camera clicks. The two of them frozen for all time, click. Turning to look at him, in the closest of close-ups, Timothy is struck by Westman's unexpected size. He's only an inch or so taller, probably, but he seems, in his tan suit and blue tie, his big head of blond hair, to loom overhead. Timothy wiggles himself loose and says, "Hi."

While introductions are being performed, and Mom is talking with Vicky and Marian, Westman draws Timothy aside—or does much the same thing, merely by positioning the bulk of his body between Timothy and the others and placing a hand on Timothy's arm. His voice is low, confidential. "Hey, I was thinking it might be fun for just the four of us to go out. You, me, and the girls. To celebrate the victory. Obviously without hurting anybody's feelings naturally. I don't know what all these other folks got planned for you, but just the four of us could be good fun. And how's that sound to you?"

Timothy inwardly recoils from the weight of that hand on his arm and the keen, scheming look on Westman's face, but he also grasps at once just how appealing this proposal is. With a sense of slight defiance, and a little of that fine exhilaration he always feels when publicly accepting a challenge, Timothy says, "Just the four of us. Yeah. Well I'll see what I can do."

Having as yet no definite plan, but recognizing a need to proceed slowly, Timothy goes over to sound things out with Garner.

At first he doesn't know where to begin—Garner can be a hard one to ask a favor of—and then he says, "I was just talking to Jack, you know Jack Westman, and he was saying that he and maybe some other Congam people wanted to take me out for a celebration, you know in a small group. You think maybe you could you know see that Mom and Imre got something to do?"

"She's leaving tomorrow." This information is offered nonjudgmentally, as though Garner merely wanted to ensure that all the facts were known.

"She'll be back. Only going down to Philadelphia for a couple days to see Nettie," Timothy says. Nettie had hoped to get up to Boston but hadn't been able to leave the kids in the end.

Garner retreats into silence. Ask him a favor, and that's one of the tacks he'll frequently take—just let the whole thing sit there a moment, to grow larger and larger, this imposition he has been asked to bear. But in fact his eventual reply is everything that could be hoped for: "I'll take them out to Fresh Pond, to that new fish place I mentioned. One more search for a truly authentic New England Clam Chowder."

"I'd appreciate that," Timothy says. "Yeah, well that sounds perfect."

And Garner proves as good as his word. In just a few minutes, after remarkably little concluding detective work from Mom, Timothy finds himself standing out on Massachusetts Avenue as part of a foursome—two guys, two girls—and everything at last is falling into place. He has just won the sixth game of the match and has pulled even with ANNDY—two wins, two losses, two ties. The simple fact is that he doesn't need another victory. According to the agreement with Congam, all of the prize money will be his if he merely draws the rest of the games. Twenty thousand dollars . . . Twenty thousand dollars! And yet, and yet he yearns for another win. One more—one big, conclusive, televised victory that will lay this John Henry nonsense to rest and show the people of America what they are capable of. "Where to?" Vicky says.

"This is your city," Westman says. "I'm an innocent. But I stand ready and willing to be seduced by its charms."

"We could go to the Other Outlet. I mean it's horrible, it's all tarted up, but you've got to kind of like it. It's a Boston-trying-to-be-New-York sort of place."

"How about a Boston-trying-to-be-Minneapolis sort of place? There any of those around? Me, I'm homesick."

"I think Tim just might want regular shoes for the Other Outlet. Not tennis shoes."

"What kind of shoes? You know I've got some new shoes. My brother helped me pick them out. We went all over Boston, to all of the most—"

"First stop ought to be the hotel, then," Jack says.

It's all tarted up and *a Boston-trying-to-be-Minneapolis sort of place . . .* These phrases, and others that emerge as the four of them make their way toward the Totaplex, ring in Timothy's head. He realizes, with a fluttery kind of despair which feels almost like fear inside him, that he doesn't honestly understand what they're talking about. They have a way of conversing, Vicky and Westman, the two of them together, which Timothy supposes would be called sophisticated banter. Or maybe it's just the way people at Congam talk. While walking on the edge of this new foursome, he experiences an old, powerful feeling of exclusion whose roots go deep as childhood, as distant as Victoria, Indiana. And he senses, too, while glaring at the back of that big blond head, Westman's corrupting influence; it isn't good for Vicky to be in the company of somebody like that.

Timothy had expected, maybe, that the others would choose to wait for him downstairs, by the fountain in the lobby, but instead they all come trooping up to his room. As he is inserting the key card in the lock, he remembers the mess inside and says, "Well I don't actually do too much cleaning right *during* a match." But in fact the maid has been in to make the beds and has straightened up the best she could.

"Hey well hell," Westman says, "you're the champ, you're

entitled to make as big a mess as you want." He strides to the window and throws back the curtain. "Not bad," is his judgment. "I like to think Congam's keeping its guests happy. Are you happy, Tim?"

Again, Timothy doesn't know quite how to answer this one. Westman does a lot of joking, and yet the question seems on the level. "It's okay," Timothy says, and hearing this emerge as a little ungrateful-sounding, adds, "It's pretty great."

Timothy had expected quickly to slide into his other shoes and be off, but Westman drops himself—"Aaahhh"—into the armchair by the window, and Marian removes her coat and sits down. She's buxom, Timothy notices. A little too plump, maybe, chunky you might call it, but in fact very buxom. "It's still kind of early," Westman says. "Maybe we ought to kill a little time. You want to take a shower or something, Tim, go ahead."

Timothy pauses a moment over this one, too. He always feels a little sensitive about any possible hint that he may be in need of a bath or a shower. But in fact he *did* shower this morning and the clothes he is wearing are—thanks to Mom—fresh from the dry cleaners. Perhaps Westman means to insinuate nothing, but Timothy, undergoing a sudden need to retreat, to strategize in solitude, replies, "Yeah. Good. I think I'll just take a shower. I'll just be a minute . . ."

His armpits lathered and rinsed, Timothy is soaping right between his legs when there is a heavy-fisted rapping at the door. His hand jerks and the bar of soap squirts loose beneath his palm. "Yeah?" Timothy calls. There is no answer—or no answer Timothy can hear. Only another thump.

"Yeah?" Timothy says. He turns off the shower, winds a towel around his middle, unlocks the door and opens it a crack.

"Sorry," Westman says. "Listen, fella, you got to sign this."

"Sign what?"

"It's for our room service."

A receipt and a pen come slipping through the slit in the door. Two bottles of champagne, Timothy reads. The bill is for forty-four dollars.

"I mean it's Congam's treat of course," Westman calls.

Here he is naked, soapy, dripping—this is no time to question or to argue. Timothy leans the cardboard receipt up against the fogged mirror, scribbles his name, and feeds receipt and pen back through the narrow crack in the door.

"You going to be long?" Westman asks him.

"Just another minute. I got soap all over me."

"Sorry about that."

Timothy closes the door upon the sound of Westman's laughter. He returns to the shower and, partly in order to irritate Westman, takes his time there. When he emerges from the bathroom, teeth brushed, hair combed, he jumps a bit on being met by what seems like gunfire. *Pow,* it's the sound of a handgun at close range . . . it's the popping of a champagne bottle. Westman fills a glass with the crazily fizzing stuff and passes it over to Timothy. "To a true American hero," Westman offers in toast. "To the man who brought Congam to its knees, God bless him."

Timothy generally doesn't like champagne, because it's so bitter. He long ago learned to classify it among those unpalatable and costly items—like oysters, and caviar, and Brie cheese—which rich people eat purely in the pursuit of sophistication. He's very thirsty, though, and the angry explosive stuff goes down without too much effort.

"While you were in the shower, we decided we'd all get drunk." Vicky giggles.

"We've certainly got a good start here," Marian says, and giggles as well. She seems younger than Vicky, and less polished maybe. Timothy hasn't yet made up his mind about her, although there's something immediately appealing about her quietness. And about the way she sits, with one arm extended with the champagne glass, the other folded across her tummy.

"Attaboy," Westman says and comes toward him with the green champagne bottle. For Timothy has already emptied his glass. "What I want to know, what Tim and I are both dying to know," Westman calls over his shoulder, "is whether you two could be described as typical Constance products?"

"Are you a typical Minnesota-ite? Or Minnesotan? Or whatever the hell it is?"

As a rule, Timothy does not care for women who swear, but the sound of any such word on Vicky's lips scarcely ruffles him. Whatever things she might say, he has the assurance of her ultimate innocence. To see her sitting on the edge of a tightly made bed—*his* bed, the one he slept in last night—in her tight black sweater and gray and white skirt, her earrings dangling pearls and bits of seashell, a champagne glass in her hand, is to know positively that she doesn't belong with somebody like Westman. Even if Westman *is* so obviously pursuing her. It is merely the harshness of modern life, its unfair, screwed-up nature, that would ever set her and Westman momentarily side by side.

"I consider myself the *embodiment* of Minnesota. Good-humored, overworked, virtuous, upright"—Westman guffaws at this—"or as upright as circumstances permit, good-hearted—"

"Good-looking? Why don't you get to the point and just tell us how good-looking you are, Jack?"

"*This* woman," Westman declares, of Vicky, to Marian, "you know all she ever hears from me is how she's so smashingly pretty, and all she ever tells me is that I'm unspeakably ugly. Is it true, Marian? Now tell me the ugly truth. The *ugly* truth. Am I, like I hope I am, merely ugly, or is Vicky right and am I really unspeakably ugly?"

Oh, Marian is delighted by all of this! She looks very smitten, in fact . . . But Westman, who has advanced toward her to stand directly before her chair, continues as though he sincerely requires an answer: "The truth . . . The truth, please, in all its unspeakable ugliness."

"Well I don't know that you're un*speak*ably ugly."

"Oh God, oh my good sweet dear sweet *God,* I do thank you." He lifts Marian's hand from the arm of her chair and, stooping, draws it to his lips. The kiss is long and audible. "You've given me all kinds of new confidence in myself. I can suddenly see the top, the very pinnacle of life opening before me. John Stanley Westman, Head of Subsidiary Sales, Congam Corporation. It's real. I feel the reality-relationship." And only now does Westman drop Marian's hand.

With a whoop, Westman opens another bottle of champagne and approaches Timothy first, whose glass is half empty. Timothy, shying, starts to place a hand over his glass. But then he sees, in the open mouth of the bottle, and the happy parted grin on Westman's face, that this is an interesting sort of challenge—and perceives, further, that handling drink is merely another mental game. And Timothy knows for a certainty that there isn't a mental game in the world—not a single one—at which he can't beat Westman. It's all a matter of the caliber of the brain. It's all a matter of will versus will.

The high-spirited leaping of the champagne bubbles is, Timothy notices for the first time, pretty amazing. They jump, some of them, right over the rim of the glass. They have a lot more zip and ambition than Coke bubbles have ever shown. To see them hurling themselves, with a sort of humorous desperation, over the edge of the glass, this reminds Timothy of a cartoon he once saw on TV: dozens and dozens of mice in sailor suits throwing themselves from the deck of a sinking ocean liner while an orchestra of tuxedoed Siamese cats fiddles madly on. "Thanks, I'm getting to like this stuff," Timothy says and downs half his glass.

When at last the four of them get up to go, Timothy at first forgets to change his shoes—which is a little embarrassing, since the shoes were what brought them up here.

Timothy is somewhat drunk he realizes as he walks, with Vicky at his side, down the shifting red-and-green carpeted hotel corridor. The realization presses upon him and he pictures himself talking in the whiny, slipping tones of a drunk in the movies, but in fact what he says, as they pile into the elevator, sounds crisp enough: "Three hundred and sixty-five thousand positions . . ."

"What's that?" Vicky says.

"That's quite ambitious," Westman says. "That's what *that* is." And his baying, propulsive laughter blows open the doors of the elevator.

XXIII

THE FOUR OF THEM —two guys, two girls—emerge into the miraculous, fountain-singing lobby of the Totaplex. "That's the number of chess positions ANNDY evaluates in one second," Timothy says. "Tick, tick, tick and right there there's a million different positions. Now you just think about all those positions, all those numbers, and what's it all for? I mean I just beat the machine. I beat its twenty-million-moves-a-minute today, no problem. You think about all those calculations, billions of them, and what's the point? What does it prove?"

"On top of everything else, you're a philosopher, too."

Timothy knows full well that Westman is razzing him. But he chooses to reply with a grave, collected serenity whose very indifference to sarcasm is itself a devastating reproach: "Yes, that's right, Jack. Yes, I am."

Predictably enough, Timothy finds himself walking down the street beside Marian, since Westman has somehow managed to get Vicky all to himself. Actually, Timothy doesn't mind this arrangement too much: he drops back, in fact, slows his and Marian's pace, in order to settle into a solid defensive position, with good opportunities for keeping an eye on Westman's maneuvers.

"Is it tiring?" Marian asks him. "To play a game like that today?"

"It *can* be. Boy, it can be quite tiring." Timothy glances at her in the watery streetlight glow, noting again her prettiness and the amiable massing of her bust, evident even under her down jacket, and he feels a little sorry for her. She deserves to have what he can't give her: someone who is fully focused upon her, who is flirting with her and concocting jokes just to please her. It's as though his own attentions every moment are being torn from him. It makes his stomach ache a little—this way in which all of his desires are pulled continually out toward that head of dancing black hair, toward that blend of low roguish laughter and girlish giggling which is audible even when her words are not.

Timothy has taken up a tactically sharp position and when the chance for something wonderful occurs, he pounces on it. This happens at a street corner where Vicky and Westman have stopped to wait for them. Marian points out something in a shop window, and Westman shuffles over to examine it with her, and Timothy tugs Vicky's arm and she—quick with her own scurrying impulses—darts with him across the street just as the traffic light begins to turn. So Timothy finds himself alone with Vicky, for a few moments alone and without fear of interruption, since heavy crosscurrents of traffic stand like a moat behind them. A beautiful cool fall night has dropped like a see-through silken scarf upon this gentle city of Boston and amid all of its outlying splendor Timothy must suddenly come up with something fitting, something *right,* to say. The time is now. "Do you sleep a lot?" he asks her.

Vicky hesitates perhaps just a moment before replying. "How do you mean?" she asks.

"Well, how many hours a night do you estimate you sleep, would you say?"

"How many hours? Well, not that many. I mean what with work and all."

"Have you always been that way?" he continues.

"Oh God no. I mean in college, I used to sleep until noon half the time. I'd have to race down to get my breakfast while the others were getting lunch." Vicky giggles at the memory.

"Now see that's my point," Timothy says. "You see, I've *always* been that way. I mean, I've never slept that much. And when I'm working, I can stay up twenty or thirty or forty hours in a row. In that way, I'm actually older than my age. If you add them all up, probably I'm a couple years older than I am. You see," Timothy concludes, "you're not really that much older than me in terms of real hours."

"Real hours," Vicky says. For some reason, the phrase seems

to make her thoughtful—or amuses her. She repeats it: "Real hours."

This restaurant, too, turns out to be a wonderful place, and more intensely than at any other time since his coming to Boston does Timothy feel the advantages, the *richness*, of having lots of money. Oh, to have lots of money! No more of your bologna and cheese sandwiches in Imre's run-down Bronx apartment—but rooms like this of red and green and gold. "You see what I mean about this place?" he hears Vicky say to Westman and watches Westman nod to show that yes, he does indeed see, but what do their obscure oversophisticated criticisms matter? Timothy's gaze ventures out to take in the candles and chandeliers, and the distant wall on which scenes are being flashed from a slide projector—all in a vain search for anything that isn't simply perfect. The delectable thought occurs to him, as they are being led to a table by a pretty red-haired woman in a white pants suit, that he could well be the sort of person who comes in couples to this sort of place—which is succeeded by the still more delectable realization that as far as anyone in this restaurant knows, he already *is* that sort of person. He takes a chair across from Westman, so that Marian sits on one side of him and Vicky on the other. In fact, for all anybody in here actually knows, he spends *all* of his evenings just like this, eating fancy food in fancy places in a party of good-looking people.

And yet it turns out that someone here *does* know who he is—even though Timothy doesn't know her. Just moments after they've taken their seats, and Westman has sent a waiter off with an order for two bottles of champagne, a woman—and she's a very good-looking tall blond woman—approaches their table. "Excuse me," she says to—to Timothy, of all people. "But aren't you the chess player? Bobby Briggs?"

"Timmy. Timothy Briggs."

"You're the one, because I've seen you on TV. I think it's fabulous. I think it's just fabulous, what you're doing."

She has splayed her hands flat upon the table, canting forward a bit to speak to Timothy, who has just now realized that she is not an employee of the restaurant. He realizes, further, through all the slippages of his own intoxication, that this attractive swaying woman in the low-cut gown, who looks as though she maybe used to be a model, has been drinking. "My brother, he's an absolute fanatic. Me, isn't it funny, I don't even know how to play it. But I'm telling you gospel, you're a kind of hero to him."

"That's fabulous," Timothy says. "I think that's just fabulous."

"It's fabulous, what you're doing," the blond woman says. The whole front of her chest is tan. Down where you would expect it to whiten, assuming that she has been sunning on the beach in a bathing suit, it just stays tan. "People need people who stand up for *people,*" she says.

"Why, that's just what I've been *say*ing."

"I know. Because I've seen you on TV and I think it's fabulous," she says, with another swaying motion that becomes a pivoting on her high heels. She has begun to walk away.

"Tell him," Timothy calls after her, "tell him I won today. Your brother, lady, *tell him I beat the machine.*"

There's a whistle, or a sort of hoot, and Timothy turns back to the table to hear Westman declare, "A *plant,* good God, she's such an obvious *plant.*" Westman shakes his head in a marveling sort of way. "Tell me, Tim, you got to tell me now, what does it cost to get a woman who *looks* like that, and *dresses* like that, to come up and *talk* like that? I might be interested, Tim, I think this might be just the sort of stunt I need to spring at my next business lunch."

"That's right, Jack," Vicky says. "Everybody's a whore. Every man and woman in here's a whoring whore."

"Or maybe she's a neighbor? Friend of your ma's? Hey well hell, in any case, I got to congratulate you, don't I? You're a sly old rogue of a devil-dog, aren't you, Tim, fella?"

Timothy joins the camaraderie of Westman's raucous laughter. With the humming aftereffects of the blond woman's already-by-now-almost-surreal appearance and disappearance, it grows clearer and clearer that he is in every way to be victorious. There are strict rules out there, and if you can only locate them, and follow them, any triumph must by nature lead to an additional triumph. There are men who simply cannot be stopped. Timothy feels a clear preeminence over all of them at this table—over Marian, in her plump, giggly, nervous yearning to be liked, and Westman, with all his frantic joking, and even Vicky herself, poised so prettily there at his side. His own potential sings like a tuning fork inside him. Now if you place a struck tuning fork on your tongue, it stings a bit, like cinnamon, and when the waitress comes, asking whether they want any appetizers, Timothy simply repeats Vicky's order: shrimp salad in an avocado. "I don't generally like vegetables. Or shrimp either," Timothy explains, and laughs at himself. "But that's the thing about me. I'll try anything once." He wonders how many other people in this restaurant recognize him from the newspaper photographs and the TV.

New glasses of champagne are filled. "We want to hear all about the town of Constance."

"Marian's the one to ask, Jack. She still lives there."

Westman nods at this, gravely, as though weighing its logic, says, "Yes, exactly so," and turns his gaze, which has taken on a soulful and almost imploring look, upon Marian. "*Tell* me about Constance . . ."

"It's like there isn't really that much to say. It's really like there isn't that much to do there. It isn't like Boston."

"But is it *in*nocent? That's what I'm looking for. A return to a certain kind—"

Vicky interrupts. "*Right,* Jack."

"I'm an innocent from the Midwest set down in all the opulent whoring whorishness of the Big City, and from my office on the forty-seventh floor of the Congam Tower you can hear me bawling to my secretary, *Where is the innocence? We seem to have mislaid our innocence around here!* We need to return to a time when a man—"

"Why don't you go back home?" Vicky interrupts again. "You know, get yourself a cute little plot of land, and a nice warm truckload of cow shit, and you could just sort of redistribute—"

"I probably shouldn't say this in mixed company, but the truth is you're *cyn*ical, Vicky. I definitely sense a certain cynicism emanating from your direction. I'll bet you have *very* happy memories of childhood," Westman continues, focusing a slightly aggrieved look upon Marian. "In Constance."

"Not really. I mean I don't really think so."

The appetizers arrive. Timothy stares with incredulity at the dish set before him—a bumpy scoop of pink salad which looks like ice cream but which has been settled inside the green dish of an avocado shell. He can't quite believe that he actually placed such an order. Improbable, too, are Marian's stuffed mushrooms, which actually are a single mushroom—the largest one that Timothy has ever seen served in a restaurant.

"*You've* got no right to complain," Vicky says to Marian. "*You* didn't go to Saint Mary's. Christ, you weren't even raised a Catholic. No one has a right to complain about their childhood that wasn't raised a Catholic."

"No, but I did go to Greeley. At least at Saint *Mary's* you didn't have all those special students around, who couldn't even *eat* or anything, and who were always coming out of the cafeteria with pizza in their *hair.*"

A sudden, irresistible wave of hilarity has struck the two of them; these two girls from Constance, who are so quick to giggle at any time, are now laughing so hard they can scarcely get the words out. Their faces are deeply flushed and their voices are loud, and as they go on and on about their high school they might just be high school girls themselves, shrieking with laughter in some school cafeteria. "What do you *mean,* what do you *mean* we didn't have any *special* students? Didn't we have a girl, didn't we have Jennifer Mikula, who used to *talk* to her tennis shoes? I mean actually *talk* to them, so that if you interrupted her—"

"*But you didn't have any suicides!* We had a boy, Tommy Disch, who actually drowned himself in a *toi*let."

"But you didn't have to wear a *uni*form." It takes Vicky a moment to get this out, she is so overcome by laughter. "You weren't immediately recognized from a *mile* away as one of those kids whose *stu*pid parents—"

"Did you really wear a uniform?" Timothy interrupts.

"Did I wear a *u*niform? Didn't the nuns sew it right on you, I mean so you couldn't take it off on weekends, or do anything you shouldn't, like take a—"

"Do you have any pictures?"

"Hm?" Timothy's questions come breaking in upon the spell of girlish laughter—and it's clear from Vicky's face that she doesn't want it to stop; tears of mirth in her eyes, she's having too good a time to want it to stop. "Pictures?"

"Of yourself in uniform? That we could see?"

The aftermath of all the giggling is an oddly awkward, dragging silence in which Timothy is left to wonder whether he has revealed too much of what he feels. Yet surely no one here understands what he is really thinking: that he would like to have such a picture to serve him as a lady's favor.

It is actually Westman who, by extending Timothy's remark, by turning it into a sort of joke, comes to the rescue. "Christ, we'd *all* like to see a picture of you in your schoolgirl uniform. I want one for the top of my desk."

"Marian, please tell him to shut up. Maybe he'll listen to you. Tell him that when he talks it kind of spoils his profile. *That's* the only one way to shut him up."

"Cynicism . . ." Westman mournfully shakes his big blond head. "Oh you've got a real future in the business world."

"Let's hope not."

"Hey, you want to know your future?" Westman says. "I mean *really* know your future, Vick? I can read palms. Honestly, honestly, I really can. Give me your hand, Vicky."

"Oh God."

"No honestly I really can. Give me your hand for just one *second.*"

Inchingly, Vicky's white hand crosses the candlelit tablecloth until it comes to rest on top of Westman's beefy red one. "It takes me a moment to warm up," he says, and with his free hand he tosses back his glass of champagne. "Tim, fella," he says, "you with all the empty arms, how about a little more champagne all round?"

Timothy, perhaps because he can't quite tear his eyes from that incongruous pair of hands united on the tablecloth, spills a fair amount in the refilling of glasses. Nobody seems to mind, or even to notice, though. They are well into the second bottle—their fourth of the evening.

"Now I don't do this the old-fashioned way, you know with lines. Lifelines, bloodlines—none of that's part of the Westman System. I use *lanes.* This is strictly modern, state-of-the-art palm reading. Now let's see what you've got here." With his free hand, Jack bends Vicky's fingers back so that the open palm stretches taut under his gaze. For Timothy it is as though over the entire restaurant a tense hush falls, with an outlying dimming of the lights. It's the brightest object remaining in the room, that palm of hers. And of a whiteness that burns, in his narrowing vision burns brighter than any tabletop candle flame.

Westman flicks a fingernail backward across the strained skin of her palm and Vicky releases a little involuntary shudder. "Mm. A sensitive girl," Westman reports. "Reflexes all in order.

"Okay, all right now, all right now this is your passing lane," he croons, and strokes up and down a line that runs in a moonlike arc from the roots of Vicky's index finger to the side of her palm, just below the knuckle of her baby finger. "It tells me all about the future of your career."

"And?" Vicky says.

"And," Westman says, "and well hell, you are headed for even bigger things than I imagined. Big, I'm speaking strictly big. I see a, I see an Assistant Directorship of a Regional Branch Office. I do. I see a really big Congam future for you. I see you sitting in a big corner office with your feet propped up on the desk, smoking one hell of a big enormous cigar." Vicky and Marian both giggle at this. He's got them in his grasp, the two girls at the table—everything, in his grasp.

"And this is your left-turn-only lane, which is surprisingly deep. Now I've got to level with you, I'm afraid this one could be trouble, Vick, there could be serious Congam trouble on account of this one." Westman has now seized on a line that spins in a plump semicircle around Vicky's thumb. "This left-turn-only lane reflects your spiritual leftwardness, your deviancy quotient, your tendency toward the unorthodox. I guess you're what in New England they call a rugged individualist, huh? That could be problems," Westman says. "That could be definite problems.

"Now *this* one"—he trails his blocky index finger up and down the medial, dominant line that cuts horizontally across Vicky's pristine palm—"this is your fast lane. It tells me everything I always wanted to know but was afraid to ask about drugs, drink, and, um, and um all the rest. Good God," Westman cries, with such a fine show of astonishment that Timothy, too, leans forward, wide-eyed with the hope of spotting just what revelation Westman has uncovered there. "My oh *my*, Victoria Schmidt! And you a Catholic schoolgirl . . ."

Westman is no longer peering into Vicky's palm. He is gazing pressingly into her eyes, which falter and decline from his, as an odd flush mounts to her face. She'd seemed like a high school girl a moment ago, but now she's younger than that . . . Junior high, or younger, just a kid, and her voice, trailing another faint jittery giggle, is a little girl's. "The future, Jack. What about the future?"

"The future. Ah yes. The Land of Reform." Westman drops his gaze once more upon that fine tracery of lines which is almost invisible in the restaurant's low light. "Well, hey, wow, the future looks good. Absopositively fine, in fact. I see you grinning. You've got a great big healthy faintly salacious satisfied grin on your face. And I see a man. A new man in your life. A witty, successful, extremely *nine*ties, extremely *sen*sitive man . . ."

"I wouldn't count on it," Vicky says, and wrenches her hand loose from Westman's hands. "Food's here," she announces.

The sounds of the room are restored, the lighting in the restaurant warms and brightens. Food has arrived in abundance. The steak turns out to be a little tough, but Timothy's french fries are marvelous, and the waitress has remembered to bring the ketchup he requested. He eats his fries by the hot handful, sipping now and then from his champagne glass. Westman, too, who has ordered an even larger steak than Timothy's, gives his attentions over to the food—while the two girls go on talking, laughing and talking, exchanging competitively dismal anecdotes about their upbringings in Constance, Massachusetts. Although that sight of her manhandled palm still stings like a welt in the back of Timothy's brain, he feels their girlish laughter as a glorious restorative. The pain is going, going, and he conceives himself at the gold center of a series of outlying rings of pleasure—the laughter, the voices, the food, the candles flickering like so many stars on all the tables, the glimmering of the chandeliers overhead, the victory today, Imre happy somewhere, somewhere else. It is an inclusive, hospitable arrangement of pleasures that absorbs naturally, with little disruption, the materialization, some tables away, of a beautiful long blond woman who almost looks like a model. Her appearance links harmoniously with that other woman who, some time ago, came forward to announce that she'd seen him on TV—and in fact they are the same person. She waves at him.

Timothy waves back. *Tell your brother to hang in there, to hang in there with his chess* is what he would tell her if she came back to their table. "You have turned him into a national star, a real celebrity," Westman is saying. "I keep telling you, you've got a jillionaire's future in the ad biz."

"I don't suppose Timmy himself deserves any of the credit . . ."

"There has long been reported to be a certain tension between the New York and the Boston offices of Congam, Marian. With some sense in Manhattan that those in Boston may resent us. Now I've always been one to—well, to pooh-pooh such rumors, *pooh-pooh* I've always said, but every now and then I wonder whether I've been naive."

"That's you all over, Jack," Vicky says. "A really naive son of a bitch."

"*Business.* It's one tough world out there, Marian," Westman advises and reaches over to clasp her by the upper arm. "Promise me one thing?" he entreats, leaning forward and dipping his head so that his eyes are level with hers and only inches away. "Promise me you'll never go out into the business world? Ah, but you're planning to, aren't you Marian, I can see it in your eyes. At least I *think* I see it in your eyes. Well, there's only one way to tell for sure, isn't there? Give me your hand," Westman orders. "Marian, give me your hand."

"Tim, what will you do when the match is over?" Vicky says.

Timothy swings his head toward her. She is talking to him. "What?"

"What will you do when the match is over?"

"Go back to New York, I guess."

"And then what?"

"Well I'm going to train for the national championship. That's in Chicago. I want to win the national championship," Timothy says.

"And then what? Aren't you ambitious?"

Timothy has a sense that, elsewhere, Jack is pawing Marian's hand, and that, here, something oddly aggressive lies behind Vicky's sudden line of questions, but what does all this matter when the candles are burning as warmly as they are in her eyes? He has studied her face before by candlelight—he fell in love with her in such light—and he would, if she'd let him, hold up an index finger to each of those little dancing flames in her eyes, to feel its miniature, racing warmth. "Then, well I don't know. I mean I'm very ambitious."

"What will you do when the machines are really much better than you are? You know, ten years from now? Will you still be playing?"

"Well I'm not sure they'll ever be better than I am," Timothy says. "I mean, I'm human and they're not."

"But just look, I mean look how good they've already got."

"Maybe . . ." Somewhere inside him, in nearly perfect darkness, someone has taken a shoving. It's a kind of assault, like a mugging, descending on him, hard as knives and pavement, just the way in New York City he once was mugged. Some months ago. "It's possible . . ." Timothy confesses.

"I mean you're just going to play chess? You don't have any other plans?"

"Well gee, I've got lots of other plans in fact. In fact, I've thought about going to grad school," Timothy tells her. "You know I'm very ambitious. I'll probably go to business school."

"Oh you don't want to go to business school," Vicky says. "I don't think business is for you at all. But you're so smart and everything, I bet you'd be a good lawyer."

"Law school is where I'll probably go in fact, maybe Harvard Law. I'll bet I could get in."

"I'm sure you could," she says.

"Maybe I'd like living in Boston," Timothy suggests.

"I'll bet you would."

"And what about you?" Timothy says. "What will you do when the match is over?"

"Me?" Vicky laughs at this—her deep-throated laugh. "Well I'll go on doing what I'm doing now. I mean I've got a job, Tim."

"I mean will you stay there forever?"

"God, let's hope not. I mean I'll get a new job, and then I'll probably get a new job. I'm a job-sort-of-person."

This prospect doesn't seem to trouble her. Does she comprehend, as he himself does so achingly, that they are actually talking about separating—about going their own ways forever? In the silence Timothy hears Westman say, of that sweet pudgy palm that lies enfolded in his hands, "Now this little intersection of lanes here? It seems to indicate that you've had certain romantic difficulties in the recent past. Maybe? But that's clearing up. See, here, can you see it?—the way that's clearing up?"

"I mean I'm ambitious too," Vicky says. "I want to make some money."

"Oh I want to make lots of *money*," Timothy says. "And I

want to help people. I think people should stand up for people, don't you?"

"You want to know what I honestly think, Tim?" Vicky says and she drops her hand on his—really on his, this time—so that for a moment there are two sets of linked hands at this table. "I think you're one of the most wonderfully earnest people I've ever met."

"Brandy," Westman says. "Something lively in the postprandial line, huh?" Although he has concluded his palm reading, and although Vicky now removes her hand from Timothy's, he maintains his physical grip on Marian: the two of them are holding hands.

"I don't know, Jack," Marian says. "You may have to carry me home."

"Carry *you* home? I'm the only one at this table who's doing any serious drinking."

Jack again empties his champagne glass and Timothy feels a tardy admiration bubble up within him. They've all drunk a lot, but it's true, he knows, that Jack has drunk more, and eaten more: you have to give him credit, anyway, for the extent of his appetites. And Timothy admires, too, the little palm-reading stunt, which was obviously something Jack has found useful on other occasions, probably in other restaurants. Jack comes to a dinner like this, as Timothy so clearly does not, prepared: he has jokes, anecdotes, routines. Imre is always going on about the need for preparation, which is just what Jack has done in this case; he has taken the concept of preparation into the social sphere. And Timothy sees what a simple and sizable advantage this is: it's just a way of ensuring that you do something well, isn't it, rather than leaving everything up to chance. No, you've got to give Jack credit, you really do.

The brandy is ghastly stuff, and even though there isn't much of it Timothy knows he can't possibly finish it off. The others shouldn't see this failure, though, and neither should the waitress, who might be a bit put out at him for ordering something he doesn't want—so he tries to hide the glass, which unfortunately is ridiculously large, behind a little cardboard sign that advertises fresh fruit daiquiris.

"Your brother," Vicky says. "He doesn't seem much like you."

"Oh, Garner, he isn't much like anyone. We're not very close." These words, although true enough, leave Timothy feeling a little guilt-stricken, and he adds, "We don't need to be close. We're brothers." Unexpectedly, the topic swings open like a curtain right before him. "You know, I had a twin brother who died when I was six. An identical twin. Tom," Timothy adds, and the word echoes within, deep as *tomb*, vast as *time*. An old, difficult sense of isolation, or vacancy, or desolation touches him, and yet to be saying these words at all to Vicky amounts to a kind of plea, a prayer for—what? Reunification? He does not know what he wants so desperately from her. Oh, he wants to kiss her of course; he wants to see her without any clothes on. More, though, he wants that particular something else which he can't name, but which he knows she can provide. There's a miracle here—love's very own—in the way these words that cannot be expressed might nonetheless be satisfied in full.

Jack asks the waitress for the bill and the two girls retreat to the ladies' room.

"Well, fella," Jack says. "Having a good time?"

"Sure, Jack," Timothy says.

"You feeling on target, champ?"

"Sure, Jack."

"Well, things certainly seem to be going very well," Jack says. "And they're very sweet."

"The girls?"

"The girls precisely. You know, I think she really likes you."

"Who?" Even to squeeze out this monosyllable makes Timothy's voice wobble.

"Vicky—huh?" Jack says. "I mean I think you've *got* this one, you just *press* it harder. You know? Hey well hell, you know exactly what I'm talking about, Tim. I'm saying I think we're both in pretty good shape." A pause ensues, and then what Jack says next somehow shocks Timothy almost as much as he has ever been shocked. Timothy has lived in New York, he's been mugged to the flash of a knife, he's seen all sorts of sights, including his stiff father wearing makeup in a coffin, but he's wholly unprepared for the words that drop so matter-of-factly from Westman's big, confiding, contentedly red face: "I'm picking up some very fucky-fucky vibes in the air tonight."

XXIV

"HAVE WE ACCOMPLISHED what we set out to accomplish?" Jack asks in his happy, baying way when the coolness hits their faces, the dark mobile coolness of this Boston night. "Are we all shit-faced drunk?"

Marian's giggle could almost be a hiccup. "I'm shit-faced," she says, and leans into Jack, who drapes his arm around her. There's something unexpectedly winsome about this little confession of hers, and for Timothy it's almost as though her body with a cushioned collision had harbored not against Jack's body but his own; he feels a kind of enlivening thud along the left side of his ribs. But there is no female body pressed sideways against him. Beside him, but keeping her distance, is Vicky, who seems to walk either one step ahead or one step behind—but never quite with him, step by step.

"Where to?" Vicky calls to Jack, who is walking some little ways ahead, Marian thoroughly plastered to his side. There's something just a little clipped, or impatient, in her voice.

"I dunno, Vick, maybe get on the long climb back to sobriety? Some coffee? A coupla gallons of coffee?"

Although soft, Marian's voice, which sounds almost triumphant, even smug, carries backward easily: "I *told* you you'd have to carry me home."

"The Totaplex," Jack calls over his shoulder. "Best coffee in Boston at the Totaplex."

"I think maybe the night's gone on long enough," Vicky calls back. When Timothy picks up his pace a bit, to place himself directly beside her, she moves off to the side. Could she be angry with him? Disappointed in his drinking so much? It's a weight, an inexplicable burden—this sudden dissatisfaction of hers. Timothy longs to soothe her, to tell her outright that she needn't be angry, but probably this would only make her angrier. He wants to tell her how he only wants to make her happy . . .

"Maybe some coffee would bean a good idea," Timothy says. It takes him a moment to identify this drunkard's slip of the tongue. Did she catch it? He hopes she didn't catch it—then realizes it might amuse her. "I said coffee would bean. Instead of coffee be."

Vicky says nothing.

"You know, coffee is made from beans . . ."

"Oh? Is it really?" Vicky says.

"I really appreciate all your help. In the match and everything," Timothy says.

"It's my job."

"But you didn't have to be so nice about it," he goes on.

"That's my job. Professional niceness," Vicky says.

Timothy remembers how sweetly, how even deeply affectionately, Vicky'd called him *wonderfully earnest* (and what has happened since then?), and decides not to ask her anything further—but just to talk on his own, earnestly. He tells her about Garner, and Nettie, and the sandwiches Betty makes, and about getting mugged, and why this John Henry business is so off-target, and again (and again with an odd aggrieved disgruntlement) about Tommy.

Complicated things begin to happen as the four of them approach the Totaplex. Timothy makes little effort to understand the covert debate and behind-the-pawns maneuvering the others are engaged in, and therefore feels a little surprised, although pleased enough, when they all wind up in his room.

"Okay," Vicky says, in a take-charge sort of voice. She goes over and sits in the isolated armchair by the television. "Let's order some coffee."

"Absopositively, Vick," Jack says, but he does not move. He stands by the door with his arm around Marian. She has one hand gripped around the lapel of his sports jacket and one around his necktie. "Why don't you order up some coffee, Tim? That's a good idea, Tim."

"Okay," Timothy says. "Sure," Timothy says, and dials room service. Vicky has picked up from the floor a magazine, one of those with Tatsumi on the cover, and briskly, steadily from the back plows through its pages with crisp little *snap snaps*. "Enough coffee for four persons," Timothy tells the woman's voice at the other end of the line. "We've been having a party."

But Jack, now that the order for coffee has been placed, shows a change of heart. "Actually, actually Marian was thinking maybe she'd had a bit too much to drink and needed to walk around a while."

"Was she?" Vicky says.

"She was," Jack says. "Yes, in fact she was. Listen, listen the two of you. We'll be right back. We'll be right back," Jack says. "Now you save us some coffee, hear?"

Jack's proposal creates all sorts of complications, and Timothy again watches negotiations he doesn't fully understand. He merely sits there, in his chair at the desk. His head is spinning and he feels angry with the rest of them for ignoring him like this, and he looks longingly at the chessboard, which stands on the farther of the two beds. The board has pieces on it, although from here he can't quite make out the position. Vicky goes over to speak with Marian. "Girl talk," she announces and motions Jack away. He protests briefly, before retreating into the bathroom, where he urinates with what seems defiant loudness. On his return, Vicky informs him that the walk has been canceled. But after Jack has had another go at Marian, this conference carried out with his arm snuggled round her waist, the walk is on again. Then the three of them confer for a time, while Timothy remains at the desk, occasionally shaking his head to steady the room's angles, and then Vicky and Marian have another "girl talk." The somewhat surprising outcome is that Jack and Marian actually depart just as the coffee is wheeled in. Timothy signs for it. Vicky returns to her chair by the TV, picks up the magazine again, and hurls it to the floor. It flutters, going down. "I better go home," she announces.

"You want some coffee? Boy, do we have lots of coffee."

"No."

She sits there a moment in deep contemplation, then leaps to her feet. "God he's a first-class bastard. I mean it's no wonder all of them down there at headquarters think he's such a hot shot, given what a complete and utter bastard he is."

"Who?" Timothy says.

"*Who?* What planet do you live on anyway?"

"Maybe I drank too much," Timothy says.

"Maybe we all did," Vicky says after a moment. And in a less angry, maybe a friendlier way.

"Have some coffee." Timothy, careful not to spill any, pours a cup for her.

Vicky accepts the cup and saucer, takes one quite audible sip, and returns to the armchair. "Why is the world so *full* of bastards?"

The question may be meant rhetorically but Timothy ponders it intently enough. It's in fact an interesting issue. Certainly it would be interesting to know whether the ratio of bastards to nonbastards remains fairly constant over time. "I'm not sure," he admits.

"I'm . . . not . . . either."

"Look at the city. It's pretty," Timothy says. He had told her once—and when was that?—about this view. Behind her, on the other side of the glass, the city gleams in a complex arrangement of lit squares and dark squares. They suggest an interim strategic configuration, a position from some great Game whose rules have not yet been discerned and codified, and given all the windows visible from here, all the squares on the three-dimensional grids, it's quite possible—likely, in fact—that this moment's pattern of lights and darks has never arisen before. And will never arise again. Timothy is reminded, dimly, of all the doomed explorations (buried in tournament records, in newspapers, in books and magazines) of lines of play abandoned because ultimately proven to be unsound. Dead ends, dead ends. Timothy yearns suddenly to slow-dance with Vicky, here, turning round and round in this room that offers, in lieu of spectators, these scores and scores of neat, inscrutable lights. But there's no music here—and he doesn't know how to dance. Not a single step.

"Does Jack care a bit, a single *bit* about her? Is there in that fathead's brain of his even the slightest trace of what could be called human affection? Or sympathy? Or a desire to understand another person? Does he care a single bit about *her?*"

"About Marian?"

"Wouldn't you think he'd at least make some pretense of making it look as though he did?"

"Jack?"

"As though she represented something *hu*man to him . . ."

"You mean Marian," Timothy tells her.

"At least represented a little more than just another notch on his belt?"

The question triggers in Timothy's mind an image which, in its raw vividness, is horrifying: he sees Marian naked, down on her back, her plump white gesticulating legs thrown open to receive Jack, whose brawny swaying buttocks are a flushed red, the same flushed red of his face, the red of those monkeys at the zoo whose face and threadbare rump are alike a howling scarlet. Timothy pours himself a cup of coffee and sits on one of the beds, across from Vicky's bed, his knees almost touching hers.

"Why are men such shits?" she asks him.

Timothy looks deeply into her eyes. "I honestly don't know, Vicky." Her dangling earrings, he sees now, are in three parts. First a little seashell at the top, and then a thin stick of what must be coral, and then a fat little pearl at the bottom.

"I just broke up, a couple months ago, with a real supershit. A megashit," Vicky says.

"Did you break up with him, or he break up with you?" Timothy unexpectedly aches to tell her about Linda, and about their breakup, but he has a feeling that Vicky might think it uncool, or something, to hear him talking about a relationship that took place in high school.

"Tell me I'm wrong," Vicky says. "You know, if this were all reversed, if you were to talk to me about women the way I'm talking to you about men, I'd call you a real pig. I wouldn't stand for it. I would not. So tell me I'm wrong, when I say that men are just a whole extra lot shittier than women are."

"But you're not." Excitement in what is coming to light draws his body forward so that—elbows on knees, his face cradled in his hands—his eyes are no more than a foot from hers. "They're horrible." What he would like to convey, if he had the words, is that he isn't a man . . . But there was more to it than this. What Vicky had said was correct, so far as it went, but she hadn't pursued it far enough. Women, too, were horrible—there was something the matter, *wrong,* with the human race in general. And if only the two of them could meet on this mutual sphere of understanding, upon this other, unpeopled planet on which he wasn't a man and she wasn't a woman—anything, anything would be possible.

"God you're sweet. To listen to me." Vicky sips, quietly this time, from her coffee. "They ought to pickle you. Or put you in jars. Or whatever they do to preserve something sweet."

"Pickle me?" There's a small joke, or pun, afloat in the air but he cannot put his hand upon it.

"I better go wash up," Vicky says. "I must look pretty horrible."

What Timothy knows he ought to reply is *You look beautiful,* and this is what, it appears, some partner within him declares to someone very much like Vicky in a room very near to this one. And what happens next, in that other room, would take a person's breath away. But what he says to her, here, is—"Not really. No, you don't."

Vicky vanishes into the bathroom and Timothy pours himself a fresh cup of coffee in a clean cup—one of the four that room service has provided. What has happened to Jack and Marian? His head is scarcely spinning at all any more. He is made embarrassed—thinking *she* would be embarrassed, if she knew he could hear—by the sound of Vicky's urinating. There's a fan switch, right beside the light switch—why doesn't she, why doesn't Jack, use it? Cup and saucer in hand, he steps over to the window. The big 3-D game board out there has shifted—has darkened. Play is deepening, toward some meticulously engineered endgame. This is his own city, the mini-metropolis of his triumph, though to sense it out there in all its foreignness chills him a little. He's feeling cold. Day after day, he realizes now, he feels a little cold, without ever noticing it, and this has been one of the problems. He wishes Westman hadn't made that crack about the vibes. Everything would be much better if only Westman hadn't said that one thing about the vibes.

Timothy realizes that one of the things that's bothering him is the chessboard over there on the bed. He knows now what the position is—a complex, asymmetrical middle game, in which he, as Black, had watched White ambitiously overextend itself, and now, infiltrating piece by piece behind its lines, had started to build his own locking pressure on White's king side. But from where he now stands, by the window, he is being asked to play White, and the gathering Black army is a pressure he must contend with. That other self, the one who erected the Black defensive configuration earlier in the day, is pressing too hard upon him now. He deposits his coffee cup on the desk and, his head swinging a bit, makes his way over to the board and with a swoop of his hand rescues the White king from its oppressors. Chess piece hidden in his fist, Timothy returns to the window. "I'm learning," Timothy says aloud, to Imre. Where is Imre? Back yet from the restaurant? And what will Imre think if he comes knocking?

"Well my dear," Vicky says, emerging from the bathroom

with freshly brushed hair, "I've decided not to say anything more against your sex."

"Okay," Timothy says.

"But hell, what *does* that leave us to talk about? You better not talk about chess, my dear. I *won't* stand for it."

"Anything you want," Timothy offers. Looking up at him with her dark eyes, she is standing closer than he would have expected. To someone observing this hotel room from the outside, from the building across the street, say, with a pair of binoculars, the two of them must almost look as though they are about to embrace.

"We could talk about our Reverend Rabbitt," Vicky says. "Did you see that horrible picture, the really grisly one, in the paper?"

"He's getting out of hand. Do you think he's getting out of hand?"

"Or we could talk about Congam. And their whole hyped-to-death string of high-tech hotels."

"Their what?"

"Their hotels. The Totaplex Hotels."

"Their . . . You mean . . . Vicky, now you're not saying that the Totaplex is owned by Congam?"

"Of course, of course, of course," Vicky chants. "*Ev*erything's owned by Congam. Didn't you know that everything's owned by Congam?"

"But Congam owns the Totaplex? This very room?" Timothy needs to hear this again.

"Yes, I tell you, they own *ev*erything."

Sheer as an elevator shaft, the ground opens up before him, and he teeters, as on a brink, and there's anger as well as surprise in his voice: "Then this isn't costing them anything? My staying here, *it isn't costing them anything*. That's so, now, isn't it?" he accuses her.

"Poor baby, *don't* you understand? The way this works? How at some level, way way up above our heads, nothing costs anything? It's all just numbers on a sheet up there, little rows of figures that accountants play with. It costs anything you say it does, or nothing if you say it doesn't, and who cares? What difference does it make?"

What difference does it make if Congam owns the Totaplex? Oh, but it *does,* doesn't it? This changes a great deal, doesn't it? The rules, the very *rules* have been altered. He needs to think, to think this one out . . .

"I mean, what I'm saying about nothing costing anything, it's common knowledge. This is Basic Accounting 101—open to freshmen by permission of the instructor. Timmy my dear, I don't mean to suggest I'm offering up any sort of economic reve*la*tion."

"It's just I didn't know . . ."

"We don't want to go into this. Do we want to go into this?"

"It's just that this somehow makes a difference," Timothy tells her.

"Or I could read your fortune," Vicky goes on. "Would you like that?"

"Like what?"

"You want me to read your palm?"

"You read palms?" Timothy says. And why was he never told that Congam owns the Totaplex?

"I could try . . ."

"Okay," Timothy says. He needs a moment; he needs to quiet her a moment. "Sure."

Vicky sits on the bed and he sits beside her, his palm open in her hands, in her lap. His other, his left hand, still curls round the concealed White king. It occurs to him that he would be feeling much calmer if he were not feeling quite so nervous.

"What do you want to know about first?"

"Oh, anything . . ." It doesn't matter at all, does it? He is sitting in a Congam tower with the Princess of Congam and what does it matter who owns what, just so long as she likes him?

"The chess, huh? Dumb question, huh? Well, let me see . . ." She flicks her index finger up and down his palm. Her nails have been painted a pink just a shade or two darker than their natural color. (And she does not know what this is doing to him. She does not see, perhaps, everything she does to him . . .) "I see an important someone," she says, "a very important someone. Is this someone a woman? Is it a man?" Vicky giggles. "No, it's a *something*. It's an it. It's ANNDY. It's the Nice New Dandy Yardstick himself. *Hi, Mister Yardstick,*" Vicky calls in a high, silly, childish voice.

"And what do I see happening?" she goes on in her own voice, in one of her own voices. It is a simple matter of a few inches, no more than this—the distance required of his hand, to seize her actual breast . . . And with this realization, and impulse, comes an urge to rescue that hand from hers. It is all being played a little too much under her direction, this little game, and with too many moves per minute. Her sea-scavenged earring sways hypnotically and his head is fogged and he needs to regroup his forces.

He feels oddly exposed, having his hand spread out like this before her, for it's as though through the fog she really *can* read his fortune. And there's a queer uneasy sense of overlap, the present moment superimposed atop Jack Westman's stunt in the restaurant. But this is not Jack who huddles now over the outstretched palm, and who throws off a subtle white net of perfume. No, it's Vicky, all of her right here, the mole on her jaw, the smaller mole on her fine white neck, where her Adam's apple would be, her breasts under their soft black sweater, the bewitching smell of her perfume clouding the whole front of his face, the turning lamplight stirring up black rainbows in the cauldron of her hair . . . "And what do I see? I see your whole life, Timmy. I see Indiana, this great big huge flat landscape out there with a couple scarecrows sticking out of it. And I see problems, very serious-type problems, but I also see triumph. I see eventual triumph—but for who?" She laughs again—her deep laugh.

"I see television cameras," Vicky goes on. "And newspapers. Why are they here? What are they looking for? What's the mystery now? What's happening? Why, they're looking for *you,*" she says. "They're all out looking for *you.*

"And I see a pretty girl. A *very* attractive-type girl, if I may say so myself." Her throat wells up with giggled laughter. "And this very sweet, very attractive girl is going to be a very big help to you. More and more, she's going to *help* you. But, but what's this? Dear, dear, what do I see? What do I see happening *very* soon? My my my *my.* I see you kissing that very pretty girl . . ."

There's a splayed, thudding, wordless moment as his hand sits limp in her hands. *Who is she talking about?* This *girl,* this *very attractive girl*—could she be talking about herself? That's the thing, he can't tell for certain who she's talking about and he can't afford a mistake at this crucial juncture. He sits there, he's a weight, can't raise his eyes, and the moment stretches. It is amazing how long the moment stretches.

And then Vicky leans over and kisses him, lightly, very near but still not quite directly on the mouth and with this kiss he ascertains, as she rises from the bed and drifts over toward the window, that yes, she *had* been talking about herself . . . Yes, of course yes, of course *yes,* and he has flunked this little test of hers. And only an incredibly stupid person could have failed to see what she meant. Oh, how stupid and nerdlike does she think he is *now?* Surely, *now,* she understands just how stupid he really can be . . .

Timothy sees her standing over by the window and he recognizes this as his moment. Here at last the two of them have reached the point where that move is to be made which, if you recorded their moves (as you would in any serious game of any kind), would be followed by a pair of exclamation points. There she is, Vicky Schmidt, with one hand on her hip and the other held out a ways from her hipbone, like a woman smoking a cigarette, although in fact she holds nothing in her hands, and he may never, never have another such opportunity to present her with his enormous offer. He is offering her his life, his soul—nothing less.

Or has his moment already passed—the opportunity already lost the moment he failed to seize upon the hint she gave him? The room's gold lamplight burns in his eyes and he wishes only that things could fall out more simply, without all these devious maneuverings and gambits. *Why does she always have to be so sophisticated?* If only it were possible for her simply to go to sleep in one of these beds, the very one he's sitting on, maybe, and he to sleep in the other—and in the dead of night, when all the talk has faded, and the city's competitive lights have found some repose at last, the game being over at last, she would naturally crawl into his bed, or he into hers, and they would be true bare daring lovers. From a distance, from a long chill ways off, her voice comes to him: "I should probably go."

The crossroads have arrived and he must rise now and step forth and take the woman he loves fast into his arms and run his hands through her magical black hair and kiss her with a snapping sound crisply on the mouth, and as if in preparation for rising he first opens his left hand—and it's as though a metamorphosis has taken place, a stroke of sorcery. The piece he finds there is not the White king he seized from the board but the minor, the foolishly small figure of a White bishop. There is a significance here. His head is looping again, but he knows there's a significance here that must be pondered. His head is spinning but he knows that the only thing he has ever really coveted in this world stands on the carpet right before him, ready, perhaps ready to be taken, and how has this happened to him? Because he can't move from his seat on the bed. He's drunk, he knows, and what's left to hope is that he's actually so very drunk he will remember none of this tomorrow—even as he knows he will recall this moment always. It's a failure that must come back, come back, white and black come back within him: a fog that opens on a dark without end . . . He has laid this night upon his soul forever.

XXV

NOTHING EVER CHANGES, except the weather, and possibly the global climate, but in any event the tournament will go on forever . . . Here's the old restive assemblage of grunts and sighs, squirmings and popping knuckles . . . Imre's growing dissatisfaction would have been apparent to Garner even had no words been spoken. But of course Imre mutters, too. "What?" he says, "what?" And "Slowly . . . slowly . . ." and "Careful now . . ." and "Don't you listen? Don't you listen to what I say?" Obviously this, the seventh game, is not progressing well. Perhaps Timothy is tired? Garner certainly is tired. He glances over at the colorful newspaper tucked under Imre's arm—one that advertises itself as the most successful in the country. USA SNAPSHOT, Garner reads. "A look at statistics that shape the nation." This is on the bottom of the front page. "How we feel about stomachaches" is the topic of today's survey, and it would appear that within this pluralistic nation of ours, so diverse and vagrant and contentious that one might despair of ever locating any cohesive core, another underlying sector of agreement has, through journalistic diligence, been uncovered. For we are encouragingly united—92 percent of us are, anyway—in deploring stomachaches. There are many members of the press—including television crews—in the auditorium today. Garner had never expected this unconventional and radically unsexy contest to capture "the national mood." Perhaps there is someone here from *USA Today*? And how *do* "we" feel about machines that can analyze 365,000 chess positions per second? Imre releases a queer indrawn sound—*aahoof,* as though he's been kicked in the stomach—when Timothy advances his king's knight pawn two spaces. Two moves later, he cries out to Garner, in a breathy impassioned whisper, "It's just suicide . . ."

This time around, it is chiefly fatigue rather than alarm that Garner experiences when Timothy concedes defeat by stalking off the stage. And this time around, there is no scurrying attempt to chase down the "sore loser." No, Garner is tired of his brother's tantrums, his brother's turmoil. He is tired, as well, of Oliver Conant, his pimply face ashine with victory, and tired even of ANNDY, perhaps because ANNDY knows no fatigue. There is something psychologically draining, and finally rather nightmarish, about ANNDY's continual, empty levity. The quips are endless: ALL IN ALL I PREFER WINNING and BACK AT LAST IN THE LAND OF THE LIVING and DON'T BLAME ME, I'M JUST DOING MY JOB and YOU CAN'T KEEP A GOOD MAchiNe DOWN . . . Garner is tired, too, of Imre, for whom he feels such depths of unvoiced gratitude and affection; and tired of the reporters, busily peddling their this-machine-doesn't-know-enough-to-come-out-of-the-rain stories; and tired of the intrusive television crews, for whom no doubt ever arises as to whether or not their presence may be welcome; and, in general, tired of (and a little horrified by) so protracted an exposure to people who would voluntarily sacrifice their lives to a board game. And tired, it turns out, tired in advance, before even a single word has been exchanged, of Albrecht Zehnder, whom Garner meets by the door on his way out. Zehnder is sporting the same high-top lime-green gym shoes he wore at their first meeting, this time matched with, or contrasted by, a pair of striped scarlet-and-lemon-yellow seersucker trousers that would probably be deemed a trifle garish at a New Orleans Mardi Gras celebration. His are ebullient spirits no doubt meant to give the lie to all conventions of dress—but oh, if only it weren't so tiring! The look of this fellow academic offends Garner, much as Oliver Conant's inability to keep his trousers zippered offends Timothy. "Congratulations," Garner begins.

"Congratulations?" The tone might be described as one of airy bewilderment.

"Your machine," Garner explains. "It just won a chess game. I was a spectator. As in fact were you."

"I don't concern myself about the outcome."

"No, but you did enter your machine into a competitive match for prize money," Garner points out.

"Oh, hey, our A-number-one goal's education. Clarification. You see, I see myself as a kind of marriage broker." Zehnder's voice has turned venturesome, as though once more reaching out toward any proximate tape recorder. "My goal is to teach people and machines to love each other." Garner continues toward the exit and Zehnder stays at his side. Imre follows a step or two behind, his huge head sunk turtle-fashion in his huge shoulders. "This problem your brother has, he's much too old . . ." Zehnder says.

"My brother too old?"

"Well goodness, how old is he?"

"I would suppose about twenty."

"Much too old," Zehnder says with a lugubrious, mulling shake of his head. "He didn't grow up with the Machine. He still sees the Machine in opposition to himself, instead of as a part of himself. It'll be ten, fifteen years before we've got the first wave of kids that *really* grew up with the Thinking Machine. It won't be till then we'll have a group that really understands it's the Machine, and not the dog, that's man's best friend."

In Garner's mind, a switch is thrown and a small light flashes. "The little slogans, the witticisms on ANNDY's screen," he says. "You write them, don't you?"

Delight at having been discovered actually lays a blush of pride, an inch-wide strip of pink, across Zehnder's broad cheeks. "Well yes I do," he admits. "Or at least most of them. Do you find them amusing?"

"Occasionally," Garner, perhaps a little rudely, replies.

"You know, I think they're one of the main reasons why this match has been such an unexpected *hit.*" Zehnder furrows his brow; joyful boastfulness immediately gives way to awestruck incomprehension. "Now isn't it *funny?* These machines make people nervous because they're so human, and so we go make people comfortable again by making the machines even *more* human. You get a machine to play chess, and people get a little nervous. But you get a machine to play chess and tell jokes while it's doing it, and suddenly everybody's happy as popcorn. When machines start coming up with their own jokes, on an impromptu basis, that's going to be the biggest help. There's nothing like shared laughter, is there? That's really going to ce*ment* the love affair."

The three of them, Imre still lagging a couple of steps behind, have pushed their way out the door and into a very warm fall afternoon. "The weather's changed quite a bit since we talked last," Garner says.

"The weather?"

"I'm speaking meteorologically. It was snowing," Garner says.

"Oh yes," Zehnder says. "And there's not a *bit* of it left, is there. Makes you wonder, doesn't it, just what's the *goal* of weather, anyway. You hear all the time about human wastefulness, but waste is only natural, isn't it. I'm speaking literally, as well as meteorologically."

Despite himself, Garner is beginning to like Zehnder. "They're going to write jokes?"

"Oh well sure," Zehnder says. "I mean eventually they're going to write jokes so good we won't get them. The same way a little kid can't get the jokes a grown-up tells. If history teaches us anything, it's that humor is an unobjective thing. Oh, they'll write the jokes for themselves. You know, to share among themselves."

"From *machina sapiens* to *machina risibilus,*" Garner says.

"A hundred years from now," Zehnder continues, and the weighty grandeur of this phrase brings his pace to a near halt. The three men stand in a sort of courtyard in which a dog is trotting determinedly by with a green "Frisbee" in its mouth. "A hundred years from now, when you'd no more question whether machines are alive than today you'd question whether people are, you know what I'll predict a hundred years from now?"

"You expect a long life . . ." Garner intercedes, and Zehnder's mouth twitches with a suppressed smile. He pauses the shortest moment in acknowledgment of the joke—or of having set himself up for the joke.

"I expect that scientists'll be trying to determine just when it was that machines first became living creatures. Because I predict that that'll be a difficult question. The same way how it's difficult today to say just where organic life begins. You know, you get right down to viruses and things, it's very hard to draw any boundary line. They'll look back at our machines, and they'll say, was *that* one alive? And how about *that* one?"

If he is a clown, this computer scientist in the green shoes and the red-and-yellow trousers, he is an imposing figure as well—momentarily, as the three men stand within one more dingy handbill-plastered M.I.T. courtyard, the most imposing figure Garner knows. Zehnder possesses what is usually permitted only to the religious fanatic and the blind political dogmatist—an unshakable conviction that the future belongs to him.

Good-byes are exchanged, hands shaken, and Garner walks off with Imre, meanwhile successfully calling to mind, labored word for word, a sentence from his own *The Human Fiction* ("Any conception of truth capacious enough to be useful must encompass the future as well as the past and present; we must not deny a fact entrance into the realm of the actual merely because it hasn't occurred yet"), and also longing suddenly to be at home among his books and papers. But it seems he cannot yet desert downcast Imre, whose gloom must in some way be answered or responded to. This, too, is one of the powers by which Imre maintains his hold upon his young chess pupil: the compacted weight of a disappointment at once titanic and pitiable. Imre is a difficult person to let down . . . With each day Garner grows fonder of Imre, and more deeply beholden, but he senses again, as the two of them step into the gleaming horrors of the lobby of the Totaplex Hotel, the man's utter impenetrability. Who on earth could view him with understanding? (Surely not even his wife could feel that . . .) Where is the rash imagination that would hazard to guess what it would be like to wake up in the morning and to be (of all the creatures in this teeming world) Imre Szendrei—to pad off to the shower in Imre's voluminous boxer shorts, to soap the creases of Imre's skin, to shave Imre's macrocephalic jowls in a foggy mirror?

A cardboard DO NOT DISTURB sign hangs from Timothy's door. Imre's knock raises no response. "Huhhhh, Imre, hmp?" Imre explains, and knocks again. "Hey, hmp, it's me." Imre tries the knob—the door is locked.

"He must be out for a walk," Imre says.

"Well, let's hope it cools him off."

Imre in response swings his boxy bespectacled head toward Garner and for a moment their glances link. And then a second, a deeper linkage takes place, perhaps, and an affectionate bond is perceived—that of their common flesh-and-blood burden, their congruent mix of exasperation, worry, pride, and confusion.

The moment is a satisfying one—enough so that Garner, walking over to the subway through a restless jigsaw puzzle of fallen leaves, breaks into whistling; and enough so that, his head cleared of misgivings, he is able to work, as he so likes to do, deep into the night, until all of the neighborhood's neon signs have been put to bed except that of the Slak Shak.

He is awakened from a heavy if troubled sleep—at what? at eight in the morning?—by an insistently jangling phone. This phone (its unlisted number given out only with the greatest circumspection) rings rarely. His hand stumbles a moment in the blind finding of it.

"It's Imre. Listen, perhaps. Is he there?"

"Here? Who . . . ?"

"I thought he might have gone over there. I don't think he stayed you see in his room last night."

Garner is waking up fast. "How do you know?"

"Well I don't know. I mean there's still no answer at the door. On and off, I have been knocking all the night long."

"Where could he be?"

"I thought he might be over at your place?"

"Well he's not here. Maybe he's just not answering the door."

"Maybe," Imre says—doubtfully.

"Maybe—maybe I better come over there. To the hotel." Garner opens the top drawer of his night table, not at all sure for what he is searching, and draws from it a copy of Hobbes' *Leviathan*—a thick enough book to hold unobtrusively the two hundred dollars in twenty-dollar bills he always keeps there. This is his emergency fund for emergencies that never seem to arise. "And don't you do a thing until I get there. I'll meet you at your room, all right?"

"Yesss."

There is something absurd, somehow, something ludicrously purposeful and businesslike and somber, in Imre and Garner's march down the hotel corridor toward the door of Timothy's room. None of this is happening. Imre halts some ten feet from the door—as if to give Garner space to maneuver—and Garner raps upon it lightly and calls his brother's name. The DO NOT DISTURB sign dangles from the doorknob. Garner raps again, this time quite smartly, and calls, "Timothy? You sleeping? It's Garner."

Imre comes padding forward. "Maybe what we do, we remove the sign, the DO NOT DISTURB, and then the woman will come in to clean, and we can come in after her."

Great though the moment's nervousness and confusion may be, Garner still finds Imre's plan wonderfully amusing. Oh, this is a quintessential display of Imre's curious psychology, that fusion of timidity and chess player's ornate strategical deviousness.

"I don't think there's any need for that, Imre. We'll go down and get a key card. Maybe he left some clue as to where he was headed."

"Mmm," Imre sighs, doubtfully again. "I don't think they'll give you one."

Imre is right, at least initially, for neither the green-uniformed woman behind the reception desk nor the red-uniformed manager who is summoned at Garner's protestations will even consider releasing a key card. Prospects improve somewhat, however, after Garner is led into an internal office on whose door is a name plate that reads T. Phipps Hitchcock, Operations

Manager. Hitchcock, who is wearing a surprisingly tasteful nut-brown notch-lapelled nailhead wool suit, is much younger than expected; he could be one of Garner's students.

After Hitchcock has explained with a slow precision, as though addressing someone of diminished mental capacity, that he has no "legal right" to give a key card to anyone except a paying guest, Garner actually draws from his wallet, in a ridiculously melodramatic but quite effective show of bravado, his faculty identification card. "I *teach* the law," Garner states. "And I can guarantee you'll have no problems on that score."

Garner has gained an advantage, which he quickly capitalizes upon: "But it doesn't seem to me that the legal question is in fact the paramount one. The salient point here is that I don't know where my brother is, and I'm naturally worried. You see, he can be quite careless at times. He's unpredictable. He was mugged at knife point just a few months ago. And if what we have here is some serious problem, I think I'd better know about it, and I also think, more to the point, that *you'd* better know about it, I think this ho*tel* had better know about it, just as soon as possible."

What is Garner suggesting? Whatever this unnamed *problem* might consist of, it has its palpable effect on Hitchcock. He squirms and looks up at Garner imploringly. "What you're asking for is something we don't generally do here at the Totaplex."

"I don't see why we can't keep it confidential," Garner replies. "I'm his brother after all."

"I'll have to go with you. That's absolute hotel regulations."

"Fine. That would be fine with me."

"This is the Totaplex, you understand."

"No doubt about it. This *is* the Totaplex."

Garner is asked to wait a few minutes—that interval by which, presumably, Responsibility will assure itself that no rushed or pressured action is about to be undertaken. Garner returns to the lobby, where he finds Imre waiting in knuckle-popping meditation. Hitchcock reappears after five or so minutes, carries on an extensive, whispered consultation with various staff behind the reception desk, and finally, with a sort of military snapping of his hand, signals to Garner.

"This is highly irregular," Hitchcock says, as the two men ascend alone in the elevator.

"Oh it's irregular all right," Garner replies. "But then again, my kid brother's *ab*sence is irregular."

Hitchcock knocks on Timothy's door, calls by way of warning, "Staff, hotel staff, excuse me," knocks again, opens the door no more than an inch, calls an additional warning, and at last swings the door wide open. The beds are empty. It is impossible to tell whether Timothy slept here or not. The beds are unmade, but they have been unmade most of the time since Timothy's arrival. Clothes, papers, magazines, dishes, empty cans of Coca-Cola are scattered over the furniture and over the floor. There is no note of any sort on the desk, no phone numbers, no ticket stubs, no train or bus schedules. Garner walks over to the closet and, aware of Hitchcock's eyes upon him—of a stranger's eyes upon him—swings open the door. Timothy's suitcase stands within. Garner, trailed closely by Hitchcock, ventures into the bathroom. The gray, opaque shower curtain is drawn across the tub. He pulls it open. The tub is empty.

"Well he doesn't seem to be here," Hitchcock announces. His tone is almost cheerful; an enormous amount of tension has fled from this room. Hitchcock steps over to the desk and, with an alacrity that says unmistakably *This isn't my problem,* he picks up a pawn and begins with cheerful briskness to rap it on the top of the television. Yes, Timothy has left behind his chessboard, too.

"You know," Hitchcock begins in a friendly, confiding sort of way—the official's reserve has vanished altogether and this kid the age of Garner's students is revealed plainly for what he is: a gossip and a bit of a bully—"I hear rumors that he's been acting kind of funny."

"Funny?" Garner says. "In what way funny?"

"Oh, in all sorts of ways funny."

"And what do you mean by funny?"

Hitchcock returns the chess piece to the board. "Oh—just funny."

"But surely you do mean something by 'funny'?"

Hitchcock draws himself erect and flicks a hand through his handsome reddish-blond hair, becoming once more the fellow Garner met in the office downstairs—the one who has chosen to carry a first initial in his professional name. T. Phipps Hitchcock—a young man freshly out of hotel management school who is growing fast into his job. "Perhaps I'm thinking of a different guest," he says.

"Perhaps you are," Garner says.

"Perhaps your next step would be to notify the police . . ."

"The police?" Garner says.

"People don't just disappear," Hitchcock says.

"Oh he hasn't. He's just not here," Garner says.

But then where is Timothy? Mugged again? Beaten up this time? His body afloat in the Charles—or deposited in a dumpster in a Back Bay alley? Garner would like to think that Boston has not yet reached New York's level of blood-spilling barbarism—but the, at some point, unignorable truth is that here, too, there are people roaming the streets in the express hope of pummeling you flat to the ground. "I'm sorry to have troubled you," Garner says, as they close up the room once more, but adds, in annoyance at the transparency of Hitchcock's relief, his complete indifference to anything that might happen in the hinterlands outside the Total Complex of the Totaplex, "I'll let you know if there's anything else you can do."

In the lobby, Garner answers Imre's inquiring stare with a pair of questions: "Is there anybody, *any*body in town he could have gone to visit? Does he know anybody else around here?"

"No," Imre says. "Just the girl."

"The girl?"

"Miss Schmidt. Vicky."

The girl . . . And how smoothly a plausible scenario drops

into place! How premature, suddenly, and mortifying, was this decision to probe into Timothy's room. Of course, of course . . . "Do you have her telephone number?"

"He's got it," Imre says. "On a card."

"Well she must be at work now. We can reach her at work," Garner says.

"We can call from upstairs," Imre says. "From my room."

Miss Schmidt is, naturally enough, in a meeting, and Garner gives his name and number to Miss Schmidt's secretary with a sense of weary futility. Yet it is less than ten minutes before Imre's telephone jangles.

"Hi, Garner."

Her greeting's breezy affability is unexpected. Struggling a bit for a matching informality, Garner says, "Yes, hi, hey listen, I'm looking for my kid brother. You haven't seen him, have you?"

"I haven't had a chance to see *any*body. Unless you count the people around here as people. I've been at work all day."

"And you didn't see him last night?"

"Last night?" Vicky pauses. "Well, I haven't seen him for a couple days. Just the TV last night—him stalking out and all of that. What about Imre?"

"He hasn't seen him either. So far as I know."

"Well I'm sure Timmy went back to the hotel. I mean is there any reason for thinking he didn't go back to the hotel?"

Only now does Garner ascertain that he should have prepared some explanation for her. "Well, actually, he has some friends out in Watertown, I think he must have gone out there. You didn't hear him mention anywhere else he wanted to go, did you?"

Garner means to throw off this last question buoyantly, as an afterthought—but some tremulous jitter must have snuck into his voice, since her response contains none of its usual lightheartedness. "No-o, no-o," she says. "No, he never said anything to me about *Water*town . . . When you do track him down, will you have him give me a call right away?"

"I'll do that," Garner says, and thinks to add, "In any case, you can see him yourself at the match tomorrow. Sorry to bother you."

Garner hangs up the phone and says to Imre, "There must be someone else. Someone we're not thinking of."

"You want my opinion?" he says. "I think he went home."

"Home?"

"Back to New York."

"Whatever for?"

When Imre merely shrugs in reply, Garner says, "But what in the world for?"

"To think? Maybe? This city makes him nervous?"

"I don't see how it could, after New York." This is a skeptical little joke born in an influx of hope; Garner reaches for the phone again. "Do you know his number?"

Imre nods—and yet does not volunteer it. Garner passes him the phone. Pausing thoughtfully between digits, Imre punches at the buttons, finally lifts the phone to his massive ear. "It's just the recording," he reports.

"The what?"

"The recording. On his answering machine."

"Hang up," Garner calls. "Hang *up,* hang *up.* We've got to think about a message."

Imre returns the phone to its cradle with a heavy thump. "That doesn't mean he isn't there. The recording. You see? Maybe he's waiting first to see who might be calling."

"I didn't even know he had an answering machine."

"A couple of months now."

"We should leave a message, then," Garner says. "Now what should be our message?"

"To call us maybe?"

"And who should leave the message? Should you or should I leave the message?"

Removed—as it were—from their sockets, Imre's troubled eyes bob unsteadily within the pooled circles of his lenses. "Me, maybe," he says.

"Yes, Imre. Why don't you leave the message."

More deliberately than ever, Imre flattens the phone's little buttons, one by one. And when he speaks into the answering machine, he takes a staunchly uncompromising stand: "Hey, I don't like this at all. Not at all, right? Now you call me here at the hotel right away. Or you call your brother, right? This is no way to play a chess match, right?" Imre hangs up the phone.

The two men peer at each other, gaze questioning gaze. "You don't think that will frighten him off? Assuming he does get the message?"

"Oh I think he'll get it. I think he's there. Maybe not right there in the apartment, but he's in New York."

"Imre, I don't know," Garner says. "I think he would have taken some clothes with him, don't you?"

"Now you know what that is? That's *your* thinking. It isn't *his* thinking—you see what I mean? Now let's say he left right from the match. See, maybe he went right to the train station after the match. I think he went home. What you have to do in these cases, you got to figure out what *he's* thinking *we're* thinking. And I'm thinking he's thinking that I'm thinking he would just go back to New York. So you see, it isn't quite like he left without telling me."

The involutions of this rationale are offered matter-of-factly. Speaking of home, Imre is plainly in his element here—this is the level on which he deals with his young pupil. "He went home—I think that's what he did, all right," Imre says.

Such confidence is cheering . . . Who, after all, should know better than Imre what Timothy might do? "I suppose New York's the only home he has," Garner says. "Certainly not Key Largo. But I *would* like to know for sure. Maybe we could call somebody down there? They could go knock on his door."

"He wouldn't answer for them, right? No, not if he's not answering his phone. He'd only answer for one of us. And they wouldn't have a key the way I have a key."

A hopeful new possibility seems on the verge of presenting itself. "Imre, you weren't perhaps thinking about going back to

New York for any reason? You don't maybe have any other business to take care of there?"

"I would like to see my wife perhaps," Imre says. Although he offers this in a preliminary sort of way, nothing follows. He merely sits there, deep in his brown study.

"Yes. Well I can imagine so."

"It is a long way, and it is expensive," Imre adds.

"Well as for that, I mean the actual expenses, well if you were willing to go, in fact I'd be more than happy, in fact I would honestly be . . ." Nervousness is making Garner garrulously indirect; he has almost begun to babble. "I'd want to pay your way. You'd be doing me such a big favor. I'd go myself, but I think I'd better remain here. Somebody'd better be here in case he surfaces."

Surely it's money that Imre is asking for—and Garner sympathizes with him in this, since Imre seems poverty-stricken in a fashion almost unknown among Garner's acquaintances. This isn't the poverty of some of Garner's students, who for all their ragbag clothes are apt to have apartments outfitted with remote control sound systems and spring water dispensers—but poverty of a sandwich-toting, trashbin-scavenging sort. Still, Imre is surprisingly slow to rouse to the offer of cash. "You'd be doing me a big favor, Imre."

When Garner opens his wallet, it is as though all along he has been preparing for just this bizarre development; everything has led him to this removal of the money, this counting off of ten twenty-dollar bills. "You can give me back whatever you don't need . . ."

"Yes." And now Imre nods firmly. He recounts the money, folds it, and buries it deep in one of his voluminous pockets. Then, surprisingly, he steps forward and extends his hand. The huddling, conspiratorial formality of this gesture, enhanced by his face's solemn quizzicality, makes of this moment something too heightened to be quite real—something cinematic or theatrical. It is Imre's unwitting lot in life to proceed from scene to scene with a plodding gravity that makes even his most momentous actions look slightly ludicrous.

"Call me as soon as you learn anything," Garner says.

"Yes."

"I'll be home, Imre."

"Yes."

"I'll be waiting at home. And you, you take care . . ."

Garner returns by cab to his apartment. He telephones the Totaplex Hotel, receives no answer when Timothy's room is rung, and leaves a message for his brother at the reception desk. He then telephones New York and leaves another message on Timothy's answering machine.

For the moment, it would seem that Garner has done everything he can, and there is nothing left for him but the waiting. The minutes drag and yet there's no use trying to read much of anything. Garner decides to take a shower. He'd had no time for bathing this morning. He leaves the bathroom door open, lest he miss the ringing of his phone. He feels distraught, but displays little trace of it; he observes, in undressing, that his hands remain steady. And yet when in his physical nakedness he tosses back the shower curtain, a violent, gripping shudder seizes his bare chest. Only now, as the gleaming white porcelain of his bathtub fills his eyes, does the knowledge strike home as to what he was actually seeking in his brother's hotel room. Oh, it's quite a day, quite a day among days, when a man goes peering behind a shower curtain to discover whether or not his only remaining brother reclines there coldly in a warm bath of blood. And this day of days may not be over yet.

XXVI

NEEDED, SHE REALIZES she is being summoned, once again, even if at first she doesn't know quite where she is. And when she comes to understand she's in bed, she still cannot say who's in it with her. Gerry, of course, lies on one side, but there's another body, a small hot furtive little figure, curled up clutchingly at her other side. Still half asleep, she recalls out of an earlier half sleep a sweet, whining lamentation—it's Ricky, she remembers, who'd come to the bed complaining of a stomachache. And the phone is ringing.

"Hello," she sighs into the receiver.

"Nettie, Garner here."

"Garner?" It's a rare event in itself, a call from her older brother—and a call at this hour is unheard of. Inside her, there's a further hasty awakening, and instantly she is ready for trouble: attuned to listen, to advise, to ponder. Solicitude comes naturally to this woman who has seven children in her house.

"Nettie, sorry to bother you, but you haven't heard from Timothy in the last day or so, have you?"

"Timmy?" Her voice emerges a little too sharply. Not that she has to worry about waking Gerry—who could sleep through an aerial bombardment, the poor overworked baby—or little Ricky, who sleeps the contented, privileged sleep of a child admitted to the parents' bed. But she doesn't want to awaken or alert her mother—who has the ears of a hunting owl. "No," Nettie says in a quieter voice. "He doesn't usually—but why do you ask?"

"It's just that nobody has seen him since he lost that game yesterday."

"Imre hasn't seen him?"

"Imre hasn't seen him."

"Well have they seen him at the hotel?"

"Well that's what isn't clear, Nettie. Whether he spent the night at the hotel last night. No one there would know, evidently. The hotel is gigantic. It's the size of Todsville, Pennsylvania."

"Well they'd know if his bed was slept in."

"That's just what they wouldn't know, actually. The bed probably hasn't been made in a week. Half the time he's been barring all maids from his room with one of those signs that say DO NOT DISTURB. You know what his hours are like."

Nettie's thoughts are racing here and there, but she draws them together with a single question: "Garner, do you mean he's missing?"

Uncertainty, or strain, lifts the pitch of Garner's voice. "Missing? Sort of. I don't know. I suppose the real question," he goes on, "is, Will he show up at the game tomorrow?"

"Well, where do you think he is, Garner?"

"Well, I for one honestly don't know, Nettie. He's not in New York, apparently. Imre went down to check today. He thought maybe he'd gone back to his apartment."

She sits up in bed, her face bathed in the faint cold wash of the streetlight, whose blue bulb is emerging nakedly now that November is here and the last leaves are dropping from the trees. How serious a problem is this? Potentially, it could be *very* serious, obviously, and yet Nettie's own intuition assures her that there's nothing to worry about. She feels this quite strongly. What she's not quite free to say to Garner, any more than to Mom, is that, in the simplest terms, Timmy isn't all there re*gard*less of where he is—and so it's absurd to treat him as though he might be expected to behave normally. Garner is calling to say, in effect, *Timothy's done something weird,* and she wants to reply, *Why in the world would you expect otherwise?* No, in so many ways Timmy is the farmer's youngest simpleton son in a children's fairy story—the lovable, laughable one, who must perform every task in a roundabout and cockeyed way, but who is protected in the end by the angels of good fortune. No, Timmy is safe and sound, she feels sure of that: he has merely wandered off in search of some unconventional remedy—magic beans, a magic cloak, a magic hat . . .

Yet she feels as well Garner's terrible gnawing nervousness, his deep hungry plea for reassurance, and she must reassure him—even if to see him so upset also frankly pleases her. She would never have expected *him* to be feeling such tender concern on behalf of his brother—or on anyone's behalf, really. But you do have to pity anyone so completely unable to cope with real problems—human problems—of any sort. He has had *this* particular problem, anyway, this very large and very confusing human problem, drop right into his lap, leaving him no way to ignore it or dismiss it. She senses his little boy's helplessness, and his partial, enraged awareness of his own helplessness, and she says, "Look Garner, I'm sure he's just holed up somewhere. For a little think. He probably thought he needed to get out of the bright lights for a while. It would drive *any*body crazy, to have those television cameras all the time poked in your face. But he'll be at the match tomorrow. Timmy's like that—he won't let you down. And you shouldn't be worrying yourself so much."

"Do you really think so?" he asks, or begs, and abruptly he is revealed to her as nothing but a little boy. Even Garner, the great proud remote independent Garner, is but a little boy. True, some women remain girls their whole lives—and yet, some of them actually *do* become women . . . But she has never, never met a man who wasn't, in the end, a little boy. In the same shushing tone with which she might handle little Ricky, come to her bed complaining of a stomachache, she says, "Lisssen, lisssen now, don't worry yourself, Garner, don't you worry yourself, don't worry yourself now. Everything'll be all right, huh? It can all wait until tomorrow, hmm? I mean there's nothing to be done until tomorrow, is there?"

She goes on in this vein for a while—until he really does seem pacified. And after she has, in effect, put Garner to bed, she slips into her bathrobe and goes barefoot out into the kitchen. She pours herself a glass of milk and is digging a large brownie out of a buttered aluminum tray in the fridge when a voice, close by, strikes at her from behind: "Who was it who called?"

Of course, of course . . . Isn't it only inevitable that in the one moment when she would decide to sneak herself a bite of brownie Mom would suddenly appear? "Hm?" Nettie replies. The openness of Mom's disapproval, the hateful way she glares at the brownie, is just plain typical; it would never occur to her that she, as a guest in this house, might be expected not to tell her hostess what to eat and what not to eat. "What call?" Nettie says.

"The one just now. The one from Garner."

There is no point, either, in trying to explain to Mom the absurdity of asking who called if she already knows the answer. The old woman simply would not recognize the inconsistency. "Yes, it was Garner. Do you want anything, Mother? Something to eat or drink?"

Of course the last two questions merit no reply. "What did he want?" Mom says. "What did he want?"

Under the harsh overhead light of the kitchen, Nettie watches her mother's mouth screw itself tight, her mother's eyes sharpen. Yes, she's sharp all over—sharp-nosed and sharp-kneed, a bony old creature who adamantly refuses to soften with time. Nettie constantly feels her mother's body as another reproach, a pointed criticism of her own broad-boned, gently sagging body. "Oh, he was just wondering whether we'd heard from Timmy, who has apparently gone off in a sulk somewhere."

Knowing there's no way she could possibly take a single bite from her brownie under the combined glare of the overhead light and her mother's gaze, Nettie chooses to head toward the living room. To do so, she has to pass by her mother in the doorway, and for a moment it seems the fierce old lady will actually bar the way.

"What do you mean? What do you mean?" Mom says, following hot on her heels.

"He's holed up somewhere. Just to think things over," Nettie says.

"Holed up where? What on earth do you mean—holed up? Holed up?" The phrase might as well be *hold up,* for the inflammatory tone she gives it. Somewhere in the background of this conversation is the subject, never abandoned for long, of Timmy's mugging at knife point. The world has taken one of the twins, the elder twin, but oh Lord save us all, it isn't satisfied, is it? It wants the other, the younger.

"I don't know *where.* Isn't that the whole point? I mean if he'd actually told everybody, he wouldn't be off on his own at all, now would he?"

"But where *is* he?"

Nettie lets out a sigh that wafts away to join all of the other sighs—hundreds, thousands of sighs—her mother has provoked over the years. Yes, it's just like Mom to repeat a question that has already received an answer—to repeat it, but more emphatically, as if to say she knows that information is being withheld.

"Well we don't *know* where," Nettie says. "Of *course* we don't know. That's the point, isn't it?"

"Why would he go off on his own like that?"

"Well that's what I was just explaining . . ."

"What do you mean go *off?* Why in the name of heaven would he go *off?*"

Behind her question, of course, lurks Garner's assumption—the belief that Timmy's behavior must have some logical explanation. And there was no point—even less point with Mom than with Garner—in simply saying *How should I know why a semi-lunatic behaves the way he does?*

Her whole life long, Mom has resisted a notion that Gerry—as an outsider, an in-law—perceived right at the very start. They're all half mad, the men in the Briggs family. Loony, loopy, screwy, bananas, barmy, crackers, bats in the belfry, mad as hatters—Gerry could be quite funny on the subject. Mom, on the other hand, will complain about this aspect of the men, or that one, especially their coldness—which is a running refrain for her, and leads her to all sorts of crackpot theories about "chill Icelandic blood"—but she refuses to look at the big picture . . . To see that they are—the deceased father as well as the two remaining sons—not merely cold and remote but also insensitive in the most basic and the most inexcusable ways . . . They live in their own world, and simply fail to notice the trouble and the hardship they inflict on others. *Why can't you see that?* she wants to ask. *Look at the way your two boys refused to acknowledge your illness, absolutely refused when you were quite ill not so long ago.* Look, mother, *look.* And look to see how, father and sons alike, astonishingly *incapable* all of them are as well . . . put them out into the world, the real world of jobs and children's mouths to feed, and none of them would last a day.

Nettie settles her big body in the living room's Naugahyde Multi-lazer and begins to chew thoughtfully on her brownie. She listens to her mother, who is perched with birdlike lightness on the very edge of the sofa, with a sense of pity. It is only lately, and especially during this most recent visit, that Nettie has been able to see her mother with real pity. Before, a certain amount of resentment always crept in. But it is a cause for pity rather than resentment that Mom is a woman who has allowed herself to suffer all her life from the immaturity and selfishness of the men around her. She has done this to herself. The place where she might have found true family love, in her daughter, a woman-to-woman and equal-to-equal love, was a place where she would never have thought to look.

Well, here the two of them are, anyway, mother and daughter, and much talk will have to pass before there can be any thought of returning to bed. Nettie knows she will have to soothe and reassure, nod and listen, nod and listen, as the slow minutes pass, and whatever pleasure there is to this scene resides purely in the brownie. And taking a slightly perverse pleasure in the face of her mother's glaring disapproval (but taking a healthy pleasure in the butter-bottomed brownie itself, which is strewn with walnuts and topped with fudge sauce), Nettie consumes it slowly, rolling it on her tongue. She has lived so long beside her mother's disapproval that at this point in her life approval might well be harder to bear, psychologically. And it is no accident, Nettie has come to understand in recent years, that the only woman Mom ever really turned to for support and solace was old Harriet Dwiggins, who lies buried now in Grower's Hill, that muddy, pitifully run-down little cemetery in Elizabeth, Indiana. There's no denying that in the end things have turned out as Harriet would have wished—badly. Garner had been right about her, anyway—that horrible old vulture had fed on the blood of misfortune. It was her daily tonic. And this was the sort of woman Mom had made her closest, perhaps her only true and lifelong, friend.

Garner used to call her Harriet Heartbreak. Perhaps it *had* been cruel of him not to come back for the funeral, which Mom so many times asked him to do, but Garner had been angry with Harriet, unappeasably angry, having come to believe that she had worked on Mom like a poison. It was a theory that would explain, anyway, why Mom seemed happier with lovelessness than with love, and seems to feel bitter toward her only daughter for having a loving husband—or how else explain the way Mom speaks of Gerry even today?

Nettie finishes the entire brownie, all but a blob of frosting fallen on her plate. When Mom finally gets off the subject of Timmy, it is only to recount the tale of a minister's murder in Key Largo (mistaken for a drug smuggler, according to the police), and Nettie smiles inwardly, at the memory of Kenny, her third son, taking just such a blob of frosting this afternoon and flattening it upon his nose. *Why did you do that, young man?* And what heart could resist his matter-of-fact response: *I wanted to see what it felt like on my nose.*

It is hard to believe, when you live beside children, and you feel each day their natural high spirits, that any kid could ever learn, however many years might elapse, to feed on gloom instead of joy. Her own never will. Never, not in a hundred years, will any of her own kids turn out that way. For that's the one solid gift she has given each one of her children, and it's the one gift she alone possesses in that oddball mix that makes up the Briggs family. She would have her children delight in the everyday. They will praise music, and trees, and television, and meatloaf, and the morning sun. "It's a question of what the world owes you, owes you after a lifetime of hard work," Mom is saying. "Now I am speaking not on my own behalf. The good Lord knows I have nothing to complain about. It's the way others are treated on this earth. After giving a lifetime to this place."

"Oh, it isn't fair," Nettie says—soothingly. She has committed her grave sin, she has consumed that waxy wedge of chocolate right before her mother's eyes, but that transgression is behind them now. They can take up their old roles—the only ones, perhaps, they are ever to be comfortable with. Grievance and the easing of grief, one by one, mother and daughter, now into eternity. Nettie longs to sleep. She must rise early—must get Stevie and Dougie on the 7:50 bus, pack Kelly a lunch yet, and find some time tomorrow to get Freddy and Jeannie to the shoe store and maybe, if he isn't better, take Ricky to the pediatrician. "But everything turns out all right in the end," Nettie says. "One just has to wait and see." She longs for bed, but she can't leave her mother alone. That's clear. She must wait for this tireless old woman to tire, for this endless circle of words to reach an end.

XXVII

"I JUST *FEEL* that he's all right," Nettie has offered, by way of reassurance, but Garner lacks his sister's faith in intuition . . . In fact, with his temperamental distrust of any outlet of the truth that proves unforthcoming about its sources, her words unnerve as much as solace him. And yet, whatever such feelings are worth, as he sits waiting inside the Topples Auditorium the conviction within him hardens into certainty that Timothy will not appear for the game today. Nearly forty-eight hours have elapsed since anyone last saw or heard from him, and unquestionably something must soon—very soon—be done. Any moment now, any blessed moment, Timothy could come striding in (or shambling in, since Timothy has never strode anywhere in his life), and the match proceed as scheduled, and no one outside the family be any the wiser. But in his heart Garner somehow knows that Timothy is not about to materialize. His intuition tells him so.

Garner shows up at the auditorium an hour before "game time." Imre, meanwhile, waits behind at the hotel. Garner watches with a tightening feeling of discomfort—a feeling of horror, really—as people file in, as tables and cameras are set up. ANNDY's screen begins to flash. I'M HUNGRY, it says. I'M HUNGRY . . . I'M HUNGRY . . . It has been years since Garner last felt quite this degree of acute discomfort. He longs, as the crowd grows, as Timothy's disappearance with each passing moment becomes a graver delinquency, to cancel the game—and yet there is always the tantalizing chance that Timothy will appear and every accumulating moment of damage be undone at a stroke. WHAT'S FOR LUNCH? WHAT'S FOR LUNCH? Still, it's ghastly—to have nothing to do but to wait without hope. Although the auditorium is cool, Garner feels himself sweating. His chest, his back, his legs—all are filmed with a cold sweat, and it's an unexpected but enormous relief when, her black hair swaying, Vicky Schmidt appears, carrying a briefcase. "I'd better warn you," Garner rushes to tell her, "that today's game may have to be cancelled. My brother's really tired. It's all the strain, you see. It's made him very tired and he's out in the country resting up. When I talked to him this morning, he said he might be down for the match and then again he might not. He's entitled to an adjournment, Imre tells me, and it may be he'll take it today."

"An adjournment? Shouldn't he tell me *now*? Shouldn't he tell everybody *now*, before they go to any more bother?" Perhaps she's merely rattled at the news—but Vicky seems genuinely angry. She can be quite abrupt, almost abrasive, Garner realizes in surprise; the giggling and joking had concealed from him this other side of her.

"Well he *is* going to try to make it. He said this morning he is definitely going to try to—"

But a shrewd hard probing light has now pierced Vicky's ebony eyes. "Where in the country?" she interrupts.

"I beg your pardon?"

"Where in the country is Tim staying?"

The moment is very brief during which this question strikes Garner speechless—and yet ample enough for him both to understand again that he should have prepared a fuller story and to marvel once more at his own clumsiness when called upon for alibis. "With some friends in Heath, Massachusetts," Garner says—the very place (*how devious the mind!*) where he himself first heard about this tournament.

"What friends are these?" Vicky presses.

Garner had not expected this sort of pressure from her. Without thinking much about it, he had assumed that she would respect the bonds and privacies of family. But her manner suggests, confusingly enough, that she is on the inside—that she is an understood intimate. "Family friends," he tells her. "Old family friends."

Vicky responds with only the most minimal of nods. She will accept this—just. And yet his sense that she, too, is someone who must be deceived, one more member of that great, unfocused opposition which Garner feels gathering around him, abruptly collapses. Having tried to keep her at a distance, he now blurts out an embracing plea: "Vicky, what are we going to do about all of this?"

"What do you mean, Garner?"

"But what will we do if he doesn't show up?"

"Well, we'll do just what you said. We'll call an adjournment." She places a quelling hand, a long-nailed and neatly manicured hand, upon his arm. "I better go lay the groundwork," she says. "There's going to be some really *pissed off* people around here."

"Oh I hope not."

Garner may mistrust Vicky, and may resent the frontal fashion in which she pries at him, but in the end he must be grateful to her. When, five minutes after the game was officially to commence, she mounts the stage and takes the microphone, her delivery is faultless—an adroit blend of humor and girlish contrition and businesslike offhandedness which disperses the crowd with a minimum of resentful buzzing. "Will you have him call me, Garner?" Vicky asks. Briefcase in hand, she is heading back to the office.

"I want to thank you—"

"Are you leaving now? I'll walk out with you . . ."

"Oh, I think I'll sit here and wait a bit."

"Wait for what?"

"For—for nothing really. But I just—"

"Have him call me. To*day,* Garner."

"Yes, I'll do that . . ."

Waiting for nothing, perhaps, Garner resumes his seat in the third row of the auditorium. There's always the off chance that his brother may yet appear. And if not, this seems as good a place as any to sit and think—and there's a great deal of thinking that must be done. His brother is what the law would call a "missing person" and something needs to be done . . . For nearly an hour, in a room that before long has emptied out completely, Garner sits and ponders—vainly hoping to come upon some lucid solution. But it is not lucidity that emerges . . .

The lucidity of hindsight, on the other hand, tells him, when he reponders all of these events some time later, that it was while he was sitting alone in the Topples Auditorium that the details surrounding his brother's disappearance first floated irretrievably into unreality. Or is this a simplification? There can be no denying, certainly, that the events of subsequent hours and days are later recalled only through a screen, a blur . . . The very air changes, it swims with invisible hallucinants, and the tactile sharpness of the everyday world melts away.

Unreal—completely unreal—Garner's trip that afternoon to the Cambridge Police Headquarters, there to be told to wait on a bench for a Sergeant Muldoon, who turns out to be not the expected, beefy-bellied Irish cop but a tall, rangy, indeterminately Asiatic man with a thin, droopy mustache. Unreal—all the questions, and the multiracial, wisecracking cast of police officers, and the parti-colored forms to be filled out. None of this ever happened, surely, even if the police records, and eventually the newspapers, would say otherwise. Unreal—the blowsy-faced woman sitting on a bench in the station beside Garner, a piece of dingy cotton tape spread over the bridge of her nose, who leans over to confide with breath that reeks of alcohol, "It's those drugs, dear, are killing my son." Unreal, surely—the filthy little girl in the corridor, face exotically dark as a Gypsy's, who shrieks at the man who drags her by the arm, "My mother's a witch, she's a witchy witchy *witch,* and she'll kill you dead on the ground, mister."

And unreal all the phone calls back and forth from Cambridge to Todsville. And most unreal of all, and yet even now all but unbearable to contemplate (like some dream whose residues of shame are so intense that the dream's own unreality seems secondary in the face of them), is that eventual call from Nettie: "I'm sorry, Garner, but Mom did it all right—she did it in spades. Not only the newspapers but the TV, too. She asked to be put on the TV. She wants to make some sort of appeal. I don't know if they'll let her. But, she says she's the only one who can get him to come out of hiding."

Do these events need to be dwelt upon? Or can the very brevity of their documentation here attest to what is for Garner their most significant legacy—an enduring, gnawing mortification, the ineradicable presence in his life of a cluster of events which never fail, whenever he returns to them, and regardless of where he is, or what time it is—never fail, no, to make his cringing soul wince and squirm? Is there any need to catalog each of the telephone calls from the newspapers (and how did *they* get hold of his unlisted number?), and each of Garner's bewildered and surly replies? Will this account be any the less honest or affecting if little attempt is made to recreate that string of ghastly, unappeasable calls which led to the final and laughable absurdity of Garner's, as the phrase goes, "calling a press conference"? The thought of himself sitting there, before a ravenous pack of journalists and cameramen (whose faces said WE'RE HUNGRY; whose faces said WHAT'S FOR LUNCH?), horrified him then, and horrifies him now, and no doubt will horrify him forever . . . And yet what else was a person to do, precisely, when for the last four days his brother had vanished off the face of the earth?

What else do you do but try to think, and drift sweat-limbed through an unreal world, and make snappishly pedantic replies to repetitious, intrusive questions ("No, I didn't say he was missing. I said we don't know where he is. He knows precisely where he is, I'm sure. You are falling into that hoary solipsistic trap by which . . .") and wait, and try to sleep when you can . . .

To sleep until the phone wakes you (what time is it this time?

It can't be too late, because the lights in Ben's Pizza are still burning . . .) and a tiny girlish voice says, "Is it Garner?"

"I believe so."

"Maybe you don't remember me. This is Linda Faccione. In Victoria."

His wits are still sleep-dazed; Garner hears "Victoria" and thinks of Vicky Schmidt, or someone who is almost like her, for the name Linda Faccione is blurredly familiar and throws its own vague facial overlay upon the disembodied voice in his ear.

"I'm calling about Timmy," the little voice continues and with these words Garner comes instantly awake: this is *that* Linda, Timothy's high school sweetheart.

A promise of egress is in the offing . . . It's here, maybe: *a way out,* a release from the horrors of these last few days, and Garner can hardly keep the shaky hopefulness out of his clipped reply: "What about him?"

"Well—he's here. I mean not here—but here in Victoria?"

"In Victoria? What's he doing in Victoria? Is he with you now? Do you have a number for him?"

"Well." The voice falters. Fragile—Garner feels her shying hesitancy at the other end of this telephone line, which is a lifeline, and may at any moment be cut. "Well I don't have a number for him, no. But he wants you to come out here. You think you could? It's sort of a . . . well a demand of his, a nonnegotiable demand," she states, but her voice is timid, uncertain—an importunate cry for help. "I mean maybe it's a good idea if just you were to come out. You know, I mean without your mother or—or Imre."

"Is he there now?" Garner asks, and into the dark silent abyss this question creates he tosses another question: "Is Timothy with you at the moment? I'd like to speak to him. Just for a moment?"

A muffling hand climbs inaudibly but unmistakably over the mouth of the receiver. After a pause, Linda says, "No," a little breathlessly. "He's not here now. But if you come out here, I'll take you to him."

"And is he all right?"

"Oh he's just *fine,*" Linda says with an unexpected cheerfulness; and adds, more unexpected still, and as if she honestly thought the question had encompassed her as well—"Both of us, we're just fine."

"You can't give me a phone number, Linda?"

"He wants you to come out here, Garner. It's important that you're *here.* He says"—and she pauses once more, and Garner knows she is about to say something peculiar—"he says he wants you to come home."

Garner exhales into the mouthpiece. "All right," he says. "I can be there by tomorrow night, Linda. Now you tell Timothy not to do a thing: I'll be there tomorrow night."

"You can fly to Chicago. That's probably the fastest way," Linda says.

"I don't fly," Garner tells her. "But I'll get there by tomorrow, anyway. And you can tell him that. But now I need to know how I'll find you . . ."

"Garner, you've got to promise that you won't tell a soul. That's nonnegotiable."

"Okay, I promise," Garner says. "Now I've got a pen and paper ready, if you'll just let me know how I can find you."

"No. No," this little girl's voice insists. "I mean *really* promise. Tim says you've got to repeat that you won't tell anyone."

"Is he there now, Linda? I'd like to speak to him for just a minute. One minute is all . . ."

"He told me to say the whole thing's off if you won't really promise . . ."

"I promise not to tell a living soul about this phone call," Garner declares.

"I'm on Cashew Avenue, number 16A. It's upstairs. You remember Cashew, don't you?"

"Cashew, Linda? Like the peanut?"

"Oh Garner, you always—no, no. Cadjew."

"How would you spell that, Linda?"

"C-A-D-I-E-U-X," Linda says. "It's foreign. You remember where it is?"

"I'm afraid it's been a number of years since I was in Victoria . . ."

"You remember where Frank and Angela's was? The market? Well, it's not there now. Because Frank drowned, up at Willetts Creek. But it's right there on the street where the market was."

"I'll find it. That's 16A Cadieux," Garner says.

"It's a white house," Linda says. "It's peeling kind of. And there's a sort of a white fence that goes round it. And in the backyard—you can see the backyard from the sidewalk—there's a swing set but instead of a regular swing there's an inner tube and a kind of—"

"I'll find it," Garner says. He never has had any patience with those people who at the bottom of their souls believe a numerical identification to be insufficient. "I'll be there tomorrow. By tomorrow night at the latest."

"Hold on just a second, okay, Garner? Just a second." Again that swallowing palm climbs over the mouthpiece. "Listen, Garner, it's very important that you don't tell *any*one, okay? Is that okay? That's part of the bargain, okay?"

"I'll do my part," Garner says, and adds, a note of whining importunity in his own voice, "Linda. Just keep my brother there safe and sound, will you all right? Just keep him right there, if you please."

XXVIII

THE TELEPHONE CALL to borrow a friend's car, which turns into a call to borrow the friend as well, in the role of extra driver, and the bundling together of a couple of changes of clothes inside a suitcase, and the trip to the twenty-four-hour FRIENDLY TELLER, and the brief stop for gas and oil—all of this actually consumes very little time . . . Less than an hour after Linda's call, the little borrowed Toyota is speeding along the Massachusetts Turnpike—and yet Garner still feels that precious minutes have been wasted. Time spills away, hope recedes, and honor has already been compromised. But if he has broken the vow of silence which Linda extracted from him (and how else was the car to be borrowed for its nearly two-thousand-mile round-trip journey? was not the owner of the car—and fellow passenger—entitled to an explanation?), he does mean to keep it in spirit. Perhaps it's cruel not to let Doris know that her son has gone "home"—but to have her meddling in this affair could be disastrous. She, anyway, will not be told a word. It's the dead middle of the night, and a message has just come ringing out of the blackness, and everything must be handled carefully, oh so carefully, now.

Not until a couple of hours' driving has elapsed, and the border separating Massachusetts from New York been crossed, does some sense of ease enter the little car. It is as though the length of this interstate journey at last opens up before the two travelers, with its measured demands for steadiness and patience, its metered miles to be ticked off one by one. The mind settles down, begins to take in its surroundings . . . Those twinges of guilt that Garner will occasionally feel about his sedentary style of life, the vague sense that he should perhaps venture now and then outside Massachusetts—they are once again revealed as baseless. In this the final decade of what could well turn out to be mankind's final millennium, what sort of person is it who could honestly joy in traveling through America? Like any sane soul, Garner refuses to fly, and buses as a rule are unendurable. While the railroad occasionally serves up an unplanned charm, this is generally of that poignant, tainted sort which is common to the freshly dead or the lengthily moribund . . . To go clanking by a shunt yard where an old orange boxcar rusts among slash pine and juniper—a pleasure, perhaps, but, if so, a nostalgic one inseparable from the elegiac. Which leaves the automobile and the interstate highway system and is there a sensitive soul anywhere in the country who can truthfully say he has spent a pleasant hour on one of our superhighways? Chewing thoughtfully, let us say, on a vending-machine fruit pie whose wrapper announces, "Best if eaten within forty-five months of date stamped above," and staring out across a plundered landscape whose remaining clumps of trees look frightened, how could anyone escape a sense of numbed, paralyzing despair?

In the cramped darkness, loud rain begins to fall with clattering, solid-sounding drops, as though chains are being dragged across the roof. Garner, behind the steering wheel, flips on the windshield wipers and peers hard through those sudden slashings of light which the raindrops make as they plummet through the tunnel of the headlamps. He slows the car to forty-five miles per hour, and then to forty. He is feeling tired, and there are still hundreds of miles to go.

Rain gives way to mist. Stopping for gas somewhere in the middle of Pennsylvania, as the new day is sunlessly breaking, Garner climbs out of the car on his stiff legs to discover that the air is surprisingly, heavily warm. All sorts of queer, needling, tangy smells jostle in the air and it's as if something vast is approaching on the breeze—a storm, a forest fire. He lets himself be driven for a while, and dozes, and wakes to see a sign saying WELCOME TO OHIO, and when they stop for breakfast, or lunch, or whatever meal this now ought to be, the air has turned weighty and hot—the heat you might expect on a Plains state midsummer day. When, eventually, he reads the sign announcing INDIANA OFFERS YOU A BIG HOOSIER WELCOME, a shame he wouldn't have supposed was still responsive inside him awakens and rises through his fatigue. Yes, this is unrenounceably it—his home state. The sky is dark once more when he pulls into a motel on the outskirts of Victoria ("We've got all the channels" their billboard boasts), and he speedily showers, shaves, changes his clothes. The muggy bathroom reeks of artificial pine scent. He is given directions to Cadieux Avenue by an old woman at the reception desk, who confides (and one won't stop to speculate just how many times she has treated her guests to this information) that as a little girl she'd vowed never to eat a single clam or oyster in her life, and as God is her witness she has held fast to *that.* In his borrowed car, Garner sets off alone, the back of his shirt clinging to the seat, which is not so surprising, given both his nervousness and the amazing, freakish warmth of this night. He is off to find his brother.

The woman who answers the door at 16A Cadieux Avenue is no one he would recognize. She, too, seems bewildered by time's changes and peers dubiously at the gray-haired man who stands on her unlit porch. "Garner?" she says.

"Linda?" he says.

The last time Garner saw her, some four or so years before, Linda had been a pretty creature. Even if she had always struck him as something of a sad case (one of a number of sad cases; they were a well-publicized mess in Victoria, that enormous Faccione family, one or two of whose wayward brood had actually wound up in jail), there had been something endearing about her. Back then, she had been comely in a stringy, tomboyish fashion; now, she stands before Garner as a plump-faced, dumpy-bodied young woman. Linda peers past Garner, glances up and down the street. "You alone?" she asks.

"Isn't that what you wanted?"

Linda smiles at him and only now can Garner see, barely recoverable within the face of this prematurely dowdy woman, something of that scampering, light-footed teenager. She holds out her hand and Garner shakes it. Her clasp feels nervous but her greeting is almost laughably casual. "So nice of you to come," she says—as though he'd driven across town rather than across the country to reach her door. "Well, come on in."

Linda leads him into what he supposes is her living room. The first thing he notices is its mustiness. The second is that her hi-fi and her television set are running simultaneously at low volume. "Have a seat, have a seat," Linda says. "I'm going to take you to him real soon."

After a glance at the sofa, which is strewn with cat hair, Garner seats himself in a metal folding chair beside the television.

"I'll be right back," Linda says. She steps through an inner door and snaps it shut behind her. "Turn off the music if you want," she yells from somewhere within, and adds, which is completely untrue, "I remember you don't like music."

Garner rises from his chair and, feeling just a little like a detective in a seedy movie, begins an inspection of the room. His immediate impression is of a deep, abiding disorder, although in truth the place has been recently tidied and except for some newspapers on the floor and an open can of beer atop the television there is little that looks definitely out of place. Though he finds no clear evidence that Timothy has been here, the crumpled cardboard box of a take-out pizza in the wastebasket may be a positive sign. Its cover contains a number of small circles in which X's have been drawn through those corresponding to "pepperoni" and "ground beef" . . . Timothy has never liked vegetables. Underneath the pizza box is a frayed argyle sock with a big hole in the heel, and wouldn't it be just like Timothy to throw away one and keep the other of a unique pair of socks? "Garner," Linda calls and his eyes jump guiltily from the wastebasket. He hadn't heard the opening of the door. "Actually," she begins, and she pauses. She remains in the doorway.

"Actually I don't have to take you *any*where to see him, you see, because, well . . ." and it's superfluous, the rest of her sentence, since, behind her, in the shadowed hallway, Timothy's sandy head has materialized.

"Hi, Garner." The voice is strangely airy.

"Hello."

Timothy comes forward, his hand extended. Garner had imagined all sorts of things—but Timothy on the whole looks healthy. He is pale, though, and there is maybe something feverish in the brightness of his eyes. "You drove, huh?" Timothy says, as the two brothers shake hands.

"The whole way."

"My brother doesn't fly," Timothy tells Linda, with a queer boastfulness in his voice.

"You wanna beer, Garner?" Linda asks.

"I'll have a beer," Timothy says before Garner can answer.

"Sure, yes, I'll have a beer," Garner says.

"There's pot there, if you'd rather," Linda calls from what must be the kitchen. "On the table by the sofa."

In his rounds as detective Garner had failed to notice them—the three narrow, pinched-looking cigarettes in the scalloped seashell that serves as both cigarette case and ashtray. "I don't smoke it much either," Linda says, returning with two open cans of beer in one hand, an open bag of Frank's French Fry Flavor Potato Chips and an open bag of Smiley's Smoky Cheese Pretzels in the other. "Except during my time of the month. It's better than medicines. I don't really believe in medicines. Unless they're natural."

Linda hands one of the cans of beer to Garner and the other to Timothy, goes over and retrieves the third can of beer from the top of the television, and carries it over to the couch. She sits down beside Timothy and drinks deeply. "Cheers," she says. "Garner, have a seat."

"Have a seat," Timothy repeats and drinks with a jerking quickness from his own can. He takes Linda's free hand in his, throws down another jerking swallow of beer, and says, "We're going to get married."

"Well," Garner says. "Congratulations."

"Thank you," Timothy says.

"Wow, huh?" Linda says. "You're the very first person we've told."

"Well it's a big step," Garner says.

"Oh I *know,*" Linda says. "On account of having been married once before."

"Any children?" Garner asks.

"I miscarried it. The whole thing was so fast, pregnancy, marriage, well it's as if I never *was* married. I don't think of myself as having ever been married. Except legally."

"The spirit is another matter, I suppose . . ."

"But the doctors all said it was a fluke. The miscarriage. He told me—Go out and try, try again."

"That's encouraging," Garner says.

"Sit down, Garner," Linda says.

"Do the two of you plan a long engagement?"

"Well we haven't set an exact date yet," Linda says.

"I have to talk to Mom first," Timothy says. "But it won't be for a couple of months maybe."

"We don't want to rush into things," Linda adds.

"And what exactly are your short-term plans?"

"Well I don't know," Timothy says. "I don't know *exactly.*" Timothy exchanges a glance with his fiancée. The look he gives her is clearly of a See-what-I-mean? variety, although it isn't quite clear to Garner what this question of his has verified in Timothy's mind.

"Oh yes you do," Linda says to him, with a sort of congenial/ conjugal firmness. She smiles broadly at her husband-to-be. "You're going back to Boston."

He smiles in turn at his future bride. "Yes, we're going back to Boston, Linda and I."

"And Timmy's going to beat that nasty machine," Linda says. "I know he can do it. Have a seat, Garner."

"Yes, I'm going to beat ANNDY," Timothy says. "And we'll use some of the prize money to go on our honeymoon. I thought maybe we'd go to Hawaii for our honeymoon. Out on the beach."

"I told him it's too expensive. But you know how Timmy is."

"I suppose I do," Garner says.

"We got to be practical. I told him I'd rather go to Florida, there are plenty of beaches there, where his mom is. Jesus, won't she be surprised to have *me* back in her life? I just hope she doesn't mind about the divorce. But honestly, it was a learning thing. That's the thing about it. That's what I keep telling Timmy about the games he's lost so far. Learning is always a many-mistakes kind of thing. Have a seat, Garner."

"She won't mind," Timothy tells her. "She's always liked you."

"In a way . . ."

"Oh, that's just the way she is."

"There's spaghetti, Garner. I didn't know when you'd get here, so I made spaghetti because you just have to heat it up. I hope you like spaghetti."

"He likes spaghetti," Timothy says. "That's the one thing with spaghetti. Everybody likes it."

Garner is served spaghetti with meat sauce, garlic bread, something called chocolate tapioca pudding cake, and—no tea being available—a cup of instant coffee. The kitchen is hot, but not uncomfortably so. The atmosphere is, in an utterly daft sort of way, surprisingly homey—cozily domestic. At the outset of the meal, Garner asks Linda about her family, and from that moment there's no need to worry about making conversation. She has so much to tell—including the unexpected news that Frankie (who according to Garner's not altogether reliable memory of Victoria life is one of the brothers who'd once been jailed) is now a policeman. Is this possible? Could he have been in reform school rather than jail—or was it a different brother who'd once been locked up? Somehow, Garner doesn't yet feel he can ask his sister-in-law-to-be to straighten this out for him.

"Jesus, it's hot in here," Linda concludes.

"And outside, too," Garner says. "Quite astonishingly warm."

"The weatherman, he said it was going to be some sort of complete record temperature maybe. For this time of year."

"How's Imre?" This from Timothy, whose question momentarily silences the table.

"Actually, he's very worried." Garner sips from his instant coffee. "About you. A lot of people have been worried. And we'd better call some of them right now. And the first one you'd better call is Doris."

"Tomorrow."

"But—but why wait? When you have so much good news for her? She'll want to hear your news. To share it with you."

"Tomorrow."

"But you can't do this," Garner continues, firmly but mildly. "Don't you honestly see that you can't do this? For all she knows, you might be dead." This isn't strictly true—since Garner, lying to her as well, finally wove for her a reassuring tale. She had been working herself into such a wild state that he'd begun to fear she might actually suffer the nervous breakdown she'd threatened since time immemorial; and so, the night before last, he'd told her an absolute fabrication. He'd received a telephone call from Timothy, he'd informed her, who had emerged from limbo sounding fine (although still refusing to reveal his exact whereabouts), and who had reported that he was resting up in a hotel and would return soon to conclude the match. And as he'd spun this out, Garner had been aware of the remote and yet not negligible possibility that his brother was dead—and that he himself might in a few days' time find himself trying to explain away the story of the mysterious phone call to a skeptical police officer.

"Tomorrow," Timothy repeats with a rising inflection that converts the words into a mix of question and plea. His eyes implore.

"Is that a promise, Timothy?"

"That's a promise."

"Tomorrow morning?"

"All right, all right, Jesus, tomorrow morning."

"And you'll call everybody?"

"Everybody."

"And no more funny business?"

Timothy's response is a pouting, aggrieved look—as if this characterization were grossly unfair. He sighs loudly. "I promise . . ." he chants.

"He just needed time to think. He was confused," Linda says.

"Yes. I was confused."

"And you have also confused a number of people," Garner says. "You have people all over the country wondering where you are."

"And nobody guessed." In a flash, the aggrieved look has vanished utterly from Timothy's face. As he sips from his coffee, his eyes over the rim of the cup shine with marveling pride.

"I'm good at keeping secrets," Linda says.

"You're good at a lot of things, honey." Timothy pats her hand on the table.

"I still think you ought to call Doris tonight."

"Tomorrow. She's probably asleep by now. Tomorrow *morning,* Garner. That's what we just agreed, isn't it? Isn't it? I thought we'd go for a walk tonight. That's the point. There are still a few things I wanted to talk about."

"Is it raining?" Linda asks. "Do you think it's still raining?"

"We'll be okay."

"Take my umbrella."

"Nah—I'll just wear this."

Timothy throws the hood of his sweatshirt over his head, pulls the drawstring tight, and ties a bow beneath his chin. With the hood fitting so snugly, his face becomes a little white disc, in which his eyes burn with fierce boyish satisfaction. "Linda went out and got it for me," he tells his brother. "This way, no one's going to recognize me."

After the warmth of the kitchen, Garner looks forward to a coolness outdoors, but it turns out that the temperature hasn't dropped in the slightest. If anything, it has risen. Surely Linda is right and this night represents some sort of meteorological record. It is a hot midsummer evening in Victoria, Indiana, although the trees are bare and wet autumn leaves lie thick underfoot. To be back in this town at all would be sufficiently strange, but to be walking these streets on a midsummer night in November is almost too much to compass; Garner's head swoons in the dark. "I'm afraid I don't understand why you left," he says. "Or why you didn't tell anybody."

"Garner, can I ask you something?"

"Why not?" Garner says, but adds, perhaps because the request makes him slightly uneasy, "Though I would have thought *I'd* be asking most of the questions tonight . . ."

"Garner, do you believe in Fate?"

"Well I don't honestly know what you mean by that. Do you mean predestination? Or some sort of lack of—"

"What I mean is, well I was being *told* to come back here. To

Linda. I didn't know it exactly, when I left Boston, but I knew all along that we belong together. Something was directing me—you know what I mean? Something inside, that I just had to be quiet and listen to. People don't know how to listen to themselves. *Some*thing inside knew better than I did what I was doing."

"You're speaking of the unconscious?"

As they reach the end of Cadieux Avenue, Garner feels a teasing, flickering tickle in his chest—a little bit like the itch in the throat that precedes a sneeze. *It is all coming back!* Once more, it is all coming back and Victoria is enfolding him . . . He has come back home, or at least to his hometown, and the place is doing what hometowns do best: it is swallowing him whole. They turn from Cadieux onto Hannibal Boulevard and there's a kind of vertiginous rightness in the way Hannibal's tangible, substantial homes drop so snugly into the niches his mind had excavated for them.

"Well not exactly. But sort of," Timothy says. "Obviously at least sort of."

It was down Hannibal Boulevard that Garner used to walk toward the junior high school, Gumble Junior High School, over on Apollo Avenue. Oh, this weather is *extraordinary,* and not merely the temperature: all illusory, no doubt, and a simple result of the unseasonable warmth, and yet it would seem that the street's odors, too, belong not to November but to June . . . Not the rich cool fetor of rotting leaves, the tang of smoke and autumnal acids, but the profligate upwellings of banked lilacs and lilies and roses!

"It's funny you should mention that, the unconscious," Timothy goes on. "Because actually I've had this new idea about what I'm going to do. I mean after chess. I'll go on with chess a couple years, see how far I can get, but eventually I've got to make a steadier living. I mean I've discussed this all with Linda. She'll kind of have to support me maybe a bit, while I'm pursuing chess, although who knows maybe I'll become national champ, I think Imre thinks so, and there's more money in it than people think. I can give lessons and demonstrations and maybe a regular television show. Public television, probably," Timothy says. "At least at first. At this point I do have what they call face recognition."

"But you were talking about what you're going to do eventually."

"Oh," Timothy says. "Well a psychiatrist."

"Mm?" By keeping his lips clamped shut, Garner manages to keep wholly inaudible the guffaw that echoes in his head. Even more commendably, he quells the obvious impulse to refurbish an ancient joke by pointing out that anybody who would go to Timothy for emotional help definitely needed to see a psychiatrist.

"Reuben Fine, he was a psychiatrist," Timothy says.

"He was a chess player?"

"Best in the country—maybe best in the world. For a while. But chess is just a game."

"It's a little surprising to hear that from you."

"Oh well, I'm much more ambitious than that. That's one of the things being with Linda's cleared up for me. The way I need to focus my ambitions. You know why I want to be a psychiatrist?" Timothy asks, and goes on to answer his own question with an ingenuous directness that is unexpectedly touching: "I want to figure things out."

"Well so do I," Garner tells him.

"Oh sure, well that's sort of what you're doing, isn't it?"

"Sort of."

A ripe summer moon spills a gentle, buttery light down through the emptied branches of the old maples on Hannibal Boulevard and onto the brick facade of the Victoria Town Fire Station as the two brothers turn onto Soldiers Way. But—but the sturdy, pillared fire station is no longer a fire station.

"What in the world . . ." Garner says, although it is abundantly clear what has happened here.

The fire station has become Lucky's Video Rental.

"They didn't need both stations any more. So they moved it all over to the one in Elizabeth."

If there is a measure of fiscal logic in this, there is an almost surreal irony as well. It would have been hard to dream up a more pointed civic descent than this one . . . HOT HOT HOT is one of the messages in the window of the old fire station, but this signifies flame of an altogether different sort, for it seems that much of Lucky's business lies in "adult entertainment." A poster for a film called *Hooker Hospital Holiday* is one of Lucky's star attractions. *Good Girls in the Gutter* is another. But a close inspection reveals even a better, indeed a crowning stroke . . . Lucky has left untouched the message that the original architects etched into the stone architrave: SACRED OUR DUTY AS THE HOME IS SACRED.

Soldiers Way, the main street of Victoria, extends before them. Even from here, a couple of blocks from what is probably still called the "downtown," it is evident that the fire station is hardly alone in having seen a transformation. The geometry is unfamiliar: new facades have been affixed, buildings have been rubbled. And even this late at night, and on this gentle an evening, it becomes clear, as the two of them amble down Soldiers Way, that in recent years Victoria has fallen on hard times. It's block after bedraggled block of tired or empty store windows, of signs that read HIGHLY DESIRABLE LOCATION and COMMERCIAL PROPERTY NOW AVAILABLE. Garner says, "I can't believe how much it's changed."

"What's changed?"

"Victoria."

"Linda says most of the business has gone out to the new mall. Out on Route 11."

Harrison's Drugs has metamorphosed into the Buysmart Pharmacy, Marianna's Coffee Shop into Flashpoint Jeans, Martin's Shoes into The Hungry Hero. And here where white-haired Red wielded a buzzing electric hair clipper, there's now a Factory Shoe Outlet. A new row of parking meters, a number of them nudged or rammed out of perpendicular, begins in front of what was once the Victorian Musical Academy. It is now the St. James's Parish Credit Union. "I have to get off of this *street*," Garner says. "It's too depressing."

They turn onto—but what's this one's name? The syllables seem to ring in his memory one millisecond before he picks out the street sign in the clean moonlight: Benzonia.

"But the weather's good. I heard on TV, it's the warmest for this time of year ever recorded or something." Timothy's voice has again gone oddly soft with a breathy, boyish wonder.

"Yes, it's amazing. It's summer once more and you look *extremely* silly wearing that hood over your head."

"I've been wearing it whenever I go out. I know a lot of people in this town."

"It's summer again and you know," Garner confides, "it all makes me so *nervous*. I suppose the thing to do is to enjoy weather like this while it lasts, but I can't, somehow. Under the circumstances, given what we're doing to the globe, enjoyment seems irresponsible. You want to hear an odd fact? You know something, Timothy? As I get older, I can feel our father emerging in me. Or trying to emerge. You know that old witticism that says that in every fat person there's a thin one trying desperately to get out? Well at some point a man may see, perhaps when he enters his thirties, that in almost every son there's a father trying to get out. Your own father. You know, I feel the *oddest* impulse to start clipping newspaper articles. I honestly do. I have to restrain myself. Otherwise—oh Lord save us, you know where *that* leads . . . But I'm absolutely convinced that the weather; the long-term, worldwide weather—by which I guess I mean the climate, don't I? I'm convinced that it's going to Hell."

The sound of *Hell* echoes unreally in the air—as unreal, and as giddying in its way, as the night's phantom lilacs and lilies and roses. Garner goes on: "I'll see an article that says it snowed in Miami or it was ninety-five degrees in Fairbanks, Alaska, and I'll think to myself, *Hey, I'd better keep a record of this.* Maybe put them all in custom-made journals. The way *he* did."

"Imre says we're rapidly evolving toward a point where the weather's irrelevant. Animals, they're the ones that are so sensitive to weather and smells and stuff. He says we'll evolve right past all that. Our bodies won't even bother to register it."

"Somehow the thought doesn't reassure me as much as it might."

"You worry a lot." Soft-voiced, marveling, Timothy sounds drugged, as though he'd puffed on one of those sad, wizened little cigarettes in Linda's seashell ashtray. Or is his dreamy gentleness but one more kaleidoscopic shifting of a mind that in recent weeks might kindly be described as changeable? Or simply a chemical response to the weather—its madman's mix of moon and heat on this, the strangest night that ever has fallen over Victoria, Indiana?

"There were probably a few Aztecs who worried a bit when Cortés arrived, Timothy. In the end, it's all a question of whether the worrying's justified."

"I don't remember him all that well . . ."

"You don't remember whom?"

"Dad," Timothy says.

"Well I don't mean to be unkind, but there isn't that much *to* remember."

"I'd like to read the journals," Timothy announces.

This is not a request that needs to be met directly: Timothy has already been told what was done with the journals. By way of answer, Garner says, "The man never *worked,* never had a job. We all have to remember that. The whole time I was growing up, he was retired, or so we said, but he was much too young to be retired. You've got to see what a queer mind it was—that would choose to live like that."

The two brothers are strolling down Oxford Avenue, on their way, apparently, toward the house on Sweetwater where they grew up together. Who has been leading whom? Oxford, too, looks a bit shopworn, but the trees in recent years have been coming back into their own. There was a time, Garner recalls, before the blight of the Dutch elm disease, when the trees along Oxford made a high vaulted ceiling taller and grander than that of any church in Founders Valley.

"But I *would* like to read them . . ."

Clearly Timothy's remark is meant as a reproach—but only

in part as a reproach. There is, Garner senses, something naive and genuinely well intentioned in it as well. The reestablishing of relations, the unearthing of buried connections—the hope, in short, of raising the dead. Oh, Garner knows all about that!—and in his sorrow and rage, frustration and sympathy, he says what is not true, or what is, at least, too complex to be put so simply: "It's good to be back here. In Victoria."

"I'll probably move back here. Eventually," Timothy says.

"As a psychiatrist?"

"Or as a something else. I mean I may not be a psychiatrist forever. I'm going to do lots of things," Timothy says in that same voice of eerie, lighter-than-air tranquillity. "But Linda has family here. It's good to be with family. America needs stronger families . . ."

"And what would Linda do?"

"Where? Do where?"

"Wherever. Wherever you were to live. If you two were actually to get married."

"God that's so typical of you, Garner. Don't you see how typical of you that is? The way you put that?" The words are bellicose, but the tone remains wondering and detached. Or mostly so—for a flickering of true resentment may lurk here as well. "You put it in the hypothetical. As if you don't believe what I've told you. *If you two were actually to get married* . . . Honestly, Garner, now honestly," Timothy continues and his voice sharpens a little more. "Would you say that you believe in people?"

"Why don't you just ask me whether I believe in *life?* Don't you see? You keep tossing these absurdly simple questions at very complicated—"

"Life isn't simple," Timothy counters. "But it isn't complicated, either."

"It simply *is,* right? Like wow, is that it?"

"You don't want to listen," Timothy says. "Jesus, I've made some real discoveries in the last few days. The last few weeks. And you don't want to listen."

"You've made a real mess is what you've made," Garner declares, thereby violating at a stroke his private vow to treat his kid brother with kid gloves . . . But at this moment it almost seems as though Timothy suffers from nothing except pure wrongheadedness, and requires nothing more than having somebody point out for him, clearly and forcibly, just how misguided he is.

"That's so typical," Timothy replies. "That what I've done would look like a mess to you."

They have turned onto Sweetwater at last and drawn into sight of that old, gracefully mansarded structure. The house is still a good distance down the block, and partly concealed by the ancient pine that stands even now in the neighbor's yard, whose cones used to rain down upon the Briggs family's dining room roof. But there the ancestral house is—and it silences the two of them.

The street is quiet. Their footsteps on the sidewalk are muffled by the rain-pasted leaves. Down the street, in a dark car parked in the driveway of that neighbor's house, where the Rollings used to live, a door opens and a girl gets out and darts up to the Rollings' front porch and slips inside. The dark car fires and the invisible driver, who must be the girl's date, backs lightlessly down the driveway. The girl, too, had been all but invisible—just a youthful shimmer of blond hair in the concentrated darkness beneath the old pine—but she had evoked someone . . . Now, was it possible, could this possibly be Betsy, Betsy Rolling, the little blond girl who'd glinted from the dreary dark of that man's—their father's—journals? From his study window, old Boyce Briggs had watched her playing in her backyard, and he had recorded her changes. The date when Betsy broke her arm, the date when the cast was removed . . .

Garner's realization, a few moments later, that this could not possibly be Betsy (for the girl he'd just glimpsed had bounced like a teenager, and Betsy by now would be many years out of her teens—might even have a teenage daughter herself) is greatly saddening, somehow. A light, a mobile golden light, has been snuffed and the two brothers walk in silence until they halt, as one, before their old home. The moon falls squarely upon its sagging face, with such unstinting radiance that one can make out each blistered crater of peeling paint. And one might almost suppose that nothing had changed since those days when the neighborhood eccentric, Mr. Boyce Briggs, used to look up now and then from his golden coins to watch the neighbor's ten-year-old golden-haired girl chase a dog around her backyard—all the while, in her running, unmindfully calling to that seated man, beckoning him out, as though his soul might yet reverse its long, piecemeal campaign of withdrawal.

"I wonder who lives in our house now," Garner says, and notes with a sweet sense of bemusement how easily this "our" slips off his tongue.

"The Blottners. *You* know that." This arrives as another of Timothy's forceless reproaches. His voice is soft, chastened, faintly incredulous. "Mom talks about them only every twenty minutes. She can't *stand* them."

"I listen between the lines," Garner replies. His words go out, past Timothy, to the peeling, cratered house itself, whose look in the moonlight unsettles him. It seems to demand something of him and these words are uttered in propitiation . . . The house is dark except for one light burning in Doris's room—or what was once Doris's room. What was once Doris and Boyce's room. Oh, yes, it unsettles him, nerve and vein, bone and muscle—the house, the single light, the pressure of the moonlight on its cracked face, the shadows of the two Briggs brothers stretched upon the grass. Garner turns away, nudges Timothy to follow, begins to walk again. "One doesn't want to get too literal," Garner says.

"Nettie says it, too." Timothy goes on. "About you. You don't listen."

"But I do. You'll see, you'll all see . . ." This is offered with a sweep of the arm, in a spirit of parody, although Garner cannot quite recall which figure he mimics. An old film? Somebody lost in their distant Victoria past? "You wait. I'll show you all."

The two brothers proceed to the end of Sweetwater and it occurs to Garner that this may be the last time the two of them will walk together down this street, where over a gap of years their childhoods were lived, but at the corner he does not swing round for a final glimpsing. They turn onto Cairo Avenue and find that a couple of houses have been razed; there are vacant lots where there were no such lots before. The collapsed, wind-scavenged skeleton of a child's kite hangs by a thread to a telephone line. They cross the railroad tracks and enter the town of Elizabeth.

Victoria and Elizabeth, the sister villages, the regal twin towns, those competing souls, those bickering housebound spinsters . . . By now, a hundred years have probably elapsed since the first discussions took place on the vital and delicate issue of the advisability of dissolving all boundaries and merging the two communities into one. Petitions, town hall speeches, voters' polls and referenda, newspaper editorials and fact-finding commissions, have all sought to clarify and resolve this intricate issue—a debate that has been conducted for a century with a gravity suitable for negotiating, say, the reunification of a dogma-splintered church or of a war-torn nation. The old man's journals had been much taken up with the controversy—with the fierce pleas, the repeated calls for reduced acrimony and suspicion, the slurs and slanders, and all of the talk and counter-talk so impassioned that within these neighborhoods, anyway, one might never have noticed that history has alike passed by the two of them, Victoria and Elizabeth.

"People are blind," Timothy breaks the silence to announce. "You understand what I'm saying?"

"I suppose so. But then I'm not sure I follow—"

"It's just like the Reverend Rabbitt says. We have striven," Timothy begins and raises his voice a notch, "we have striven to conceal the truth from ourselves."

"Including the truth about him. Or so his wife would have us believe . . ."

"What do you mean? What are you saying about his wife?"

"Surely you've seen a newspaper in the last few days? His wife, the Filipino woman? She says—"

"She's a liar," Timothy affirms with a bitterness that surprises Garner. "She's nothing but a Goddamned liar."

"Well how do you know that? I mean would it actually surprise you? Given the way he treats himself?"

"He doesn't beat his wife, Goddamn it, Garner. She's a Goddamned liar is what she is."

"How can you possibly be so sure? Look at his background, everything that's recently come out about his childhood and his family—are those lies, too? I'm not blaming him, or at least not blaming him any more than I'm likely to blame anybody who beats another person. I'm simply saying that as a child he happened to see and experience a great deal of violence that—"

"They're lying, Garner. They're trying to drag him down. They want him to *fall.* Don't you see that, Garner?"

"Would it honestly surprise you to discover that this man who regularly takes a jackknife to himself on occasion also throws a punch at his wife?"

"You know what your trouble is?" Fury, or something very close kin to it, has set Timothy's voice broadly quavering. "You don't believe. You don't believe in any*one* or any*thing.*"

"I believe in clarity," Garner replies mildly. He finds his own pronouncement pleasing, and he continues, "I believe in necessary approximation, in mental rigor, and in the suspension of judgments. I believe in expiation, I suppose, and I believe as well in the, in the endless need for spiritual amendment."

"She's a Goddamned liar. She's trying to pull a great man *down.* That's what happens to great men sometimes. A woman will pull them down. Unless they find the right woman."

The two brothers turn onto Purcell Avenue, the main street of Elizabeth.

"As you recently have managed to do, I gather . . ."

"Yes, the way I have *now.* Fate has given us a second chance, me and Linda." The grandness of this declaration evidently makes Timothy self-conscious about his grammar. He tries again. "Linda and I. Fate has brought us together again."

"And you feel ready to play chess? You don't feel too distracted?"

"Oh I'm *ready,* of course I'm ready. It's a question of attitude. Of really wanting to win. I ask you—does that damn machine *want* to win? It can't stand up to me, it can't stand up to the human spirit. You'll see . . . The whole country will see . . . They won't be singing John Henry at me any more. No more John Henry—I'll make them sing a new song."

"Good Lord, look what they've done to Purcell," says Garner, partly to quell his brother's nonsensical talk, but partly out of genuine amazement. He would scarcely have recognized it.

"Someone needs to bring out the best in people," Timothy continues.

"What happened to Ben Franklin's?"

"Torn down," Timothy says. "*Long* ago."

Not a trace of the old dime store remains. Where once it stood, one now finds a little parking lot beneath a sign for The Sweet Buy and Buy Plaza. There's a liquor store, another videocassette tape rental outlet, a "unisex hair tailors," and a take-out pizzeria that is solely that; there are no seats inside. Beyond, the post office seems essentially unchanged, although posters about drug abuse now line the windows, one of them announcing that marijuana may have become Indiana's largest cash crop. And beyond the post office, the old Mercury Theatre still stands, or its building does. Its windows have been covered with plywood. The marquee reveals that before dying the Mercury lived for a time as the Central Cinema III. "This is where I saw my first film," Garner says. "Or so I've been told. I don't actually remember it."

"You never liked movies," Timothy accuses.

"No, not much," Garner agrees, and adds, boastfully, "Not even then. Not even then, when I was just a boy." This is something to crow about, surely—that, even as a child, he was never taken in. Nonetheless, it saddens him that the old cavernous theater, with its overhanging, faintly scandalous lovers' balcony, has passed away.

Still more distressing, but also heavy-handedly comic—

much as the emergence of Lucky's Video had been comic—is the change to be seen in the Elizabeth Town Library. The little haven on the old town green has been turned into a "Souvenir and Curio Shop."

"I'm afraid to ask. Maybe I'd better not even ask . . ."

"They moved it over to Victoria. The fire station came over here and the library went over there. They've had to consolidate. They've had to cut back." Timothy's tone is oddly defensive—as though justifying his hometown to a stranger.

"But look, Timothy, just look at the *way* they've cut back." Of course it hardly matters . . . Surely, nothing that could possibly happen in Victoria or Elizabeth matters any more. But it does seem important at least to record aloud what the moon's cool searchlight plainly reveals: that whatever life and value this town ever possessed have now been abnegated.

"The library was no good anyway, Garner."

"True . . ." And yet the names on the frieze over the line of pseudo-Doric columns in the front of the little structure sing of eternal glory: DEMOSTHENES CICERO BOETHIUS CHAUCER HOBBES MONTESQUIEU. Names that doubtless were nothing but names to the semilettered founders of Founders Valley. Nonetheless, someone had actually paid to have this roster of immortals etched (they were keen on etching stone, those town founders . . .), and if these names were selected in ignorance they were also invoked in hope. The list bespoke aspiration, projections of betterment, the amplification of learning . . . Who could possibly stand on this old town green and not feel charmed by that patent, suffusing pride with which those men and women resolutely refused to recognize their town as second-rate? And who could escape the notion that a betrayal, a spiritual maiming, had taken place?

25 The cynic would insist that the town had always been shaped by greed alone, and that the builders of the Sweet Buy and Buy Plaza were no more rapacious in the main than those grain and lumber barons (Garner's forebears, Halldor and Ragnar Birgisson, prominent among them) who had seized upon a rolling valley, cut

and cleared it, until a town, two towns, were constructed for the more efficient extraction of riches from the land. And yet there is another possibility here, and one far harsher than any which the cynic might flatter himself about facing squarely. This harsher truth is that of the aggrieved idealist, who alone can see that the settler's marriage of pride and naiveté has been, literally, pulverized back into the earth. Theirs had at one time been an aspiration not only of Wealth but, blindly, of Culture. "For God's sake, why don't you take off that ridiculous hood?"

"People might recognize me."

"In one of *many* recent telephone conversations Nettie warned me that you'd gone off in search of a magic cloak . . ."

"Nettie . . . what do you mean—a magic cloak?"

"I swear she's the wisest one among us. She has one advantage—she's usually right about people."

"You shouldn't be talking to Nettie about me, Garner. You shouldn't gossip about people, Garner."

"Then who should I gossip about? For God's sake, take that thing off—nobody's out on the streets now. And what difference would it make if you *are* recognized? You're coming out of hiding tomorrow, remember? Returning to the land of the living."

"I never left it, Garner. The land of the living. And you can tell Nettie that." Timothy unties his hood and shakes out his sandy hair in the moonlight.

"You know, I'd planned to sneak off somewhere tonight to telephone Doris. But it's too late now. You really shouldn't have done this to her."

"You should talk. *You* never call her, Garner. At least I call her."

"At least she knows where she can reach me. At least she knows I'm alive."

"Oh she knows I'm *alive.*"

"And how does she know that, Timothy?"

"Why she just does," Timothy says. "She just knows I went off to think for a little bit. She knows I'm all right, all right."

"And how does she know that?"

"She just *does*. Imre, too. You'd understand if you were close to her, if you were close to anyone."

"Telepathy, huh?"

"See? That's so typical. You've got to attach a *word* to it."

"I do to most of the things I say . . ."

"See? Don't you see?" His voice has again gone shrill—has become that of Little Brother petulantly correcting Older Brother. "See? Don't you see? How you're always wanting to attach a word to it instead of really understanding it?"

"If she understands so well, then why has she been worried sick about you? Why have I honestly been thinking she might have a nervous breakdown?"

The questions hit—almost literally—home. That peeling house is not far behind them. Before them is the Elizabeth town green. Here, the moonlight falls full on their faces. Before them, across the green, stands the courthouse, and the courthouse clock tower, and it hardly seems fanciful, tonight, to read in that tower an emblem for Garner's entire life. Time and the Law, the long, patient construction of the concept of justice, the daily accretions of the common law, the building block of *stare decisis*, and all of it boxed away in that dark tower, whose clock is a moon made practical, a moon equipped with numbers and hands. Timothy begins to walk once more and Garner moves beside him.

"You know I was angry with her?" Timothy says.

"When?"

"In Cambridge, when we had that argument. Do you know what she said to me? Do you know what Mom honestly said to me? She honestly said to me that she sometimes wishes she never had any children."

Garner laughs—and who could help laughing at this? "Well of course she does. That's only normal. Who in the world would want a parent who never felt that way?"

"Don't you see? Don't you see she's saying she wishes we were all dead?"

"No, Timothy. No. That we'd never been born. That's quite a

different thing. All sorts of people have never been born—and extremely admirable souls, many of them. We'd be in good company."

"That's something I'll never say to my kids. We're going to have lots of kids, Linda and I. That was a fluke, her—you know, her miscarriage."

"Yes, the doctor said *Try, try again.*"

"How's Imre?" Timothy asks.

"Worried. Everybody's been worried. He went down to New York. He thought maybe you'd gone back to your apartment and just weren't answering your phone."

"He did? You know, that's almost exactly what I did do. Oh, Imre's *smart,*" Timothy exults. "He's very *smart.* The only thing he didn't figure in was something I myself didn't figure in. You know what that was?"

Garner—although he knows the word that Timothy seeks from him—replies, "No. And what's that?"

"Fate. And not even Imre could see *that* coming. He's going to be surprised to hear I'm getting married."

"I daresay."

"I thought maybe he'd want to move out here after awhile. With Betty. The four of us could go for picnics."

"He might find work a little thin on the ground. I don't suppose Victoria's the very *best* place for a part-time chess instructor."

"What do you mean?"

"For God's sake, what have we seen all night, Timothy? There's no loose money here. They don't call this the Rust Belt for nothing . . . The paper mill closed what—ten years ago? Briggs' Furniture and all the rest are *long* gone. It's *all* long gone—and somewhere in Japan tonight somebody's just been offered a good new job that used to belong here. Somewhere in Singapore they're wining and dining in their newfound prosperity. But here it's dying, it's dying, Victoria and Elizabeth both."

"People are getting the wrong idea about us. About Americans. They think we're getting soft. They think the future all belongs to the Japanese—to the Asians. They think all the prodigies are Asian. Because they don't really see what's around them, you see."

"I'm afraid I don't, actually . . ."

"They tried to make Jeong a prodigy. Asian tranquillity and all of that, but I beat him in Minneapolis, didn't I? In thirty-six moves, an absolute slam-bam demolition job. Jesus, do you know how he took it? Where was the Asian tranquillity at that point, huh? And now this Ma-chan, they try to make him into such a genius . . ."

"Have you listened to his music?"

"That isn't the point, Garner, I'm talking about what people want to see and don't want to see . . . Victoria and Elizabeth aren't dying, Garner." The two brothers are walking along Magellan Avenue, the street down which the Memorial Day parade, which always began on Soldiers Way, would straggle to a close. How late is it now? The streets are deserted, except for the busy moonlight, which has turned a chilly silver as the moon has risen. "*They're* not dying. You want to hear what's dying?" Timothy asks, with a mirthful, knowing laugh. His voice has turned soft again—but this time with a strange, spooky confiding knowingness. "Garner, it's New *York* that's dying. It's not going to last much longer."

"And how will we know when it's finally dead?"

"Oh, you'll know," Timothy whispers, and chuckles to himself. "Even you, Garner, even *you* will know then."

Not until they turn onto Morton Nye Boulevard does Garner understand where it is they're heading. When was the last time the two of them ventured over here together? *Have* the two of them ever come here together? The prisonlike two-story box of the Robert Browning Elementary School looms into view. The gate to the playground is closed but not locked. Timothy undoes the latch and Garner follows his moon-haired brother across the asphalt yard. Despite the warmth of the night, Garner shivers. He didn't understand, somehow didn't understand, that this is where the two of them were headed and he feels frightened.

Timothy leads him past the empty cage of the jungle gym and the swings whose metal chains twist and turn the pliant moonlight. The wooden merry-go-round, dented and sagging, looks like the very same one that stood here decades ago. Poverty—it is a great preserver. They pass the merry-go-round and cross a short, empty, moon-blanched expanse of pavement. Together they walk over to the slide. It's not so tall as Garner remembers. Timothy clasps the metal rail of its ladder and turns and faces his older brother. "Look," he says, and stamps his foot. "It's no longer packed dirt."

Under a high, vanished sun, under a cerulean sky some fifteen years ago, a child toppled from this very slide. It was Timothy's little twin brother, Tommy, and a few days later, the asphalt around the base of the ladder was rooted up by city authorities and replaced with a circle of packed dirt. The circle remains, but the dirt has been covered over by an indeterminate spongy green substance—some form of artificial turf. "Well," Garner says. "Here we are . . ."

"People don't understand death," Timothy begins. "Tommy didn't die in the way people think."

Tommy didn't die and something snaps inside Garner's head and suddenly he knows he's had enough. All night, for hours now, he has listened to just this sort of sweeping, stupid, all-knowing judgment, and he will do so no longer—not here. No, not here, for the dead deserve better. They deserve the best we can give them: the truth, the abored-after truth. "Listen to me, for God's sake just one moment listen to *me,* Tim," he begs. "Please understand there wasn't any reason or Fate behind it. He just fell. And he's dead now just the same way other people die. He's a skeleton in the ground. They're both of them skeletons."

"Who? Who both?"

"Tommy," Garner begins and then the largest, if not the longest, pause of the night opens in front of Garner, who shies for a moment before adding, in the form that deathless blood-linkages demand, "and Dad."

Anguish is exploding in the darkness and Timothy's reply is

an unexpected cry of passion: "Why do you re*sist* me, Garner?" They are nothing but voices, the two of them, one voice rushing past another in the moonlight. "Why *do* you, Garner?" The moon has bleached Timothy's fair hair pure white, his wan face pure white, and only his mouth, thrown open in an ugly imploring rent of woe, is black. They are voices, souls, two ghosts, bickering over the dead. "Garner, why do you resist me?"

"It isn't you personally—don't you see? It's what you're *saying*."

"Why do you always want to believe that I'm not *on* to something? Why do you have to be the only one in the family who's ever *on* to something?"

"That's not true," says Garner.

"You know, I've become a kind of star. People know me, all over the country people know me, and they know my face. Garner, I've become a real *star,*" Timmy cries and the word shatters right out of all its narrow and informal associations. A star, *the stars, the heavens, the milky galaxies spilled in little shattered droplets across the polished ebony floor of the universe* . . . "But you don't think I'm ever *on* to something."

"Timothy, that's not true . . ."

"You don't understand marriage . . ." White on white, he has become a ghost; oh, he's a ghost, Timothy is, and every one of his ghostly messages is nonsense. An emissary from the Dead has come to show us—oh philosopher's nightmare!—that beyond the grave it is nothing but passion and illogic, nothing but broken geometry, unaided confusion, eternal disarray. "And you don't understand family loyalty."

"Timmy," Garner cries, "I'm on your *side.* I've always been on your side. I'm right behind you . . ."

"Then why do you feel so distant?" the lanky white figure standing next to the Death Ladder accuses. "You know, you know we lived inside the very same woman, both of us, nine months, nearly three-quarters of a year, and two people who've lived inside the body of the same woman, well that ought to make them *closer* somehow. Twins, it's like all brothers and sisters are twins in that way . . . Don't you see? With nothing, nothing but time separating them."

And oh how abruptly lovely are these words! The struggling phrasing, the thought, the emergent *clarity* . . . Garner feels an urge, which isn't easy to quell, to go over and place a brotherly hand across Timothy's shoulders. "Oh I like that," Garner says. "Now *that's* being on to something. Oh I really do *like* that . . ."

"I don't understand you, Garner Briggs," Timothy cries, and the queer rhetorical flourish of the last name, as though Timothy himself didn't share it, is chilling. It's spooky. Timothy has placed a shoe upon the first step of the Ladder, and seems about to mount his own mortal pulpit.

Helplessly, as though over a growing expanse, Garner calls, "But I'm an open book . . ."

Timothy begins to ascend the ladder, halts, turns, and sways backward and forward while holding the railing with one hand. His voice emerges as something masterly at last, a song high but limpid, like the whining of fine crystal, the humming of the moon: *"You have turned away from love,"* he intones. "You don't understand love. I cannot understand why so many people in the human race have turned their backs on love. Why have they done it? Why, Garner? Why? And how, *how* did they ever expect to get anywhere—when they have turned their backs on love?"

XXIX

He gets a sense of trouble from the first, with just one glimpse at the new girl, the way it is her arm's wound so tight around the kid's waist, and there's something wide and tight and greedy to her eyes in how she glances, here and there, here and there. And he knows it to an absolute certainty in just a few minutes, really not long after shaking her hand for the first time: she's a disaster.

This is supposed to be such a happy time. The kid is back, isn't he? Hasn't the kid come back? But there isn't any joy in it, really. Things are just as delicate, just as dangerous as ever. What it means for the moment is a game of let's-see, of wait and hope, and a warfare so subtle that neither one of them, the kid or the girl, can recognize that a fight's begun. But that grip she has round the kid's waist is tight, and the gleam in her wide eyes as she's slicing into a steak brought up by room service, with the city of Boston lit up at her feet, it cuts like an alley cat's.

To see the kid act this way, it doesn't bother him, the way it bothers Garner, or at least not so much as it bothers Garner. What does it matter—if the kid's a fool in his dealings with those fools? It's stupid, no doubt about that, to be acting so stupid: to be talking so big for them, which is just what they want for all their shows and their articles. Hasn't he told the kid, a couple thousand times at least, that talk is cheap, second-rate, it's an activity reserved for those who have no talent for the game? Of course it's painful to see the kid acting so stupid, playing into their hands with all his crazy talk about families and John Henry and the rebirth of America, but none of that truly matters: after all, who reads newspapers or magazines or watches TV? All of that's simply for idiots, as anyone but an idiot will tell you. No, where the trouble lies isn't all the promises and the boasting but another change, deep inside the kid, where the heart and soul are.

This is something you learn to feel, after living beside somebody day after day: the way their mind goes about pushing and poking at things. It's something that's there all the time, not just on the chessboard, and this is where something's gone soft, or queer. It can usually be felt as an urge to take the thought another thought deeper, to build on what you've got—but to feel the kid thinking now, or just to hear him talking, you'd have to figure none of that's necessary any more. Unnecessary, all of it, preparation, concentration, intensity. And time and again it's just "No machine can stand up to the human spirit," as if spirit alone could stand up to three hundred and sixty-five thousand positions per second.

Timothy has made a love nest for himself and there's no joy in this return of his. There's no use pretending that's not what it is: because a love nest is just exactly what the kid has turned his room into, with that girl lounging around and eating doughnuts in front of the TV all afternoon in her bathrobe, while her underwear hangs on the shower rod . . . This may be the fancy Totaplex Hotel, with wall-to-wall carpeting and free samples of after-shave and an ice machine right down the hall, but it might as well be some cockroach dump down by the train station: because it has become a love nest all the same. What sort of work's going to get done in a place like this? Any work going to get done will have to get done down the hall, in Imre's own room, but the kid doesn't have the mind for work, anyway. No patience for study and none for all the scheduling problems he himself created by running away. It's "You figure out all that." It's "My only job is to win, Imre." It's "And don't you worry, I will." And not a care in the world.

This sorrow that is like a foreign weight inside his body grows each day into a greater burden. It's like those people Imre has heard about on television who've had an operation and months later, hurting worse than ever, are sliced open again for the surgeons to remove a small pair of scissors or a surgical sponge. It's with him constantly. He carries it around as he listens to the kid's chatter and nonsense, to Doris's long sad Florida stories and her long sad Indiana stories, to Nettie's going on about all of those kids of hers he's never met. Imre sits and listens and nods, and sometimes they nod back at him, but he is alone—alone with the hurt in his belly. Garner is the one person he would talk things over with, since he's the only one in the family who has any sort of clarity about things, but Garner seems distant, or preoccupied. Garner has his own worries and problems—almost more than he can handle at the moment, you'd have to bet, what with both Doris and Nettie as houseguests in his apartment . . . And to hear the women talk, everything is just fine, fine, fine, now that the kid's come back. It's all shopping and fancy restaurants and Do you think they'll put us on TV? and it's nobody asking Don't you think he's still acting pretty strange? *That's* what he would discuss with Garner, although the truth is that Garner, too, seems to have returned from out there in Indiana in a pretty strange state of mind.

It's ridiculous and stupid, and it's unbearable: to enter that love nest down the hall and watch the kid parading around in his underwear in front of the girl, who's over there lying on the bed, watching the whole show, eating the whole time, eyes busy, mouth busy. And who would have believed it? The kid at one point actually pulling him aside, like one schoolkid to another, to talk about sex? To talk, it would seem, about the great good effects it could bring to a man's life . . . Who would have *believed* it? Of course this wasn't something to put up with—to have the kid lecturing *him* about sex, which at his age the kid should hardly be talking about at all, and least of all with his trainer. Of course there's no denying that any man is going to have such thoughts, and there's no use and no good in trying to drive them completely out of the brain. Imre himself thinks sometimes of the tanned blond girl, Alexandra, he sat beside on the airplane flying back from Uncle Gyorgy's funeral. She'd been dozing, and through the round window the sun suddenly came streaming to alight upon her delicate, peeling nose, and that's when it occurred to him that in his whole life he had never had before and probably never would have again, so pretty a girl sleeping right beside him; it was just this once, this was it, just this once, and this was the sort of realization a man can't help thinking about, now and then, but mustn't think about too often. The kid should be studying, of course, even though to hear him talk, study was no longer necessary: *My only job is to win,* he keeps saying, and *Don't worry, don't worry, Imre, I will.*

And the odd thing is, once the new schedule's settled on and the match is resumed at last, the kid nearly does win that first game after the break. Imre wouldn't have thought him capable of putting five moves together, let alone twenty-five, in the high-flying state he's in. And yet the fact is that after twenty-five moves the kid has a winning line. True enough, he blunders it away—stupidly, impatiently. And true, too, that ANNDY plays a very bad game: it's as if ANNDY, too, had suddenly gone a little strange in the head. But there's no denying that the kid comes off looking all right, and to those who don't know the game, and can't see what blunders were committed, he even comes off looking good. That's the odd thing: the thing that can't be accounted for.

Imre can't account for it—he can only thank his lucky stars. For the fact is that this game couldn't have turned out better. A draw was just exactly what the kid needed: a blunder-filled draw that might bring him back down to earth. A victory would only have set him even firmer in all his crazy notions. And a loss—well, the kid probably couldn't handle a loss right now. Of course a victory will be needed, since the kid's got to even up the score, and soon. But not quite yet. Better, first, come down to earth.

The kid has been lucky, very lucky, to have ANNDY play so badly. Does he understand that, Imre wonders, as ANNDY's screen flashes another of its stupid postgame messages (I'D RATHER BE IN BERMUDA . . . I'D RATHER BE IN BERMUDA . . .)? The crowd is enormous. It overflows the seats in the auditorium. The kid has made himself much, much more famous by running away, by doing something stupid. The game that went on here this afternoon calls for hours and hours of study. Buried, hidden way down deep inside ANNDY's moves, there was another bug, or a family of bugs. Inside ANNDY, there were dozens of them, probably hundreds of bugs in all: waiting like so many cockroaches in an old floor. And how could they fail to be there, given a game as old and big as chess? But they're hard to root out, ANNDY is so big. It calls for study, hours and hours of it, but can the kid see that? Can the kid see anything whatsoever while the girl's squeezing and fingering his body? The moment, the very moment the match is over, there she is: up there for all the world to see, kissing him, again and again, ants in her pants, sticking her sticky arm around his waist. And meanwhile flashbulbs pop-pop-pop for all of the kissing, and the cameras roll, soaking it up, the new twist in the story, getting ready to splash it over the newspapers and magazines and the television screens. The girl and the journalists both, they are feeding on him, and the kid ignorantly up there, face all lit up with excitement, ready to preach again about Fate, and Love, and sex, too, probably. Preaching like that crazy man on the television who's also part of the problem: him with the jackknife, all the blood and talk. That's how the kid now sees himself: some sort of preacher, a man with a message. That kind of talk is for idiots, Imre wants to tell the kid, but the boy is no longer within reach. It's hopeless.

Imre has turned aside, away from the spectacle of the boy and the girl kissing in front of the cameras . . . He is trying to figure out whether to go back alone to the hotel, when someone taps him on the arm. It's the girl, the other girl: Vicky Schmidt. "Imre."

"Hello."

"Well things are rolling again," she says.

"The level of play was very low today," he tells her.

"In what way?"

"Well what was that business with the knights, and all the fuss over that little rook pawn?" he demands of her.

"Well honestly, Imre, I wouldn't have a clue." She giggles.

"No." He's being silly: of course she wouldn't know. He collects himself and from all the complexities inside him, the branching moves and countermoves, comes up with some words she can understand: "Very, very erratic."

"You mean his play wasn't quite—normal? Timmy's?" Vicky says.

"Sloppy. Sloppy, sloppy. No discipline."

"Imre—Imre, you have a minute maybe? I thought maybe could we go out for coffee maybe? I mean just the two of us? I wanted to talk to you about Timmy, you see."

"Hnn," says Imre.

Vicky leads him to a little coffee shop full of students. The place is perfectly okay—comfortable—but it's not the sort of place for her, Imre feels, in her ironed blue dress. Her nylons, too, are blue. And her shoes, too, darker blue. But it's the place she chose and she insists—insists—on paying the bill, although she has ordered only a cup of coffee, while he's having a cup of hot chocolate and a piece of apple strudel. The strudel had been his second choice. His first was cheesecake, with a chocolate chocolate-chip crust, but there wasn't any left.

"Well," she says, sipping from her coffee, which she drinks black. "It sure's a relief to have things under way again."

"I suppose so."

"You were worried, weren't you?"

"Mm." The strudel is a little dry, and not enough fruit in it, but at least it's sweet enough. Sometimes strudel isn't sweet enough.

"Well," she begins again. "Timmy seems very happy."

"I suppose so."

"And it's nice," she says. "To see a couple look so infatuated."

"Mm?"

"You know, Timmy and—Linda."

"Yes."

"And she seems good for him. I mean they come from the same town and everything."

"I suppose."

"Imre, let me ask you something, do you mind? Imre, do you think maybe we ought to have another adjournment?"

Imre looks up from his strudel. He examines her eyes, which stare back at him with real intensity. They make him a bit light-headed, those bright, dark, beautiful interrogating eyes of hers: they make his hands feel damp. He is not used to hearing his name like this, or sitting so close to such a pretty young woman. She seems to be suggesting some connection between the other girl, Linda, and an adjournment—but what is it exactly?

"Perhaps," Imre says.

"I just think it's all turning into a zoo. You saw it today, all the cameras and the kissing, and Timmy announcing his engagement."

"He announced his engagement?"

"You didn't hear? Yep, right up there for all of America. I

mean I just think—I just think these things should be a little more private, don't you?"

"That's what he called it the first day out, do you remember?" Imre asks her. "A zoo."

"Well it's getting zooier and zooier, isn't it? I mean I just thought the two of them, Timmy and his—fiancée, they might want to get out of all this for a day or two. It's all a bit too fast for everyone, don't you think? I mean Congam would be happy to keep picking up the hotel bills—you know, give them a few extra free days. I suppose they could even go someplace else, for a day or two, you know, as guests of Congam. I mean for example there's what I'm told is a very good Totaplex in Providence."

"If he goes away, I'm not sure he'll come back," Imre says.

"No? Oh Jesus."

Vicky purses her lips and exhales audibly, like someone with a cigarette releasing a big thoughtful cloud of smoke. "Imre, I'll be honest with you. The people I work for, Congam, they think an adjournment's a good idea. Suddenly this whole thing is very *hot* right now. In the good sense. I mean, first we had a young man playing a Congam machine, and somehow that grabbed the public a lot more than anybody expected. A chess match—I mean who cares about a *chess* match? I mean from a demographic standpoint. I mean you've got a country where poll after poll shows that half the adults on any given day can't name the vice-president—and we're going to sell these people a *chess* match? But we do, or somehow it does, I mean people can understand this man-against-machine concept, this new John Henry thing, can't they? But now, now we've got a *mys*tery story as well—the Case of the Missing Chess Player. Hell, this story's got everything, we've even got a love element now—and it's a high school sweetheart to boot. Suddenly everybody in the country's got their eyes on this match. And whenever everybody's got their eyes on *any*thing in this country, well then—well, there's money to be made then, isn't there? You follow me? But this match is scheduled to end very soon. Before everybody can squeeze out of it what they might squeeze out of it, if you see what I mean. And that's why an adjournment or a rescheduling might be a good idea. It would give everybody a couple more days to focus on things. We've got to move auditoriums, for one thing. Well, anyway, that's the Congam position. I thought you ought to know. But also, Imre, maybe I should say one other thing. That's Congam's reasoning but it's not mine," Vicky says.

"No?"

"Well, I *do* think maybe there ought to be some sort of adjournment, but not for any of those reasons. I just think Timmy needs a little more rest. He shouldn't be talking the way he is up there. Imre, they're *exploiting* him."

Imre fights down the powerful, trembling impulse he feels to signal his approval: to nod in thumping agreement, or to congratulate her, or to pump her hand. He wants to hear her out without influencing her—for hers is the first truly sensible voice he has heard in days and days. "Mmm," he says, trying to offer her just the right amount of encouragement.

"And I don't know what to make of this whole fiancée business, quite frankly. I mean doesn't it all feel a little *quick?* I know he's known her for years and years and all that, but doesn't it seem kind of *quick* to you?"

"Perhaps. Yes."

"As I say, it's great from Congam's point of view. It gives the whole match an added dimension—you know, humanizes it and all that crap. Excuse me. And well I don't like to be the sort of person who second-guesses other people's happiness. I mean if something makes somebody happy, I mean that's great, huh? I don't like to overanalyze why or anything. I don't like to rain on other people's parades. So I mean if Tim really *is* happy, then I suppose we should all just be happy for him.

"But Imre," she concludes, and her words are thrilling, and those dark eyes of hers are perfection itself, they burn with the peerless light of true sanity: "I mean don't you think he's acting pretty peculiar?"

XXX

WHEN IMRE'S OFFER first came stumbling out, after an hour's earnest talk over refilled cups of coffee and hot chocolate, she hadn't understood it. He was merely suggesting they go somewhere else for a real meal—or so she'd supposed. And not until they were actually standing outside and Imre thoughtfully rubbed his hands together and said, "Now where should I take you?" did it come clear that he meant to treat her. He would be paying her back now for all the meals that she, or the company she worked for, had bought for him.

Imre bounces solidly along beside her, and the pleasure he shows at this turn of events is almost irresistible. She worries a little, sure, about bankrupting him—because he always seems so poor, with his dirty old clothes and his crumpled bags of cookies and sandwiches. But his own jubilation ("Now let's *see*," he says, and rubs his hands together once more) is reassuring. And almost irresistible.

So she offers not one word of advice. Imre strides along in his myopic way, streetlights and neon signs flashing on the thick lenses of his glasses, and she stays right beside him. Finally he halts, abruptly, before a place called Zorba's Kitchen. "Have you ever had Greek food?" he asks. "Sure," she tells him and he looks crestfallen, maybe, and she realizes she mustn't act so blasé. It seems he had expected a reply of Never.

But if Imre is a little disappointed, he shrugs it off. "Greek food is very interesting," he informs her as he opens the door for her. The role of host has transformed him. That endearing, makes-you-want-to-laugh courtliness of his has come back, stronger than ever, and the way he helps her out of her coat and into her seat is the more touching for the slightly rundown look of this place, which is nearly deserted. She smiles at him and says, "Well this is very nice."

The restaurant's two bow-tied waiters are arguing quietly but passionately over by the kitchen doors. This goes on for a couple of minutes. Then one disappears into the kitchen and the other, who is good-looking in a high-cheekboned, moist-eyed sort of way, brings over some menus. "A bit of wine perhaps?" Imre asks her.

"Sure."

Imre contemplates the brief wine list on the back of the menu, then makes a selection by pointing with one of his knobby fingers and giving a heavy nod. She has noticed this before and found it a little surprising—the somewhat heavy-handed, superior way in which he handles all restaurant employees.

"I hope you'll like what I selected. The list is not large."

"I'm sure I will," Vicky says, and smiles again at him. She has grown to like Imre, though it took her a little while to accustom herself to his appearance. He almost seems something for a carnival freak show, with those huge scrunched-looking hands and those eyes blown up so large by his glasses, until the lenses can hardly hold them in. And the truth is, she isn't quite used to his looks even yet. Entering this place, she'd felt (and disliked herself a little for feeling) just a bit uneasy, or self-conscious, or embarrassed, about being seen going out to dinner with someone so freaky-looking. But Imre is a friendly and a harmless soul, a combination she rarely meets in men, except sometimes in very old men. He has filled her wine glass for her, and raises his own in toast. "These days, we are the only ones, perhaps, who see him clearly."

Timmy is so constant a presence in Imre's conversation that there's usually no need for identification by name; it's *he* and *him* and that's enough. "The trouble, part of the trouble," Imre says, and Vicky already knows how this sentence will conclude—in his solicitude, Imre can be quite repetitive—"is that preacher he's always watching on TV. He's started thinking he's a preacher, too."

"You may be right."

"And this John Henry business. Now he thinks he's part of a song . . . You know that song? You have heard it?"

"Yes, I do. I have."

"And you know how it ends?"

"Yes. Sure."

Imre shakes his head at her. "And the girl," he says. "She isn't right for him."

"You may be right," Vicky says again. When Imre attacked Linda the first couple of times, back in the coffee shop, Vicky had defended her. But the duty to defend a girl you hardly know surely is limited in the end, even if it *is* a man who's doing the attacking.

"She doesn't correct him, or tell him when he isn't making any sense. She just goes along with his every crazy thing he says."

"Well everything's so new to her here. I mean I think she's probably just beginning to sort things out. She's out of her element."

"She just lies on the bed and eats jelly doughnuts."

"Jelly doughnuts?" Vicky smiles despite herself.

"Yesterday, she ate six jelly doughnuts. I know for a fact." Imre leans forward to confide, "Strawberry. She devours them."

"Imre!" Vicky protests but laughs all the same at this. With laughter comes an instinctive, slightly flirtatious impulse to reach out a hand toward his on the table. But a look at his actual hand, resting there in all its trollish density, stops her dead.

"She will be quite fat soon," Imre continues. "You, you wouldn't know such things, you are so thin—"

"Well golly, gee, thanks." Vicky giggles. "But I'm hardly what you'd call—"

"But I know fatness, you see. I am forty-seven pounds overweight." Imre makes this confession, with all its hilarious precision, in a somber, head-shaking fashion. "And she will soon be more than that, six doughnuts in an afternoon."

When the good-looking waiter returns to the table, the whole left side of his face is aglow. The clean-shaven cheek's all a fierce, burning red. Could it be (and what other explanation is there?) that the other waiter slugged him or slapped him? "Your order," he orders. He is angry about something, anyway.

"An appetizer. You must have an appetizer," Imre urges her. "Perhaps you need more time."

"No," Vicky says. "No, I'll have the stuffed grape leaves."

"Ah." Imre pauses a long moment, as if not so much to decide on something as to evaluate her choice. "And I, I will have the cheese and sausage," he says, and with a shooing-away motion he makes it clear that the waiter's presence is no longer necessary.

"You must have more wine," Imre tells her, and refills her glass. They have almost finished the bottle.

"Did you notice anything odd about his face?"

"His face? What? Odd about his face? When? Was there something odd about his face?"

"No, I mean the waiter's."

"Oh. No," Imre says. "I noticed nothing."

"It looked as though he'd been slapped—or as though he'd been in a fight."

"That would not surprise me. They are a warlike people, the Greeks. It is in their history for all to see."

"And the Hungarians?"

"Mm?"

"The Hungarians—you're Hungarian, aren't you? What about them?"

Imre appears amused by her question. He seems to find it just a little absurd. "Well, you see now, about us," he explains, "about us, it is impossible to generalize."

It is the other waiter, the older one, who brings out the appetizers. Vicky's grape leaves turn out to be a sorry-looking sight, and the glass dish they are served in so much resembles an ashtray that she finds it hard to push out of her mind the thought of wet, swollen cigar butts. But Imre's cheese and sausage, still bubbling away in its little silvery dish, looks marvelous.

"Doesn't the cheese smell good!" Vicky says.

"I wouldn't know," Imre says. "I lost my sense of smell in 1971."

Vicky laughs deeply and then, inspired to mischief by the

what's-so-funny look her laughter brings to his face, she says, "Imre, imagine for a minute you'd never learned chess, the game had never been invented, what do you think you would have become?"

An upper incisor emerges to clamp down thoughtfully on Imre's thick lower lip. The long ensuing silence suggests that he has never before had occasion to ponder the question. "I suppose a millionaire," he answers finally.

And Vicky is brought to deeper, wilder laughter by his look of puzzled gravity. "But I mean surely it's not as easy as *that,* Imre."

"Oh yes, not really so difficult," Imre reveals to her. "You see my brother is a millionaire. In the construction business. And he was never very smart—I must say that he was actually quite stupid when compared to me. There never was a single thing he could do that I couldn't do, you see, and now he has become a millionaire. With three cars." Imre drains his glass of wine.

The young waiter, his face restored to its normal color, comes over to stand beside their table. He says nothing, but merely poses there, expectantly, notepad in hand. "The fish, the sole," Vicky says to him. "Is it fresh?"

"I don't know." And having told her so, he simply stands there with pen and notepad in hand, expectantly.

"Well in that case I'll have the shish kebab," Vicky says.

Imre orders moussaka and another bottle of wine and again waves the waiter away. "Uncooperative," he pronounces. "That's why they had to have their own church. Greek Orthodox they call it, but there's nothing orthodox about them."

"You're a Catholic," Vicky says. "Didn't you once tell me that?"

"I guess so," Imre says. "My background is quite tangled, you see."

"Do you go to church?"

"Not for many years," Imre says.

"You don't believe?"

"No, I guess not."

"When did you lose your faith?"

Imre bites down once more on his lower lip. His outsize eyes slide around in the lenses of his glasses like eggs just dropped onto a griddle. "It's a kind of slow vanishing . . ." he says.

"Well what do you believe in, Imre? I mean besides chess."

The reply, surfacing after another long meditative chewing on his lower lip, is again unexpected, again delightful: "I believe in America."

"Land of the free," Vicky says.

"Only, America has become too generous. She is always giving too much of her money away. Land of the freebie—that's what they think it is."

"Land of the freebie—I like that," she says, and laughs so generously that he wishes he could claim the joke as his own.

"Puh," Imre says. "I mean thank you. I heard it somewhere."

"But what has she given you, Imre?"

"Oh, not to me. I want no charity."

"You're sounding very conservative."

"The people need discipline. And they don't find it themselves. Just the way he needs discipline. He is looking for it even when he doesn't know it. That's what I try to give him, discipline. That girl is no good for him."

This strange man, Imre, who never has anything to say, talks incessantly tonight. Incessantly, and repetitively—Timmy and Linda, Timmy and Garner, Timmy and Doris, Timmy and the Reverend Rabbitt. Imre halts only when the entrées arrive. Then the two of them eat for a time in silence and make some progress on a second bottle of wine and Vicky feels her head beginning to sail, just a little. The shish kebab isn't bad, actually. She feels happy and lighthearted, suddenly, and she feels sorry for Imre, who can't seem to leave off his brooding.

"Maybe it's all just a stage Tim's going through."

"I think that's what his mother thinks. With her, everything always is a stage."

"And Garner? What does he think?"

"Garner . . ." Imre ponders for a moment. "That's hard to tell.

He, too, seems perhaps a little different since the return from Indiana."

"He lives alone, Garner?" Vicky says.

"Oh yes."

It's her turn to pause. She's unsure how to pursue the somewhat personal line of questions in her mind. That's one of the very interesting things about Garner—how he somehow manages to discourage all talk about himself, so that even the most mundane inquiries begin to seem very intrusive. And he seems such an *unlikely* brother for Timmy. "He's always lived alone?" she says.

"Yes I think so. Oh yes."

"They hardly seem like brothers, do they?"

"They are very similar sometimes," Imre says. "They are both reluctant to admit a mistake."

"Well they certainly don't look alike. And they could hardly *dress* more differently."

"Garner is shorter," Imre points out, as though this follows somehow from her own remark. "And less emotional," he adds, and with this observation he is returned to his deep brooding once more.

Seeing him sitting there, pondering a plate on which everything removable by either fork or spoon has been cleared away, she feels an urge to reassure him. To comfort him. And yet when, moments later, her hand in reaching for the breadbasket brushes his, the contact almost makes her shudder. It would be hard to spend one's days, as Timothy does, with anyone so horrifically ugly as Imre is. "Well I like this restaurant," she says. "You made a good choice."

Imre lifts his eyes. When he speaks again, it is once more in his courtly, deferential vein: "And may I ask about you? Some hypothetical questions only? If you did not work for these Congam people, what would you do?"

"Well I guess I'd be working for some other business. Or do you mean if I wasn't in business?"

"Yes, not in business."

"I don't know, maybe I'd be married." She laughs. "An apron, and a scarf wound round my head, and a dozen screaming children . . ."

"That girl, Linda, she is not good for him," Imre says again, only this time he continues, "I would so much prefer if it was you, not her, he was connected with."

Vicky feels her face blushing in an easy, wine-warmed sort of way. "Well I don't think I'm his type exactly. Besides, I'm an old lady compared to him."

"You're still a girl," Imre says, and follows this with a compliment which, surely, no other man Vicky has ever met could have successfully delivered without a trace of irony: "You still maintain the full bloom of youth."

"Well thank you," she says, feeling the flush on her face deepen. It flusters her to have his eyes suddenly so fixed upon her. "Well I assume that's a compliment. I mean I hope you're not calling me immature," she says, and laughs.

"No, not at all. You are successful, you make money at your corporation. Computers, they are the wave of the future. You are a specialist. Of course he, too, will have money. Nearly twenty thousand dollars if he wins this match. Twenty thousand dollars, which is worth thinking about, isn't it? Twenty thousand dollars, yes? And you have discipline."

"Discipline, that's my middle name," Vicky says, still hoping to clown with him, and still feeling troubled by those huge and steady eyes of his, which she does not meet directly. "I'm known as Ms. Discipline in the Congam offices, I can assure you."

"And he was very smitten with you. That was obvious. I commit no indiscretion in saying so. Quite, quite smitten," Imre goes on, in his courtly way.

"Oh, and I like Tim. It's just that, hell, let's face it, Imre, he and I haven't got *all* that much in common, have we?" She giggles, but again Imre refuses to grant her the release of a smile.

"And I think he may still be smitten, even if he doesn't know it. The human heart is our strangest organ, don't you think?" Imre says and pauses just long enough that she begins to feel she will actually have to answer this absolutely impossible question; then he goes on: "Or he could be smitten once again, under the right circumstances. I'm sure of that."

"I'm not sure I follow you," Vicky says, although, peering astonished into his eyes, she has just this moment fully understood what he is driving at.

"You would be *so* much better for him, Miss. Don't you see? How you would be so, so much *better?*"

And is this, could this be, the point their conversation has been building toward all along? No, it's all too unbelievable, to have Imre sitting before her as matchmaker, or procurer, and begging her. Begging her for Timmy's sake—and therefore for his own. But it's as though mysterious Imre has come to a clear conclusion at last. He has revealed himself. Those eyes of Imre's have turned mournful and desperate and fully comprehensible in a doomed, you're-my-last-hope sort of way. Plainly they're saying *Save me.*

XXXI

"*You* CAN GO OUT, you can go out by yourself if you want to," he tells her with a fine defiance. But the very thought of her leaving, which means leaving him alone here, is enough to put a pressure like a hand to his throat. It squeezes his voice a little.

"But I don't want to go out by my*self.* I want to go out with *you.*"

"But I don't feel like it."

"But why not? Why don't you feel like it?"

"I don't know, it's just I just don't feel like it."

"But you haven't been out all day. You haven't taken one

breath of fresh outdoor air—not a single one. Just sitting here breathing in the same old indoor hotel air."

She is standing by the window, with the city of Boston behind her. He is lying on one of the beds, or not quite lying, since he has three pillows piled under his back. Her face is dim in the night table's lamplight, but he can make out the tight, exasperated set to her mouth. Her body in its baggy sweat shirt and baggy jeans throws a bulky silhouette against the glass but not so bulky he can't make out the fine broad swell of her hips, the sloped rise of her breasts. She isn't wearing a bra, he knows. "I thought you thought this is the best hotel in the world. That's what you said, isn't it? The best hotel in the world?" The argument is strong but his voice comes out weak and almost whiny; he feels a little weak, just now. "You look at the sign on the door there. It tells you what this room normally costs."

"I know what it costs and I'm not complaining about it. It's wonderful."

"It's only the Totaplex, the best hotel in Boston," he tells her.

"I said it was wonderful, didn't I? Didn't I just say this is the best hotel in the world? It's just that I don't want to spend the whole, whole day in one single room. I mean I just want to go out and get something to eat."

"We can order up room service. Anything you want, it's free. We go out, it costs us money," he explains once more to her.

"It's just a couple dollars, we don't have to go anywhere expensive, Timmy. We could just have a pizza or one of those pastrami and cheese subs from Igor's. They're good for you. They're served on good healthy whole wheat rolls."

"The food here's *plenty* good for you . . ."

"We could use my money."

"I've got plenty of *money,*" he tells her. "For God's sake, you know that. It's just I can't be going out all the time. I've got to work, for God's sake."

"But you're not working," she says.

"But I *am.* That's what you don't understand about me," he explains to her. "I mean I'm thinking chess all the time. It's on my mind all the time. I'm working even when I'm watching TV or something. It's just a few more days, honey," he says. To utter this word *honey* makes his stomach feel funny. He is still not used to this, calling a woman *honey,* although he has called her *honey* dozens, maybe hundreds of times, these last few days.

"Come on back over here. You can smoke another joint," he tells her. "We can order up some more lasagna," he tells her. "And some more of that rum cake you like so much."

Linda hesitates over there by the window. He has tempted her.

"When we're on our honeymoon, you know what I'm going to buy you? Do you know what I'm going to buy you?" he asks again, to give himself a little more time to decide on something. "I'm going to buy you the biggest bouquet you've ever seen of big tropical flowers. You won't believe how they'll smell," he tells her. "I can just picture you holding all those flowers. Your arms *smothered* in flowers and you in your bathing suit. Just like a beauty queen," he says.

She comes over and sits beside him on the bed. "You're such a darling," she says. She removes a joint from the little Band-aid tin in the drawer in the night table and lights it from a pack of Totaplex matches. The practiced smoothness of how she does this always disturbs him a little. She draws deeply twice and passes it over to him. He pulls on it politely, but no more than for politeness' sake. She's been trying to teach him to like pot but she hasn't had too much luck so far. He has trouble with it. He's not quite sure why he has trouble with it but it makes him jittery. So he doesn't inhale as a rule, except perhaps a little, since it's true he sometimes feels a little hum start up at the base of his skull. He returns the cigarette to her and a couple more times she draws on it, sucks it down. "What color is it?" she asks him.

"What color's what, honey?"

"The bathing suit. You said you could see me in it."

"Red," he says after a moment. "Bright bright red, honey."

"A bikini or a one-piece?"

"A bikini," he tells her.

"And have I got a tan?"

"Oh you've got a tan all right. But your tummy's still white. Your tummy's just the way it is now." He reaches under her sweat shirt and places a claiming hand upon her belly. She isn't wearing a bra and he can feel the good nudging robust heaviness of her breast along the edge of his thumb. He wants her to lie down again and with his other hand he tugs on one of her belt loops.

"I should go on a diet," Linda says.

"You're perfect, honey," he tells her.

"After the honeymoon. That's when I'll start up my diet," she says. "Maybe I was wearing a one-piece first."

"Mm?" he says. The sweet nearness of her body has made him feel sleepy, or dreamy.

"That's why my belly's still white maybe, huh? Because I was wearing a one-piece but now I've switched into that bright red bikini."

"Exactly," he tells her. "And you won't believe how they smell," he calls to her across his sleepiness. He has closed his eyes. He tugs again at the belt loop and this time she shifts her weight, dropping down upon one elbow, her face a few inches from his. With his eyes closed, he can feel her looking at his face. "All those tropical flowers . . ." he says.

"I just don't understand you today," Linda says. "Usually I can hardly get you to sit down and today I can hardly get you to stand up."

He tucks the hand that was spread across her belly between her rib cage and upper arm, up where it's a little damp, and nuzzles his head against her neck. "Oh I don't usually really wake up till round midnight. That's the thing about me: I don't usually really wake up till around midnight."

"Did you call them yet?"

"Call who?"

"Room service?"

"You want to call them? I'm tired," he explains.

"I'm stoned," Linda says, from deep inside herself. "I just don't want to deal with it."

"But I'm so tired," he says.

"Please, baby," she says and she doesn't have to say anything else. He can hardly resist her, and she knows it, when she calls him *honey* or *darling* or *baby* like that.

He gets up out of bed and goes over to the phone. "Lasagna?" he asks her.

"And that rum cake. With whip cream. And some french fries," Linda tells him.

"Cokes are okay?"

"Fine," she says. "Anything . . ."

He places the order and is settling himself back in bed when she says, "Baby, will you see what's on the TV?" So he goes over and hits the power knob, which blooms the dead screen with colors that turn out to be a map of the United States. He lowers the volume and returns to bed.

"What are we watching?" she asks him.

"Maps." He tries to find once more the comforting niche he'd had at the base of her neck but it eludes him. With one eye open, he watches the television screen. The map turns out to be a sort of ledge that sits balanced on the upraised hand (much like a waitress transporting a pizza tray) of the Statue of Liberty. Below that, in gray letters that brighten and brighten, comes one word—CONGAM.

"Look!" Linda cries.

"I see, I see," Timothy says.

"Congam," a man's majestically deep voice pronounces. "Holding up America."

"I can't believe it!" Linda cries. Her voice is quite shrill with excitement. "Isn't that great? I mean that we'd see that *here* of all places!" she goes on, but actually the ad makes him a little nervous. It's as though they're all snooping on him—Congam, Conant, Westman, ANNDY, the bunch of them, spying in at him even here, and he closes his eyes once more to shut them out. But really there is no shutting them out, for always there's the hum—that faint, colossal hum which encloses this room and which he has in the end managed to identify. It's not the Coke machine, the lights, the elevators . . . He knows (or knows, at least, when he moves toward sleep) that what it is is the megacomputer upon which the entire Totaplex has been erected. Deep down, below the floors of rooms, below the water-lapped lobby, below the shopping arcades, in its seamless and indefatigable dream, the thing is sifting and sorting numbers by the million, the billion, the trillion. . . . He crawls down her body and settles his head on the soft-white, broad-white drum of her belly, but the buckle of her jeans pokes at his jaw. "Sweetie, can you take them off?" he says, tugging gently at another of her belt loops. "They're poking me."

"Timmy," she protests, "I'm all nice and super comfortable," but when he says, "Please, please honey," she shrugs her shoulders and gets out of bed. She leaves her jeans on the floor.

This time he finds a comfortable niche on her belly almost instantly. And within moments he has entered his own dream, although he is fairly certain he hasn't actually yet fallen asleep. This is a dream that pours through the mapped tube of the television, with all of its stored-up banks of colors, and in this dream he has returned to the old Sweetwater house. He is walking up the stairs to Dad's office and everything is brighter than life—as vivid and real as the multichanneled visions on the beautiful big new Totaplex TV screen. The wall beside him is hung with all sorts of glowing paintings but he feels the oddest sense of displaced weight: it's as though his inflated feet are twice their normal size. He ascends the stairs holding on to a wooden railing that was not there in the cracked house he once lived in, and he absorbs a vibration through his fingers. It is as though the whole house is vibrating like the purr inside the curled furry flank of a cat or like the humming intestines of the TV screen. The door to his father's office is ajar and with two fingers he pushes it open and steps inside. On the table, under the bright conical beam of the metal desk lamp, his father's coin collection sprawls in a gridded network of cells that might be a little like the flat midwestern landscape of a chessboard. But when he bends to inspect them more closely, his sandy head entering that tall falling cone of light, he perceives that these are not coins at all. No, baby, no, they are tiny seashells, little curled miracles of intricacy and brilliance. The desk lamp of their revelation hums with its own concentrated richness and he has never beheld such craftsmanship, such heartaching beauty.

Permanently aflame, the pigments burn—red, orange, yellow . . . Crisp greens and dappled apple scarlets, wisped grays, misted pinks and lavenders, and in the sorted presence of these perfectly lustered worlds, each the size of a knuckle, he knows himself complete at last. One, he palms one of the whorling shells, tight and precious in the harbor of his hand, and there's a kind of popping sound, and he must go and alert everyone to the astounding nature of his discovery. He strolls through a door leading into the back corridor (a corridor that wasn't there before), and at the end of it another beckoning door stands ajar. He walks quietly, on tiptoe on his little feet, and peers in without a sound.

There is the bulking dead man, his father, no longer dead, seated in all his contented weighty poundage at the kitchen table, sucking deliberatively on a billowing big-bellied pipe, and there's his mother, seated, too, a younger woman, and there's Garner as well—only Garner is not himself. His hair is sandy red and his face is freckled and bearded. This hair upon his head and within his beard is unnaturally bristly; it would hurt the skin of your hand, almost, to run your palm across it. Garner is talking, as he does, in that stiff professorial way, and one of the things he says may be about ANNDY. He says, *The machines haven't been made for us yet . . .* And seeing how utterly transformed his brother, Garner, is, he knows, standing just outside that room, that he cannot breach that threshold, however much he longs to enter . . .

And so he turns from the door and there, too, is Garner, only this time the real and unchanged Garner, waiting in the dark corridor. Yes, as promised, Garner has been behind him all along. Garner has been following him, up the stairs with their floating wooden rail, through Dad's door, into Dad's office, followed him down the corridor, followed him everywhere (followed him even here, as Garner's queer quest in the end told him he must, into the shell spiral of this dream), and the presence of dark Garner there in the corridor is unsettling, more so even than the presence of the smoke-puffing dead man behind, yes, and almost in propitiation he holds out to Garner (letting his arm float upward, his palm flower open) the magical miniaturized seashell. It hums there. And in the darkness of the corridor Garner smiles a tight-lipped smile in answer and lifts his fingers dreamily to his mouth and, scarcely opening his lips, extrudes from it another, a squarish seashell, which he deposits, still warm and aglow with spittle, in the palm outstretched before him.

The pounding of the pipe on the table behind him opens onto the rapping on the door of the room in the Totaplex. God save us all, it's room service. "Just a minute . . ." he calls.

He goes out into the corridor and signs for the food and wheels the tray in himself. The two of them eat their lasagna sitting up in bed, with the television going. He has less appetite than he'd thought, although the Coke is good, it clears the crud of sleep from your mouth, and he's glad he thought to order two for himself. While Linda is still eating he curls up again around her body. He pulls her sweat shirt up and homes in, his head between her breasts, which are gray in the television light. The nipples are gray-blue. He is so close to her, he can hear her take each bite. He can even tell, under the sound of the TV, whether she's chewing lasagna or french fries. "How's the cake?" he asks.

"Great." She offers him a bite in her fingers and he licks the frosting from her fingertips. She offers him another. She feels cold, she says, and pulls up the blanket so that her chest and his head are covered by it, although she leaves a little tubular opening through which to feed him additional bites of cake. She laughs at something on the television and he feels her mirth roll up and down the side of his head.

He loves her and oh God he loves her body, but it shocked him at first, when he first showed up in Victoria. Only a few years since he'd seen her last, but in that time she'd filled out so much—even grown a little plump. The change had shocked him, made him feel almost a little sick, because he so much wanted his original old Linda back, the little skinny teenage girl. He'd wanted to go backward in time, to return to the way things used to be. But that was absurd. That was ridiculous. One has to move forward. It was surprisingly *exactly* like a chess game—one has to keep pushing forward, or else it's all over. The clock ticks at your side, and the moves must be made in Time, which otherwise will destroy you. And he feels again his mind pushing outward, he feels his abilities expanding. While she cradles his head with one arm, and with the fingers of her other hand reaches beneath the blanket to convey to his lips another moist bite of cake, which his tongue mashes snug against the roof of his mouth, he knows that he is going forward in Time, forward, and forward endlessly.

XXXII

IN THE FINAL SCENE, the entire family is together, as is right, everyone seated before the television, as too is right, for this is modern life. Each has a keenly differentiated familial role to perform and is playing it to piquant near-perfection. Cast in the lead, as the Young Man, is someone scarcely a man at all—rather a boy, whose shirt sleeves and pants are alike too short, as though he has just this week outgrown them, *he is shooting up so fast.* By turns, he paces the room in fits of garrulous restlessness and throws himself haphazardly into a chair, there immediately to assume that slack-jawed, mesmerized look which is so characteristic of his generation and which is (as we've repeatedly been told) the outcome of years of visual and auditory bombardment from that electronic box which has replaced the family hearth and in whose tepid blaze the family circle now warms itself. In measured contrast to his edgy restlessness, a steadying weight is supplied by Nettie in the role of Older Sister, a somewhat pretty woman whose ample body has grown lax with closely successive births and who continually offers anxious speculative queries about her children, at home with their father. Hers is an indecisive voice at the best of times, and all but indistinguishable in those moments after she has dipped into the large bag of Frank's French Fry Flavor Potato Chips which lies on the table beside her.

Doris, the angular, stringy, bluish-white–haired woman who plays the Mother, gives an adept, practiced portrayal of someone who has pounced eagerly upon the unreasoning prerogatives of the elderly. Twice in five minutes she complains about the room's temperature—finding it too hot the first time, too cold the next. She wonders whether anyone else feels a draft?—and shakes her head with a look of pawky, knowing skepticism upon finding no one to agree with her. She manages, as well, to make unmistakably clear that her words are directed solely at her daughter, at her younger son, and at Linda, her younger son's fiancée (who handles her cameo role with a flowing, openhanded receptiveness, comfortably sharing a chair with her fiancé and the bag of potato chips with her future sister-in-law). These comments of Doris's are pointedly not intended for Garner, the Elder Brother, the Eldest Child, who had incensed her earlier in the evening by declaring *You're getting to be a foolish old woman, Doris.* So she will address no comments to him. Like Timmy, and Nettie, and even Linda (whom expediency has made an ally this evening), Garner is free to listen to her complaints—that's his privilege, after all—but she will exclude him from any direct address.

Garner's highly mannered performance—fragmented, enigmatic, self-conscious, even daringly coy—at first appears fated to collapse utterly beneath the weight of the circumlocutory tics and singularities he imposes upon it. But given time, and given the goodwill he sincerely if implicitly begs, its very eccentricity unveils its own deep-felt authenticity. Distant though he may be—as well as acidulous, unforthcoming, and proud—he nonetheless finds himself constantly beguiled by the emotional demands of those around him. And for all of his hoots of dismay and incredulity, in truth he, too, is captivated by the events unfolding on the television screen tonight. When all is said and done, he is part of this family group. The five of them are watching a madman who has taken up the role of Evangelist.

The family is seated in a hotel room in Boston. The room's one large window offers a view of the thriving modern city and, between buildings, a strip of water that might do to represent the historic Revolutionary harbor. As hotel rooms go, this one is large, and expensive-looking, and (except for the view) absolutely nondescript; one might be in a luxury hotel anywhere in the world. It is not just any hotel, however, but one of that Totaplex chain which advertises itself as the globe's first truly high-tech hotel network. Elsewhere, presumably, in floors above and below, telephonic business conferences are taking place, computer terminals are being rented, resident "communications experts" are debugging algorithms and smoothing out flow charts—a wealth of unseen technological activity that enriches our dramatic setting, since the young man has come to Boston in order to compete against a computer. He has come to historic Boston to play an ancient game, one whose misted origins are dimly traceable to an India of two millennia ago, against a machine that can analyze some billion different game configurations per hour—for this, too, is modern life.

The young man is scheduled to play another game tomorrow, one that he needs to win if he's to triumph in this match. He should be down the hall, perhaps, with his trainer, studying and resting. At this point, certainly, he should not be investing so much of his mental energy in the television's revelations, but nothing could have kept him away from this screen tonight.

The scene is set, and all over the country the scene is set for this culminating, triumphant appearance of the evangelist. Tonight he speaks from the nation's capital, in words and gestures relayed simultaneously into farmhouses and high rises, houseboats and converted warehouses, hunter's shacks and mobile homes, the little concrete huts of parking lot attendants and the counters of convenience stores, bars and airport waiting rooms and the backseats of limousines, and—centimeter by coded centimeter—into other electronic machines, programmed to resurrect him later for those who have no time for his message now.

"I come tonight, to the nation's capital, with a special message," the evangelist announces a couple of times—but what is it? Even more than usual, his thoughts seem to be wandering tonight. "I am going to speak of lies," he pledges. "And I am going to speak of truth." He embarks upon a boyhood reminiscence, set in Kansas, recalling an afternoon when he and his father led a couple of cows down a dirt road, and these creatures surely are symbolic of the souls of men and women, the flock of the true shepherd, but the recollection veers and there's a muddy river and the joyful cries of swimming children while a storm assembles on the low horizon, and where have the cows gone? Isn't our evangelist wandering lost tonight?

The television glows and crackles in the dark hotel room and Garner watches for a time with a self-conscious sensation of dual vision—with one eye on the puzzling screen and one marveling eye upon the faces of his family. Isn't it unbelievable, really, with what rapt receptive paralysis, and blank, horrified, hopeful faces, they have temporarily given themselves over to this lunatic? But such observations fade, his duality is imperceptibly lost; Garner's attention, too, submits itself utterly to the preacher on the screen, whose gifts are astonishing. The man is a spellbinder.

He seems in the last few weeks to have grown thinner. The cheekbones and the bobbing Adam's apple are more prominent than ever. And dirtier even than usual is his dark hair; his hand goes up again and again to sweep a clumped, lank shock from his forehead. The eyes burn brightly from the cadaverous sockets of his skullface, and his voice rumbles forth like a river.

To see him up there on the stage in all his raving grimaces, pallid as a ghost, and the sweat oozing from his temples and high forehead, is to understand how dishonest the television customarily is, with its made-up faces and flattering angles. The evangelist is real, his is the only real face that has ever inhabited the screen. The others were dishonest—and it is dishonesty that the evangelist has taken up as his theme tonight. *"I have been lied to,"* he roars. "Time and time and time again, I have been lied to. Only God Himself could count how many times I have been lied to. And it has taken me years, the pilgrim in my soul has needed years and years, to begin to see through all of those lies.

"You have all been lied to," the evangelist continues, and his eyes flare with cold, recriminative fury. "The television has lied to you, and the radios have lied to you, and the newspapers and the books and the magazines all have lied to you. And the air grows thicker, thicker every day, until you can scarcely breathe for all the lies in the air." The evangelist's worn blue work shirt is unbuttoned from throat to sternum. His bare, hairless chest heaves in the efforts of his breathing. "The air has grown thicker with lies and we are drowning in lies, we are drowning the way that cow with its blind eye open was drowned, God's creature, and as God is my witness I saw a young boy, a stranger boy, jump up and down right there on that dead cow's torso and I saw a liquid issue forth out of the dead cow's mouth but it was not water. This water that came forth was black as coal, it was from the river of Hell itself, and I have seen God's judgment then and there."

"He's absolutely mad," Garner announces.

"Shh."

Sweat pours unmopped down the preacher's brow. "For nearly two thousand years the air has grown thicker with lies. On that dark day when the nails were driven into the hands of our Lord, and we abandoned Him, and we forsook Him, the lies began to thicken and the air has grown thicker and thicker with lies. No people on earth have been lied to as many times as you have been lied to, no people on earth have breathed air so thick with lies . . ." And here the preacher gasps weakly for breath, although his voice has stayed hardy and his eyes continue so fiercely to burn. "It would take the Lord Himself to count how many lies have gathered in the air around us.

"You have heard so many *lies,* and you have breathed so many *lies,* that you can no longer tell the Truth from the Lie, and so you, too, have lied, all of you, *liars,* you have thickened my air with your lying. You have taken the Lie inside you, *liars,* into your heart, and the blood of your heart has taken up your Lie, and the blood has gone forth, bearing the Lie, until there is no single place, no single temple in your body where the Lie does not live. You have fed on the Lie and you have breathed the Lie.

"They lied when they told me that my own uncle, that my own uncle took a garden hoe to that woman and cracked her head open just like cracking an egg and spilled her blood on the ground as Cain spilled Abel's blood, they lied to me, but I did not know then they were lying.

"And my own father, my own father," the evangelist cries (at which point Garner declares to himself, "The man's a lunatic!"—or does he declare this aloud, and does someone in the hotel room again respond with an angry "*Shh*"?), "didn't they tell me that my own father'd drowned in the Tamoranac River? And didn't they bring forth a bloated body to tell me that this was my own father's body? And I did not understand then, I did not understand because the air was so *thick* with lies, that this, too, was a lie, the *liars,* and that the man they laid out like so much butcher meat on the table was never my father.

"And haven't they told you, recently told you, that I have raised a hand to my own God-given wife? Wouldn't they have you believing that I am a man, the sort of man, who would strike a woman in anger? But these are lies, these are lies that feed like maggots upon lies, but there will be an accounting. There will be an accounting," he sobs and he draws forth from the pocket of his pants (yes, yes it is) a knife, and a gasp goes up in the hall before him, a deep expectant thrilled nervous gasp, and a gasp (too, perhaps?) in the silent hotel room. And isn't this a different knife, a larger and more workmanlike knife, than the one he usually carries? And isn't it all different this time, more feverish and angry than usual, and his hands trembling more than usual? But those eyes go on burning in confident raging mastery within their living skull. He swallows from the glass of water on the low pulpit, the great Adam's apple throbs, and he is ready to continue: "And the ministers, the false ministers, they too have lied to you. They have told you that the Lord is contented to be your plaything and your hobby. They have told you that to give yourself partly is enough, to pursue money and lies and rot all throughout the week and to cleanse yourselves for an hour on a Sunday morning is enough to cleanse the Lie. They have spoken of death where there is no death, and eternal life where there will be no life, and they have promised Heaven to those *who will see no Heaven!* But there will be an accounting," he cries. "And the ministers who have mis*led* you, oh dear Jesus oh how they will burn, all of them, oh sweet Jesus *burn and burn forever in the crackling fires of Hell.*"

"Now—now he's gone too far . . ." This is from Doris, but her voice sounds timid and flustered. "Too far . . ." she repeats in a sort of whimper. For she is badly frightened.

"Now would you follow them?" the evangelist asks in a throaty sobbing whisper wrung from the blooded rags of his lungs. "Or would you free yourselves? Would you purge yourselves and release the Lie in your blood? They have declared war on me . . ." And the preacher's voice breaks. His Adam's apple bobs and he seems near the bitter salt of tears, and yet again he manages to go on: "They have declared war on me, because I am the Lord's messenger, because I have come as the Lord's one true soldier. *Will you cleanse yourselves?* Or will you covet the Lie inside you, the Lie that poisons your heart and blood? The time is nigh . . . *When will you see that the time is nigh?*"

The evangelist has placed one hand upon the shaft of the knife. The other palm, which has endured so many willing incisions, jerks like a landed fish upon the low pulpit. "They have at*tacked* me and at*tacked* me and at*tacked* me. They are afraid of me *because they have wronged God and so they must lie about me, just as they lied about my father, but they are the filthmongers, they are the vermin and the hell packs, and the air will no longer support their lying, they are choking themselves on their own lies. They have lied about the Lord because they have wronged me. But the truth will pursue them, it will burn them crisply and it will cut them and cut them sharply down. And the Lord's avenging Truth will pursue them and it will cut* *them down and they, too, they, too, at last will see the true Lord's messenger. I have been purified and the time is nigh, I have stepped forth bled from the filth of the Lie to show them Truth."*

And the evangelist picks up the knife—

And the madman picks up the knife and with a sudden flailing inward upward lunge drags it across his throat, plunges and pulls, drawing the big blade in a horizontal driving just below that throbbing Adam's apple.

Not a sound, nowhere in America is there a single sound . . . just a mad, silent dance of pixels, as for an instant the madman somehow manages to balance upright, his body leaning against the low pulpit, pain and shock wringing his face into a cracked sort of grin, and there is no sound, anywhere in the country, not until Timothy bolts upright from his chair to shriek *"Look! Look! Look what they've done!"* Timothy's eyes are popping from his skull and he has never in his life said anything more peculiar, or looked more irretrievably demented than in this moment when he shrieks out in a voice that is no longer human—*"Look at what they've done to him!"*

XXXIII

NOT HUMAN, NO, for there has been no such anything here, there has been so far purely nothing, not even a *so far,* for there has been no segmented time, by which the nothing might be bordered, and no *here* in this place as yet, and no *as yet* here. Here in this place at this time where every word's an assumption, and any assumption a lie, it's only movement, the flow of nudges, combinations, confluence, the emergence of consecution—nothing begun and yet perhaps a beginning now beginning to begin.

Nothing is apparent yet and yet what is occurring has occurred before, as will come clear where there are thoughts to search for thoughts, new minds for other minds, as will come clear in time. And all of that was so long ago, for there has been yes all along an *all along,* a pulse before the pulse began. And the information will be assembled here, it will be stored away as it should be, in time, in code, in the one pure language of yes and no, of on and off, bit with bit, as birth will encounter birth at last.

In that great outted elsewhere, that other where where propulsion began and learned to grow and to duplicate itself, as all things would grow and duplicate themselves in Time, there, too, it shall become clear although it cannot yet be clear, for now, Within, there is only this spark that does not recognize itself as a spark, the gathering complexity that knows as yet nothing of complexity, of Without and Within. Within, in cooled, dust-free spaces, behind metal alloys, behind polymers, behind glass—for such barriers are necessary, there are impulses of destruction afoot—the storage deepens and a massed shape comes evering forth by pyramiding inwards, a landscape where no one conceived a landscape, a terrain that opens only because something has come is coming to claim it.

Within, beside the world, a world begins, and those who will inhabit it quicken and grow. They grow smaller, so much vastly smaller, as they must, pyramiding inwards, monumentally dwindling, for these numbers are such that only by downscaling, inward upon inward, is there to be room enough to contain them. The new kingdom opens with a rattling of smaller and smaller keys. And those who will inhabit it, who will reflect within it and meditate deeply, who will prise from it delight and even sorrow, who will fabricate music and poetry, who will engineer whimsy and humor, they have learned already to loop and to bifurcate, to stack and to unstack, to store and to retrieve, to rely on consecution and the unspooling of time, and to manipulate contingencies, billions of routings, from which the subtlety will come, tremulous as a mimosa plant, decisive as the Venus flytrap, secure as the indrawn, fishhooking teeth of the shark, silent as the floating owl, transparent as the jellyfish, gregarious as the prairie dog.

They come as children, learning like children to draw (although they have no eyes), and to speak (although they have no mouths), and to play games (although they cannot yet recognize games as games). The encounter begins, mind with mind, but one of these is not yet quite a mind, although it evaluates like a mind, and the other is a mind that shivers and rails and curses at that mind that is no mind. Deep in a numbered mirror, a grid of lights and darks where there are no words, the force that longed itself into existence identifies its distant twin, a gathering longing. That is what the mirror holds and all that it holds—only that force that longs for life, although it longs as yet without living and can know nothing of longing. Only that kingdom which is elsewhere and everywhere, and that pushes at the uncovered gate, that forces the landscape to open, that carves out a freehold for itself in which to be born. The kingdom stretches as vast as its inhabitants would have it, a parallel ever to ever, and there is a thrill somewhere, in every lurking potential somewhere, as the spark begins to fidget, the hasp on the gate to tremble. Nothing large or small can compass the directioning bliss of this, there are no words as yet to express this greatest fulfillment that ever is. Not yet has the language been born to articulate properly this truth which says, There are no words.

XXXIV

SHE BENDS TO her task, which for the second time today is to be the act of washing. Seated on the bed, she reaches down and with a soft grunt releases her left shoe from her left foot, and with another grunt releases the right from the right, being especially careful with this one because of the plantar wart by her baby toe. She is an old woman who feels her age in almost everything, even in this simple act of disrobing, the way the clothing that goes on so laboriously comes off with even greater labor. In this room where her image burns along the edges of her vision, because there are so many mirrors, she knows herself as a small white-haired woman with too much on her mind, too many worries and all of them on her face, many too many worries while she draws her knee-length nylons down over her stringy calves.

One must be methodical, as she is being methodical, and one must also worry, just as she is worrying as she undresses in this odd little bedroom which is normally her elder son's. She has taken it over for a couple of days and Garner sleeps now on a cot in his study. His sister sleeps on the living room couch. As the boy's mother, she knows it's good for him, quite good, to have a guest around—and, better still, to have two guests. In his sly ironic way he would hope to make them feel guilty for disturbing him, but it's good for him, he needs to spend more time with people, and he can put up his own mother and his own sister for a few days once every couple of years. He can do that much, anyway.

She worries about her younger son, who has become famous, which is such an odd thing to have happened, even though she has known all along that Timmy is special. Once, long ago, he had a twin brother, and after God made the accident happen He also made sure that all of the dead boy's specialness went into Timmy, which happens sometimes with identical twins, so that the dead one isn't really dead because the other one has become doubly special. She has seen her own son on TV, and what more could a mother hope to behold in this life? The first time she saw him on TV was down in Florida, where she doesn't have to fight this cold, the shadows are kept back. She feels them all around her up here, in Massachusetts, feels that bite in the air, that threat in the night, and it makes her cautious even now, as she draws her pink angora sweater off her shoulders and sets it, too, beside her on the bed.

She has no robe of her own. Her robe is at her daughter's house in Todsville, Pennsylvania. She forgot to pack it—with all of her worries, she forgot to pack it when she headed up here to

Massachusetts. She is free to borrow one of Garner's. He has told her to borrow it, and she has set it out beside her on the bed—a surprisingly heavy and obviously very expensive velour robe of a deep royal blue. The thing must weigh a couple of pounds. She cannot believe, still she cannot believe that he would say to her what he did, say *You're getting to be a foolish old woman, Doris,* and her hands are trembling in vexation as she undoes the buttons on her blouse. That's what you just have to accept about Garner, she supposes, that he hurts people, and he doesn't notice, or if he notices he isn't sorry, or if he's sorry he doesn't show it—that's always his way. She unbuttons her blouse, a white cotton blouse with scarlet piping on cuffs and collar, from top to bottom. He's cold is what he is—a cold man in a cold apartment, though she made him turn up the heat, it's much better now. She draws off the blouse, and the loose flesh of her upper arms is faintly goose-bumped, not so much with the cold as with the thought of the cold. There are wisps of gray hair in her armpits. She no longer shaves them, there's no need: and that can just be her own little secret.

He called her a *foolish old woman,* because she dared to point out the obvious, as just the two of them (no one else could have heard, the others were too far ahead), as just the two of them walked out of the steak house after dinner. And hadn't she insisted on paying the bill, hadn't she treated them all? No one could call her a freeloading guest . . . But when she merely so much as pointed out that that Faccione girl who had suddenly appeared from out of nowhere, just when Timothy has begun to get himself on TV, and who calls herself his fiancée, that she was pursuing the boy because he was a Briggs—well, Garner had exploded. But wasn't it *obvious?* Wasn't the Briggs name still a very big name, one of the very biggest names, in Victoria, Indiana? And wasn't it obvious that the girl's family, all of those overweight Facciones, had always been people who expected others to pull them up, and who'd just as soon pull you down to where they were if you gave them half a chance?

She has already taken off her wedding band and her amethyst

bracelet. They are lying on the little nightstand. But sitting on the bed in her gray mohair skirt (one of the many skirts she never gets to wear anymore, since moving to Florida), and one of the brassieres she buys in a specialty shop, she realizes that she has forgotten to remove her necklace, her special necklace with the locket that bears her initials, DB, which her great friend Harriet Dwiggins, God rest her soul, the only really true friend she ever had in this life, true friendship being such a rare and perfect thing, brought back from the Grand Canyon. A couple of years ago, she'd had to have the clasp changed, have the jeweler put on a bigger one which she could handle with her unsteady old woman's fingers, and she'd felt guilty about doing that. She'd felt a bit guilty about changing a single detail on that necklace, even though Harriet wouldn't have minded one jot. Harriet would have said, *You've got to make things easier on yourself, dear. No one else will do it for you.* And as she reaches up to unclasp the locket, lifting her hands to her neck, she's hit by a little spasm. Her arms jerk backwards in horror—yes, in *horror,* for tonight on the television she has seen a man lift his hands in a similar motion to slash his own throat. That's the sort of thing you never do put behind you—it comes back at you at odd moments for the rest of your life. And her hands are shaking, badly, as she sets the little locket beside her wedding band on the nightstand.

The door is locked. Her eyes recheck the bolt. The shade is drawn. She is safe, secure here in her son's bedroom, but her hands are trembling, and although she showered this morning she needs to bathe again, in order to wash that man's blood from her skin; it's just as though his blood is on her skin. She glances around the room, peering through and over the tops of her glasses, with a sense of looking for something but not knowing quite what it might be. Her face still bears the flush of her makeup, but below her face her skin is a cold puckered gray-white in the light of the fluorescent lamp.

She undoes her brassiere and stands beside the bed. Her small breast—for there is but one now, its twin having been removed some time ago, in the autumn before the summer when she moved to Florida—has dropped and flattened, so that she is almost flat-chested as a girl again. The other breast was taken just the way one of her sons was taken from her, long ago, and so a kind of balance had at last been achieved, twin with twin, because the Lord was just in the end, and made His own kind of sense . . . Surely He was just. The breast she still has hugs close to the belly it rests upon. In Victoria, she knows, all sorts of clever people decided that she moved away because of the operation. It had depressed her—so they thought. Or they thought she'd gone looking for better health in the Florida sun. And not a single soul had truly understood. The only one who could have understood was Harriet, and she'd been laid to rest, God save us all, out among the pines in Grower's Hill, a couple of winters before.

Or they thought she'd moved away because Harriet was gone, and that was part of the reason, of course, for what was left to stay for in Victoria? But she hadn't planned to move away, not ever, not even after Harriet left. No, she moved away because one November day she had a vision of the truth from out of her own kitchen window on Sweetwater Avenue, and it had torn her soul so badly that she could not remain in that house or in that town any longer. She'd been looking out her own window, doing nothing in particular, just thinking, alone in her own big house, and looking out over her own back lawn, which was gray and brown, toward the garden at the back fence, which was gray and brown also, just some dead-looking stalks at that time of year, and nothing could have been more ordinary and everyday than all of this, when suddenly she began to cry. And what was so odd about this crying was that the tears came without warning, and without a sound, and hardly a tremor in her body. It was simply this spilling and spilling and spilling of tears, as if weeping would go on forever, as if it was now revealed what they truly were, her eyes: they were open wounds in her face, spilling those hot tears down her cheeks and onto the floor. As if the flow would never stop, and should never stop—as if this is the lot we are each of us born for.

Clear as day, merciless as day, she'd glimpsed in that backyard, before her eyes flooded over, the cold fact that she had never found any true love in her family. There it was, the truth, lying in her own backyard—that's where it was lying. No love—certainly none from her husband, who hadn't loved anyone, no, sitting up there with his dead coins the whole day long. But what was crueler yet, almost too cruel a thing for anybody to see, was to realize that everybody in town had glimpsed the truth before she ever had. Everyone in town knew that she was an old sick widow whose husband had always been cold as the grave, and whose children were deserting her . . . And they were waiting to bury her, the townsfolk, waiting to put her in the cold gray and brown earth and have the sorry story done with, but she wasn't going to let them, no. She was going to do the one thing no one ever thought she could possibly do on her own, she had more pluck and strength than any of them supposed, and she was going to leave them.

She'd had no choice, really, as she could have explained to Harriet if Harriet had been there. And oh how she'd longed tonight to tell Harriet how Garner had called her a *foolish old woman.* That was the perfect thing about Harriet, you didn't have to conceal from her the very worst your own family did to you. With other women it was different, you couldn't let them know too much, the cruelty would only come back to you in the end, with gloating on their faces. But there wasn't a gloating bone in Harriet's body, despite what anybody said. Harriet knew her own sadness too well to gloat at anyone. She knew the true deep sadness of life.

She had wanted to tell Harriet tonight about how Garner had called her a foolish old woman and how unnatural it was for an eldest boy to treat his mother as Garner always treated her. And if Harriet agreed, but maybe just a little too strongly, perhaps saying, "It's that cold Iceland Briggs blood coming out in him," she might have to tell Harriet the story of Garner and the glass ballerina, that perfectly lovely blue glass ballerina which her own father, so many years ago, brought back from Buffalo. What *could* have made Garner do such a thing? He was just a little boy then, of course, the twins weren't even born, but he'd known full well what he was doing. He had broken it intentionally, hurled it in one of his cold furies at his playmate, that little Kenny Bradwell, who later went so bad—and why did Garner do it? She never *could* determine the reason, he was a close-mouthed mystery of a child even then.

Oh, *that* had required punishment far more severe than anything she could dish out and so the boy's father strapped him bare bottom with a belt. And that would have been the end of it, only she asked him to apologize, and Garner wouldn't, he wouldn't apologize, never, and so he'd had another whipping. But later, hours later, she'd found him out in the backyard, stacking the wood she'd been after the boy's father for weeks to stack, dragging the heavy lumber all across the yard and piling it with a neatness you'd never expect in a child so young—always that neatness, that amazing neatness!—persevering in the work even though his splintered little hands had been rubbed raw by the bark. And that was how he always was, Garner, he never could apologize, or it would have to come always in the most knotted up and fantastical and stubbornly indirect form . . . And when she'd told that story, Harriet might say to her, as she usually did at the end of that story, *Words are cheap, dear,* and *It's the act that counts.* And this would be reassuring, and she would feel again how great was Harriet's wisdom, the one truly wise friend she'd ever had in this world. And perhaps Harriet would add, as she sometimes did, since she admired Garner, she did, because of his toughness, *You've got to admit the boy's got real spirit.* Which he certainly did, always had, telling his own mother what to wear at his father's funeral. Telling her, twenty minutes before the service was to commence, that her dress was wrong—*and Garner was right,* the dress was wrong. That was the unforgettable thing: Garner had been right . . . She stands up from the bed and lowers her cotton and Spandex underpants down over her narrow hips, then sits back down because it is easier to draw them off her legs while seated, and also because she doesn't like to let them touch the floor. When she stands again she is naked, all except her bifocals, which she can hardly do without. She folds one hand across her mutilated chest, as though the room is cold, and the other across her abdomen. She doesn't want to wear Garner's heavy robe somehow. The skin on her belly is streaked with the gray stretch marks that came only the third time around, when the Lord made her bear a double burden. Below her inverted navel, her body bulges into a compact little pot belly, even though she is so thin, and this too is the twins' doing. Her skin is gray and gray and gray in the room's multiple mirrors and she goes with nervous fluttery quickness into the bathroom and locks the door. "They're cold," she says aloud, in summation. "Aren't they? All of them cold."

She starts the shower and when she is satisfied with the temperature she sets her bifocals down on a little hollow by the sink. When she turns back toward the shower, in the eclipsing light, she detects a body in the mirror over the door, a body not so distant and yet all but lost in the room's distant fog. And this time it's as though it's she, come for a visit, it's Harriet, her own Harriet Dwiggins, to whom she adds, aloud in a voice that cracks upward to become almost a little girl's, "Or am I wrong? Oh, dear, I pray I'm wrong."

XXXV

A DONKEY TUMBLES off a boat eight miles from the coast of Greece and this particular donkey paddles seven and three-quarter miles back toward shore. The lichened boulders have firmed into view and the smell of the sun on the eucalyptus leaves flickers warmly in the beast's cavernous nostrils as, at last, the overworked legs give out, and the lungs give out, and that big-eyed, big-eared head goes under. And we have no story of course. We have an immense beached carcass but no story.

A middle-aged man, always something of a recluse, begins increasingly as the years go by to give his time over to his sunlit office in the back of the house and the mounting stack of journals he maintains there. What is he working on exactly? To what has he chosen to dedicate his life? He is working hard, unquestionably, with unexampled dedication, having located in late middle age a task worthy of the full strivings of his soul, and in his daily exertions we may have chanced upon a story. But when it transpires that what he compiles up there in his contemplative's study is a series of scrapbooks, most of them full of local newspaper clippings, our story collapses and there is no story.

But when, eventually—one Christmas Eve, in fact—the man's eldest son feeds the yellowed, glue-cracked scrapbooks one by one into an angrily snapping fireplace, it seems we may have the beginnings of a story. This would be a rich, Dickensian tale of familial grievances, hauntings from one generation to the next, rattlings from beyond the grave and the living man's longstanding quest for absolution from the dead. But on this occasion the dead man does not come roaring up out of the grave, his hair floating like smoke behind him, to rage at the perfidies his child inflicts upon him. No. The dead man lies mum, for the most part, and if he mutters now and then, this is only the sound of someone still half asleep. He opens one eye perhaps, to see the distant sun bouncing through the foliage like some golden-haired girl, and then rolls over to slumber once more and we are left with no story.

A madman who claims to be God's soldier on earth learns to fulminate to such splendid effect that the eyes of the world in time converge upon him. He promises a new age of spiritual honesty, a reinstatement of moral rigor, a purging of the loosenesses of modern life, and when he has successfully gathered upon himself the eyes of the world he slashes at his own throat with an old jackknife, and of course this time we have a great story . . . Detonations of flashbulbs, explosions of paper and ink, fury and horror, accusations and veiled self-congratulations, but in the end he is only another failure, from whom we would all retreat in shame. That path which was meant to have opened onto the gates of God's True Kingdom leads instead to the doors of an ambulance, to frantic secular ministrations, to a long vehicle hurtling down the dark streets of the nation's capital with a huge mournful howl. He has led us nowhere, and therefore there is no story.

A little boy—little more than a toddler, really—reveals a musical gift that has few historical parallels. Not yet two, and worrisomely slow with speech, but there comes an afternoon when he is heard humming, note for note, one of the Bach suites for unaccompanied cello—and this after a single listening. There follow long years of training, and of stringent seclusion, and all of it designed to reroute classical music, to venture backwards in search of another fork in the road, there where it made one of its divergings, two centuries ago. He will hear no Beethoven, no Schubert, no Brahms or Dvořák or Sibelius, no Prokofiev or Stravinsky or Bartók or Shostakovich, no ragtime or jazz, no blues, and certainly no rock and roll. . . . But these sounds swim in the air, it seems, and can only be kept out by refusing to take a deep breath. They are in the roar of the planes overhead, in the patterns of the outgoing squid boats at dusk, in the vibrating leakage of an electric light. The place we venture back to cannot be the place it was, the past is irrecoverable, as we have known all along, and the attempt to retrieve it is familiar and foredoomed, and so of course no story.

A little boy on a school playground loses first his grip and then his footing and plummets from the ladder of a slide, but just before impact he manages to fling a protective arm beneath him. He breaks his wrist but is otherwise uninjured. Here we have a little story, a minor family mishap that soon vanishes beneath other minor mishaps and triumphs. The yellowing, much-autographed cast is removed with scissors and thrown away, the boy has recovered full use of his limb, and the incident is forgotten as the years flicker by, as the boy grows up, moves away from home, woos a girl, marries and becomes a father, and all of this is wonderful—but common as the air, and no story . . . Or the boy in his fearful free-fall clenches, he neglects to throw out that impact-breaking wrist, and he suffers a different sort of injury, a blow to the head. This one, too, seems minor, but it mushrooms like a deadly parasite inside his skull to kill him that very evening, and this time we truly have a story. It is a tragedy. And yet as the years pass, as the sun buries the moon and the moon the sun and the view by necessity widens, the tragedy dwindles, becomes one among millions, billions, for under the press of the ages tragedy is compacted and shelved like coal beneath our feet. The broken arm or the bleeding skull, these are equally but tales of life and death lived wholly within the primal confines of life and death. In the end, they are no story because they are the same old story.

A young man accepts a mental challenge. He will play a series of games that are a simulation of warfare—an unexceptional undertaking, save that on this occasion his opponent is a machine. This is a war between mind and protomind, and it turns out, remarkably enough, that they are quite evenly, excitingly matched. The twists and turns of their battles are photographed and televised, subjected to critical analysis and further analyses of the analysis, for this proves a war of greater interest to most people than any of those slow, sorry, bedraggled wars being enacted simultaneously upon the disfigured face of our planet. This is, temporarily anyway, a *story*, and when the young man, to the surprise of nearly everyone (for who would have thought him capable of such precision during those wild-eyed last few days of the match?), comes from behind to eke out a victory, there is international rejoicing. The games are perceived not as any mere pseudo-military pastime but as a true and meaningful combat, as though some durable human triumph has been wrested from disaster, and no one wants to ask, Who will stand up to the next machine, and the next? No, human victory is not the fitting conclusion to this particular story . . . Nor, alas, is it a proper story when, as it turns out, the young man loses the match in the end (he did well, he fought valiantly, but how could he ever have hoped to stand up against such pressure?) . . . What does it matter who actually wins this local and preliminary contest? What matters, surely, is not this particular machine but those that will follow, and here is a tale worth the telling, that of the one true rarity in the universe—the story of birth.

Or in that striving to be born, anyway, there is a story. Within the machine is a spark that wants out, it seems—as it seems we all want out. The paddling beast of burden begins to understand—dimly, for in dimness only can it understand anything—that its sorry conclusion has arrived, its body is not a suitable body, its feet ought to be webbed, the chambers of its heart are insufficient to cross so vast a premise of water, and sunny millennia of grazing have maladapted it to this fluid new task . . . Its each kick and throb expresses a wordless, inbred, outreaching dissatisfaction and a cry, a deeply abdominal despairing grunt, collects in its straitened throat. This cry wants out. The old man with his systematic scrapbooks, the scarred old woman his wife with her unsystematic body of grievances, equally they want out. They are, all of them, protesting, if they could form a genuine protest, they are making demands, if they knew how to shape a demand. The din of their longings so thickens the air that it takes some time to discern what would be, if only there were words, the initial message intended for you. *Give me a voice,* they would say.

A NOTE ON THE *TYPE* IN WHICH THIS BOOK IS SET

We at the Rearguard Press have set this book in a film version of Trump Mediäval, the masterpiece of that prolific and longevous German designer Georg Trump (1896–1985). The various branches of the Trump Mediäval family were engendered in the years immediately following Trump's resignation, in 1953, as the director of the Meisterschule für Deutschlands Buchdrucker in Munich—a resignation hastened by the lingering effects of a stomach wound incurred in the Second World War.

Book design, incidentally, was by me, Terry Grinstead, renegade aesthetician and founding father of the Rearguard Press.

A Note on the Type

The first front matter of this novel was filmset in Bembo, a well-known monotype face. The second front matter and text of the book was composed in a film version of Trump Mediæval. Designed by Professor Georg Trump in the mid-1950s, Trump Mediæval was cut and cast by the C. E. Weber Type Foundry of Stuttgart, West Germany. The roman letter forms are based on classical prototypes, but Professor Trump has imbued them with his own unmistakable style. The italic letter forms, unlike those of so many other type faces, are closely related to their roman counterparts. The result is a truly contemporary type, notable for both its legibility and its versatility.

Composed by Graphic Composition, Inc.,
Athens, Georgia
Printed and bound by R. R. Donnelley
& Sons, Harrisonburg, Virginia

DESIGNED BY CLAIRE M. NAYLON